In Loving Memory

of

Dianne Price

(1933 - 2013)

Never Say Goodbye

Dianne Price

BOOK FOUR OF
THE THISTLE SERIES

Ashberry Lane

Ashberry Lane
P.O. Box 665, Gaston, OR 97119
www.ashberrylane.com

Published in association with Terry Burns of Hartline Literary Agency, LLC.

ISBN 9781941720271

Cover design by Miller Media Solutions
Cover images by Ashlee Murr Photography and iStock.com

The Thistle Series
by Dianne Price

Broken Wings, Book One
Wing and a Prayer, Book Two
The Promise of Dawn, Book Three

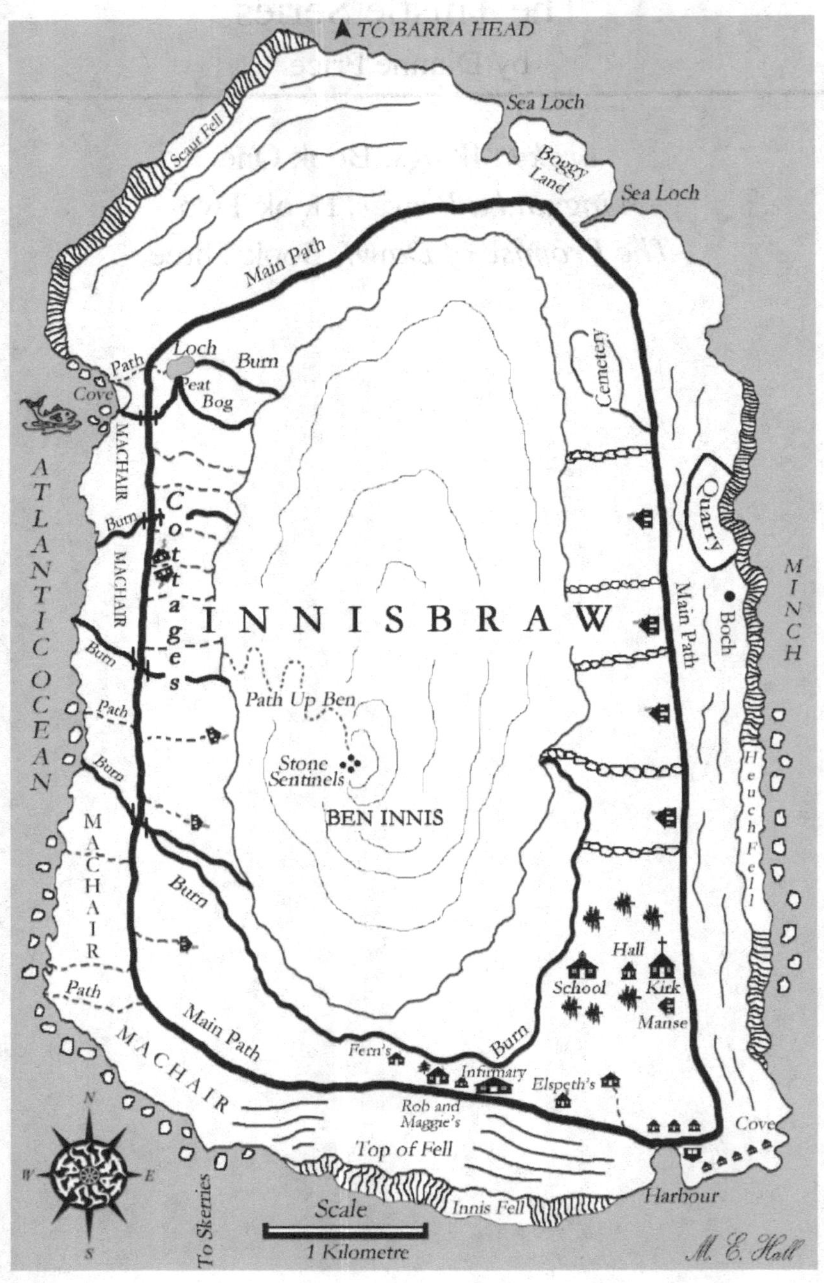

Written with some British spelling, this book also includes a Scottish Gaelic glossary.

Dedication

For the glory of my Lord, Jesus Christ.
And, as always, for my True, who lived
up to his name in every way.

In Loving Memory

Dianne joined her beloved Savior and
her husband in heaven one week before
her first book released.
She is probably dancing a Scots reel
even as you read this.

Chapter One

Isle of Innisbraw, Outer Hebrides, Scotland
Early September, 1947

Rob Savage wiped raindrops from his face and shambled across the stubbled ground.

The devastation wrought by a night of pounding rain and gale-force winds was unbelievable. Sheaves of machair hay—most broken apart into sodden clumps—lay scattered across the vast expanse like uprooted graves.

He'd been on the island six years and never beheld such destruction—even the hurricane little more than a year ago had not occurred during harvest time. And the oats and barley in the nearby fields ... They were used for coo and cuddy feed, aye, but the oats also provided a hearty breakfast and grain for bread. Granted, this was the second oat crop, but how many would suffer empty bellies before spring?

Alec MacDonald and Lachlan MacCrae, waxed jackets and breeches stiff with sandy mud, laboured nearby, tying the least-damaged sheaves together with string and draping them carefully over a drystone dyke.

Och, how would they feed their Hieland coos this winter with no hay? Substitute cut-up neeps?

The thundering surf pounding on the western shore like the tolling of the death knell, and the rain tasted as salty as the tears of defeat.

Rob scooped up an almost-intact sheaf and carried it to the men, his wellies sucking against the drenched soil with each step.

"Hoy, Rob." Alec grunted and wiped rain from his forehead with his arm, rivulets of water darkening the white in his hair. "Told Lachlan you'd show up to help."

The younger crofter wore a grim smile. "Didn't argue with him, for I knew you would too. We could use a hand."

"That's why I'm here."

The three were soon joined by other crofters, all dour-faced, the light of hope dead in their eyes. They worked in teams, one to hold the sodden sheaf together, the second to snip and tie the towie. After hours, the top of the large, square dyke was covered with stacks of sheaves, tied side by side to keep them from being blown off the jagged capstones.

Alec kneaded the small of his back. "No reason to try to save the oats and barley. Once they're wet, they rot." He raised his face to the dreich sky. "If this rain stops, we've a glimmer of hope for saving the hay. If no', 'tis all for nowt anyway."

Rob nodded. "Have you a guid supply of neeps laid by?"

A long, ragged sigh. "Aye, sacks of neeps, just no' ..." He waved his hand over the sheaves of hay.

The crofters all thanked Rob for his help, bringing a flush to his cold cheeks.

Why did they still treat him as somebody special? He put his breeks on the same way they did.

A disaster, that's what it was. Skailwind and plomping rain had fallen on the meadow hay, barley, and late oats which lay cut but not yet carted to sheltered byres. Maggie Savage dropped the corner of the lace curtain and sat at the kitchen table, worrying her lower lip. Just yesterday morning, word had gone out across the island that the machair hay and grain crops, ripened early by a warmer-than-usual summer, were ready for the cutting.

Last night's gale struck the island with the stealth and fury of a horde of banshees, rain soaking the stacked sheaves and winds toppling and grinding them into the sandy soil of the machair. How many island folk would go hungry this winter?

Sighing, she rummaged through the pile of laundry on the table and pulled out all the hippens to fold. Rob would surely be home after dark if the pounding rain on the slate roof was any indication. She dropped the cloths back into the pile, rested her chin in her cupped palms, and closed her eyes. How could she tell him what a midden the day had been, especially their laddie's part in it?

A tentative knock on the door brought her to her feet.

"Come away in," she called, raising a warning hand to Shep, who leaped up from the rug in front of the fireplace. "No bowf," she commanded.

Though the dog didn't bark, he reached the door before her.

Neighbours Fern MacNeill and her lass, Katie, hurried inside, brushing the rain from their hair and scrubbing the soles of their shoes on the rag rug.

"Where are your coats?"

Fern wiped a wet strand of black hair from her cheek. "On the entry. They're soaked almost through."

"Och, bring them in and hang them in the coat closet. I've already laid a towel on the floor to catch the rain from Rob's waxed jacket."

"Can you hold this dish, then?"

Maggie took the plate from Fern, pulled aside the damp tea towel, and sniffed the spicy aroma. "Your only day off work all week and you steamed a clootie dumpling?" Her nose wrinkled with delight at the dessert. "And I have just enough clotted cream to go with."

Her friend winked conspiratorially. "And if we want any of Rob's favourite, we'd best have ours before he puts a fork to it."

Katie brought in their coats, and Fern hung them in the closet. The lass knelt and hugged the dog's neck, then jumped up, wiping her cheeks. "Och, Shep, you slubbered all over me." She looked around the room. "Where's Robbie, Aunt Maggie?"

"Abed."

"Abed?" Fern asked. "Is he sick, then?"

"Only a nap."

"But he gave up napping no' long after you birthed Annie."

"This is his first in months, but he had a tantrum after I paddled his bum for biting Annie's finger." Maggie busied herself setting a fresh pottle of tea to steep.

Fern put the cosy over the teapot and led Maggie to a chair. "I thought he was over being jealous. He usually ignores the lassie."

"That's true, he does. He was full of himself, pressing me to go ootside and play on the entry like a big lad, but I told him it was too wet. He was in a rare fash from then on."

"You mean he bit Annie when he really wanted to take a bite oot of you?"

All Maggie could manage was a weak, "Aye."

Fern squeezed her hand. "We'd best come up with something to keep the bairns busy. You can't watch Katie while I work if Robbie's going through another bout of giving you fits."

There was no one else nearby to watch Katie while Fern saw patients at the infirmary, plus, having Katie to distract Robbie made a big difference in his behavior. "The day got off to a bad start, that's all. When we woke later than usual and found it storming, Rob threw on his clothes and dashed off to help the crofters, only twa scones in his pocket for breakfast. Then Annie and Robbie both fussed when he wasn't here to kiss them when they woke, and I burned the brose and had to start all over, making their breakfast late, and it was just porridge, no' proper brose since the oats hadn't soaked overnight."

Mischief sparkled in Fern's blue eyes. "You're no' biggen, are you?"

Maggie gasped. "Och, of course no'. Twa bairns in hippens is more than enough. Three would have me cairted off and committed as a daftie."

Katie skipped up, copper curls bouncing across her back, dimples dancing in her rosy cheeks. "But I'd help you like I did with Wee Annie, Aunt Maggie. I promise."

"I know you would, lassie. And a big help you were. I missed you this morning."

"Mither!" Robbie shouted.

Followed by a wail from Annie's room.

"I'll get the lass," Fern said. "You see if you can settle things with your laddie before Rob gets home. I've seen his patience, but even a saint can slip in the face of Robbie on a tear."

Rob turned his steps toward home. He shouldn't have taken the time, but after helping the crofters and checking the thatched cottage roofs of the widows who lived alone, he'd stopped in his office at the shed and telephoned each of his volunteer rescue lads, reminding them to be on alert. With the seas running high, they could be called out to a rescue at any time. Then he'd looked at the progress on the two rescue boats being built for Barra and Harris Islands, though he needn't have bothered.

As always, the keels were taking shape a few days ahead of schedule. Taking Graham MacDonald on as a partner was turning out better than Rob had ever thought possible.

Crossing to the side of the path, he peered through the rain at the shore. Almost high tide and only a few feet before the water reached the main path and threatened to flood the boatshed, the howff, the post office, and the Cottage Weavers—the newest industry on the island. He'd have to keep an eye on that, rounding up a crew to fill bags with sand at the next high tide, if needed.

He climbed the hill quickly, stomping an inch of wet sand from the soles of his wellies every few metres. What a midden of a day. A few of the smaller crofters had cairted their grain to coo houses the een it was cut but no' near enough of them. And if this storm kept up, he'd have to delay production in the shed and send some of his lads around to help repair the leaking thatched roof. He'd found no major damage and had hung water buckets 'neath each leak to catch the intermittent drips. He grinned. One advantage of being six-five? No need for a ladder.

The lamp Elspeth NicAllister kept lit all night to guide those climbing the path to the top of Innis Fell cast a fractured, hazy glow through the rain. Guid, she was abed and safe. Despite her spirited arguments it wasn't needed, he'd had a few rotten thatches replaced after the hurricane.

I ken at over one hundred she's the auldest on Innisbraw, but let her bide a while longer on earth, Faither. We still need her prayers and wise words, and I can't imagine living without the luve and encouragement she gives so freely.

The infirmary windows were dark, but a light shone in Doctor John McGrath's wee cottage. Maggie's faither was probably poring over medical journals, or writing up some new ground-breaking orthopaedic procedure. Though running the infirmary often kept John too busy to take supper with them, he spent Sabbath afternoons playing with his grandbairns and exchanging news over cups of tea and Maggie's shortbread or a rare clootie dumpling.

Home. He eased the gate open, fastened the latch, and stepped along the flagged walkway. Lights blazed from the front window. Pray God Maggie was still up. He'd waited all day to feel her tiny body pressed to his, to tangle his fingers in the black hair slipping down her back, to taste her soft, sweet lips. He crossed the flagged entry, toed out of his boots, and peeled off his waxed jacket. His hand was on the latch when the door flew open.

"Rob! You're home."

"Aye, I'm home." A sigh of relief burst from deep within his chest as he gathered her into his arms. The heather-honey sweetness of her kiss brought a groan. Could any man ask for a warmer welcome? He ran his lips over her silken throat, another groan building.

She pulled away with a laugh. "You've mud on your face. Give me your jacket. Your supper's on the warming shelf, shower water's hot, and I've hung your dressing gown in the bathing room."

"Trying to get rid of an unwanted suitor, are you, wife?"

A fond pat on his bottom punctuated with a pinch was her answer.

Maggie spooned her back against Rob's belly, warm and relaxed.

He pulled the bedquilt over her shoulder and kissed the tip of her ear.

Och, she'd thought him asleep.

"Sleeperie, lass?"

He wanted to talk. And she knew why. He'd eyed Annie's bruised finger when they'd checked their sleeping bairns before seeking their own bed. He hadn't said a word. Just kissed the wee bairnie's hand, tucked it 'neath her cover, and turned out the lamp.

Now 'twas time for her to pay the fiddler. "I'm awake."

"I was surprised to see Robbie sleeping with his stuffed rabbit again. Thought he gave that up months ago." Rob's voice was a low, calm rumble in his chest.

"He ... he pulled it from his toy box before his nap the day."

His fingers trailed over her shoulder 'neath the quilt. Soft as the brush of butterfly wings, that touch. "You mean the nap he took after you paddled his behoochie for biting Wee Annie's finger?"

Och, how quickly he'd put it all together. She nodded, unable to voice an answer.

He stroked her back and kissed her forehead. "I'd hoped the lad was no longer jealous, that he'd accepted she had a place in this family and learned to luve her."

Maggie pulled away and looked up into Rob's face. "I don't think he's jealous any longer. Annie's finger was close, 'tis all … and an acceptable substitute."

"Substitute? For what?"

"For mine."

"Yours? Why would our lad want to bite you?"

"Because I wouldn't allow him oot to play on the entry with the blowsterin wind blowing rain against the front window." She put up a hand to stop Rob from interrupting. "It was a frustrating day, with me burning their brose, Shep keeping to his spot on the hearth rug and no' wanting to play, Katie no' here because Fern had a day's holiday ..."

"On with it, lass."

"I should have seen the signs—him stomping about the living room, gritting his teeth and making that low growl in his throat. Like he's about to explode with frustration because he doesn't know the words to make his wants known. When he asked for at least the tenth time about going oot on the entry, I told him to stop whinging and get a book for me to read to him as soon as I was through suckling Annie."

"And he lost it."

"Aye. He bit Annie's finger, then stomped off into his bedroom, slamming the door."

"And you paddled him."

"No' before I calmed Annie down. Poor lassie, she was rouping like her heart was broken. I'd sung most of the lullabies I know before she dropped off to sleep and I tucked her into her cradle."

"Where was the lad during this?"

"Robbie was sitting on the floor in the corner of his room, holding that rabbit, his face to the wall. I told him what I was going to do. That ... that was the hardest thing I've ever done, Rob, for the anger had left me and he looked so miserable."

"But you had to, luve, no' only for Wee Annie's sake, but for his. He needed to feel physical pain too."

"You'll no' punish him further?"

"Of course no'. In a way, I feel responsible for his frustration. We have onshore storms from the east so seldom I thought roofing the entry would give the bairns a guid place to play oot of the rain. Mebbe I'll fasten a tarp from the eaves."

"Please don't. With the days shortening and getting dark earlier and earlier, 'twould make the kitchen and living room feel like a cave. And ruin our view of the harbour and Minch."

He pulled her up into his arms. "You realize 'tis only September, with a long wait till spring?"

"Fern and I have come up with an idea to keep both Katie and Robbie busy."

"What, add them to my boatbuilding crew?" His grin was catching.

"Of course no'. I'm going to teach them to cook."

How quickly that grin faded. "Cook? You want our lad to learn to cook?"

"Aye, you know yourself how many times you used to say you wished you could fix the family something to eat, and you're getting verra guid at it." She held up her fingers, ticking them off. "You can brew tea and coffee—"

"And pour milk from the jug withoot spilling it."

"Haud yer wheesht. And you can fry eggs and minced sausage and even fix a pot of brose and a plateful of sandwiches."

"But that's no' cooking. 'Tis just fixing things."

"Things to eat. That's the kind of thing I want to teach our Robbie—och, no' the frying part yet, but sandwiches, how to spread bramble jam on a buttery—easy, safe things like that."

"Och, I don't know—"

The rescue siren pierced the night air, drowning out his words.

He leaped from bed, pulled on his denims and socks, and rummaged in the closet for a shirt.

Maggie held out his gansey sweater. She couldn't control the tremors shaking her body. A rescue shout with high seas in the mids of a storm—just what she feared most. She pulled on her dressing gown and followed him to the front door.

The siren uttered a final, strangled wail as he shrugged into his waxed jacket, yanked the door open, and stepped into his wellies.

She handed him a torch and threw herself against him. "Promise me you'll take care and ask our Lord's guidance."

"You know I will, luve." His kiss was fast and urgent. "Monitor our radio transmissions with Control to find out what kind of shout we're facing." He vaulted the front gate and tore down the path, his torch a smitch of light bobbing in the darkness before it disappeared behind a curtain of rain.

Maggie stood in the doorway, shivering. *Be with him, Faither, please. Hold my Rob safely in the palm of Your hand, far above the raging waters.*

A cold nose pressed against her palm. Shep always seemed to sense her fear.

That fear that always threatened to grip her heart and take her under.

She rubbed his silken ears. "He'll be home, lad. He promised he'd always come home." Stepping into her baffies, she tied her dressing gown tighter, then made her way into Rob's office, Shep at her heels. He'd no' leave her until she went to bed or Rob returned. She snapped on the Anglepoise lamp.

The shortwave radio sat on a shelf behind Rob's desk, already set on the right frequency.

She toggled the switch to Receive.

Now the wait. At least Rob had talked her through the initial phase of every shout: first the all-volunteer crew arrived, by ones or twas, and immediately changed into their wetsuits, Rob included. Once they were all aboard and suited up, Rob contacted by radio whoever was working the Control desk in the shed, asking for a complete update on the reason for the emergency call, the coordinates of the vessel in trouble, a contact radio frequency, and went over everything again to make certain there were no misunderstandings before they left the harbour.

Which meant it could be a long wait. The crew all lived on the western side of the island. After the turn o' night and in the mids of a storm, it would take them time to dress and fight their way through the teeth of wind and rain to reach the *Maggie* at her berth.

Keep each and every lad safe, Faither. Give them Your strength if they have to go into the water. She rubbed her forehead. She wouldn't borrow trouble now. It could be a medical emergency or a tow, like the last shout. *Please, Lord, just a tow, only a tow.*

Rob's deep voice interrupted her frantic prayer. "This is the *Maggie*, Control. What do we have, Stephen? Over."

"'Tis a large trawler with six hands aboard, Commander. She lost all power to her engines and steering, and is at the mercy of the sea. Barra will be first responder, but has asked us to stand by to assist as needed. Over."

"I copy that. Large trawler, six hands, Barra's first responder, we stand by to assist as needed. What are the coordinates? And a radio frequency for the trawler? Over."

"They had no radio frequency for the trawler. Barra has them at fifty-six degrees north, seven degrees west. Over."

"Confirm, fifty-six degrees north, seven degrees west. But we're almost as close to them as Barra, and a lot faster."

"The call went directly from the trawler to Barra Control, no' Maritime Rescue. Barra's already left Castlebay and are on their way." Stephen's voice rose an octave. "Hold, Rob, Graham's just walked in. He'll take my place at Control. I'm on my way oot to the *Maggie*. Over."

"Give heels to, then, and tell Graham to contact me if there's any change. *Maggie*, oot."

"Will do, Rob." Graham's voice. "Godspeed to all. Control, oot."

Tears blurred Maggie's sight. *Almost as close to them as Barra.* Rob had told her that it didn't matter who received the initial call. Whoever arrived first would act as primary rescuer. And a much smaller lifeboat didn't have much to offer against Rob's rescue boat, even in calm seas. With his determination to save as many souls as he could, Rob would keep the *Maggie* at full throttle all the way.

Would she live the rest of her life trapped in this nightmare of fear? Hadn't she suffered enough when Rob flew bombing missions over German territory while she paced the halls of the base hospital, yearning for—yet dreading—the roar of B-17s circling the base to land? Every emergency flare sent up by a landing Fortress stopped the breath in her throat. Was it the *Bonnie Maggie*? Was Rob's crew working frantically to save his life while his blood spread across the cockpit floor?

She dropped to her knees beside the chair, hands clasped tightly together. An in-sea rescue in dark, storm-tossed waters, the waves washing over Rob's head. Hadn't she already given this to the Lord?

Chapter Two

Waves crashed over the *Maggie*'s deck, obscuring the windscreen with salt water and spume. Rob checked their position. Exactly fifty-six degrees north by six-point-nine degrees west. He rotated the radar antenna. As he expected, no sign of the trawler.

Without steering or power, she had either been caught broadside by a wave and sunk, or been carried far to the west. And where was the Barra lifeboat?

He glanced at Neil MacLean, his second coxswain. "Cut engines to half speed. New heading—due west. Train those spotlights dead ahead. We'll have to go looking for the trawler or what's left of it."

Neil nodded, executed a slow turn to the west, and activated their outside spotlights. "What about the Barra lifeboat? We'll have to keep close watch so we don't run her over. No' an easy task in these seas."

"I'll keep a sharp lookout and try to raise her on the radio. We'll have an advantage turning our stern to the storm. It should keep the waves from washing over our windscreen."

None of the usual chatter came from the crew, who stood braced against the violent shudders buffeting the *Maggie*. With Graham filling in for Stephen, they were ten strong for the shout. In this gale, 'twas biddy certain they'd all be needed. But this was their first attempt at a rescue in the mids of high seas and plumpin' rain. *Keep us focused, Lord, and if it be Your will, help us find that trawler before it's too late.*

After fifteen minutes with no contact, they received a faint radio transmission. "Barra lifeboat to Innis ... Rescue. Can you hear ... Over."

Flipping his radio to Broadcast, Rob replied, "Barra lifeboat, this is Innisbraw Rescue. Your signal is verra weak. What is your position? Over."

"Having problems with ra … Have you located traw ...?"

"Negative. What is your position? Over."

Silence.

"Barra, do you read me?"

No response.

Rob pounded his palm on the helm. "Och, there's no telling

where they are, and with a failing radio ... I hope they turn back before they capsize in this sea."

Neil's face looked grim. "Do we keep looking?"

"Aye. Running with the wind and sea at our backs, we should be off the shores of Mingulay soon. With no harbour and a rocky shore, if we don't find the trawler by then ..."

Another nod from Neil. Thank God, he knew this sea and its islands better than most navigators knew their own faces.

Ten minutes later, a faint smudge showed on the radar screen.

Rob leaped to his feet and grabbed his binoculars. "Kill the interior lights. There's something oot there." He cupped the padded eyepieces to his face and pressed the lenses against the windscreen. There. Something ... "Steady ahead slow." He looked away, blinked, then peered through the glasses again. "There she is, the trawler! Stern's facing us. Don't think she's moving."

"But she has to be … unless ..." Neil's voice cracked. "Och, Lord, if they put oot both anchors and the flukes caught on some rocks—"

"Manoeuvre a bit closer till I can see her better. Steer aport. More ... more … a bit more. Reverse engines, full stop!" Rob reached for the rope hanging from the cabin ceiling and gave it three slow pulls.

The *Maggie*'s shrill siren throbbed into the night.

He motioned his crew closer. "I don't see anyone on deck, but her stern's being savaged by waves. We'll go roped together in pairs—Artair with Duncan, Ewan and Paddy, and I'll pair up with Graham. Danny and James, stand by to pull in our ropes. Remember, three tugs means to start pulling. Matthew, prepare for casualties. Help with the ropes only if they can't do it withoot you. Start roping together." He gripped Neil's shoulder. "Turn her prow to the south. 'Twill be hard holding her broadside to the waves, but we can't use the aft deck with waves washing over it. As soon as she's steady, rotate the spots to light the trawler." His fingers tightened. "Any questions?"

"I'll keep her steady. Godspeed."

The *Maggie* rolled as it took a wave amidship.

Don't let her capsize, Lord, but if she does, bring her back up. Rob took the tethering rope from Graham and tied it around his waist. "Lads, make your way slowly aft and be verra careful climbing down to the aft deck. Hoods up, check your ropes one last time." He took a few seconds to meet each lad's steady gaze. *Thank Ye, Faither, for this brave crew. Guide my thoughts, Lord, please guide my thoughts.*

He unlatched the cabin door.

It flew inward with the ferocity of the rain-laden wind.

Five minutes later, all six men had their lifelines tied to the taffrail. Rob waited until the boat wallowed in a trough between waves before leaning close to Graham. "We'll go first," he shouted. "Don't climb the rail, just slide under it and jump. Head straight north. I'll be right behind you."

Maggie awakened to find Shep licking her chin. She pushed him away and crawled to her feet, knees burning. How could she have fallen asleep in the mids of her prayers? She looked at her watch.

0400.

Surely she'd have heard the radio if there'd been a broadcast. She checked.

Still on Receive.

After turning the volume to high, she threw more peats in the fireplace and hurried into Robbie's bedroom to make sure he hadn't kicked off his bedplaid.

He slept soundly, one ear of his bedraggled rabbit clutched in his hand.

Her heart ached. So much like his faither, this laddie, always craving action. *Bring Rob home, Lord. His lad needs him—we all need him.*

Annie had slept through a feeding. Poor lassie, still exhausted from all that rouping.

Maggie covered one bare foot and tiptoed from the room, her knuckle caught between her teeth.

Where was Rob? Why hadn't he brought the *Maggie* in yet? Should she call her faither at the infirmary? But wouldn't Fern have dropped Katie off if they needed a nurse?

She paced the living room floor. *Guard my heart, Lord. Help me believe Ye are watching over my Rob.*

A burst of static brought a stab of pain ratcheting through her chest. She raced back to Rob's office.

"Control, this is *Maggie*. We're on our way in with six victims, all in need of treatment for near-drowning and hypothermia. Six cairts and John and Fern at the dock. Over."

Neil's voice, no' Rob's.

Chapter Three

Graham's voice broke through the roar of blood pounding in Maggie's temples. "Control to *Maggie*. Will have six cairts waiting along with John and Fern. What is your ETA? Over."

"We should dock in about half an hour. *Maggie*, oot—Och, hold, Control. Commander says to pass on none of the crew are injured. *Maggie*, oot."

None injured.

Her Rob was safe.

Maggie cradled her face in her hands. *Thank Ye, thank Ye, thank Ye, Faither, and forgive me for doubting.*

Shep rested his chin on her lap, tail thumping on the wooden floor.

A loud wail from Annie's room propelled Maggie to her feet. She scooped the lass from her cradle and kissed her dimpled cheek, relief over Rob's safety so palpable she could fly. "Hushie-baw, lassie. I know you're fair hungry, but you're soaked through." After gathering up a hippen, gown, and blankets, she hurried to her rocker, changed the fussing bairnie, and set her to nurse.

Shep circled the rug at their feet and plonked down, nose beneath his tail.

Maggie stared into the glowing embers. Once again, their Heavenly Faither had kept her Rob safe. But this was only the *Maggie's* third shout, with winter gales sure to lash the island for months. There would soon be another shout, and another ...

The front door opened and Katie stumbled in, yawning and knuckling her eyes.

Fern followed, peeling off the lass's coat as she guided her toward the staircase. "Up to bed," she said. "I'll be back for you at the usual time unless I call." She hugged Maggie's shoulder. "I can tell you've heard, then. You're smiling."

Maggie nodded, eyes filling again. "My Rob's safe—this time."

Fern fingered Annie's soft curls. "Do you realize what this means? No matter the weather, Innisbraw has a rescue boat with a crew who can save countless lives. I know how you fear for Rob's safety, but hang on to your faith and allow our Lord to work His perfect will."

Annie squirmed and Maggie put the bairnie over her shoulder, patting her back. "You'll call me if you need another nurse? I'm sure Flora or Morag would watch the bairns for me."

"Of course, though 'tis doubtful we'll need you. There's John and I, and you know Rob won't have allowed Matthew in the water—his medic skills are too valuable—so we'll have his help too."

A loud burp, followed by two more.

"Och, she's been a wee piggy," Fern said, putting her hands out to the glowing peat embers in the fireplace. "I'd best go. John's waiting."

Settling Annie to her other breast, Maggie looked up at her dear friend, heart overflowing with gratitude. "We're so lucky we have you."

"Aye, you are." Fern laughed. "The wind's died but the rain's still plomping down. I'll send Rob home the minute I can. You ken he won't leave until all six of those fishermen are oot of danger."

"Aye, and him oot on his feet from no sleep and all that ... swimming."

"But alive, Maggie. Alive."

Fern's parting words brought tears flooding Maggie's eyes. Fern was most likely thinking of her Edward, buried in an unmarked grave somewhere in France, another victim of Hitler's insanity. "Bring someone to luve her, Lord, and Katie too. The lass and Rob are close, but 'tis no' the same as having her own faither."

Rob sipped his coffee and stretched his long legs beneath the infirmary's kitchen table. If only he could shed his hot wetsuit. The dried salt water inside irritated his skin and sweating didn't help.

Five of the battered trawler's crew were settled in the infirmary, skillfully cared for by Fern and John. Only one patient remained in danger, a young apprentice fisherman with fuzz on his chin and a stubborn stomach that didn't want to release the last of the seawater trapped there.

Muscles complaining, Rob drained his cup and pulled himself to his feet. Och, he was so tired even the spaces between his toes ached. He grunted. "Half blootered on coffee," he mumbled as he set his cup in the jawbox.

Ewan stopped him in the hallway. "Commander, that last lad's going to be fine. Barra lifeboat's coxswain is after you on the telephone. Fern said to use Doctor John's office."

This was the first time Rob had smiled in hours. "So they made it back to Castlebay, then?"

"Sounds like it."

He turned into the hall leading to John's office, pushed the door open, and grabbed up the receiver. "Rob Savage here."

"David Hamilton, first coxswain of the Barra Lifeboat. Good to finally talk to you, Commander, though knowing we'll have a rescue boat like yours next year, I'd hoped to see the *Maggie* in action."

"Call me Rob, David. I was worried you might have capsized."

"We've an inflatable bladder on deck, but we didn't have to use it. Our biggest problem was our radio. It was spotty from the mouth of the Castlebay harbour until we lost contact with you. Must have chased your wake toward Mingulay but never did see you—or the trawler. We scouted the western shore of Mingulay for a long time, but finally gave up, knowing we could never find that trawler without a radio fix."

Rob sat in John's chair and leaned back, rolling his stiff neck. "That's had me puzzled, David. How did the trawler contact you if their radio wasn't working?"

"They had a working radio. It's just that Stuart Cullen, our lad who took the distress call, has a cousin crewing that trawler. He got so excited, all he asked for was their coordinates. Then our radio started acting up and the rest was a very messy ... I'm sure you've heard the military term before, but I'll leave it to your imagination."

Rob chuckled. "I can think of several that would work and none fit for company." He flexed his cramping legs. "Glad to hear you're safely back home."

"You too, Rob. Thanks for doing our job for us. I'll be over there one day to check out our new rescue boat."

Maggie hardened her voice. "You can go oot on the entry to play once you've picked up all your books, balls, and stuffed animals. No' before."

Robbie gazed at his mither, eyes narrowed. "But I just got them oot."

She swallowed a laugh. His eyes might be blue, no' hazel, but his faither narrowed his eyes that same way when arranging an argument for his side.

Katie pulled on her sweater sleeve. "I'll help, Aunt Maggie. Being inside all the day is wearisome."

When Robbie ran for the coat closet, Maggie headed him off and deposited him in the middle of his toys. "Katie said she'd help, no' do it all, lad. Your faither could be home any time. You don't want him walking into a midden."

"I want him home now."

A sudden memory from long ago flooded Maggie's mind. She knelt and crept toward Robbie, hands raised, fingers splayed like claws. "I am the Midden Mouse. I live in midden piles, and I'm going to eat my way to a certain laddie and rub my tum-tum-tum, I am-am-am."

He hid behind Shep, shrieking and laughing, hopping from foot to foot.

Katie picked up a book and a ball and dashed into Robbie's bedroom. "Hurry," she shouted. "The Midden Mouse is after you. Help me clean up the midden!"

Cannie lass to catch on so quickly.

Maggie crawled toward a book, mouth opening and closing. "Yum-yum-yum for my tum-tum-tum."

Robbie picked up that book, then another, and snatched a ball out of her reach. He suddenly stopped, a shout of triumph stiffening his sturdy body. "Hoy, help me, Faither. 'Tis the Midden Mouse."

Maggie froze in mid-crawl and looked over her shoulder. She wanted to fly into her husband's arms and feel his hands in her hair.

Rob, still wearing his wetsuit, stubble on his jaw, eyes blurry with fatigue, and those delightful dimples dancing a jig beside his lips, nodded at her and grinned, giving Robbie a thumbs-up. "Clean up the midden, man. I'm the Hero of Innisbraw. I'll take care of the Midden Mouse."

So hoarse, his voice. Och, how much seawater had he swallowed?

Rob got down on his knees and crept slowly toward her, licking his lips, green-flecked eyes flashing.

Her flesh tingled and her heart pounded. *Chase me. Catch me!* She raised a beckoning paw at him before advancing toward the two bairns, again chanting, "Yum-yum-yum for my tum-tum-tum."

Robbie and Katie scooped up the rest of the books and balls and took them into the bedroom, then returned for the stuffed animals, racing to keep them from her clutching hands. The bairns disappeared into Robbie's bedroom.

Rob pounced. He pulled her into his arms and lifted her into his lap. "I've got you, wee Midden Mouse," he said, voice a low growl. "Now I'll feed *my* tum-tum-tum." His lips sought hers. He tasted so guid, of coffee and the sea. His kiss gentled and moved to her forehead, cheeks, throat.

She clung to him, savouring the feel of his muscular body, his soft lips. He had come home to her.

"Faither!"

She opened her eyes.

Robbie stood beside them, hands on hips, Katie at his side. The lad stomped his foot. "Faither, that's no' the Midden Mouse. That's Mither."

Rob groaned and raised his head. "Of course she's your mither now the midden is cleaned up."

Katie tossed her copper curls. "Come on, Robbie. Let's go play on the entry. Our Innisbraw Hero needs to rest."

"That no Hero. That's my faither." He pulled on his heavy sweater and let Katie button it.

"Of course that's your faither," she said, sounding so much like Fern. "But he really is the Hero of Innisbraw. My mither told me so this mornin." She buttoned her own coat before taking Robbie's hand and opening the door. "Your faither saved six fishermen from drowning last night. That's why he's a hero."

Shep slipped out the door before it closed.

Maggie evaded Rob's roving hands and pushed his hair off his forehead. "You need a shower and sleep, luve. I know you're spent."

He cupped her chin in his palm and looked into her eyes. "Was spent." He nibbled her earlobe. "There's nowt like the sight of my Maggie slinking across the floor, eyes sparkling"—another nibble—"verra shapely behoochie wriggling"—another—"to bring a spent man alive."

She settled her cheek against his chest, feeling his chuckle before hearing it.

"Where did your Midden Mouse come from? Another auld Scots tale?"

"'Tis a game my mither thought up so I'd have everything put away before Faither came home. You know how sma' that cottage is. I'd forgotten all about it."

"I wish I'd known her, your mither."

And your own. She struggled to her feet and held out her hands. "Up you come. I hear Annie stirring. I'll suckle her while you shower."

He didn't move. "I don't think I can. Och, I should have stayed on my feet."

Though her heart ached, she knew the last thing her Rob needed was pity. "Rob Savage, get up. You can't stay on the floor all the day."

"I don't want to hurt your back pulling me up. Just fetch one of those chairs."

She held the chair steady. When he was standing, she unzipped his wetsuit and peeled it down his arms. "Into the shower with you. I'll bring your dressing gown."

"I should dress. Graham could use some help at the shed, and I need to check the tide. There may be flooding the next time it's full."

A niggle of irritation. Such a stubborn man. "You'll have your shower and a lie-down. Then, after some food for that empty belly—and don't tell me you didn't swallow and retch up seawater, for your voice is as hoarse as a raven's—you can talk about checking the tide."

No argument. He fingered a tendril of hair on her shoulder, then shambled into the bathing room.

Rob yawned and stretched, reaching for his watch on the bedside table.

1515.

Och, he'd slept the day away and high tide had come and gone. Mebbe he should call Paddy at the howff and ask him how things looked.

The Irisher was always wary of his business flooding.

Rob sat up and swung his legs over the side of the bed.

His head must be full o' mince. Paddy was a member of the rescue crew. He was most likely still asleep, resting himself up for a busy night taking care of the folk who frequented the howff for their nightly "wee drams" or half-pints of the local ale and a dance or twa.

Best be getting on with it, then.

His legs felt strong. And he didn't hurt anywhere. Well, mebbe his throat was a bit sore, but that was to be expected after all the retching he'd done. His belly was so empty, the sides were rubbing together.

His denims, shirt, socks, and gansey sweater lay in a neat pile on the chair in the corner. Someone must have brought them up from the *Maggie*.

He dressed, going over the shout in his mind. They'd found the six fishermen huddled together in the trawler's small wheelhouse, wet, certain they were doomed, and too cold to be of any help. The skipper, a young man who cared only about losing his boat, refused to cooperate, arguing it was his decision to stay with his boat, not abandon it like a stinking rat. And there were no life preservers aboard.

An ominous, deep-throated creaking signaled the approaching breakup of critical timbers—if the frayed anchor ropes didn't part first. No time for arguing.

Rob ordered his lads to strong-arm the men, force them across the heaving, slippery deck to the railing, and jump, each holding a fisherman.

He and Graham were last to leave the stricken trawler. Graham half-carried a young, white-faced lad across the deck while Rob followed with the skipper, who struggled to free himself from the iron grip on his arm.

"You can't do this!" he shouted. "It's my boat. You can't force me to leave!" He lunged, teeth bared.

Though he'd never hit a man deliberately, instinct kicked in. Rob's right fist connected with the skipper's chin.

He dropped like a stone.

Now, Rob flexed the fingers of his right hand as he pulled up his socks. Hadn't broken anything, but his knuckles were sore. He lifted the lace curtain and looked out the window. Only a light wind and a mist of rain. Thank the Lord, the storm had blown over.

If Neil hadn't been an experienced coxswain, some, if not all, of the crew and victims could have been lost. He had sent Matthew to the railing to look for anyone in the water. When the medic reported he'd seen several jump overboard from the trawler, Neil ordered Danny and James to pull the slack out of all the lifelines and keep them taut above the churning propellers. Then Neil slowly backed the *Maggie* closer before idling the engines.

Those few feet made the difference. Blinded by the heaving waves, muscles seizing, at the end of their endurance from holding tight to dead weights as waves broke far over their heads, plus fighting panicking men with bellies full of seawater, the rescue crew agreed they could not have lasted much longer.

Artair Frazier had summed it up best. "When Danny pulled my rope to the boarding ladder, I was one breath away from my last."

Rob wound his watch. *And so was I, but my Maggie will never know.*

Arms piled with folded towels, Maggie stopped beside Rob's rocker on her way to the bathing room. What a bonnie sight. Annie bounced in her faither's lap, light-brown curls framing rosy cheeks and a wide smile allowing a glimpse of two new bottom teeth.

Rob put her over his shoulder and nuzzled the back of her neck, bringing giggles and a shriek of delight. His gaze met Maggie's.

She returned his smile.

"She's surely the bonniest lassie on Innisbraw," he said, "if no' in all of Scotland."

"You'll have no argument from me."

"When can you sit, lass? That's why I decided to stay home the rest of the day—so we could have time together."

His pensive tone sobered her. "This is the last of the laundry. Be back in a tick." She stacked the towels on their shelves in the bathing room closet and took time to brush her hair. There was still the ironing to do, bread to proof, drawers to straighten, and a pile of mending, but that could wait for the morra when Rob went back to the shed. 'Twas a rare day, indeed, when he took any time off but the Sabbath.

She'd just sat in her rocker and reached for Rob's hand when the front door crashed open. Robbie and Katie dashed in, followed by Shep, who raced into the kitchen and shook himself, water flying in all directions.

Rob lifted Annie into Maggie's lap. "Stay, you. A certain lad and lass—and dog—need to be reminded about no' bringing the rain in with them."

Katie studied the floor, but Robbie and Shep raced around the living room, leaving a trail of water behind them.

Rob caught the back of Robbie's sweater and swung him off his feet. "Enough!"

The harsh whisper stopped Shep in his tracks.

Rob plonked Robbie down on the kitchen bunker and stripped off his sopping sweater and trews. "I want you to go put dry clothes on, then you'll find a rag and start mopping the floor."

"But, Faither—"

"No 'but, Faither.' Didn't your mither tell you to stay on the entry? You don't go plowtering about in puddles and expect your mither to clean up the midden you make."

"We did stay on the entry, Uncle Rob," Katie said. "But the wind started blowstering and blew the rain all over us, and we had to call Shep because he was oot nosing around Aunt Maggie's garden and didn't want to come."

Laughing, Maggie sat Annie on the hearth rug and ordered Shep to guard her.

The dog crawled across the rug and bared his belly, a sure sign he knew he was in trouble.

"Och, you're as impossible as your laddie," she chided, scratching his belly. She hurried into the bathing room and returned with a handful of freshly folded towels. "Robbie, dry your hair and get into clean clothes like your faither said. Then you can dry Shep. Katie, get oot of your wet coat and tights before you catch your death. There's dry things in that clothes-press upstairs."

Rob lifted Robbie down and patted his hippened bottom. "Hop to it, laddie, before your mither turns into the Midden Mouse again." Eyebrow raised, Rob asked, "And what are my marching orders, Mither?"

Maggie stifled a laugh. "To make a fresh pottle of tea."

He gave a brisk salute and a hasty, "Aye, Commander Mither, fresh tea and a dry floor."

Chapter Four

Maggie nestled in Rob's lap, watching peat embers cast their warming glow about the room. The light swept shadows from corners and bathed the limed walls with flickering tongues of yellow and orange. She pressed her cheek against Rob's chest, listening to the steady thrum of his heart. Such a grand afternoon and een, filled with food and laughter and luve. Now the bairns were abed and with the long night ahead ... She shivered with delight when his long fingers traced the outline of her cheek and chin. How could hands so large have a touch so light?

He kissed the top of her head. "Do you think the Proctors will really come to Innisbraw next summer? 'Tis such a long way to travel just to show us their lad and how he's grown."

"I'm thinking they want to thank you again for saving their lives and helping Jill birth their laddie." She stayed his protest with a finger to his lips. "I know Stu Proctor helped too, and Den, but 'twas you who saved them, Rob. Without you, they'd have all died. What if you hadn't taken the boat out that first time?"

"I was hoping we'd have heard from Den by now."

Rob, always diverting the subject of his bravery. And such a yearning in his voice. He and Den had been close since they were young lads. She laced her fingers through his. "He'll write. 'Twas obvious when he was here that you're still his verra best fr—"

The rescue siren wailed, shattering the warmth with its scream of impending danger.

Maggie froze. *No, Lord. Surely no' so soon.*

Rob lifted her to her feet and stood. "I have to go, Maggie." He gathered her close, his breath ragged against her cheek. "With the wind blowing a gale again, every boat at sea's in peril."

She hugged his waist, frantically searching her mind for a logical argument—the only thing that could change Rob's mind. "But you're still too spent. How can you help someone else if your own crew is exhausted? Let somebody else answer the shout—like Tiree."

His muscles tensed. "We can't refuse a shout. They're depending on us."

Didn't he understand? Couldn't he see how terrified she was—

how she couldn't go through this again so soon?

He dropped his arms, stepping away. "I need to go right now, luve. Lives depend on a quick response."

She clutched his shirt, holding him back. "What about your life, Rob? Don't you think that's important? Don't you know how much you mean to me—to our bairns?

He jerked his shirt from her grasp. "Monitor the radio, Maggie. I'll be back as soon as I can."

"Monitor the radio?" She raised her voice at his retreating back. "Do you think that helps when all I'm seeing in front of my eyes is you sinking below the waves?" She dashed across the floor and stood in front of the door. "I've lived years fearing for your life. I've watched you bleed to death, seen you take your last breath. I've mourned over your dead body, buried you a hundred times, faced a life empty of luve, of *you,* time after time. Don't I mean owt to you, Rob? Are you so set on saving the world your own wife means nowt?"

His pale face a blur, head bowed, he reached around her and opened the door. He was leaving. After all she had said, after laying her soul at his feet, he was still leaving.

The cold wind and pounding rain lashed at his body, threatening to lift him from his feet and send him flying off the fell onto the strand far below. His feet plodded on, eyes unseeing, heart turned to ice. How could she ask him to choose not to save a life? His feet turned down the pier.

Spume-laced waves dashed against the dock, roaring in protest when mere wood impeded their way. "We're stronger than you," they mocked. "Stand aside and let us show you the power of the sea."

A spark of protest stirred his frozen body.

No. The sea could not win.

He forced his reluctant legs to move. "On you come, Commander. Most of the crew's here, waitin' on you." He staggered into the light.

The *Maggie's* cabin. Where he belonged.

Maggie felt warmth and the rise and fall of a chest. She opened her eyes and found Shep's furry body pressed close to hers, his pale blue eyes begging for approval. Scalding tears slipped down her cheeks. She buried her face against the dog's neck as a keening cry burst from her throat. Why had she been so blinded by fear? How could she have sent Rob on a shout with unkind words ringing in his ears?

They could never be taken back.

Elspeth had often warned her, "Hasty words can be forgiven, but no' forgotten." Maggie had been so selfish, thinking only of how she felt, how she suffered, how much she sacrificed.

She couldn't have hurt Rob more if she had taken a knife to his heart. He needed her approval, her understanding. After years of withdrawing to avoid rejection, he'd learned to trust, to bare his innermost thoughts, to reveal his painful memories. Thought by thought, memory by memory, he had crawled from that place of inner safety and opened his heart to her and given all he had to offer—his luve and constant support.

She was worse than Peter, who denied the Lord.

Worse than Thomas, who doubted.

She was Judas. Who betrayed.

Shep whined and tried to pull away.

Och, she was squeezing the breath from him. She struggled to her feet and opened the coat closet door. As she'd feared, Rob's waxed cotton and leather A-2 jackets hung there, above his rubber boots. He'd gone out into the gale wearing only a light linen shirt, denims, and what he called "socks."

Another coin to add to those thirty pieces of silver.

Her head throbbed, scattering her thoughts. The radio. She needed to get to the radio, find out what kind of shout. Then she would wait until Rob reported in, giving a time of the *Maggie*'s arrival back at Innisbraw.

Tomorrow, she'd seek out Hugh and ask his help. But tonight, she would be waiting on the dock, no matter the time or the weather.

She doubled over, a searing pain in her chest. What if he turned from her with that same look of indifference she'd seen on his face so long ago? The thought stopped her from reaching the radio.

It couldn't matter. She wouldn't let it.

She'd be there. Waiting.

Rob ignored the startled looks of his crew and reached for his wetsuit. So he was starting a call soaked through and shivering. What never mind did that make? He stripped and pulled up the rubber suit, fumbling with the zipper.

"Let me be helpin'," Paddy said with a grin. "I've often wondered how you can do it at all, with hands big as supper plates."

"Thank ye." Rob tapped the Irisher's shoulder before he made his way to Neil's side. "Who are we missing?"

"Only the Frazier brothers, but they have the farthest to run."

As though on cue, Artair and Duncan Frazier rushed in, panting and mumbling apologies.

Rob grabbed the radio mike. "Control, this is the *Maggie*. What do we have? Over."

"This is Control, Rob." Graham's voice. "'Tis the *Sonsie Susan* with five aboard, including the skipper. His engine lost power. Coordinates are fifty-three degrees north by seven degrees west. Mark says you know his radio frequency. Over."

Rob repeated the information. "I have it on my clipboard. Leaving the dock now. *Maggie*, oot."

"Godspeed, Rob. Control, oot."

Rob exchanged looks with Neil as the second coxswain steered the *Maggie* into the harbour and upped the engines to full power.

Mark Ferguson's boat, auld and always in need of repair. They'd practiced rescues together before the *Maggie* was certified. Though young, Mark was an experienced skipper.

Rob took his seat, bracing himself as the *Maggie*'s prow plowed through the rough sea, waves washing over her deck. He found the *Sonsie Susan*'s frequency and hit Broadcast. "*Sonsie Susan, Sonsie Susan,* this is *Maggie*. Do you read me, Mark? Over."

"*Sonsie Susan* to *Maggie*. Aye, Rob. Do you have our coordinates? Over."

"Aye, they're locked in. We're only about five minutes from your position. What's your condition?"

"I'm keeping the prow into the waves, and we're all vested up with safety lines tied, but the sea's running high with some waves over thirty feet. I've never seen a gale like this so early in the year."

"Guid work. Keep your prow into the waves, no matter what it takes. See you in five minutes. *Maggie*, oot."

The *Maggie* pitched and rolled, shuddering as each wave thundered across the deck. Rob's mind raced. He knew each man aboard the *Sonsie Susan*, and Mark and Susan Ferguson were good friends of his. He had to do this right.

Normally he'd use the transfer sling and put Neil aboard to look at their engine. If the engine couldn't be fixed, they'd do a tow. But a transfer at night? In the mids of a gale? Just shooting tow lines would be hard enough.

Where was the logic he'd always used to solve problems? Was it a casualty of Maggie's piercing words?

When she finally made it to the radio, Maggie's fingers shook as she checked the connections. All solid. She'd waited too long and missed the initial call. Pressing her thumbs into her throbbing temples, she sat back with a groan.

Shep nosed her hand.

Her fingers moved through his soft coat as she went over her plans. She couldn't leave the bairns alone when she went to the dock. And who could she call in the mids of the night? No' Fern if there were casualties.

Casualties.

How could there be more tears when her handkerchief was already sopping? She wanted to pray, to pour out her grief and plead with the Lord to keep Rob safe. But her shame was too great. *Her* shame. Once again, her wicked thoughts concerned only herself. She knelt beside the chair and poured out her sins to God. Five minutes later, she wiped her eyes on her sleeve. "I know Ye have already forgiven me, Faither, but I fear Rob won't be able to. Please keep him safe. 'Twill be so hard for him to concentrate on the shout without knowing I support his dream. Give him guidance and a clear mind. I know Ye control the sea, like all of nature. Hold him up, Heavenly Faither. Bring my Rob home."

BELIEVE appeared before her closed eyes in brilliant red.

For the second time in her life, Maggie had received a visual answer to a prayer. "Thank Ye, Faither. Och, thank Ye." She leaped up and turned off the radio. She needn't be at the dock when the *Maggie* returned. She'd be right here, where she belonged, waiting for her Rob's footsteps on the entry. He might no' accept her apology. But he would be home.

Chapter Five

The tow was difficult, long, and fraught with danger. The waves were so high, Rob couldn't see the trawler behind them. Wiping the sweat from his forehead, he gazed ahead, anticipating the impact of each wave as they approached Innisbraw Harbour. Once inside the broad mouth, he flicked the radio to Broadcast. "'Tis Rob, Mark. We'll shorten the lines and tow you as close to the south dock as we can, then winch you alongside. Watch those lines closely. We don't want them to snap and leave you adrift in the harbour. Over."

"Aye, Rob. We're watching them now."

Rob radioed Graham at Control and told him to call his boatbuilding crew to winch the trawler alongside the south dock. There were no injuries as yet, but 'twould be good to have a cairt and cuddy standing by in case something went wrong during the winching.

Once the *Maggie* was secure in her berth, Rob climbed down onto the shuddering dock. The wind had died, but rain came in torrents. He made his way to the south dock, shielding his face from stinging raindrops big as ha'pennies. Still a lot of work to be done, but the end was near.

An hour later, the *Sonsie Susan* was tied fast to the dock. Mark raced to Rob and hugged him, pounding his back. "Thank the guid Lord we have you and the *Maggie*. We never would have lasted if we'd had to depend on Barra. I'd have lost my boat for certain and mebbe my crew."

Rob brushed aside the skipper's effusive thanks. "What were you doing oot there in a gale, Mark? I've never known you to take chances like that."

"Och, never have, never meant to. I've spent the last twa days in Oban, unloading my catch and waiting for the weather to clear." He lowered his eyes and toed the boards. "After the wind died, I sailed for home, never thinking another gale was on—"

Susan, wet, black hair tangling around her cheeks, raced onto the dock and launched herself into Mark's arms. She ran her hands through his dripping red hair before turning to Rob. "We can never thank ye enough." She caressed her husband's cheeks as they shared a long, heartfelt kiss.

Rob's stomach cramped as he eyed Susan's protruding belly. Come Hogmanay, she'd deliver their first bairnie. After losing twa before birth, they'd finally be the family they wanted to be. He stared out at the harbour, but almost didn't notice the dark, turbulent waves. Maggie waiting on the entry, a smile of welcome lighting her face—that's what he wanted to see. He turned on his heel, brushing the water from his face—not tears, just rain—and walked down the pier.

Alec MacDonald hailed him from the path. "Need a ride up the fell, Rob? You look fair spent."

He couldn't face anybody now. "Thank ye, but I have some things to talk over with Hugh. I'll wait in my office for first light before I bother him."

"You won't have to wait, lad."

Hugh climbed down from Alec's cart, the outside lights of the boatbuilding shed revealing his face. "We can have that ride up to your home or ...?" The light glinted off his eyeglasses but not before revealing the concern in his brown eyes. He took Rob's arm and led him across the path. "The Cottage Weaver's empty at night. How about a blether there?"

"Should I wait for you, Hugh?" Alec called.

"No' necessary. Get yourself oot of this storm and back to your warm bed. Guid night, friend."

Rob stopped for a moment. He wanted to talk, but not when he was so tired.

A firm hand on his arm urged him forward. "On you come, Rob. That rubber suit can't be all that warm, and we're both getting wetter by the minute." Hugh opened the door and led Rob inside, switching on the light.

The musty odor of wool filled the cavernous space packed to overflowing with looms covered with varying stages of woven cloth.

"Why were you waiting with Alec, Hugh?" Rob asked. "I told Graham there were no injuries."

"I felt compelled to see you." Hugh pulled over two benches and wiped his eyeglasses with his handkerchief. "Sit. And talk. What has you looking like a dead man walking?"

Rob sat and buried his face in his hands. "Because that's what I am."

"Why, Rob? Why do you say that?"

Och, the words were as reluctant as the tears. "I had to make a choice."

"Between?"

Such a simple one, that word, yet so hard to answer. *I have to go, Maggie*, he'd said. And *lives depend on a quick response. Monitor the radio.* Such cold words, those. So selfish in the face of her agony.

Hugh removed his waxed jacket, shook it, and placed it on the bench at his side. "Answer me, lad. I'm here for a reason."

Rob leaped up and paced. "A choice between Maggie living with the constant, gut-wrenching fear I'll drown, or letting countless victims drown instead." He leaned against a loom and closed his eyes.

"So Maggie's fears are your fault, no' hers?"

Maggie's fault? "How do you control fear, Hugh? I've never felt it for myself. Not bodily anyway. And when I feared for my crews, I shut it oot of my mind, no' wanting to cloud my decisions with something I had no control over. But I've seen what fear can do. I've watched men, guid men, choke at their guns, unable to return fire when the enemy was blasting away at them. I've stepped through the vomit of men who didn't want to die, who were so afraid they wouldn't live through that twenty-fifth mission they were willing to face a court-martial before they'd follow orders. Fear's a destroyer of lives, Hugh. I should know."

"You're right. Fear is the destroyer. In this case, Maggie's fears."

"But I just told you. She can't help it. It's just there, inside her, threatening to tear her apart every time there's a shout. Och, I should have known you wouldn't have the answer, because there isn't one."

"I don't have the answer. But God does."

"Aye, the same God who mandated I build and command that rescue boat, even knowing—since He knows everything—that Maggie would be tortured by fear?"

"You doubt your mandate too?"

Rob jerked away and threw himself down on the bench.

"You're verra bright, Rob, and well educated, but you have a blind spot that's led you to the sin of arrogance."

"Arrogance?"

"Aye, arrogance of the most insidious kind. Once again you've taken the blame for something caused by another. The Word tells us it's arrogant to assume our words or actions are the cause of another's pain."

Hugh's fingers dug into Rob's arm.

"You and Maggie share the same fears—just twa sides of the same coin. For years, she's feared losing you physically, while you've feared losing her emotionally."

Rob grunted. "I suppose we've both lost the coin toss, then. I'm still alive, but I've threatened her luve."

The minister reached for his hands. "Look at me, Rob. Maggie telephoned me. I know what happened the night, the hurtful way she sent you off. That's why I was waiting on the dock."

Hugh's quiet words resounded like a shout. "And?"

"She left a message for you. She'll have a fresh pottle of coffee perked, the shower water hot, and a nice, hot meal waiting for you."

His tired, worn-out brain could hardly comprehend a warm welcome. "But it will just happen again. With the next shout."

Hugh reached for his waxed jacket. "I've been remiss in no' seeing a growing need here on Innisbraw. I'm starting a Bible study group for women whose husbands, lads, or brothers face danger in their lives—fishermen, your rescue crew, you. Though the war is long over, the women are still emotionally scarred by the fears that haunted them then. I'm confident the Word of God will help them face their fears and conquer them."

A glimmer of hope. The confidence that God's will would prevail.

Could Rob step out on faith on this? He took a deep breath—and that first step. "Will you pray with me before we go? I didn't pray for God's guidance during the shout like I always do. It could have cost Neil his life. I feel like I've slapped a verra dear Friend in the face by feeling He'd abandoned me when 'twas me who'd turned my back on Him."

Hugh's usual elfin smile returned. "Of course we'll pray, then you'll get that ride home. Knowing Alec, he's sitting ootside in his cairt in the plomping rain. He can be as stubborn as you."

Fresh coffee waited on the back of the stove, a clootie dumpling on the cooling shelf. Rob's shower water was hot, and Maggie, hastily bathed, hair brushed, and clad in her auld white nightgown and dressing gown, sat in her rocker, twisting her fingers as she stared into the blazing peat fire. She wouldn't look at her watch again. Her breath caught at a rapping sound.

Och, only a fresh spate of rain on the slates.

She had waited so long. Had the *Maggie* returned to port, or was Rob, at this very moment, fighting for his life in monstrous, gale-driven waves?

Believe.

The word impressed itself upon her heart. G*ive me Your faith, Faither. And if—no, when—Rob returns, give me Your words. Mine* *have made such a muddle of things.*

A sudden gust of wind.

She turned. Breath froze in her throat.

Rob leaned against the door, water dripping from his hair and wetsuit, arms limp at his sides, narrowed eyes probing deep into her soul.

Thank Ye, Faither. Smile tentative, steps hesitant, she walked toward him. "Welcome home." Only a whisper, but all she could manage.

They were standing only centimetres apart, but it looked like a chasm, dark and bottomless.

Your faith, Faither. She closed the distance and threw her arms around him, pressing her body against his, a sob catching in her throat. "I'm so sorry."

A hand pulled her face against his chest. Another fisted itself in her hair.

Now, Your words. "Och, I'm so happy you're home, luve!" No' a whisper this time.

He engulfed her in an embrace so tight she could scarcely breathe. Strong, trembling arms wrapped around her body and lifted her until she could look into those hazel eyes.

No words needed now. Her mouth sought his. She moved her lips slowly, savoring the taste of the sea and the essence of the man she luved. A sob escaped her lips, but still she kissed him, the salt of their tears mingling, merging, melding into one.

Rob slid to the floor, cradling her in his lap. His lips left a trail of scalding flesh across her forehead and down her cheeks before nipping her chin, her throat.

Her body tingled, blood pulsing to the rapid beat of her heart.

He groaned. "We need to talk, Maggie."

Disappointment threatened to push her over the emotional edge. She took a deep, calming breath. "First coffee and a shower. The water's hot."

"I'm fair parched."

"Help me up. I'll pour you a cup, then help you oot of your wetsuit."

He steadied her arms until she gained her feet. "Och, look at the water on the floor. I've made a midden."

"It's seen worse."

"Hand me a towel. I'll clean it up while I'm down here."

She poured a cup of coffee and held it under his nose. "You'll do no such thing. Up you come, and drink your coffee before your shower."

The rain seemed to be easing. Mebbe the gale was finally blowing itself oot. Rob smiled in the dark.

Maggie lay quietly beside him, but he knew she didn't sleep. She was waiting for that talk he'd mentioned.

He propped himself up on one elbow and snapped on the bedside lamp. Was she as nervous as he? He toyed with a strand of her hair. "I'm thinking we need to clear the air." He fought to steady his pounding heart. "A lot of things were said the night by both of us—hurtful things."

"'Twasn't you who said the hurtful things, Rob, but me."

He lay back down beside her where he could look into her eyes. "Please, Maggie, I need to say this now, while I can."

She nodded.

"I knew you feared for my life when I was flying, but I didn't know how much." He cleared his throat. "Once I was back in command of the 396th, most all I thought about was making it the best group in Wing again. And when that finally happened, we started bombing Germany itself, making the missions longer and more dangerous for my planes and crews." He picked up her hand and rubbed his thumb over her knuckles. "I don't want you thinking I never thought about you. I did, probably more than you can imagine. But you covered your fear well, always meeting me with a smile when you came off duty, never nattering about my long hours or late meetings with Wing, never questioning why I led the bombing strikes I did, only pestering me about losing weight."

A fleeting smile showed she remembered.

"I guess what I'm trying to say is that you didn't talk about your fear, so I thought you'd overcome it. I know now I was wrong. When I think of how you suffered in silence, I ... I feel like I've failed you for years."

"I couldn't tell you, Rob. There was nowt you could have done, and you had enough to worry about."

"Right. But that was in the past. Now, the rescue boat." He rubbed the side of his nose. "You hid your fears about that too, no' revealing them until the mornin of the capsizing trial. I offered then to find another first coxswain to take my place, but you said it wasn't needed, that you could overcome your fears through prayer."

She averted her eyes.

He couldn't have her believing she was at fault. "Like an eejit, I believed it was that simple, even though my own fears about the boat sinking when launched haunted me for months, no matter how much I prayed." He took her hand and laced his fingers through hers. "We've had four shouts since the *Maggie* was certified. And I didn't find out until this last one how terrified you are of me drowning." He met her tear-filled gaze, the muscles in his jaw cramping. "And what did I do? I made some daft remarks about my duty, told you to monitor the radio, and left you alone to fear the worst."

A tear touched her cheek.

"I've failed you Maggie, and I won't blame you if you say you can't handle it again."

She pulled her hand from his and sat up, face pale. "So this was all your fault?"

"I forced you to it, Mag—"

Her palm covered his mouth. "I laid there and listened to you. Now you're going to give me the same courtesy." She slowly removed her hand.

"You don't have to smother me. I'll listen," he said softly.

"Guid, because I'm going to tell you what really happened." She pulled the sheet over her bare shoulders. "First and foremost, you cannot take responsibility for my fears. They're mine, twisted and wrong as they are. I should never have flung Edenoaks in your face, for that was a lifetime ago. No, I didn't tell you then because that would have distracted you—made you even more vulnerable to making a mistake that could have cost no' only your life but others'. But that was my decision, no' yours."

He wanted to remind her of what she was always telling him, that a burden shared was a burden halved, but she deserved her say.

She pushed the hair from her eyes. "Second, I meant it when I said I didn't want you to find another first coxswain. I've never wanted that. You designed the *Maggie*, built her, and you should command her. I've never doubted that was what God wanted. I've only doubted God taking care of you. And that's my sin—doubting our Lord.

"Third, I'm deeply sorry I forced *you* to choose, knowing how many lives depend on you answering a shout, no matter when, no matter how often, no matter how dangerous."

He reached for her, but she pulled away.

"Now you know what a selfish shrew you merrit, perhaps 'tis you who should regret returning. I won't fault you if you've had enough of my wicked tongue."

He grabbed her shoulders and pulled her down. "I'll never get enough of you." He buried his face in her hair. "But what about the next shout? I can't leave you, knowing how you fear my drowning."

She punched him in the chest.

He blinked. "That stung, lass."

"I hope that got your attention, Commander Savage, because I want you to listen verra carefully. Hugh is starting a Bible study group for those of us who fear for our men at sea. 'Tis time to face this problem head-on. We need to meet, to voice our fears and have them answered by the Word of God. Men might not share their troubles, but women do. There have to be many more fearful women."

"So you're telling me you won't be sitting in front of that radio, just waiting for bad news?"

"That's exactly what I'm saying. Once I know what kind of shout you're answering, I'll be on the telephone, probably to the wives and mithers of your own crew. 'Tis amazing what a little blethering can do for a shared problem."

Rob had never been prouder of his Maggie. Aye, *his* Maggie. She'd faced her fear and was about to do battle.

Chapter Six

Rob unfolded the letter from Den and read it again.

> *Bucko,*
>
> *Just time for a quick note. I want to thank you and Maggie for the great time you showed me on that piece of rock you call home (just kidding). Busy as ever, risking life and limb teaching idiots how to take off, keep the bird in the sky, and land, hopefully in one piece.*
>
> *Say hi to your kiddos, Fern, Katie, and everyone else for me. Will write more when I get a minute to breathe.*
>
> *Ciao, Den*

Rob slipped the letter back into his pocket. No' a mention of a partnership or when Den would return for a visit. Probably had a new "conquest" and was spending every night on the dance floor—or in her bed.

Rob looked up at the louring clouds and sighed before turning north, then west toward Alec's croft. With most of the hay, barley, and late oats lost to the constant rains, he'd offered to help the crofter cut up his neeps for coo feed. He upped his speed, fighting disappointment over Den's note. "Help me rest on your promises, Faither." The words of 2 Peter 3:9 ran through his mind. *The Lord is not slack concerning his promise, as some count slackness; but is longsuffering to you-ward, not wishing that any should perish, but that all should come to repentance.* "Bring Den to Ye, Faither. Please send someone to speak Your words of salvation."

The loud wail of the rescue siren stopped him in his tracks. Och, their first shout in twa weeks, and he wasn't home to reassure Maggie. He turned and retraced his steps toward the dock, belly churning.

Though she'd taken the names and telephone numbers of the other women attending, she'd only experienced two Bible study meetings. Surely not enough to help her through the first shout since that terrible night.

He slowed in front of the shed. Should he call her?

He looked at the clouds hovering close overhead, ready to release their havoc any moment, pounding the island with more rain. No time.

"Katie, take Robbie oot to the entry for a game of keep-away while I listen to the radio. And put your heavy sweaters on." Maggie eyed her son, waiting impatiently while he made up his mind.

"I don't want to play keep-away," Robbie protested, lower lip fat with a pout. "We played it yesterday."

Katie headed for Robbie's bedroom. "Come help me carry the balls," she urged. "We'll use the ones too big for Shep to carry off."

"Can I go first?"

"Aye, but hurry."

The second Robbie's pout turned to a smile of victory, Maggie hurried into her bedroom, scooped up her Bible, and raced into Rob's office to turn on the radio. "I can do this, Lord. I have to do this." She sat in Rob's chair, heart beating a wild tattoo. "Make it another tow, Faither, just another tow." She pulled a paper from her apron pocket and laid it on the desk, smoothing out the creases.

All the names and telephone numbers of Rob's crew. Pray God she didn't need them.

She closed her eyes and waited to hear Rob's voice, thinking back on the days since that last shout. To anyone else, their life would appear the way it always had, filled with luve and harmony. Even her faither, as perceptive as he was, had never acted like there was anything amiss during their Sabbath afternoons together.

But she'd seen a shadow in Rob's eyes—a question, even—and known what he was thinking. Would she fall apart again? Could he leave on a shout knowing she still suffered from paralyzing fear?

With trembling fingers, she leafed through the Bible to the passages she had underlined. A verse in John. "Peace I leave with you; my peace I give unto you: not as the world giveth, give I unto you. Let not your heart be troubled, neither let it be fearful." One from 2 Timothy: "For God gave us not a spirit of fearfulness; but of power and love and discipline." Another in 1 John: "There is no fear in love: but perfect love casteth out fear—"

"Control, this is the *Maggie*. What do we have, Duncan?" Rob.

She leaned forward, eager for Duncan's response.

"A request for an assist from Barra, Commander. A steamer's been reported aground and breaking up off the east coast of Mingulay. They're having squalls and heavy rain and need you on standby to assist in the rescue of forty-nine souls. Barra's towing their boarding boat."

"A steamer, forty-nine souls. Coordinates?"

"They're fifty-six degrees forty-seven minutes north by thirty-seven degrees forty-one minutes west to fifty-six—"

"Och, sounds like the entire east coast of Mingulay. We'll find it, squall or no'. Leaving the harbour now. Advise if anything changes. *Maggie*, oot."

Maggie sat back, uncertain whether to be relieved it was an assist, or frightened it could lead to an in-water rescue of all those souls. She reached for her telephone list.

Duncan Frazier was safe in the shed, but his brother Artair was aboard the *Maggie*. Their mither, Julia, had been one of the first women to admit her fears for her lads' safety.

Maggie prayed for guidance and picked up the telephone receiver. Soon they had shared Bible verses, quoted Jesus's promises, and prayed together.

The squall hit Innisbraw an hour later, forcing Katie and Robbie to forgo their game.

Maggie hummed as she did her chores. Hummed! How much the time spent with Julia had helped. She allowed the bairns to help prepare their dinner, congratulating both on how well they spread the butter on the bread, then laid cheese and pickles atop in fanciful patterns.

Though Maggie tried, she couldn't swallow more than a few bites. She did drink several cups of tea, heavily laced with milk and heather honey. Determined not to show her unease, she laid out paper and pencils on the kitchen table, asking Robbie and Katie to draw a picture of Shep.

The afternoon dragged on, filled with stories and games of Hide and Go Seek, Annie's feedings and playtime, and preparing a supper of chicken bree. Many times Maggie pulled aside the front curtain, watching for a break in the rain, praying for something, someone to interrupt the long hours of waiting.

Fern appeared at a few minutes gone 1700 to pick up Katie.

"Why don't you stay for supper?" Maggie asked. *Please say you will.*

"If that's chicken bree on the stove, 'tis a definite aye." Fern shed her coat. "I'm feeling guilty serving toasted cheese and coddled eggs almost every een." She looked at Robbie and Katie busy drawing another picture. "Have you heard owt?" she whispered, hugging Maggie's shoulder.

"No' a peep." Maggie cleared the tears clogging her throat. "I have the radio tuned as high as it will go."

"John said 'twas an assist for Barra. He sent me home, but I could be called back if the *Maggie* brings any survivors here. No' that they will, with the Cottage Hospital on Barra."

Supper was a superficially gay affair, the bairns interrupting one another to tell Fern all they had done the day. And quiet Annie, in an unusual display of raucous good humour, entertained them all with belly laughs and coos.

Maggie tried to laugh at all the appropriate places, sometimes succeeding, often not.

The *Maggie* had been gone for ten hours. What was taking so long?

After Fern and Katie took their leave, she bathed both bairns, suckled Annie for the last feeding of the day, and tucked her into her cradle.

Robbie, much quieter than usual, settled into her lap in her rocker. "Where's Faither?"

"Oot helping folk in trouble."

He turned and hugged her. "But 'tis raining. He'll get all wet and catch his death."

Her lad's use of one of Elspeth's favourite sayings brought tears to Maggie's eyes. She should telephone Elspeth. Her dear, auld friend had a way of easing burdens.

Robbie buried his face in the hollow of her throat. "Why are you crying? Do you have an owie?"

She hugged him close, breathing in his wee lad scent, taking strength from his concern. "No, lad, they're happy tears."

He stretched and yawned. "I'm sleeperie. Can Shep stay in my room the night?"

"Only if he stays oot of your bed."

"He will."

Maggie helped Robbie say his prayers, tucked him into bed, warned Shep to stay on the rug, and closed his door. She checked her watch again. Over eleven hours. None of the other shouts had taken so long.

Rob lifted the radio receiver. "Control, this is the *Maggie*. We're entering the harbour. No survivors aboard, just a verra tired crew. No injuries."

"*Maggie*, this is Control. Did you find the steamer, Rob?"

"After near nine hours of searching. We finally saw a flare and traced it to the south-east tip of Sanderay, almost five miles north of Mingulay. The steamer's crew had all made it ashore with the steamer aground nearby. They were loaded onto Barra's boarding boat and should have been in Castlebay long before now."

"This is one shout I want to hear all about."

Rob grunted. "No' much more to tell if you leave out one problem after the other. I'll fill you in another time. *Maggie*, oot." Fifteen minutes later, Rob trotted up the path to the fell.

Och, Maggie was sure to be in a rare fash. Almost twelve hours was a long time for anyone to wait, but for a lass with as many fears as Maggie, it must have seemed like an eternity.

His stomach cramped. Would he find himself in trouble again? *Help me face whatever it is, Faither.* He paused at the gate and peered through the rain. Lights all on and no sign of Maggie pacing behind the curtains. He unlatched the gate and stepped through. Might as well get on with it.

The door opened before he reached the entry. Maggie stepped out, her arms wrapped around herself against the cold night air.

Or was it to keep from showing her anger?

"Rob! Och, Rob, you're home at last!" She launched herself into his arms.

All doubts evaporated with the warmth of her greeting. He pulled her up the steps and into the house, covering her face with kisses. Her heather scent, her soft skin, her sparkling eyes, the hair spilling down her back, attacked his senses. He tore off his jacket and dropped it on the floor. *Faither, thank Ye. Ye've done a mighty work in Maggie.*

At 2100 hours, after another satisfying shower and a change into their dressing gowns, Rob pulled Maggie into his lap in front of the fire. He couldn't get enough of her and kissed her again, inhaling her scent, tasting her lips, tangling his fingers in her hair.

She pulled away with a breathless gasp. "I want to hear all about the shout. Everything."

Everything? "That's asking a lot, luve. After a while, searching for that steamer got so tedisome, I had a hard time motivating my crew to stay alert."

"But why was it so hard to find? Isn't a steamer larger than a trawler?"

"Much larger. The problem was, we didn't have good coordinates. We went up and down the shores of Mingulay, blowing our siren and flashing our outside lights. And Barra didn't have any better luck. But you were most likely listening to my conversation with Duncan, so you know how we found them."

"Was anybody injured?"

"No' a one. That was a fine, well-seasoned skipper." He kissed her forehead. "Now you know how I spent the day. What about you, luve? How did you fare? And no fibs."

She nestled her cheek against his chest. "'Twas hard, I'll admit, but while I was waiting for your first transmission, I spent time in the Word, going over all the verses Hugh had called to our attention. Then, after I knew what kind of shout it was, I telephoned Julia Frazier, and we blethered for almost an hour."

"And where were the bairns while this took place? Tearing the house apart?"

She giggled. "Oot on the entry, playing ball with Shep. Then the squall hit, and they helped me fix their dinner—och, Rob, you would have been so proud of your lad. He spread the butter on the bread and even made designs with the cheese and pickles. 'Twas a guid idea, teaching him how to make sandwiches. He ate every bite without me prodding."

At least the lad would never starve for lack of a cook. "And the rest of the day? How did that go?"

"Verra well. Both Katie and Robbie were cooperative. Annie entertained us."

"My quiet Wee Annie? What did she do, blow bubbles with her spit?"

"Your Wee Annie decided she liked to laugh. And I don't mean dainty, lassie laughs, but big belly-jigglers."

Rob raised her chin. "Verra guid. Now, how did *you* do, especially after such a long time passed?"

"Quite well. Really. Och, I had some jittery times when it was hard to take a deep breath, but I never felt the panic I experienced before, just twinges of fear as the hour grew late."

That's what he was hoping to hear.

Over a month and three rescues later—twa tows and one in-water—

Rob stopped dreading the sound of the rescue siren's wail. The only thing he could fault was the constant rain. He'd never experienced a wetter autumn on Innisbraw. Lachlan MacCrae, a coo crofter and expert thatcher, along with a crew of young lads he'd trained, worked for weeks replacing rotting thatch on auld cottages.

The rescue boats for Barra and Harris were taking shape, and the *Maggie*'s record of six successful rescues with no lives lost garnered further interest in the Hebrides and even the coastal communities of Scotland. If this kept up, there should be further orders for his unique rescue boat that could right herself if capsized.

On the fifteenth of October, Control picked up a message from an Innisbraw trawler in trouble. Thomas Campbell, an auldtimer with a decrepit boat bearing the poetic Gaelic name *Tir A' Mhurain*—Land of Bent Grasses—had suffered a seized engine and lost power between the Isles of Coll and Innisbraw.

Rob had always had a liking for Thomas, who often bantered in the Gaelic with him after kirk, tossing out unusual words and expecting the same in return. The spry, auld man would slap his knee with delight if a word caught his fancy, crooning it softly 'neath his breath as though tasting each syllable.

It was another tow, and though long, not as difficult as the others had been. The sea was still running high, but the waves were much smaller. It was late afternoon before Rob reached home. His arms ached from wrestling the helm, still he leaped over the front dyke, whistling.

Another successful rescue.

He went into the house by the side door and stripped off his muddy boots.

Maggie, who had been folding laundry at the dining room table, ran to him and hugged his waist. "You did it again, luve. Fern came for Katie just as you contacted Control. You saved five more Innisbraw souls the day."

He grabbed her, kissed her, warmed himself in her fervent welcome.

"You're freezing cold. On you go then, into the shower. The water's hot."

"Care to join me?" he teased.

She wrinkled her nose. "No' if you want supper."

"What a dilemma for a man who's gleg as a gled."

She laughed and patted his hip as he made his way to the bathroom.

"Where's Robbie?" he called over his shoulder.

"Over at Fern's. Katie wanted to play 'doctor' again and needed a patient."

Rob chuckled as he removed his boxers and stepped into the shower. Maggie's faither had given Katie an auld stethoscope, which she'd draped around her neck. It hung below her knees, but she was so proud, no one had the heart to mention how comical she looked.

And Robbie was awestruck.

Washing quickly and toweling dry, Rob put on his dressing gown and made his way to the bedroom for fresh clothes. When he came out, Annie was fussing in her cradle, so he picked her up and put her over his shoulder, nuzzling her light-brown curls. The aromas coming from the kitchen made his mouth water.

Maggie stood at the stove, stirring a large pan of skirlie.

When she opened the oven door, the smell of roasted beef made him moan with anticipation. Meat pasties. He sidled up to her and nibbled her ear. "I don't know which smells better." He groaned.

"What, the skirlie or the pasties?"

"No, the supper or you."

She swatted at him. "Go get Robbie from Fern's house, luve. Then we can eat."

"What about this wee lass?"

"Give her to me. I'll change her hippen while you're gone."

Only minutes later, Maggie jumped as Rob dashed into the kitchen, peeling off Robbie's sweater, impatient to share his news. "Alice Ross just delivered a special delivery letter to Fern."

"Our postie? Who from?" Maggie bounced Annie on one hip while mashing Robbie's tatties.

Rob took Annie, who grabbed his nose and squealed with delight. He pried her fingers away and kissed them. "Den. Can you believe that? The Barra mail steamer brought it."

"Den? What did he have to say that couldn't go by regular post?"

"She hadn't read the letter yet."

Maggie put a towel around Robbie's neck and seated him in his highchair.

He grabbed a spoon from the table and pounded it.

His blue eyes sparkled when Maggie tickled his chin and took the utensil away. "Do you think there's something special between those twa?"

He shrugged as he cut up Robbie's pasty. "I've been hoping so, but it can't be much or he wouldn't have left last summer."

"I miss him. He made me laugh."

"Me too. I just wish he'd taken me up on my offer of a partnership."

"He may yet."

"Don't count on it. Den loves flying every bit as much I did. I can't see him ever giving it up."

Five minutes later, a knock sounded on the door.

Rob jumped up from the table and answered it.

Fern and Katie stood on the entry flags.

He pulled them inside. "In you come and stand in front of the fire."

"Thanks. The wind's finally died, but the rain's still pouring down." Fern's black hair sparkled with raindrops and her blue eyes danced. "I'm sorry to interrupt your supper, but I just had to share Den's letter."

"Have you had your own supper?" Maggie asked. "There's galore."

"I fed Katie, but I'm too kittled up to eat." Fern's cheeks flushed red. "Go finish your supper," she said to Rob as he took their coats. "I'll pour myself a cup of that tea and Katie some milk. Then I'll read you the last part of the letter."

Rob's eyebrow rose. "Last part?"

"The rest is ... personal." She smirked.

"Hurry up with the tea," he said. "You've got me on heckle-pins."

Fern prepared her tea, sat at the table, and unfolded Den's letter. "Here goes ... 'I'm going to send you an extremely large, special-delivery package for Christmas. Don't try to guess what it is, I just hope it's something you really want.' There. What do you think?"

"That's all?"

"Aye. He enclosed a note for Katie, but so far she's unwilling to share it."

"'Tis a secret." Katie giggled and tossed her long, copper-coloured curls. "A verra, verra special secret."

Rob frowned. "You've got me flummoxed. I can't imagine what it could be."

"Mebbe he's bought you something for your house," Maggie said. "Something from America, no' still rationed like everything is here."

Fern shook her head. "I thought of that, but Den doesn't seem like the type to buy that sort of present."

"Did he ask you any questions while he was here?" Rob took a swig of coffee. "You know, about things you'd like to have?"

"No, and I'm in a fair fash. All I have for him is a sweater I knitted. I'm going to post it this week."

Rob took Annie so Maggie could finish her supper. "Don't get yourself in a fash. Knowing Den, it could be owt. He has a daft sense of humour sometimes."

"There's shortbread in the food press," Maggie said to Fern.

Fern pushed back from the table. "Afraid no', thank ye. The night's bath night for a certain lass."

Katie rolled her eyes. "Again? I'm always having to bathe."

"You haven't had one since Sabbath night. On you come, into your coat."

After Fern and Katie quit the house, Maggie nursed Annie while Rob cleared the table and rinsed the dishes. Kitchen redded, he picked up Robbie and sat in his rocker with the lad in his lap. "I wonder what Den's up to, though he's always pulling jokes."

"Has he always been such a tease?"

"Aye. He could think up some of the most ingenious schemes at the Point. 'Tis a wonder he wasn't booted."

"Why wasn't he?"

"Because he's one of the best military tacticians around." Rob lifted Robbie to his lower leg. "Ride the cuddy, lad." He bounced his foot. "I've always had a pretty good grasp of tactics, but Den could think ootside the norm. Some of my best ideas came from brainstorming with him."

"Then why wasn't he given a group of his own to command?"

"Faster, Faither, faster," Robbie squealed.

"Och, laddie, this auld cuddy is getting long in the tooth. Go spend time with Shep. 'Tis almost time for bed."

Robbie tumbled to the floor and crawled over to cuddle Shep.

"I was asking why Den wasn't given his own group ..."

"Don't think he wanted one. Too much work and no' enough downtime. He didn't want to spend every night organizing strikes, unless it was at a pub and the mission's target was a local Edenoaks lass."

"Has he always been a flirt?"

"As long as I've known him."

"Then he isn't right for Fern. She still hasn't gotten over losing her Edward in the war. Den would break her heart, wouldn't he?"

"Och, 'tis just a present he's sending, lass. He didn't say anything about coming back. If he were, I'd be the first to know."

Maggie touched his arm. "Will you carry Annie's cradle into her bedroom? She's fast asleep. And so is our lad."

And so he was, fast asleep with his head on Shep's side.

"I'll ready him for bed and tuck him in. It'll only take a tick."

The bairns abed, Maggie sat in Rob's lap in front of the fire. She snuggled closer and sighed. "I'm glad you were never like Den."

"So am I. Just the thought sets me on heckle-pins."

"Did you ever feel something special for a particular lass?"

"Other than you? Only one."

"Who was she?" Such a soft-spoken question, but loaded with flak as dangerous as a battery of German anti-aircraft guns.

"Her name was Peggy Blankenship."

Maggie stiffened.

Better finish the mission quickly. "We were both four years old and she had freckles."

Her laugh broke his tension. "Och, I didn't mean when you were a bairn. I meant when you were grown up."

Thoughts filled with humiliating memories replaced those of his youngest years. "I didn't know how to talk to women. They scared me to death."

"I'm glad." She pressed soft lips to his neck. "You saved all you are for me."

"Was there ever anyone special for you?" Why had he asked that? If there had been, he didn't want to know.

"Never. I used to think there was something wrong with me. It took meeting you to realize there wasn't."

"How?"

"I realized the first time we danced, I just hadn't met the right man before."

Chapter Seven

The weather remained windy and wet into the month of December. Rob and his crew responded to shouts; twa more towing rescues and several in-water rescues, one involving another Innisbraw trawler. Because Graham couldn't stay up all night at the Control desk and oversee the building crew by day, Rob hired and trained an older lad to act as Control when the wind was blowing a gale and he needed all nine hands aboard.

Maggie continued attending the Bible study group and interacting with its members when the boat was out. She still prayed constantly while Rob was on the water, but her stomach-twisting dread that he would drown no longer threatened to overwhelm her.

By Christmas Een, the *Maggie* had been responsible for saving forty-four souls. Rob dug into his dwindling bank account and gave each of his rescue crew a Christmas bonus. Though their work was supposed to be strictly voluntary, he appreciated their hard work and dedication.

So far, Den's package had not arrived. When Malcolm MacNeill docked with the post late on the evening of December 24, Rob met the *Sea Rouk.*

"No package for Fern," Malcolm said, "just a card for you from the Proctors and some post for other folk."

Though Rob mulled it over in his mind all the way up the fell, he couldn't imagine what Den was up to.

Rob stopped at Elspeth's on his way home. He'd missed blethering with her, hearing her throaty laugh, seeing the luve shining in her eyes. Och, he had to make more time for the woman he considered his grandmither.

She greeted him with a warm hug. "You're looking well, lad. Come away in. Thanks to the peats you cast for me, I've a warm fire."

So wee and frail, this dear, auld friend, like a newly hatched bird, all bones and little flesh. "We'd like you to join us for a late dinner on the morra." He quickly closed the door to keep the cold out. "Alec and Morag will be coming, along with Hugh, Rinait, and Graham. They can pick you up a bit before 1300."

Elspeth's smile deepened the creases around her twinkling,

faded-blue eyes. "I can't think of any place I'd rather be than among guid friends. I'll bring some of those special scones you like."

"Sounds guid." He kissed her cheek. "Fern and Katie will be joining us also."

"Of course. Couldn't Calum make it home?"

"He said he'd try. We'll just have to wait and see. Maggie sure wants to see her brother."

Her gnarled fingers stroked his arm. "You'll be at kirk for the turn o' the night service?"

"We will. Angus is picking us all up so we'll most likely ride with you."

"Do you have time for a wee blether with this gone-auld woman?"

Though eager to get home, the yearning in her voice shamed him. "Always."

Hugh had two reasons for scheduling a midnight service: to recognize the birth of Christ and to ask for special prayers for the *Maggie*'s crew. He didn't know why he felt an increasing urge to call a special prayer service for them, and he didn't want to alarm the folk. The turn-o'-the-night service would do nicely.

A feeling of luve and gratitude swept over him as he gazed out at his congregation. How many other ministers could expect such a turnout on such a night, especially in Scotland where few such celebrations were held? His eyes lingered on Rob and Maggie, each holding a bairn. *Protect Rob, Faither. Hold him up with Your mighty hand. And quiet Maggie's heart so she doesn't lose herself to fear.* He bowed his head until his heart quieted.

Rob offered a silent prayer, giving thanks for his Maggie and for each of his bairns. His heart overflowed with thankfulness and joy. He squeezed Maggie's hand and his pulse leaped when her fingers responded. How he wished he, that lonely lad in the orphanage in New Hampshire, had been allowed a glimpse of what lay in store for him. It would have saved so many years of heartache.

The service was filled with music and praise and a special prayer for the *Maggie*.

Rob's eyes filled with tears when Hugh asked his congregation to pray daily for each rescue lad by name. That's what he and his crew needed—constant upholding before the throne of God.

Miraculously, though Christmas Day dawned dreich, it wasn't raining. Maggie pulled her dressing gown closed and settled deeper into her rocker.

Robbie played with the wooden troke Rob had made him. Annie sat on the hearth rug surrounded by her favourite toys—spoons. Shep lay close by her side, chewing on a large beef knucklebone but constantly watching how close Annie got to the flames.

Maggie took a sip of tea, sneaking a glance at Rob.

No tapping fingers, no jiggling foot. So relaxed, nursing his third mug of coffee.

Och, if only every mornin could be spent rocking, watching their bairns play, and enjoying each other's company instead of hasty breakfasts and even hastier guidbye kisses. "This is the first day you've had off other than the Sabbath in months." She laced her fingers through his.

"Aye, and I'm enjoying it, though I feel a bit guilty sitting around in my dressing gown on a Wednesday mornin."

"Don't you dare. You're no' going to do a thing all day but relax. Didn't you once tell me everyone needs a little R and R?" She got up and went into the kitchen, returning with the coffeepot.

"I can get my own coffee, luve."

"You may be able, but I won't let you. I'm declaring this Rob's Day, so enjoy it while you can."

He laughed and touched his brow in a salute. "Aye, Commander."

The ringing telephone propelled him from his rocker.

He wore a puzzled frown when he returned from his office.

"Who was it?"

"Graham."

"Graham? What did he want so early?"

"He took a verra strange radio message from Oban a few minutes ago."

"He was manning the Control radio? But why? He's your partner, no' one of the crew."

"He's covering for Alec. The lad's wife is due to give birth later the week, and you know Graham. He didn't want Alec worrying about her going into labour while he was away."

"Rinait will be in a fair fash. She's jealous enough of the late eens he spends at the shed."

"She will that, but that's a never mind to us. The man who called said he was delivering a large package to Innisbraw and that it would arrive by floatplane."

"Den's package."

"That's all I can figure, but it can't be verra heavy or even verra large to fit inside one of those sma' planes."

"Shouldn't you call Fern?"

"The man said only Rob Savage was to meet the plane, nobody else."

Rob looked at his watch. "I'd better throw on some clothes and get down to the dock. The plane's due in about ten minutes."

Maggie fretted. Only her luve for Fern kept a full-blown fash at bay. Why now, when what Rob needed was to sit and enjoy the mornin?

That Den, always raising a storm in a teacup.

Rob, returned moments later, dressed in his denims and gansey sweater. He pulled his A-2 jacket from the closet, and leaned over to kiss Maggie. "Sorry, luve. I'll be back in a tick. Mebbe you should dress so you can go with me to deliver the present to Fern when I get back."

Robbie pulled on his pant leg. "I go, Faither."

"No' this time. Help Shep. We don't want your sister too close to the burning peats."

Rob gave up trying to figure out what was going on as he trotted down the path. It was so like Den to get everyone in a fash over something just for the fun of it. He spied the plane just as he was nearing the end of the pier—a sparkling, new red floatplane with black trim. He waited on the dock while it circled the harbour once, most likely checking for debris, then landed and taxied up.

A figure slid from the cockpit onto the pontoons and jumped onto the dock. It looked like ... Couldn't be. But it was.

"Den!" he shouted. "What are you doing here? What's going on?"

Den tethered the plane to the small dock, and removed his luggage and several boxes from the cabin. He boosted the boxes up the ladder to Rob. "So this is the greeting I get? Not even a *ho ho ho*?" He threw his suitcase onto the dock and stood looking at Rob, a wide grin on his face, his short red hair a mess of spikes. "Merry Christmas, bucko." He slapped Rob's shoulder. "You're looking at dear old Saint Nick himself."

Rob pumped Den's hand. "When you say special delivery, you

mean it. But where's that extremely large package you wrote Fern about?"

"You're looking at it."

"Come on, Den, even soaking wet you don't weigh over twelve and a half stone—och, one seventy-five."

"Not me, you idiot, the plane."

"The plane? What are you talking about?"

"Is that partnership position still open?"

A burst of joy flooded Rob's soul. "You know it is."

"Then you're looking at the Innisbraw Boatworks new transportation. She's a beauty, isn't she?"

This was too confusing. "I'm still at briefing, and you've finished your bombing run. What are you talking about?"

"You always were a little slow. I'm telling you you're looking at your new partner, and my buy-in to your little venture is that plane right there. If I'm going to live on an island without a single automobile, at least I'm going to travel in style."

Rob choked down tears and laughed, pounding Den on the shoulder. "Are you serious? You're really moving here?"

"Lock, stock, and pajamas, bucko."

"But what about Fern? She was the one expecting an extremely large package, no' me."

"I'm sure Katie told her it was a floatplane. I asked the lass—I'm talking like a native already—to keep it a secret. But I know how the female mind works. One mention of the word 'secret' and they can't wait to share."

"No' this time. Katie's a very serious lass. She wouldn't tell Fern a single word of your note."

Den whirled around and kicked his suitcase. "To coin one of your words, 'och,' I'm in trouble."

"Big trouble."

"What do I do?"

"You could give her the plane and teach her how to fly," Rob suggested with a grin. This was turning into a grand mornin. No' only had Den accepted his offer of a partnership, but one of his pranks had backfired.

Den's eyes darted to the floatplane. "But notice how the colors match the *Maggie*? I was planning on putting some sort of company logo on it. You know, use it as a tax write-off."

"You'll have to work that oot for yourself. I'm sure your devious mind'll come up with something."

"Do you really think she'd like to learn to fly?"

"Haven't a clue. But she's quite a woman, as you already know, so it wouldn't surprise me a bit." Rob eyed the boxes. "What did you bring, Faither Christmas's entire sleighful?"

"You're looking at all of my earthly possessions. Not much to show for almost thirty-two years." It wasn't like Den to look so downhearted.

"Och, until I married my Maggie, you had me beat. Let's haul your boxes to the shed. I'll phone Angus and see if I can borrow his cairt to move them up to the house later."

"I did bring a few presents." Den looked at Rob, his forehead creased. "I hope you were serious about that partnership business."

"Dead serious." Rob clasped his arm. "Welcome aboard, Den. You've made me a very happy man."

Maggie's heart leaped when Den walked into the house with Rob. "Den! You've come back for another visit." She dropped a tea towel and hurried to greet him.

"No' a visit," Rob said, grinning like a daftie. "You're looking at my new partner."

A laugh gurgled in her throat. "'Tis what Rob wanted with his whole heart." She hugged Den. "I'm so happy to welcome you to Innisbraw. You've made this a glorious day."

He returned her hug and kissed her cheek. "Let's hope Fern feels the same way."

Maggie stepped back, hands on hips. "I'll skite yer lug if you hurt my friend. She doesn't need a man who's always looking at other lasses."

Den's mouth opened and closed. He cast a helpless look at Rob. "Ouch. I don't know what you threatened to do, but I get your point."

Robbie attacked Den's legs. "Come see my new troke," he shouted. "Faither Christmas brought it."

"No' now, lad." Rob picked up Robbie. "Uncle Den's verra tired. Let him rest a moment, then he'll look at your troke."

Den rumpled Robbie's hair. "You bet I will, sport. Then I want to say hi to that sister of yours. She sure has grown." Den walked to the window and looked out. "As much as I like this island and look forward to working with Rob, it's Fern who really brought me back. I tried to get her out of my mind, but I couldn't." He turned to face them. "I'm not fooling around this time. That girl's got me so pie-eyed I can't tell up from down. Even living on an itty-bitty piece of rock surrounded by the Atlantic, and not a single automobile in sight doesn't faze me anymore." He pushed his hands into his pockets. "I never thought flying could take a backseat to anything. I've never felt this way before, not ever."

Maggie blinked and looked to Rob for his help.

"Then why don't you wash off the traveling grime, and I'll go next door and tell Fern her package has arrived," Rob said with a bemused smile.

Den nodded and picked up his suitcase. "Same bedroom?" he asked Maggie.

She managed a weak, "Aye, same bedroom," and watched him plod up the stairs. Could she believe him? Granted, she'd never seen him so serious, so solemn. She sighed and melted gratefully into Rob's arms.

"No' ours, but the Lord's perfect will, luve," he whispered.

Chapter Eight

Though Rob was enjoying the predicament Den had gotten himself into, he didn't want Fern hurt. Maybe he should tell her the truth. But wasn't it Den's place to set things straight?

Fern answered the door, wearing an apron, flour covering her hands. "Rob, what a surprise. Nollaig Chridheil." She stepped aside after the Christmas greeting and motioned him in. "Katie and I are making cookies for your dinner the day. Edward's mither sent me the receipt from America years ago."

Katie stood on a chair at the kitchen counter rolling dough, towel tied around her waist and smudges of flour dusting both cheeks and chin.

Rob kissed the tip of her nose. "You look guid enough to eat."

"No' me, Uncle Rob." She giggled. "The cookies."

He drew back in mock surprise. "Och, I thought you were a cookie."

She swatted at him. Picking up Maggie's bad habits, was she?

"Are you at a stopping point?" he asked Fern. "There's a surprise for you over at our house."

What looked like a forced smile. Nervous, was she?

"So it came after all." She took off her apron and scrubbed her hands. "On you come, Katie, let's have a cleanup. Den's surprise has come."

The lass squealed and clapped her hands, sending a puff of flour into the air. "What fun!" She smiled and winked at Rob.

"Hurry, then." Fern washed Katie's face and hands in the jawbox, took off her own apron, and ran a brush through her hair.

Rob eyed Fern's skirt and sweater. Both had seen better days, but he couldn't suggest she change just for a quick visit to his house. His stomach cramped. Should have sent Maggie—she would have known what to do.

Och, Den and his surprises.

Fern grabbed their coats as they went out the door. "Did it come by floatplane? I thought I heard one earlier."

"It did," Rob said, with some hesitation.

"Is it as large as he said?"

How could he answer that without lying? "Well ... mebbe no' quite," he stammered.

"I didn't think so. Den does exaggerate."

Katie grabbed Rob's hand and squeezed it, smile so wide her dimples were deep holes in her cheeks. "I can't wait to see it."

"Then you really do know what this package is?" Fern asked her daughter.

The lass clamped her lips tight and gave her mother a pert smile.

Rob led the way to the front door, then stood aside so they could enter. When he stepped inside, he collided with Fern, who had stopped suddenly.

Den stood in front of the fireplace, smiling broadly.

Appalled, Fern's hands flew to her hair. She whirled around to face Rob. "Look at me," she hissed. "I'm a mess! Why didn't you tell me?"

"It was supposed to be a surprise, remember?" Rob shrugged.

"Men!" she exclaimed, eyes spitting fire.

Den came forward slowly, smile fading, as he caught Katie mid run. "Merry Christmas, Fern," he said. "I didn't mean to upset you."

He'd come back. She stared at him, cheeks burning.

He took another step forward, gaze probing hers.

What could this mean? "So your employer gave you a holiday?" Och, so weak, so daft, like a clerk greeting a customer.

"I'm taking Rob up on his offer of a partnership. I'm here to stay."

Her mouth opened and closed like a hen with the pip. "To stay?" she whispered.

"Yes."

"For good?"

"Yes."

Fern clasped her hands, studying the flour trapped beneath her nails. "I don't understand." *You're no' a green lass with stars in your eyes. Look at him.* She raised her eyes. "Why didn't you tell me you were coming? Why did you tell Katie and not me?"

He ran his hands through his short red hair. "Can we go somewhere private and talk? I have some explaining to do."

"Indeed you do." She couldn't look into those pleading blue eyes.

Rob pulled Den's A-2 jacket from the closet. "Use the entry. I hear Maggie and the bairns in Robbie's bedroom. Katie and I'll join them."

Fern strode out to the entry, Den at her heels. When she was sure Rob and Katie were out of earshot, she closed the door and whirled around. "So talk, and it had better be the truth."

He tried to take her into her arms, but she backed away.

"You were going to explain?"

"All right." He put his hands in his pockets and gazed at her longingly. Memories of holding her, kissing her, had haunted him for weeks. He leaned against the railing, looking out at the white-capped sea. "I've made a mess of things. The biggest package was for Rob."

"Rob?"

"We've always played little tricks on one another, but this one backfired."

"Why did you tell Katie the truth in your note to her, and then ask her to keep it a secret? I don't understand any of this."

He turned and looked at her. Her cheeks were so rosy, her eyes so sparkling blue, his knees felt weak. "I didn't think she'd keep it a secret from you."

"And why not? You asked her to."

He threw up his hands. "Because I thought ... I was sure ... I didn't think she could keep a secret from her own mother. I was wrong. I'm sorry."

"But why mention this extremely large package to me at all since there obviously wasn't one?"

"But there was—there is."

She looked at him, confusion clouding her eyes.

He took her hand and pulled her down the steps. "Come with me. I know it's cold, but your coat looks warm enough."

She pulled her hand away but walked by his side as they took the path leading down the fell. "Where are we going?"

"To show you what I was talking about."

They were silent as they made their way down the hill. What a mess. When would he learn to stop playing games? When they reached the pier, he led her out toward the boatshed dock.

"I don't see anything but the plane you rented."

"The plane's the extremely large package. I bought it for ... for the Boatworks, as my share in the partnership."

"Partnership? Och, I should have realized that. It's painted the same colours as the *Maggie*."

"Then you understand?"

A shake of her head dashed his hopes. "No, I don't. Why couldn't you have written to me with the whole story?"

He took her by the shoulders and looked into her eyes. "I didn't want you to know I was coming. The plane and partnership were Rob's surprise, but ... but ..."

"But you were my surprise."

What a fool he'd been. "Not one of my better plans."

She laughed. She actually laughed. "Oh, Den, Den, when are you going to grow up?"

"Probably never," he mumbled.

"In that case, you should be ready to accept your punishment, don't you think?" Smile dazzling, she had never looked more beautiful.

"My punishment?"

"Aye." She put her arms around him and raised her face. "You need to know what you're in for, Den Anderson. For one, I'll never wed an unbeliever. And I'm a one-man woman, and I expect my man to be a one-woman man. The first time you flirt with another lass will be the last time, or I'll ... I'll ..."

"Skite my lug?"

"Aye, I'll skite yer lug."

Their lips met.

He couldn't get his breath, heart pounding, as he gave in to the sensations washing over him. Lips so soft, caress so warm. He groaned. There wasn't anything he wouldn't do for this woman—even look more closely into that God thing. When their lips parted, he smiled down at her. "I want to marry you, Fern. I want Katie to be my daughter. Someday, maybe we can give her a brother or sister."

Emotions flitted across her face. Was that fear? It couldn't be. Why would she fear him? Hesitation, maybe?

Why had he blurted that out? He'd left himself wide open to rejection by the only woman he'd ever loved.

Fern squeezed his hand. How could she have fallen in luve with an unbeliever? Somehow, someday, she'd lead him to the Lord. "We'll talk about that later, when we know each other better. Since you're going to be living here, there's no hurry. Right now, there's something else I want from you."

"What? Anything, Fern."

"I want you to teach me to fly that extremely large package."

"You want to learn to fly? Really?"

"Of course. How else can I keep my eyes on you? I've heard all about pilots and their roving eyes. Not all pilots are like Rob, you know."

Den grinned. "Rob thought you might want to learn. All right, it's a deal. As soon as the weather's settled down, you'll have your first lesson. I promise."

When they reached the house, they walked in to find Rob, Maggie, and the bairns gathered around a book.

Katie darted to the door, looking anxiously at Fern and then Den.

"Don't I get an even longer Merry Christmas hug from my favourite lass?" Den went down on one knee.

Katie threw herself into his arms.

Rob and Maggie followed into the living room, each carrying a bairn.

So her lass still felt the same about him. "Den's going to teach me to fly your company plane," Fern said. "'Tis the least he could do, under the circumstances."

Rob eyed Den, then matched her smile. "Good. I've a feeling that floatplane's going to get a lot of use."

"The first thing we have to do is get you licensed to fly it," Den said to Rob as he got to his feet. "And it could use a hangar of some sort. With the winter weather like it is around here, we don't want her outside all the time."

"My thoughts exactly. We'll build an extension off the *Maggie*'s dock. If the weather allows, I'll have a crew get on it first thing in the mornin."

Fern winked at Maggie. "These men and their airieplanes," she whispered.

Maggie bumped her hip against Rob. "After dinner, you're going to have to take me down to see that airieplane. Who knows, I might even want a few lessons myself."

John was the next dinner guest to arrive. He shook Den's hand, and when told of the new partnership, welcomed him back to the island and offered his congratulations. The twinkle in Den's eye suggested another partnership in the making as well.

Guid. Now Rob would have some much-needed help, hopefully with the rescue boat as well. Perhaps that would lessen Maggie's fears.

John scooped up Robbie in one arm and Annie in the other, and warmed himself in front of the fire while Rob and Maggie greeted the other guests, agreeing with everyone that it was grand news, especially since they were already fond of the congenial redhead.

Maggie placed each woman's basket or plate on the bunker: Elspeth's almond scones, Fern and Katie's frosted cookies, Rinait's crème cookies, and Morag's large platter of mincemeat tarts. "I'm glad I didn't make any sweetenins," she said with a laugh. "There's enough here to satisfy even Rob's appetite."

"Could you put Annie in the highchair?" Rob asked John. "This will be Robbie's first dinner seated at the table." He leaned closer. "On a stack of books, of course."

John plonked Robbie onto his chair, whispering, "Now you're a big lad," then lifted Annie high, kissing her belly before guiding her legs behind the highchair tray. His heart melted when she gave him a sweet smile. Was there ever a more fortunate man?

After everyone was seated around the table, Rob carried in a large beef joint surrounded by root vegetables. Fern poured milk for Robbie and Katie while John gave in to Rob's insistence and carved the joint. Plates were soon piled high with meat, vegetables, salad, and homemade pan bread. They all held hands as Hugh said grace.

John's heart might have burst with love when he felt his grandbairn's wee hands in his. After the prayer, his gaze swept over Maggie and Rob, then Robbie and Annie.

Calum must not be coming after all. Och, what would it take to have his family together permanently?

Several toasts were drunk with coffee and tea to the host and hostess, to the new partnership, and to the coming New Year.

Rob was filling his plate for the second time when the siren on Innis Fell wailed.

Conversation stopped and all eyes turned to Rob.

He leaped up and embraced Maggie. "Monitor the radio if you want, luve." He kissed her, hugged Robbie and Annie, and grabbed his A-2 jacket. "Coming Den? If you're game, you can see how an official shout is handled."

Den took his own A-2 jacket from the front closet. He paused a moment, then went to Fern and kissed her cheek before ruffling Katie's hair. "See you later."

Graham donned his jacket. "I'll take over monitoring the radio at the shed for Paddy. Since he's a bachelor, he's filling in for me." Seemingly ignoring Rinait's glare, he planted a kiss on her lips and ran after Rob and Den.

John looked at Maggie.

Pale, she was.

Och, why a shout on such a special day?

Maggie turned to Hugh and Elspeth. "We need to pray." She hurried to turn on the radio.

They all left the table and gathered around Maggie.

Only static, then a voice. "We're not sure how long she'll last. We're fast on the rocks and the sea's grinding my boat to pieces."

"The *Maggie*'s crew is arrivin' as we speak, skipper." Paddy's lilting brogue. "What are your coordinates? Are you sure 'tis the northern skerries?"

Maggie's breath caught. No' the skerries. Many a life had been lost on those rocks.

"Aye. We're at eight degrees west by fifty-six-point-seven-oh degrees north. Hurry, man!"

Graham's voice replaced Paddy's. "This is the *Maggie*'s Control, Skipper. How many souls aboard?"

"Six."

"Are you all vested up?"

"Of course."

"Then keep your radio tuned to Receive. The *Maggie*'s commander will want to talk to you."

"I will, but if you don't hurry, we'll be in the water."

"Where are you out of, and what's the name of your boat?"

"This is the *Anna Gregor* out of Harris Island."

"Roger that. Hang on for Rob Savage. The *Maggie*'s casting off her lines now."

Her faither gripped her shoulders.

She turned to him.

His face was ashen, body trembling. "That's Calum's boat. My lad's on that boat."

Chapter Nine

A rising wind whistled around the cabin as the *Maggie* plowed through the surging waves. Rob peered out the side windscreen as the steep, rugged cliffs of Innis Fell faded from view. Thank God the call had come from the northernmost skerries, close to Innisbraw. Near twa hours of daylight left. Plenty of time to affect a rescue before the gloaming swallowed the light, making objects in the water almost impossible to see.

His watch read 1345. About ten minutes to go.

He called Den to his side. "Get into a wetsuit and help Artair and Duncan set out the stretchers. Stack all the blankets on one."

"Will do, Commander." Den shot him a thumbs-up.

Rob returned the gesture and tapped Neil's arm. "You're in charge of the *Maggie*. If you need help, use Den. He's done it before."

"Won't you need him on deck?"

"No training. Don't want him in the way, but you can send him oot to help pull in the lines."

The radio crackled.

He took the mike from Neil.

"Innisbraw Rescue, this is the *Anna Gregor*. Can you hear me?"

"Aye, *Anna Gregor*," Rob replied in crisp English. "This is the *Maggie*. What is your condition?

"We're breaking up fast. Can't stay aboard much longer."

"We're less than ten minutes out. If you have to abandon ship, jump as far away from your boat as you can. I repeat, jump as far away from your boat as you can. Understand?"

"I'll follow your instructions."

"Make certain your lads' vests are secure."

"I will, but they'll have a hard time keeping their heads above water in these waves."

"Understood. Keep this frequency open as long as you can. We'll activate our siren when we spot you."

"Commander Savage, did you know you've kin aboard the *Anna Gregor*?"

His heart stopped for a moment. "No. Who?"

"Calum McGrath."

"Calum?" Rob's breath caught in his throat. Och, no' Calum.

Den gripped his shoulder. "Isn't that Maggie's brother?"

"Aye. I should have remembered he crewed aboard the *Anna Gregor*. They must have been on their way to Innisbraw to drop him off."

The fingers on his shoulder tightened. "Don't do anything stupid, bucko. He's Maggie's brother, but you're her husband. Take care of yourself out there."

Rob prayed for Calum's survival and the Lord's help in making sound decisions during an in-water rescue fraught with danger. After ten minutes, Rob spotted the trawler.

She was held fast amidships, prow out of the water, listing badly to starboard. He activated the *Maggie*'s siren, and his lads rushed out the door while Rob moved the *Maggie* as close as he dared. Heavy winds and high tide sent waves crashing over the rocks, the water exploding into a foaming, blinding cauldron.

The keel of the *Anna Gregor* screamed as the rocks slowly ground her apart.

"Take over, Neil. Keep her steady."

"Steady, aye."

"Give Neil all the help he needs," he told Den as he pulled up his hood.

"Let me spot for you." Den's eyelid twitched, a sure sign he was upset.

"You're safer in here. You're not trained."

"My eyesight is. I'm used to spotting. Use me, Rob."

It was true. Experienced wartime pilots had a highly developed ability to see objects others missed. Rob let out an explosive breath. "All right, but stay on the main deck and tie a lifeline." He keyed his mike to Broadcast. "*Anna Gregor*, *Anna Gregor,* this is *Maggie*. Over."

"*Maggie*, I've just given orders to abandon ship. We'll use the port side. It's higher, but closer to you. Have to go."

"Godspeed, Skipper. *Maggie*, out." Rob left the cabin at a run and found the rescue crew waiting on the lower fantail deck, lifelines tied. He slid down the ladder, tied his line, and leaned on the aft railing, assessing the doomed trawler.

Men jumped into the sea, throwing their bodies away from their boat. One jumped short and glanced off the side of the *Anna Gregor*.

Wincing, Rob counted. He pointed out the positions of the victims and ordered four of his men to jump, reserving three to pull in the lifelines. Rob scanned the water as he pulled on his flippers.

Four victims struggled against the waves, not making much headway, but still away from the rocks. There appeared to be a fifth victim, and possibly a sixth, close to the listing trawler. Turning to Den, who stood on the upper deck, binoculars to his eyes, Rob shouted. “Is there a man in the water close to the boat—mebbe two?”

“Affirmative. One’s struggling. Looks like he’s helping somebody.”

Rob checked his lifeline, fixed his eyes on the two stragglers, and jumped into the water, striking out hard the moment he surfaced. He rode the crests of the waves as they swelled toward the rocks.

Reaching the victims was the easy part. Even with the help of his crew pulling them in, getting himself and two victims back to the *Maggie* against the flow of the tide would be difficult—if not impossible.

He shook his head to clear his vision. Where were the two victims? He rode the next wave as high as he could, straining to see through the roiling water. When he spied them, his heart plummeted.

They were being carried toward the rocks so quickly.

He reached out as powerfully as he could, pulling with his arms and kicking hard, until he spotted them again. He was gaining on them rapidly, but the sea ahead boiled with currents and crosscurrents, slowing his progress to a crawl. He swallowed a mouthful of water and choked. Blinded by the clashing waves, he paused and shook the water from his face.

There they were, only metres ahead.

Do it, Savage. Do it now! He reached them in less than a minute.

One, white hair plastered to his scalp, struggled to hold an unconscious man’s face out of the water.

Rob grabbed the comatose man’s arm. “Give him to me.” He took hold of the man’s life vest with his left hand.

Och, no, it was Calum—a gash on his forehead streaming blood.

Rob’s fingers probed for a pulse, but his hands were so cold. He pressed harder. *Alive! Thank Ye, Lord.* He grasped the older man’s arm again. “Can you keep his face out of the water if they pull you in?”

The man nodded.

“Take him.” Rob untied the lifeline from his waist and tied it around Calum’s. “Hold the line with one hand, and keep his head up with the other.”

Another nod—weaker.

Was he asking too much of a man already exhausted and half

frozen from the icy water? Rob had no choice. He took the slack out of the rope and gave it three hard pulls.

It slid through his hands as his lads received the signal to pull in the lifeline.

Hope Den's helping with the ropes. He battled to hold his position as the two men inched back toward the *Maggie*. He was in trouble.

Even two men couldn't pull three men in against the violent surge of the surf, especially when one was unconscious—and Calum was bleeding and probably had a belly full of water. He needed medical attention fast. There was no choice but to send them ahead and make his own way back to the *Maggie*.

Taking several deep breaths, Rob stroked and kicked so hard his muscles cramped. Waves pummeled him. Currents roiled around him. He was losing ground—took a wave full in the face and swallowed water. A large wave loomed above him. He tried to dive into it, but his reflexes were too slow. It caught him and tossed him back.

A rock rushed closer.

He slammed into it. His left side felt as if it had been crushed. Yelling in pain, he swallowed more water. He tried to avoid the rocks but couldn't move his left arm. Memories of his Maggie tumbled through his mind, rapid as the tick of a clock, yet vivid in their clarity: her violet-blue eyes gazing up at him with such luve, the blood in his veins turned to molten lava so hot a breeze brought hens-flesh coursing over his body; her smile, filled with mischief or joy, returning an upside-down, wrong-side-out world to its axis; her soft, sweet breath whispering life and luve and the morra against his throat.

He grabbed onto the closest rock with his right hand. *Be with my Maggie, Faither. I luve her so—*

A wave washed over his head.

Chapter Ten

"Be with our lads as they battle the sea," Hugh prayed. "Give them courage and strength and the knowledge they aren't alone, for Ye go before them, showing them the way with the bright beacon of Your perfect luve. I pray this in the name of Your Son, Jesus Christ, our Redeemer and Fortress in time of need. Amen." He raised his head and looked around the room for Maggie.

Still on her knees, she was, hands clasped, knuckles bone-white, eyes shut. What horrors was she seeing behind those closed lids?

He pulled himself to his feet and touched Elspeth's shoulder. "Come," he mouthed, helping her up. The two stopped by Maggie's side and went to their knees again, each reaching for a hand.

She grasped their fingers and looked up.

The pain in her eyes shattered Hugh's heart. *Don't allow her to give in to despair, Faither. Write Your promises on her every thought.* "I believe I hear Annie rouping," he said. "Morag has the wee lass, but if it's hunger she feels, you're needed."

"Yes, your lassie needs you," Elspeth said. "And you need her."

Maggie tried a deep breath. Failed. Both Rob and Calum in peril. "Robbie?" she asked, voice hoarse.

"Your faither has him oot on the front entry—with Shep."

"'Tis cold oot there."

Elspeth smoothed a curl of hair from Maggie's face. "I'm certain they have their warm jackets on. On you go, lass. Take care of your bairnie."

"'Tis cold oot there," Maggie repeated. "In the sea."

Elspeth's words were firm. "No' if our Lord's holding you in the palm of His hand."

Binoculars to his eyes, Den watched the two men Rob had been helping being slowly pulled back to the *Maggie*. Why wasn't Rob with them? The realization hit him like a blow to the stomach. Rob had given them his lifeline.

Den dropped the binoculars and untied his line, then pulled up his hood as he raced to the fantail ladder. When he reached the bottom, the first victims were being helped onto the rescue deck. He retied his rope on the railing beside one of the men pulling in another crewman. "I'm going after Rob. Give me your flippers."

"You take this rope and pull it in. I'll go after Rob."

"You're tired, I'm not. Now give me those flippers!"

The man on his other side, also pulling on a rope, leaned closer. "Listen to Stephen. He knows what he's doing."

Ignorant islanders. "You going to let Rob drown while you mess around?" Den grabbed Stephen's arm. "The flippers. Now!"

Stephen toed out of his flippers. "When you reach him, take up the slack and give three jerks. We'll be standing by."

After slipping into the flippers, Den climbed onto the railing, took a deep breath, and jumped.

The shock of the icy water stunned him. He surfaced and swam as hard as he could toward where he had last spotted Rob. He hadn't been in the water for years. Never been an expert swimmer. Why hadn't he exercised more? His life was a joke—on him. Out-of-shape flyboy with a warped sense of humor and little else to offer.

The passing minutes seemed like hours. His muscles burned, chest heaved. He'd never make it. Though he'd never prayed in his life—had secretly scoffed at those who did—a sudden urge to pray overwhelmed him. *I don't know how to do this, God, so cut me some slack. Give me the strength to find Rob. And keep him alive. Please, I'm begging You here, keep him alive.* The words Hugh had spoken after a prayer echoed in his mind and he added them now. *In Jesus's name.* He crested a wave. Caught a flash of something red in the spray ahead.

Rob's wetsuit. It had to be. He gave it all he had, muscles trembling with fatigue. *Hang on, Rob*, his mind screamed. *Hang on. I'm coming!*

A wave caught him.

He put out his hands and bounced off a rock.

A pain shot up his right arm, but his outstretched fingers touched something soft. He shook the water from his face.

Rob!

He put his arm around Rob's shoulder and pulled him close. His eyes were closed, and there was a tinge of blood staining the foamy water around him.

The breath left Den's chest.

Rob couldn't be dead. He couldn't.

Den gulped in air and took up the slack in the rope until it stiffened. Ignoring the sharp pain in his right wrist, he gave three strong pulls and tightened his grip on Rob's chest.

They left the rock. The pull against his waist hurt, but so what? They were going in the right direction. He tried to shield Rob's face as waves washed over them, but in the roiling current, his efforts were futile.

Rob suddenly choked and gasped.

Den clasped him closer, his own chest heaving.

Alive. Rob was still alive!

It took a lifetime to reach the fantail. "Careful," Den cautioned the men who stood by to pull them aboard. "He's hurt, but I don't know where." Using a final burst of energy he didn't even believe he had, he boosted Rob high until they had a good grip on him.

As Rob was lifted from the water, his torn wetsuit came into view. The rocks had chewed it to shreds.

The instant they had Rob aboard, Den pulled himself up the short ladder, again ignoring the pain in his right wrist. Probably a sprain. Big deal. He lay on the platform, gasping for breath while four of the crew lifted Rob to the main deck.

There wasn't much blood on the deck. Maybe the rocks had only scraped Rob's skin.

He slowly climbed up the ladder and stumbled into the cabin.

Rob lay on a stretcher, Matthew bending over him and looking as though he was checking for a pulse.

Den pushed his way to Rob's side. "How is he?"

"Alive, though I don't know how." Matthew grabbed scissors and cut Rob's wetsuit away. "I need blankets!" he shouted.

Someone thrust two blankets at him.

He peeled the wetsuit off and covered Rob's shivering body. "Give me that pressure cuff," he told Den, pointing.

Moving as quickly as his exhausted muscles allowed, Den handed the blood pressure cuff to Matthew.

The young man placed it around Rob's right arm and inflated it. "Too low." He slapped Rob's cheeks. "Come on, Commander, wake up. Wake up."

Rob groaned and moved his head but didn't open his eyes.

Matthew prepared an IV. Once the needle was inserted into Rob's right forearm, he secured it with tape, grabbed for a bottle of saline, and snapped the connections together. "I don't like the looks of his left side," he told Den. "He's swallowed water, but I can't push too hard on him with his dislocated shoulder. And there's deep abrasions from his ankle to his upper arm. He's going into shock."

"Can you help him?"

"I can't reset his shoulder. All I can do is try to stabilize him till we reach port." He reached for more blankets and piled them under Rob's feet and legs. "So the blood will flow to his head."

For the first time since he'd entered the cabin, Den took his eyes off Rob. The *Maggie* was underway with Neil at the helm. Den glanced around.

All of the fishermen, most with IVs, lay on stretchers beneath blankets. Calum McGrath looked so much like Maggie, Den recognized him immediately. A bloody bandage covered his forehead, but his eyes were open. He must be concerned about Rob, looking over at him and trying to get up, but Paddy McDonald pressed him down.

Den turned back to Rob who groaned, teeth chattering. "Can't you give him something for the pain?" he asked Matthew.

"No' with his pressure so low. Can't risk it. All I can do is secure his left arm to the top of his head, but it takes four hands. I could use some help."

"You've got it."

Ignoring groans of protest, Matthew lifted Rob's arm until his elbow rested against his head. "Hold it there while I get everything ready." The medic grabbed a blanket, folded it into a rectangle, and tore off several long pieces of tape. He pressed the blanket beneath Rob's arm. "Don't let him move. I have to tape his arm down."

Rob's pasty-gray face was bathed in sweat. He opened his eyes once, then closed them again, panting.

"That should hold it." The medic's sweeping gaze made Den squirm.

"You look a bit shocky yourself. Sure you wouldn't like to lie down?"

"I'm staying right here."

Neil activated the siren.

They must be entering the harbour.

Rob opened his eyes, tried to talk but only groaned, twisting and turning on the stretcher.

Den grabbed his right hand. "Hang on, bucko. We're almost there."

A stream of seawater spewed from Rob's mouth.

Den turned Rob's head to the side so he wouldn't choke.

Rob panted, squeezing Den's hand so hard it hurt. "Calum," Rob croaked. He tried to sit up but fell back, writhing.

"Don't move," Den ordered.

Rob retched again.

Den wiped Rob's chin with a corner of the blanket. "Calum's all right, Rob. He's conscious."

"Thank Ye, Lord." Rob shuddered. "How many saved?" he rasped.

"All of them."

"My crew?" Rob groaned.

"All safe. No injuries. Except you."

Neil flipped on the radio and asked that John meet the *Maggie* at the dock. "We've one crew member and one survivor injured," he said. "Be sure you put the fastest cuddies at the front. Those twa need transport immediately."

"John, Maggie, and Fern are at the dock," Graham replied.

Den's heart twisted. Too bad Maggie would be there. Not only was her husband injured, but her brother was as well.

The instant the *Maggie* docked, John leaped aboard before the lines were secured. In the cabin, his gaze swept from stretcher to stretcher. He saw Calum first, then Rob. Och, his worst fears come true. "Triage!" he shouted to Matthew.

"Rob. His shoulder's dislocated and his left side badly abraded."

"Help Rob," Calum groaned.

John went to Rob's side.

The lad was obviously in agony.

He checked the position of Rob's arm, nodding approval at the makeshift brace. Matthew's assessment of a dislocated shoulder was correct. "Did you give him morphine?" he asked the medic.

"Pressure's too low."

John nodded to two of the crew. "Get this stretcher to the first cairt in line."

Maggie and Fern rushed into the cabin. When Maggie saw Rob, her pale face blanched even whiter.

John grasped her shoulders. "'Tis no' life-threatening, lass. We'll transport him first."

She nodded and looked around, eyes wild. "Where's Calum?"

"On yon stretcher. I'll check him next. You go with Rob. His left shoulder's dislocated. On you go."

Maggie rushed to Rob's side. She pressed Den aside and took Rob's hand. "I'm here, luve," she said as the stretcher was lifted. "I'm here. Hang on."

Though Rob tried to smile, his extreme pallor and shallow breathing were clear signs of shock.

She stood aside as they carried the stretcher through the cabin door, then took Rob's hand again. His pain ratcheted through her body. Hadn't he suffered enough during the war? Wiping the tears from her eyes, she forced herself to take deep breaths. "I've got it." She took the saline bottle from Artair, who trotted on the other side of the stretcher. "Go help transport Calum."

Fern ran to catch up with her. "John says it looks like Calum has a concussion and a stomach full of seawater, but he should be fine. They're transporting him next."

"Thank ye."

Fern grasped Maggie's elbow as they loaded Rob into the cairt. "He'll be all right. He's strong." As Maggie climbed in, Fern called to her, "And everyone's still praying. He'll be all right."

Rob writhed.

If he fainted from the sheer agony, he might be better off, but the dangers of losing consciousness ... She shuddered. *Och, Lord, no' a coma. Don't let him go away from me again.* She pressed her body against Rob's, trying to cushion him against the rough ride.

Every bump brought a moan, and his lower lip bled from the gnashing of his teeth.

"It won't be long, luve," she soothed. "We're almost to the infirmary."

When they carried the stretcher into the foyer, Maggie directed them to the operating room. She hung the saline from the stand beside the operating table, cradled Rob's neck and head in her hands, and moved them carefully while the two lads transferred him from the stretcher. She grabbed two pillows and propped his feet and legs up again.

He rolled his head from side to side.

Maggie held his arm against the blanket. "Faither's on his way, luve." She caressed his face. "He'll put your shoulder back in place. Just hang on a few minutes longer."

"Sorry, Maggie," he panted. "But I couldn't leave Calum to ..." He tried to sit up and yelled out in pain.

"Calum's fine, Rob." Maggie pushed him down. "Don't move. It only makes it worse."

John rushed into the operating room, followed by Den and Matthew. He took Rob's right hand. "I'm going to manipulate that shoulder back into place, lad. You need to hang on as hard as you can." He nodded at Maggie. "You're needed out there. Den and

Matthew will help me." When she hesitated, he pushed her toward the door. "Go help with your brother."

"Go ... Maggie," Rob panted.

She ran back to Rob, stooped, and kissed his forehead, tears spilling again. "I'll be right back."

John leaned over Rob. "I'm going to untape your arm, then we'll turn you onto your belly. Try to relax. Don't tense your muscles. I'll support your arm." He pulled the tape from Rob's arm, and the three men manoeuvred him over onto his belly. John placed Rob's right hand at the edge of the table, then eased his left until it hung over the side. "Hold on and brace yourself. We're going to pull that shoulder back where it belongs." He ignored Den's pleading eyes and nodded at Matthew. "You and I'll try it first. Pray God it doesn't take a third man."

The two men got on their knees beneath the operating table.

"Hold him tightly, Den," John said. "Keep him from sliding." John grasped Rob's left hand with both hands.

Rob's raspy panting filled the silence.

"Take his elbow," John instructed Matthew. "Apply even pressure downward as I pull on his hand. On the count of three. One, twa, three. Pull."

Rob cried out as they both put their weight into it.

John felt the arm give. He exerted more pressure, slowly and evenly.

A muffled pop.

Rob screamed again, then relaxed.

John nodded to Matthew. "'Tis back where it belongs. You can let go now." John held on to Rob's hand as he climbed out from beneath the table and helped turn him onto his back. He straightened the elbow and flexed it, placing Rob's left arm across his waist. "Hold his arm here, Den. I need a restraining sling."

Rob was barely conscious and sweat streamed down his face.

John raised Rob's waist enough to get the sling in place, then secured his arm and wrist in the straps. "I need a pressure, Matthew."

Matthew took the reading. "Still low, but higher than before."

"Let's get you a little relief," John said to Rob. "We can't take all the pain away, but it will help while I see what other damage you've done to yourself." He administered the shot and waited for it to take away the sharpest pain. Moments later, he patted Rob's right shoulder. "It won't take long for the morphine to work. Try to rest."

"Sorry for all the trouble."

"Stop apologizing, lad. You did what you thought had to be done. I just wish you'd stop and think about yourself one of these days."

"But Calum ..." Rob shook his head.

"What about Calum?" John asked as he raised the blanket and studied the injuries to Rob's left side.

"He was knocked oot. Couldn't let him drown."

"You did this saving Calum?"

"I tried."

Den, face flushed, pushed his way to Rob's side. "He tied his lifeline around Calum so they could pull him and another man in. By that time, Rob was too close to the rocks. A wave caught him and ..."

Despite his years of medical training, John's hands trembled and tears sprang to his eyes.

Rob had been willing to make the supreme sacrifice to save John's son. Someday he would find a way to repay this lad, who had the heart of a lion. He leaned over the table. "Thank ye from the bottom of my heart." His voice broke.

Maggie heard Rob's screams. Her hands shook as she took Calum's blood pressure.

Still in shock, but pressure rising. The gash on his forehead would require a few stitches to close, and both eyes were turning black and blue, but his breathing was less laboured and he appeared lucid. "Was that Rob?"

"Faither's putting his dislocated shoulder back in place. 'Tis verra painful."

"He saved my life, Maggie. I was knocked oot, but Paddy told me after I came to. Rob gave me his lifeline. Without him, I'd be feeding the fishes."

She put her hand over his mouth. "Don't talk anymore. Just lay still and rest."

"Find out how he is for me. Then I'll rest."

Another stubborn man. *Man?* It seemed so strange to think of her baby brother that way, yet a man he was. "All right. I'll go now if you promise you'll lie still while I'm gone."

"I promise."

That sounded more like the wee lad she remembered. She smiled and kissed his cheek before dashing toward the operating room.

Her faither placed a gauze pad and roll of tape on a tray as she walked in. No sign of Den or Matthew.

"You got it back in place?" Maggie's gaze scanned Rob's face. So pale it was, and he looked exhausted.

Her faither nodded. "It took twa of us, but I knew it would with all that scar tissue from his past surgeries."

Maggie took a towel and blotted the sweat from Rob's forehead. She leaned over and kissed his bruised lips. "Is it better, luve?"

"Much." Och, his voice was hoarse again from all the seawater he'd swallowed.

"Everything's going to be all right," he added, trying to smile.

She looked at her father. "What about his left side?"

"I've bandaged some of the deeper lacerations. I don't think anything's broken, but I'll take some pictures just to be sure."

"Nothing broken," Rob croaked. "Just sore as—"

"The de'il," John said quickly.

Maggie smiled. That was the closest she'd ever heard her faither come to swearing. "Calum's going to need some stitches on his forehead. Other than that, he seems to be doing well."

"I need some lads to help get Rob into a bed."

"Want to go home," Rob rasped.

John threw up his hands. "Of course you do, but you'll be here several days. I'm giving you penicillin as well as saline. Your lungs are still weak after that last plane crash, and you may have breathed in seawater, no' just swallowed it."

Maggie pushed the forelock back from Rob's forehead and trailed her fingers over his cheek.

His pupils dilated. The morphine was working.

She took his hand and kissed his palm.

He sighed and closed his eyes.

Chapter Eleven

The first two days of Rob's stay at the infirmary passed in a haze of pain and morphine-induced nightmares. Only Maggie's presence made it bearable. Each time he woke in a sweat, she bathed his forehead with a cool face flannel and spoke soothing words, assuring him that Morag and Flora were keeping close watch on Robbie and Annie, and that she was exactly where she wanted to be—with him.

A clear mind came on the third day. Maggie had just gone home to suckle Annie and fix a supper to whet his appetite, when Den appeared in the doorway wearing a navy-blue jumpsuit with *Ryan Air* embroidered in gold on the breast pocket.

Rob grinned. He'd score a point with this one. "So your name is Ryan, now? Anderson's no' Celtic enough for you?" He waited for an explosion of teasing Nordic pride.

Ignoring the jibe, Den leaned against the doorjamb, a picture of studied nonchalance. "X-rays show anything broken?"

He pointed to Den. "I'm certain Fern told you they didn't."

Den plonked down in a chair and propped his feet on the bed. "So when can we spring you outta this place? Or do you like the lazy life of leisure?"

Rob chuckled—and winced. Had to remember no' to do that. "Reading poetry to Fern, or is she working you to the bone?"

A quick smirk, but that eyelid was twitching again. Given enough time, he'd have Den answering the question that had kept him awake most of the night.

"It isn't Fern who's had me working." Den leaned back, laced his fingers behind his head. "I've been helping your building crew put up a hangar for the floatplane. Should be finished in a day or two. Then, if the weather cooperates, which is a pipe dream on this piece of rock, it's off into the wild blue yonder." He flew his hand through the air.

The opening Rob had been waiting for. "What's that bandage around your wrist?" *Almost to the target.*

Den pulled his arm down and scrambled to his feet. "Nothing. Just a little strain."

Rob pinned him with a stare. "I had a dream last night, only I think it was more than a dream. A memory, even."

"You getting delirious or something?" Den squirmed and averted his eyes.

"You were in the water with me. Are you the one who pulled me off the rocks?"

"What of it?" Den shrugged.

"And you hurt yourself doing it."

Den stabbed his fingers through his hair. "You're the one who got hurt, not me. It's only a sprained wrist for Pete's sake."

"Now it's a sprain, no' a strain. You didn't answer me. Did you go into the water after me?" He'd seen Den in the pool at the Point. A great man to have on one's side for a game of water polo, not because he was a great swimmer but because he was so tenacious and sneaky.

The effort it had taken to fight through those waves, with no training or experience, was beyond comprehension. When Den's eyes met his, Rob was shocked by the look of pain on his friend's face.

"Somebody had to. You were drowning. Drowning, Rob, and nobody saw it but me." Den walked to the window and looked out.

Just what he'd feared. He could have cost Den his life. "Turn around. I've never liked talking to a man's back."

Whirling, Den blinked the tears from his eyes, grin crooked. "So we're even-steven, bucko. You saved my bacon when I had those Perspex shards in my eyes and couldn't see the runway at Edenoaks. You talked me down to a perfect landing."

"That was different. I was on the tower, in no danger." The enormity of what Den had done squeezed Rob's voice to a whisper. "You could have drowned."

Their gazes locked, neither wavering.

Den looked away first. "Calum's been wanting to talk to you."

"No' until I've thanked you."

"Try to kiss me and you're dead meat."

"Kiss you? I wouldn't kiss that ugly mug if they paid me a million pounds."

"Ugly? Me? At least I'm not ten feet tall!"

"No, stumpy, you're not."

"Stumpy! Why I've a good notion to—"

"What on earth are you twa fighting about?" Maggie stood in the doorway, hands on hips, eyes darting between Rob and Den.

Rob grinned at her.

Den did the same.

"Ach, you twa!" she exclaimed. "I thought you were serious."

Den's chin thrust out. "He called me 'stumpy.'"

"And he saved my life." Rob held out his hand to Maggie. "Why didn't you tell me it was Den who pulled me off the rocks?"

She squeezed his fingers. "Because you've been in no condition to hear it. Calum told me." She turned to Den, eyes bright with tears. "I'll never forget what you did. Thank ye."

"I'll take a kiss from a bonnie lass like you any day."

Maggie blew him a kiss and squeezed Rob's hand again. "We've come near tying Calum to his bed to keep him from barging in here. He thinks there's something verra wrong or he could have seen you sooner."

"I'll go tell Calum you're back in the land of the living." Den headed for the doorway.

"Thank you for saving my life," Rob called.

With a dismissive wave of his hand, Den beat a hasty retreat.

"Do you want more morphine?" Maggie asked.

"No' now. Mebbe some APCs later."

"We could try the APCs since you're no' bleeding now. I'll get both ready. You're looking so much better, but I don't want you suffering through another night."

Rob lay back and closed his eyes while he waited. So Den had saved his life. He felt a swell of affection—no, more than affection—of luve. In the past fourteen years, they'd been through far more than friends usually shared: the Point, training Air Corps Cadets to fly, well over a hundred bombing missions between them. Now their lives were interwoven again. What would the next fourteen years bring?

Calum cleared his throat and walked up to Rob's bed.

One look at the black, green, and yellow bruised flesh around his eyes and Rob choked back a laugh.

"I know, I know," Calum said. "Biggest and best set of keekers you've ever seen."

"They are that. Sit you down. How are you feeling, lad?"

"Too guid to stay here." Calum turned a chair around and straddled it. "But Faither's being his usual overly cautious self."

"I'll testify to that."

"How are you feeling?"

"Sore and bored."

Calum grinned. "That about sums it up."

"How's the rest of your crew?"

"Most are already away home. Only the skipper—he has a bad ticker—and I are still here."

Rob grimaced as he tried to get comfortable. Should have asked Maggie for those APCs when he had the chance. "So how was the fishing?"

"Pretty guid, but you know how it slows in the winter. A lot of mending nets and checking gear so we don't have a breakdown hauling in a load of fish later. I'm saving every pence. Going to have my own trawler someday."

"I know. I'm going to build it."

"Of course you are." Calum leaned closer. "That rescue boat of yours is a marvel, Rob. That's the first time I ever traveled at eighteen knots and 'twas smooth and easy."

"There'll come a time when eighteen knots is as slow as walking." Rob warmed to a subject he could talk about forever. "Technology's creating breakthroughs in materials and techniques every day."

"Can you build a trawler that'll right herself?"

Och, right to the heart of one of his worst frustrations. "No' yet. Trawlers need room for fish storage and the air baffles take that up. Maybe someday ..."

Calum untangled his long legs and stood. "I didn't come to talk boats, Rob. I came to thank ye for saving my life."

Seeing the lad's discomfort spurred Rob to hide his own. "You're verra welcome. I'm just glad I got there in time."

"I can't believe I did that."

"Did what?"

"Tripped just before I jumped. I was all ready to jump as far out as I could, and suddenly my feet got all tangled together and I was going over the side head first."

"So that's what happened."

"Aye. What a bumbling eejit. And it almost cost you and the skipper your lives. And Den, as well."

"But it didn't." Rob reached for Calum's hand, gripped it. "Things happen, lad. Don't dwell on the past. Just be thankful things turned out all right. I know I am."

Tears filled Calum's eyes. "I can never thank ye enough."

"You just have. 'Tis a shame it took something like this to bring you home for a few days, but God works in mysterious ways."

Calum leaned against the bed, grin restored. "I was going to tell you all later, but I'd like you to be the first to know."

"Know what?"

"I'm coming home. To work. To stay! I've been talking to Tormad on the radio almost every day. He wants me to sign on with him as a partner. 'Twill be a forty-sixty split the first year, then fifty-fifty. What do you think?"

What grand news. Calum home to stay. "I'm thinking you're going to make a lot of people happy. And Tormad's a guid man."

"Aye, he is, and a cannie fisherman. He always gets the best catches on the island, and that's working short-handed. With another crew member, we'll set the world on fire."

"That you will. You need to tell your faither and Maggie. They'll be verra happy."

"I'm going to tell them tonight."

"Expect some tears. Maggie always leaks like a broken spigot at guid news. Tired as she must be from nursing me, she could cry a rainstorm." Aching all over from lying in one position for so long, Rob tried to move slowly, but a pain in his knee brought a groan.

"I'll be off now. If ever you need owt, let me know, and I do mean owt."

Rob didn't mean to snort so loud. "If you can think of a way to get me out of here, let me know. That's what I really want."

"I'll work on it. See you later."

Rob lay back, staring at the ceiling. Life was so strange. On second thought, no' strange, but complex. So many lives entwined—luves, loyalties, kinship, all taken together in small snapshots to form a larger picture.

Den was here to stay and mebbe he and Fern would marry. And Calum was coming home. Their family would be complete.

The rain came down in sheets, rattling against the windowpanes like a thousand thundering feet of the ancient Celtic "wee people." The wind moaned mournfully around the eaves of the infirmary, reminding Rob of the auld tales of the banshee who lured travelers to their doom with her siren wails.

Rob sat on the bed, face turned to the window, frustration building.

Raining again. John would never release him in such a downpour. He grabbed the crutch leaning against the bed and pulled himself to his feet. Six days he'd spent away from home, and just when he was finally going to escape the smell of antiseptics and the tedium of doing nowt, he'd have to wait again.

He limped over to the window. Couldn't see a thing, couldn't even hear the roar of the surf over the keening wind. He wanted to slam his fist into something. How could he run a business from a hospital bed? He missed the activity at the shed: the smell of new-cut lumber, the sounds of power saws, Graham shouting orders to the crew.

And the rescue side of the business. There hadn't been a shout in the past few days, but one couldn't be far off. Neil was qualified to handle the Maggie in any weather, but who would plan the rescues and see them carried out without loss of life?

Only Graham, with his experience during the war, knew anything about motivating and directing a crew. But he got seasick.

Most of all, Rob missed his bairns. Though they visited him twice a day, it wasn't the same.

Maggie was exhausted. He had finally convinced her to spend the last three nights at home with the bairns, but she had undoubtedly slept as poorly as he when they were apart. Flora and Morag still watched Robbie and Annie during the day so Maggie could spend time with him, but the strain was beginning to show. Pale, she was, and drawn. His heart ached for her. Six days of this was too long.

Steps came from the hall.

He turned just as Angus and Hugh came into the room, their jackets dripping water on the polished floor.

"'Tis pishing down fair hard." Angus wiped his face with his kerchief. "But we've come to take you home."

Home? Did he say I'm going home?

Hugh eyed Rob. "Are you sure you're up to it, lad?" He reached beneath his waxed jacket and dried his eyeglasses on his shirttail. "You still look dead tired."

"I'm tired all right. Tired of doing nowt. John really said I could go home?"

Angus hooted and slapped his knee, sending a splatter of water in all directions. "He's been so busy birthing bairnies, he just told us to have at it and get you oot of here."

Bairnies? Rob's mind raced. Och, 'twas late for Catriona and early for Susan, but he knew from experience bairnies often made a mockery of schedules and such. "Are the bairnies birthed? How are Susan and Catriona?"

Hugh, face aglow with his elfin smile, patted Rob's arm. "Steady on, lad. They're birthed, bathed, and with their parents as we speak. A bonnie lass for Susan and Mark, and a hardy lad for Catriona and Alec."

Och, what a relief. Rob hadn't been concerned about Catriona, a sturdy, young woman who'd laboured on her faither's croft before marrying Alec. But Susan—sunny, gentle, luving Susan—had already lost twa bairnies before birth. He grabbed Hugh's elbow to steady his trembling legs. "You're certain Susan's lassie is healthy? She couldn't take another loss. 'Twould devastate her and Mark."

"John assured me when he telephoned that both bairnies are healthy and eager to suckle. Ready to go home, lad?"

"Absolutely. You bring my jacket?"

"And this." Angus held up a waxed cotton tarp. "We'll just tie it round you and be on our way." He pulled a loop of rope from his pocket. "'Twas Maggie's idea. Said no' to get your sling or dressings wet."

The two men settled Rob's A-2 jacket over his shoulders and draped the tarp over his hair and body, tying it around his waist.

Hugh handed him the crutch. "See if you can move with all that on you."

Rob took a few steps. "Can do. On we go."

"Watch the flags. They're slippery," Hugh cautioned as Angus opened the door.

Old Jack stood patiently in the traces, steam rising from his broad back.

"I'll get in first and give you a hand up," Angus said.

Using his right hand and foot, Rob managed to climb onto the bench with little difficulty. He moved over to make room for Hugh. It seemed daft to ride such a short distance, but he could never make it through the mud on his crutch.

A few minutes later, Hugh jumped down, opened the gate in the dyke, and sloshed through the stream of water to wait by the door.

Getting down was a little more difficult for Rob, but at last he climbed the steps to his front entry. Sheltered from the rain, he untied the tarp and handed it to Angus. "I can make it on my own now. Come you in for a hot drink."

They both declined in one voice.

"Thanks for the help. You don't know how much it means to be home."

Hugh patted his arm. "Take care, lad. We're having a Ne'er's Eve service at the kirk before the Hogmanay ceilidh. You'll be in our prayers."

"I'd like to come, but I don't think I can," Rob said.

"Of course no'. Just enjoy being home. 'Tis with grateful hearts we celebrate the night, for we have much to be thankful for. What could have been a tragedy, our Lord turned into a triumph."

"He did that."

Maggie opened the door, Annie in her arms. "Rob," she cried, "Faither called and said you'd be coming. I thought you'd at least wait till the rain let up a bit."

He returned her hug, burying his face in her hair. "Never. I couldn't wait another minute."

She looked up, blue eyes sparkling like summer sun on a loch. "Why doesn't that surprise me?" She waved to Hugh and Angus as they drove off. "Have you heard about the new bairnies? Och, Rob, I'm so kittled up. Susan finally has the lassie she's blethered about since we were lasses ourselves. We'll have to visit them as soon as you're able." She reached for Robbie's arm as he tried to run past. "Inside with you, skellum, 'tis wet oot here."

The lad put his arms around his faither's legs. "Oop, Faither, oop."

Rob tousled his hair. "Let Faither sit first, then I'll hold you."

Maggie pushed their son inside and stayed at Rob's side while he made his way to his rocker.

"'Tis so guid to be home." Rob sat, his gaze traveling over the familiar, comfortable room.

Burning peats flickered in the fireplace, casting a warm red and yellow glow across the white walls.

He laid the crutch on the floor and reached for Robbie.

The lad climbed up in his lap and laid his head against Rob's shoulder.

"There's a guid lad." Rob rocked, burying his face in his son's hair, savouring the scent of boy, dog, and that unique aroma that identified Robbie.

"I've scones fresh from the oven," Maggie said, "and a pottle of coffee."

Rob laid his head back. "Och, Maggie, luve, this is where I belong."

Tears sprang to her eyes. She bent down and kissed his cheek. "Aye. It is that."

Robbie soon tired of the inactivity and slid down. He careened around the room on his wooden troke, his raucous shouts and squeals bringing smiles to his parents' faces.

Maggie placed Annie in Rob's lap.

He cuddled her, fingering her soft curls. So sweet and innocent. Such peace, such a sense of belonging, fell on him, moving him to tears. This was his home and this was his family. Nowhere else nor anybody else could ever take their places in his heart.

After Annie dropped off to sleep, Maggie put her in the cradle and brought Rob scones and coffee.

He hadn't thought himself hungry, but they went down such a treat he ate three of the scones and drank almost the entire pot of coffee.

With a smile of soft summer breezes and the scent of heather, Maggie sat in her rocker and reached for his hand. "This lovely house you built us is no' a home without you in it."

He brought her hand to his lips. He wanted to tell her it was her face he was seeing when that wave washed over his head. But he couldn't—no' now, no' ever. "I luve you, Maggie. With all I am and ever hope to be, I luve you."

"Our Lord was faithful, Rob. He spared both you and Calum. I'm so grateful."

"So am I, lass. I hope it strengthened your faith as much as it did mine."

Chapter Twelve

"How many hours are you willing to put in?"

Den's blue-eyed glare sliced into Rob like splintered glass. "What do you think I'm here for? To sit back in a cushy chair and prop my heels on a desk? Or maybe work on a tan when the sun shines three times a year—or is that four?"

Wow, Den was wound tight as a wet anchor rope. Rob could either explode or explain. But the Word said that soft words turned away wrath. It was worth a try. "John says it'll be weeks before I can lead a shout." He kept his voice soft, tone conciliatory. "I need a second-in-command, and I'd like it to be you. But, like any job, there's training you'll need before you're ready."

Though the fire was gone from Den's steady gaze, his hands fisted. "As you oughta know, I can swim, bucko. Even sat in on your first-aid classes last July, and listened to that guy explaining how to use the radar." Den reached for his coffee and drained the mug. "So, what else is there to learn?"

Bucko. That rare show of recalcitrance was cooling fast.

"No' a lot." Rob shrugged. "Learning enough to pass your medical test, the quickest way to find a victim who's sunk below the waves …" He reached for his mug, took a sip. "And how to plan a rescue when it's blowing a gale, the sky's black as a mid-winter night, and your deck's awash with forty-foot waves."

Den sank into Maggie's rocker. "That's a lot to expect of me. At Edenoaks, you planned and led most of our bombing strikes. I just flew support and took the lead on the milk runs."

Was Den afraid? Och, all these years, Rob had thought his pal too interested in dancing or sweet-talking another female into bed to be bothered with having his own group. But he had everything it took to command: intelligence, tenacity, logic, the ability to think under pressure. No more tiptoeing around.

Den needed to be set straight.

Rob leaned forward, finger stabbing. "Milk runs, you called them. Where's the guts it took to lead those three squadrons through flak thick enough to walk on? Or jump into the sea, battle waves coming from all sides, to pull me from the rocks? That siren could sound at any time, with nobody to command the *Maggie*. You going to play your comfortable 'backseat Charlie' role or show me the leader we both know you are?"

No anger in Den's eyes now, only a dark shadow that bloomed and disappeared so quickly, it might have been imagined. "You'll be risking a lot of lives, Rob. You sure I can do this? Really sure?"

Ah, he was not afraid for his own life, then, but of failing others. "No' as many lives as you're risking by waffling. Of course, I'm sure."

The shout siren remained silent—a miracle Rob attributed to the fervent prayers being offered by folk all over the island. He spent two days plotting scenarios, making diagrams, and talking Den through the steps required to plan rescues for each situation. High seas, no wind, or blowing a gale. Visibility zero to clear. Rocks or open sea. Which crew members to use and when. How to motivate his crew to do their all without foolishly sacrificing their own lives.

"It's a lot like the information you heard at every mission and weather briefing you ever sat in on," he told Den, as they sat in the rockers. "Now, you take that information and use it to make sure you bring back every survivor and every member of your crew."

Maggie confronted Rob after a particularly intense session. "You sound so stern, luve. Are you certain you're no' expecting more from Den than he can give?"

Rob let out a long exhale. "He didn't survive the Point or all those strikes he flew by luck. I've told you before, Den's a tactician. Once he learns to handle the *Maggie* as well as he did a B-17, it'll all come together."

Neil sailed the *Maggie* out of the harbour into the Minch and handed Den the helm, taking him through exercises in speed, turning, sudden stops, backing up, how to keep the prow into the waves, what to do when wallowing amidships in a trough, and the use of radar for zeroing in on coordinates.

Paddy tethered him to a lifeline and showed him how use his flippers when diving for a submerged victim, what to do with combative ones, and how to orient himself by riding the crests of the waves.

Matthew familiarized him with where all the medical supplies were kept, what to use when, and how to evaluate and triage survivors under chaotic conditions.

Den returned to the Savage home late every afternoon, exhausted but excited. "This is like taking flight training and ground school at the same time," he told Rob. "My head feels like it's full of mush, my belly's churning, and my arms and legs ache worse than after I pulled you from the drink. But it's finally making sense." And every night, he plodded through the rain to the infirmary for John's advanced lessons in how to insert an IV or plasma needle into collapsing veins.

"But that's what Matthew's for," Den argued the night before his medical test. "And I'm hurting you, jabbing that needle into your arm. Isn't there another way to do this without turning you into a pin cushion?"

John loosened the tourniquet around his upper forearm. "Who do you think we practiced on in medical school—cadavers? Matthew can't be inserting IVs into multiple victims at the same time. Get a clean needle. We'll try another spot."

"That's another thing. I see lots of fatter veins. Why choose such a small one? My hands are too big."

"No' near as large as Rob's." The doctor moved the tourniquet lower on his forearm and tightened it. "I'm using smaller veins because when a victim's in shock, his blood supply decreases." He wiped his arm with cotton soaked in surgical spirits. "That vein right there. Insert the tip of the needle and move it verra slowly. Don't lose your nerve now. I've had worse bites from a midge."

Den swallowed, inserted the needle, and moved it up the vein.

"More. A wee bit more." A grunt of satisfaction. "You're in. Congratulations, Den. We'll make a medic of you yet."

Rob stared up at the bedroom ceiling. He shouldn't have spent the last few hours memorizing the final pages of the floatplane's flight manual Den had given him. Lying in bed, reliving all the sensations of flight, always brought a sleepless night. Why did remembering that vast expanse of blue, the peaceful solitude, the casting away of earthly responsibility, awaken a yearning that tore at his soul?

The wailing siren startled him from his reverie.

He shrugged into his dressing gown, fumbled in the dark for his crutch, and limped into the living room, flipping on the light. Muttering under his breath about having to use one hand, he jerked his waxed jacket off its hangar.

Den stumbled down the stairs, pulling his sweater over his unbuttoned shirt.

"Take your time on the path." Rob tossed Den the jacket. "And take my torch. It's still pouring rain oot there."

Den hopped across the floor, pulling on his socks. "What else is new? Hasn't stopped raining since the day I got here." He pulled on the jacket, shooting Rob a wicked grin.

Rob handed him a torch. "Your wellies out on the entry?"

"Right by the door. Best buy I ever made."

Squeezing Den's shoulder, Rob propelled him to the door. "Then on you go. And Godspeed, Den. You'll do fine."

"You betcha."

That cocky, confident grin told Rob all he needed to know. Den thought he was ready and that's what counted. Rob waited until the blurry figure disappeared into the rain before closing the door. *Give him Your wisdom, Faither, and a steady mind. Lives depend on it.* He added peats to the fireplace and made his way into his office, grumbling at how much the crutch slowed his progress. He turned on the desk lamp and the radio, plonked into his chair, leaned back, and stretched out his legs. This could be a long, gut-twisting night. And he was about to find out how Maggie felt with every shout, having to depend on the radio for information. No' a pleasant prospect.

Maggie came up behind him and cupped his chin in her palm. "You're barefoot, luve." Her sweet breath caressed his cheek. "As soon as we know what kind of shout it is, I'll fetch your socks and put coffee and a pottle of tea on."

The fingers of his right hand glided over the silken skin of her throat. "Go back to bed, lass. There's no need for both of us to sit here till Den's back."

"Get used to having somebody breathe over your shoulder. Knowing Fern, she'll be here in a tick and won't leave till he walks in our front door."

"Control, this is the *Maggie*. What are we looking at, James?" Den's voice.

Rob's pulse quickened.

"*Maggie*, Control. 'Tis an assist request from Mull's lifeboat. They picked up a radio signal from a trawler. Coast Guard placed it on the northwest side of Coll, four souls aboard. Skipper says their fish hold's filling with water. They have a pump going, but it's flooding too fast to do much guid. Over."

"Copy that. Give me the coordinates and radio contacts for Mull and the trawler."

Rob ran his finger over the map on the wall at his side as James recited the numbers.

Nothing but open sea to the west, if they got that far. Might have torn a hole in their hull on rocky Eag na Maoile near Coll's northwestern shore.

Den radioed the numbers back to James. "We're leaving the harbour now, Control. Let us know if anything changes. *Maggie* out."

Rob studied the map again. With Mull's lifeboat based in Tobermory, far east of Coll, Tiree's to the south was much closer. Why call Innisbraw for an assist with Tiree only miles away? Och, too many unanswered questions.

He arched his back and stretched. No matter how fast Den pushed the *Maggie*, that trawler would be little more than floating debris by the time she arrived.

Fern and Maggie's voices filtered in from the kitchen. He hadn't even heard Maggie leave the office. No reason to stay glued to his chair for hours. Somebody had made a mistake calling Innisbraw, but it wouldn't reflect badly on the *Maggie*, no matter the outcome. Shame brought a flush to his face. *I'm being selfish, Faither. Please be with the crew of that trawler and whoever arrives to help them—and bring Den, my crew, and the* Maggie *safely back to Innisbraw.*

Fern, assured by Rob that Den was in no danger, chose to spend the night, rather than rouse Katie from bed again. "You'll wake me when he comes home?" She stifled a yawn.

Maggie handed Rob a mug of coffee. "We will."

"Then I'm off to bed. I'll sleep with Katie. She doesn't know the shout was such a muddle. She could have bad dreams."

Rob watched her climb the stairs before he drew Maggie into his arms. "You're no' staying up the rest of the night." He smoothed tendrils of hair back from her forehead. "It could be dawn or later before the *Maggie* returns."

"And you?"

"I'll use the time to start drafting plans for that seventy-five-foot trawler. Och, luve, I was dumfoondert when Graham showed up here last een with no' only that order, but twa rescue boat orders too. The rescue boats won't be a problem, but I've never designed a trawler, let alone one so large."

She rubbed her cheek against the mat of hair on his chest. "We could smoorich," she whispered, batting her lashes against his flesh.

Light as a nestling's feathers, those lashes. He suppressed a groan. "And get me into trouble with your faither again? He already scolded me for doing too much." To soften his protest, he lowered his lips to hers, eager to show how much he loved and treasured her.

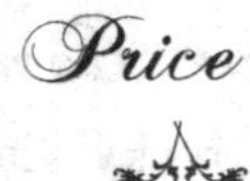

Den stormed through the doorway at 0515. “What are you doing up?” He tossed the waxed jacket onto the kitchen bunker. “Or didn’t you hear about the wild goose chase we were sent on last night?” He took the mug of coffee Rob held out and gulped it down so fast he scalded his tongue.

“How could I help hearing? You didn’t need a radio to reach Control this mornin. Your yelling carried all the way up the fell.”

Rob’s quiet censure did nothing to soothe Den’s ruffled feathers. “You bet I yelled, bucko. I’ve seen a lot of harebrained mix-ups, but that one took the cake.” He poured another mug of coffee and took several deep breaths before chancing a cautious sip. Och, his mouth burned as bad as the fire in his belly.

“No reason to take it out on James.”

“James? What does James have to do with it? It was that crazy Coast Guard with their ‘we didna make the decision to call you,’ and Mull telling me they were ‘only following orders.’ Whose orders, for Pete’s sake? God’s?”

“Stop your shouting, Den Anderson.” Fern hurried down the stairs, cheeks red, eyes spitting fire. She pulled to a halt in front of him. “You’ll wake the dead.” She poked his chest. “And the bairns.”

He hung his head, anger deflating fast as a punctured balloon. “Sorry, Fern. I forgot where I was.”

“Obviously.”

Rob filled his mug with the last of the coffee. “It’s hard to take, having a shout go so sour when you’ve spent a long time sweating over a rescue. I went through the same on that assist for the steamer supposedly aground on Mingulay.”

“Yeah.” Den sneaked a peek at Fern.

A smile played on her lips.

How could she be mad as a hornet one minute, and smiling like a kid on Christmas morning the next? Women—he’d never understand them. He stalked off for a shower, licking his wounded pride with every step.

Chapter Thirteen

Den slammed down the telephone receiver and sat back in his office chair, rubbing his left ear. Hoo-boy, Graham might be working his tail off with that boatbuilding crew, but that didn't make filling in for Rob a picnic.

If he heard one more excuse from a supplier about a late shipment, he was going to explode like a Roman candle gone berserk on the Fourth of July.

He glanced at his watch and reached for the list of radar specifications Rob had given him that morning.

Not many notes, just the size of the trawler and the usual weather conditions it would face, especially in the winter.

Almost 1500 here, so about 0700 hours in San Diego. Dale Taylor, an old friend and electronics whiz, should be getting ready for a hard day at work in that cluttered but surgically clean garage he called his "electronic manufacturing facility."

It didn't take Den long to convince Dale that he was the only man on earth with the smarts to design and build a radar system for a fishing trawler operating in the Atlantic Ocean and North Sea.

"You know, Den, this sounds like something I can sink my teeth into," Dale said, excitement quivering in his gravelly voice. "I'll get busy and start researching." He laughed. "I may just have to fly over there and install it."

"Sounds good. And bring that lovely wife of yours. Who knows, you might decide to stay." He'd actually said that? Lovely wife? Maddie Taylor was so plain she made vanilla pudding look fancy.

Dale's loud hoot startled him. "Stay? On a tiny island in the Atlantic with all those gales you told me about? Not a chance. We live in sunny California, remember? I'll give you a call and let you know when I've got a schematic to send."

Den grinned, hung up the receiver, and popped his knuckles. Now he had to call that company in Glasgow and light a fire under them to fill the order for six diesel engines. But first, he'd earned a break. He poured a mug of coffee from his thermos and reached for one of the scones Fern had tucked into his pocket when she'd brought Katie over to play with Robbie.

Fern. What was he going to do? Just thinking about her made his heart pound. He couldn't see her often enough, couldn't hear her voice without wanting to touch her, feel her soft lips on his. This waiting was so frustrating, he found himself blowing sky high at the slightest thing. Being her friend wasn't enough. He'd all but proposed, for Pete's sake.

"I can't marry an unbeliever," she'd said.

But he still couldn't get his mind around that "faith" thing. Sure, Hugh's lessons every Sabbath sounded good, even made sense most of the time. But they weren't like lectures on advanced mathematics or physics, based on proven, scientific facts.

Once, he'd audited a philosophy class out of curiosity. He'd sat at the back of the half-empty hall, mouth open in disbelief. This was West Point, a bastion of scientific teaching, and this professor was spouting tripe—nothing Den could grasp and rope in, nothing solid, just "believe what I'm presenting because Socrates, Plato, or Aristotle spoke these pearls of wisdom centuries ago, and they were much more learned than you." Pure pie in the sky.

But what about the time he'd prayed? Sure, he'd been desperate, muscles quivering, lungs straining for breath, certain he'd never reach Rob in time to save him from drowning. And the answer? No trumpets from on high. No instant spurt of energy—he'd had to struggle through the next wave, and the next.

But he'd been able to. And he had found Rob alive.

Since that day, he'd replayed the rescue over and over in his mind, searching for a logical explanation for his strength not giving out until he got Rob back to the *Maggie*. There wasn't one. Even the strongest will couldn't overcome an exhausted body once the adrenaline ran out.

Too bothered now to eat the scone, he pushed it aside and sipped his tepid coffee as he telephoned the diesel engine provider, listed the suppliers he wanted to call tomorrow, made a schedule of expected delivery dates, and filed invoices.

At 1630 he looked at the papers remaining on his desk and shook his head in disgust. What a waste of time. Too discombobulated to concentrate on another task, he pulled on his jacket and left his office—a broom closet, more like it.

Graham and his crew were gathered around one of the rescue boats under construction, pointing and having a lively conversation, their rapid Scots as incomprehensible as jabbering gibbons in a zoo. Graham raised a hand and Den returned the wave.

Nice guy, Graham. Never beefed about Rob taking another

partner, and he could speak pretty good English, probably from his stint in the British Army.

It was almost dark outside. At least the rain was only a light drizzle, though it was blasted into his face by the cold wind. Lights were on in the weaving shed and Paddy's howff, but the path was deserted.

He shoved his hands in his pockets and started up the hill.

Maybe Fern would ask him to supper.

His thoughts circled back to his problem. Somehow, he had to give up his bias against what he'd always called "Bible thumpers." His deep-seated distaste had started when he was a kid and new neighbors moved next door. The first Sunday afternoon post move-in, he and his youngest sister were turning cartwheels in the front yard while his dad washed their Packard. Just a normal, lazy Sunday afternoon—until the new neighbor stepped out onto his porch, wearing a stiff black suit and a scowl to match. "You are an abomination to the Lord," he'd thundered, thumping his fingers against a black book. "The Sabbath is a holy day, to be spent praying and reading the Good Book, not on frivolous games and vain labors." Variations on that diatribe took place almost every Sunday for years, and though the subject was avoided by his parents, it left a blight on what he considered an otherwise happy childhood.

Even if Den overcame that aversion—Fern and Maggie and Rob were nothing like that man—the next step would be harder. Giving control of his life over to a God he couldn't see or hear?

Hugh had used an example of faith that made sense.

Den kneaded his temples, trying to jog his memory. Maybe if he concentrated on something else, like the roar of the waves on the rocks below the fell or the hazy glow the lamp in Elspeth's front window cast across the path

Lamp. Electricity. That was it! A man turned a switch and trusted the light to go on. Could he see the wires behind the walls? Hear the power surging through those wires? No, it was faith.

Made sense and sounded so simple. Maybe that was the problem. Too simple. He paused in front of the infirmary, jumbled thoughts circling one absolute: he couldn't lose Fern. He'd have to worry this thing until he had it licked.

Fern sprinkled the last of Den's shirts, rolled it up, and wrapped it and the others in a towel. Though it might seem daft to spend one of her rare free afternoons ironing, what better time was there? Maggie had balked when asked to give over Den's ironing, but Fern had insisted. "You have too much work already with Rob home all the day needing quiet so he can work and Katie insisting on playing with Robbie," she'd argued. "Besides, you have Den underfoot every night. 'Tis the least I can do."

She poured a cup of tea, added milk and heather honey, and sat in her rocker, head back, eyes closed. Och, what was she going to do? Every day that passed, her feelings for Den deepened.

He was so bright, passing his medical test with no' a stumble and already taking over as commander on the shouts. Always helping her, he was, drying the dishes when he took supper with them, keeping her stove and fireplace baskets filled with peats, reading a bedtime story to Katie, even oiling a complaining door hinge.

She smiled, picturing his blue eyes sparkling with laughter, that red mop of unruly hair standing on end from his nervous fingers, hearing the yearning in his voice when he bid her goodnight. And he never grumbled about attending kirk with her on the Sabbath. It was unfortunate he had no English Bible. But would he even use one?

What am I going to do, Faither? I'll never marry an unbeliever, so I have to trust Ye to open his heart to the salvation Ye offer. Please don't ask me to walk away from the only man I've ever loved since Edward.

Rob rubbed his aching knee, tossed the pencil on the papers scattered across his drafting board, and reached for his crutch. "Just twa more weeks, and you'll be walking on your own," John had told him the day before. He grunted.

Just twa weeks, was it? An eternity, especially when he didn't know how much longer he had to wear the restraining sling.

He glanced at the radio. "Hope I don't have to spend many more hours waiting through a shout with my heart in my mouth," he muttered.

So far, they'd been lucky. Just one shout after that fiasco on Mull, and only a medical emergency, at that. Graham had telephoned to tell him the rescue crew seemed to be taking to Den as commander. But that was ultimately Rob's responsibility, no' Den's. Rob snapped off the lamp and limped into the living room.

Empty. Where were Maggie and the bairns?

"And I'll only close the door if you promise no' to tease Annie," Maggie said, coming out of Robbie's bedroom. She turned to Rob and hugged him. "'Tis about time you came oot of your office. You look spent."

"No' spent, just in a bit of a fankle." He rested his cheek on her head.

Her arms tightened. "What about?"

"Och, that trawler design is harder than I thought 'twould be. I've about worn out those books on Scots trawlers your faither brought when I was designing the *Maggie*. I'll have a lot of questions to put to some of the fishermen before I can go much further."

Eyes sparkling like sunlight on waves, Maggie danced away and plucked the coffeepot from the back of the stove. "Then you can start with Calum this een." She filled a mug. "He's joining us for another game of Monopoly. Said he's come up with a way to make sure Den doesn't cheat. If we—"

A loud thud, followed by a squeal.

She rolled her eyes, marched to their lad's bedroom, and threw the door open. "What are you doing in here?" she asked, hands on hips.

Rob limped over and looked in. Robbie and Annie sat on the floor, Annie with a large rubber ball between her dimpled knees.

Shep stretched out on the rug, ears twitching, tongue lolling, a picture of innocence.

Annie squealed again, smiling up at her mither.

"She threw the ball at the door." Robbie said, his anxious gaze darting between his parents. "You said we could play keep-away, Mither."

"I did, but don't be throwing the ball. You could break your lamp."

"But she—"

"That's a big ball for a sma' lass to be throwing so hard," Rob said, trying hard not to laugh. "Sure she didn't have a wee bit of help?"

Robbie frowned, scuffing his foot on the floor. "Aye, Shep—"

"Shep helped her throw the ball?" Rob shook his head. How far would a lad so young go to stay out of trouble? "I'll let you play in here, just no more throwing. Roll the ball like you've been told."

Annie chortled and hugged the ball, saliva slicking her chin.

"Are you certain you should let him get away with that?" Maggie whispered, closing the door.

"Och, he knows he didn't fool us. Why ruin a guid een by making a mountain out of a molehill? 'Tis American slang. It means—"

She wrinkled her nose and swatted at him. "Turning a wee fash into a rare fankle. On you come. Drink your coffee while I check the pasties."

"Beef pasties?"

"What else? I know you hate mutton."

Rob plonked down on a kitchen chair. The aroma of roasted meat, onion, and pastry made his stomach growl. He reached for his mug and drained it, hoping the coffee would help tide him over till supper. "Finish telling me how we're to keep Den from cheating," he said. "To him it's a joke he's pulling, but 'tis no' funny to the rest of us."

Maggie returned the pasties to the oven and adjusted the heat. "We won't let him be banker. That's when he does it, you ken, blethering on about the wooden tokens giving him splinters, how awkward the wheel is instead of dice, and the London names for the avenues, hoping we won't see him palming notes from the bank and adding them to his own." She poured more coffee for Rob and a cup of tea for herself.

"But he's no' used to the Waddington, UK version. And using pounds instead of dollars can be confusing."

"You're doing it again, Rob, making excuses for Den."

Is that what he was doing? He ignored the coffee, stomach cramping.

She sat in his lap and brushed her lips across his cheek. "Mebbe I misspoke. You don't do it often, but he's been your friend so long, I'm thinking you're used to covering up his 'jokes' to keep him oot of trouble."

He didn't want to talk about this now. Her heather-scented hair, soft fingers trailing over his cheeks, made his body tingle.

"Am I wrong?"

Her quiet question brought reluctant memories. Maggie wasn't wrong. It had become such an ingrained habit, he never thought about it anymore. He remembered the stove black Den added to tins of boot polish at the Point, knowing it took days to get rid of the stains. Rob had used a tin himself and forced Den to smear some on his fingers to throw off suspicion. Or when Rob had made an excuse to pull Den away from a card game at Randolph Field after he'd dropped his cards, using the confusion to palm an ace. Granted, that was long in the past, but Den was still playing pranks—and cheating to do it.

"You're no' wrong, luve. Den's been such a guid friend, acting the fool, calling attention to himself, so the firsties wouldn't make me stand at attention for hours, poking me in the chest and calling me a 'tall, worthless nobody with rocks for brains.' And he played Major to my Colonel at Edenoaks, with never a sign of resentment." He buried his face in Maggie's hair. "I wouldn't be here if he hadn't saved my life on that shout."

"But why are you still protecting him?"

"I've known for years Den's joking is a way to cover something else, something deeper, but I've never discovered what. Now I'm thinking he might be searching for the God he's been running from so long." He held her away, looking into her eyes. "I hope you understand I can't embarrass him by accusing him of cheating."

"That would be cruel." She rested her cheek against his throat. "Just tell him using pounds instead of American dollars is too confusing to make change quickly."

That might be stretching it, but it could be a way out.

Chapter Fourteen

May, 1948

Outside a light breeze salted the air, and best of all, the first sun in months warmed Maggie's face. The bairns' exuberant squeals made her smile. She pulled a towel from her washing basket and pinned it to the line.

Robbie raced across the girse, Shep at his heels.

Katie skipped behind, tossing her long copper curls as if shaking off the winter's gloom.

Annie sat at the back of the croft, eyes wide, wee fingers exploring the bright green blades of girse. Last summer, she'd lain oot here on a blanket, practicing smiles and trying to suck her bare toes.

How Rob had luved finding his Wee Annie ootside. He'd knelt beside her, fingering her silken curls, kissing dimpled elbows and knees, tracing the delicate arch of an eyebrow with his fingertip.

Maggie roused herself from the mind-picture and stood on tiptoe to hang the last sheet. If only Rob were here to share this rare spring day. But he was at the shed, doubtless checking the boats under construction or going over a list of orders with Den.

She smoothed the corners of the sheet and nudged the empty basket out of the way, smile fading. Every shout, he'd sat in front of the radio, eyes narrowed, muscles tense, as though trying to will himself aboard the rescue boat.

And her? She'd been so relieved he wasn't in danger, the passing days had sheltered her in clouds of happiness, as fragile and subject to the winds of change as those in the sky. Now, her brief respite from fear was over. Her faither had released Rob for in-water rescues the day before. The next shout belonged to him.

Don't put yourself in a fash, Maggie Savage.

Spurred to act before the prickle of fear grew, she sang a Scots ditty, her feet hopping and skipping to the tempo as she ducked the sheets flapping in the wind and danced from trews to towels, blouses to sheets, leggings to linens, touching each with a forefinger and a pinkie.

By the time she finished, out of breath and ready for a cup of tea, the same joy flooded her that she'd experienced as a lass when Elspeth taught her the dance. Glorious! As soon as Annie was auld enough, she'd teach it to her.

"Mither," Robbie shouted.

She shaded her eyes as he raised a stick high and sent it sailing across the girse.

Shep leaped after it, feet flying, ears flapping, tail raised high.

"Guid one, laddie," Maggie called.

Annie tugged on her skirt, blades of girse clutched in one grubby hand.

She pulled the lassie into her arms and wiped a smudge of dirt from her chin. "What a nice present. We'll put these in water to show Faither when he gets home."

Fern brushed aside a flapping sheet. "Enjoying the sun, are you?"

"Och, I didn't hear you coming." Maggie pulled a blade of girse from Annie's hair and bounced her on a hip. "The sun's still high. It can't be that late already."

"Mither." Katie launched herself at Fern's legs. "We've been ootside since before dinner. We had a picnic with bacon butteries and shortbread, and Annie didn't spill her milk."

"Ready to go home, then?" Fern asked, eyes sparkling with mischief.

"No. 'Tis too early." Katie rolled her eyes and dashed back to play more.

Fern smiled and gestured to a blanket spread nearby. "Let's fauld our fits. I've been on my feet since early mornin, inventorying the medicaments in the pharmacy and everything in the supply room."

Maggie carried Annie to the blanket.

The bairn squirmed and kicked her legs. "No, no," she said, shaking her head.

"Down you go, then, but don't get too near Shep and Robbie." Maggie lowered the lassie to her feet. "They'll knock you on your behoochie."

Annie batted at the seat of her leggings, and walked to her spot by the back dyke where she plonked down, still clutching her handful of girse.

"There's a bright lassie," Fern said, "but she's so quiet. No' like your lad who never sits still." She sat on the blanket and patted a spot next to her.

Maggie joined her with a grateful sigh. "Robbie's just like his faither, always on the move, but Annie's more content to watch. I'm grateful she's no' a climber like Robbie was at her age." She plucked a blade of girse and twirled it between her fingers. "Now, tell me what brings you home so early."

"A guilty conscience—and don't raise your eyebrows—John's, no' mine. He said, and I quote, 'You've been standing all mornin while I sat at my desk. On you go, enjoy the sunshine.'"

"Faither does have his moments of insight," Maggie said. "Or mebbe I should say hindsight, since 'tis usually after the fact." She pushed aside a strand of hair tickling her cheek. "Has Den said owt about Rob being released to command the *Maggie*?"

"No' a word at supper last een. But he's so busy helping Rob and taking Scots lessons from Elspeth, I haven't seen him much, and when I do, he's spent."

"Rob told me about the lessons. He said Den reminded him of himself when he was learning Scots, having trouble placing his tongue behind his front teeth so he didn't roll his *r*'s so much as swallow them."

Fern laughed, hugging herself. "Have you heard what he said to Elspeth when she told him to stop wasting her time with his blether, that he's no' a lad and should act his age?"

"No, but I'm thinking you're about to tell me."

"He told her he'd start acting his age the minute she acted hers."

"He didn't! Did she take her walking stick to him?"

"I doubt it. Elspeth told me at kirk, and she just gave me one of her sly smiles and shrugged."

A sudden gust of wind sent the laundry billowing and snapping. The women fetched warmer sweaters for their bairns, cups of tea for themselves, and sat on the top step of the side entry for a broader view of the croft yard.

"Has Rob said how he thinks Den's doing?" Fern buttoned her sweater. "Is he finding it a help having another partner?"

"He says 'tis exactly what he's needed. No' only did Den step in for Rob with the shouts, but he's freed him from all the paperwork and telephone calls that kept him from working on the trawler design." Maggie sipped her tea, thanking God for the opportunity to blether with her dearest friend. "Why? Surely he ken's how much Rob appreciates his help."

"I'm certain he does. 'Tis just that Den's been so quiet the past few weeks, no' full of his usual nonsense." Fern put her cup on the step and drew her legs up, hugging her knees. "And he's always looking at me, like he wants to say something but doesn't know how—or is afraid to."

Maggie worried her lower lip. Should she delve into something so private? But Fern herself had revealed Den's awkward attempt at a proposal. And her adamant reply. "Has he said more about getting merrit?"

Fern plucked at a loose thread on her tights. "How could he? I told him I'd never marry an unbeliever." She straightened her legs and sighed. "Each Sabbath he leans forward in the pew like he doesn't want to miss a word Hugh says, but he's no' willing to discuss the lesson on the walk home. 'Tis like he has something on his mind he's determined to work oot for himself."

"Mebbe he's too busy listening to the Holy Spirit to have time for a blether."

Was that a spark of hope in Fern's eyes—or a teardrop reflecting the sun? "I pray that's true."

Rob stood at the *Maggie*'s railing, looking out at the wind icing the harbour's waves with white foam, erratic gusts tugging at his short hair. Finally, a sunny day. No' verra warm, but bright with promise. He closed his eyes and pictured Maggie ootside with the bairns, turning her bonnie face to that lemon-yellow orb in the sky, celebrating an early return of what the islanders called the "steady weather."

His gaze wandered to the new floatplane shed at the end of the dock. Why wasn't he flying high in that limitless sky, no longer bound to rocks and girse, but soaring free above it all, the vast expanse of the heavens his—

"Hoy, Rob!"

Reverie shattered before he could lose himself in it, Rob turned.

Den rounded the cabin and adjusted his aviator's sunglasses higher on his nose, teeth flashing a wide grin. "Thought I'd find you here." Wearing rumpled denims tucked into wellies, red hair tangled like a discarded mop, Den Anderson looked a mess.

Rob laughed. "Aren't you getting ahead of yourself with the glasses? And what's with the wellies? Hedging your bets the sun won't last the day?"

Den hooted and clapped Rob's shoulder. "I'm celebrating, bucko. Haven't seen this piece of rock look so guid since I was here last July." He zipped his A-2 jacket and shoved his hands into his pants pockets. "If somebody could find a way to stop that wind, we might be able to feel those weak rays instead of just imagining how warm they are."

"Dream on." Rob leaned his hip against the railing. "Summer's a guid twa months oot."

"What's turned you into such a Gloomy Gus on the first sunny day since I landed here?"

Gloomy Gus? Rob hadn't heard that one in a long time. "I'm no' gloomy—just a realist. Rain is still to come. And that new addition to the shed for the trawler is scheduled for construction as soon as the rescue boats are launched and oot of the way." He took a deep breath and exhaled noisily. So much to do and so little time. "Then I need to help Graham break in another new boatbuilding crew for the trawler after we put the Barra and Harris boats through their sea trials."

Den yanked off his sunglasses. "We? Is that 'we' as in you and me, or the imperial 'we'?"

Was Den feeling uncertain about his role in the business now that he no longer commanded the *Maggie*? Och, Rob had done it again. When would he learn to share his plans with the folk they involved—especially Den, who'd worked so hard to make this partnership work? "The both of us. You'll take one boat, and I'll take the other. And we'll do the same when it comes to the capsizing trials. With all your experience on shouts, you're more than ready."

Den pounced, pounding Rob's shoulder.

He grabbed the railing to keep from going over backward.

"You bet I'm ready! Wait till I tell Fern. She's been wondering when I'll get oot of that office and start earning my silver."

The bear hug that followed was no surprise, only the tears filling Rob's eyes. How many times had Den's hug revived his flagging spirits?

Made a bad pass on the football field? Had to swallow an unearned reprimand from a firstie? Strike films destroyed by flack?

"No problemo, bucko. There's always tomorrow." And the hug.

Rob embraced the warm memories and threw his arm over Den's shoulder. "Let's get back to the office. I've a few more ideas I want you to—"

The wail of the shout siren split the air.

Chapter Fifteen

"I don't want to go in," Robbie shouted, his protest muffled by the shrill siren.

Maggie swatted his bum and pushed him toward the house. "In you go while I get Annie." She ran across the girse, palms pressed to her ears. *No' now, Faither. Please no' the day.*

Fern intercepted Maggie's mad dash. "I'll get Annie and Katie," she yelled. "Get yourself to the radio."

Minutes later, Robbie pouted in his bedroom, Katie sat in Maggie's rocker with a drowsy Annie in her lap, and Maggie and Fern stood in front of the radio, listening to a steady hum of static.

"Shouldn't be much longer," Fern said.

Maggie battled the fear trapping a reply in her throat. *I will no' do this again, Lord. I cannot allow it.* She pulled a tattered list of names and telephone numbers from beneath the ink blotter on Rob's desk. The carefully printed words blurred, replaced by the image that had haunted her for so long—Rob's face, disappearing beneath the waves.

Fern's hand closed over hers. "The sea's no' running high. We must have faith."

Her friend's trembling voice cut through Maggie's growing panic. She'd been so selfish, thinking only about Rob. Of course Fern was also afraid. Though Rob would command the shout, he'd take Den.

"Control, this is *Maggie*. What do we have, Ewan?" Rob's deep voice, so calm and steady.

"*Maggie*, Control. 'Tis a strange one, Commander. Maritime Rescue reports a yacht in trouble with nine souls aboard, but they say the radio transmission's so bad, they only got partial coordinates. They put the yacht someplace in the skerries. We're still working on the exact location. Over."

"Copy, Control. We're clearing the harbour now and will head southwest. Get us that location ASAP. *Maggie*, oot."

Maggie hugged Fern. Rob and Den had rescued the Proctors from the skerries without a crew to back them up. But the skerries were so dangerous ... *Be with my Rob, Faither—and Den. Keep them safe, please keep them safe.*

Rob relinquished the helm to Neil and zipped up his wetsuit. If that yacht was in the skerries, and with nine needing rescued ... He turned in his seat and counted his crew. Nine, including himself and Den. If they had to go into the water, that wasn't enough. At least twa lads had to be left aboard to man the ropes, plus Neil at the wheel. That was cutting it thin. Pray God they could get close enough for a sling transfer.

Neil tapped his knee and handed him the mike.

"*Maggie*, this is Control. The clearest fix we can get is fifty-six degrees north by eight degrees west, which would put them in the central skerries. Maritime Rescue confirmed 'tis the *Princess*, an Inverness yacht, with nine American adults aboard. Over."

"Roger, Control. I'll talk to the skipper on the hailing frequency. *Maggie*, oot."

Rob dialed the local hailing frequency. "*Princess*, this is *Maggie*, Innisbraw's rescue boat. Come in. Over."

Static, then a male voice sounding close to the edge of hysteria. "Rescue boat? Did you say rescue boat?"

When Rob tried to reply, it was obvious the man on the yacht still had his mike keyed to Broadcast.

"Dear God, help us!"

A woman screamed in the background, and a man slurred curses and ranted about foreigners and their accents.

Rob waited a minute, then tried again, using his clearest English. "*Princess*, this is *Maggie*. When you want to hear me, push Receive. To make me hear you, push Broadcast. Do you copy—understand? Repeat, do you understand? Over."

"Finally, somebody who speaks English. Help us, we're sinking! Now he said I push Receive."

This skipper knew nothing about radio protocol. He'd have to simplify things. "*Princess*, you're doing great. Do you have life vests on your passengers? I repeat, do you—?"

"We have life vests, but we're one short. Push Receive again."

"*Princess*, if you have women aboard, put the life vests on them, and those men who are poor swimmers. Do you understand?"

"I already have. I'm not an idiot. Where are you?"

Rob fought an urge to shout. "*Princess*, we're about ten minutes from your position. What is the condition of your boat?"

Silence.

A hand kneaded Rob's shoulder and he glanced up.

Den.

Rob mouthed his thanks for the show of support, then broadcast, "*Princess*, I say again, what is the condition of your boat?"

"We're stuck on a rock, leaning to one side."

"*Princess*, I'm going to give you some instructions, so listen carefully. You must follow them. I repeat, you must follow them. Are you ready to receive?"

"Of course I'm ready."

"*Princess*, listen carefully. Do not, I say again, do not abandon ship. Stay with your boat. Have everyone hang on. I repeat, hang on. Do you understand?"

"You don't have to keep repeating yourself. And what do you mean, don't abandon ship? We're sinking." More curses.

"Do not go in the water. We may be able to transfer you directly from your boat to ours." Rob ran a hand over his face. Who rented a yacht to this incompetent? "*Princess*, do not go in the water!"

Silence again.

"*Princess*, this is *Maggie*. Did you read me?"

No reply.

Rob turned to Den. "What's your take on this?"

"If he's as bad with navigating as he is on the radio, 'tis no wonder he hit the rocks. And he sounded drunk to me, slurring his words and losing his temper. A mean sot, is what he is."

Rob nodded. An inexperienced skipper trying to navigate the Atlantic, and blootered, at that. Alcohol and seawater—a deadly combination.

Rob pressed Den's forearm. "How are we going to use the transfer sling, if we can get close enough?"

"We're at least twa men short. But what other choice is there?"

"Then help the lads get it ready."

"Aye, Commander."

Rob grinned. Den's crisp, correct reply was exactly what he needed after that daft radio interchange.

Moments later, a shout from the deck sounded.

Rob stood and peered through the windscreen.

There she was, grounded amidships on a single large rock and listing to port.

He activated the siren and his crew raced out the cabin door. "I'm going oot on deck," he said to Neil. "The sea's calm as I'd hoped, and the boat's caught on a rock no' far from us. Slow ahead and get as close as you can. If they're still aboard, we'll try the sling."

Another brisk, "Aye, Commander."

Three of his crew stood ready with the transfer sling, and the others waited on the fantail, rescue lines tied. Den stood at the railing, binoculars to his eyes.

"What do you see?" Rob shouted.

"Men and women fighting for a place at the railing."

Rob raised the bullhorn. "Ahoy, *Princess*. Skipper, clear your deck and prepare to receive a line. Clip the line to your railing securely. I repeat, fasten it to your railing securely."

One of the men, hopefully the skipper, waved his hands. The crowd slowly deserted the railing and disappeared from view.

Rob signaled his crew.

Duncan took aim and fired the line. It shot over the yacht's railing.

After a moment, the skipper clipped the rope to the railing. Within seconds, he was joined by the passengers. They were shoving one another, their screams faint, swallowed by the roaring sea.

Rob nodded at Artair. "Women first, lad."

Artair seated himself in the sling and activated the transfer. Moments later, he reached the yacht, scaled the railing, and secured a woman in the sling.

Duncan, Paddy, and Den pulled her toward the *Maggie*. When she was safely aboard, they unsnapped the harness, helped her to her feet, and sent the empty sling back for another victim.

Matthew bundled the sobbing woman into a blanket.

"My husband!" she screamed, pounding on Matthew's chest. "I want my husband!"

Rob returned his attention to the yacht. The sound of the rock grinding into the hull was unmistakable. Eight more to go. Would she hold up that long?

Another woman came across, then another, both so hysterical James came off the fantail to help Matthew.

Den grabbed Rob's arm. "Artair's in trouble."

A large man struggled with Artair, pushing him against the railing.

Rob raised the bullhorn again. "Women first," he shouted. "Step back now! Allow the women to come first." He dropped the bullhorn to his side.

The man stopped struggling and Artair was able to fasten the last woman in the sling. She was brought aboard the *Maggie*, followed quickly by four men. Belligerent, despite the cold, spume-laden wind and their brush with death, and still so blootered they stumbled into the cabin, the men cursed and shoved aside the blankets offered.

Artair appeared at the empty railing and raised his arms in a shrug.

The yacht listed farther to port.

Eight souls had been brought aboard the *Maggie*. There remained only one.

Rob raised the bullhorn again. "Can't find him?"

The lad shook his head.

"Come back," Rob ordered. "Right now!"

After Artair had been helped onto the *Maggie*'s deck, the skipper, clad in a white shirt and trousers and no life vest, groped his way to the yacht's railing. He waved a bottle in a sloppy salute and shouted something. The sounds of the yacht's screeching timbers and crashing waves drowned out his words.

Rob tied his lifeline and positioned himself in the sling.

"No, Rob!" Den shouted. "I'm lighter. Let me go!"

Shaking his head, Rob activated the sling. He was over three quarters of the way across when the man tumbled over the railing, hit the side of the yacht, and plunged into the sea, head first.

He disappeared in the roiling water.

Rob waited a few seconds to get closer, unclipped himself, and dropped. He hit feet first and clawed his way to the surface. Couldn't see the skipper. He struck out toward the yacht, giving it all he had. A wave picked him up and slammed him against the hull. A searing pain in his forehead. The breath left his lungs. Waves lashed at his body.

Blinking his eyes to clear his blurred vision, he spotted a flash of white and reached out. Another wave slammed him against the hull, driving him underwater. He held his breath, groping. His hand closed around an arm. He hung on, fighting toward the surface. His head broke free. Gulping air, he pulled the man close to his chest. Another wave loomed high. No time to take the slack out of his lifeline. He tightened his grip on his victim, raised his arm, and waved.

The rope around his waist jerked and tightened, pulling him away from the hull.

Though the trip through the sea only took minutes, it seemed like an eternity to Rob. His head ached, arms felt numb. Hanging on to the unconscious man took all his remaining energy.

When they reached the *Maggie*, two lads jumped off the taffrail, one taking the skipper and the other helping Rob.

"I'm all right," he panted. "Get him ... aboard."

The limp man was lifted onto the fantail and carried to the upper deck.

Rob accepted Den's hand pulling him aboard but brushed aside his help after that and climbed the ladder to the upper deck alone, though his muscles screamed and his head pounded. He stumbled into the cabin.

The space reserved for Artificial Respiration was filled with men and women sitting on the deck, a few huddled together beneath blankets, all staring at the man on the stretcher.

"How is he?" Rob asked Matthew.

"He's dead, Commander."

"No." Rob grabbed the side of the door to keep from falling. "He can't be dead. I got to him in time."

"The back of his head's crushed. Must have hit a rock when he went into the water."

Den grasped his arm. "Let Matthew take a keek at that cut over your eye."

Rob looked into Matthew's grim face. "He's really dead?" Only a whisper, but all he could manage.

"Aye, Commander." Matthew took his other arm. "Den's right, I need to see to that cut. You're dripping blood on the floor."

Too tired to argue, Rob allowed the two men to lead him to his chair, where he sat down heavily. Dead. He'd been too late.

Matthew pressed a piece of gauze above Rob's left eyebrow. "How many fingers?"

Rob glanced up. "Three. I'm all right, Matthew." Numb with disbelief, he sat while the medic sterilized the cut and covered it with a plaster.

Whispers and a few sobs intruded into the silence he craved.

Dead? Though he'd known it could happen on any shout, he felt sick.

Den pulled a blanket over the man's face.

All the better to cover Rob's failure.

Stars winked awake as Maggie walked Rob to the house. "You should have stayed the night at the infirmary."

"I only needed three stitches and a few APCs for my headache."

"Mebbe. But you're fair spent."

He grunted and plodded on, head bowed.

Rob looked so miserable, yet there was nothing she could do for him except listen when he finally felt like talking. 'Twas a guid thing Fern had taken Robbie and Annie to her house.

"Den will be here long before Rob," Fern had said. "It will take

John a while to treat that cut on his head. Go to the infirmary. I'm no' needed, so your bairns can spend the night with me." She'd attempted a smile. "'Tis my turn after all the times you've kept my Katie."

Maggie opened the front door and led Rob inside. "The shower water's hot, luve, but let me wash your hair. We don't want water on that plaster."

He soaped himself and allowed her to wash his hair, bending back so his face was out of the stream of water. So quiet he was, and his eyes dark with pain—no' physical pain, but something deeper, harder to reach.

His hands trembled when he drank the mug of coffee she offered, and he still spoke no' a word. She led him into the bedroom, slid the dressing gown from his shoulders, and pressed him onto the bed, joining him the moment she shed her gown. *Help him, Faither. He can't see the eight he saved, only the one he lost.* She pulled up the bedquilt and pressed her back against him, spooning close.

Her Rob needed time, no' talk.

Comfort, no' empty platitudes.

His fingers brushed her cheek and tangled in her hair.

Aye, comfort.

She awakened to find Rob sitting beside her, dressed and shaved. He pulled her into his arms, kissing her neck and shoulders. "Thank ye, my Maggie," he said. "You always know what I need."

Tears threatened. Her Rob was back, his eyes no longer dark with pain. *Guide my words, Faither. Help me know what to say.* "Then how about some breakfast. You missed your supper."

"A bit later, and I'm no' hurting. I've been trying to write a report on the shout. I know there'll be a sheriff's inquest at the least, what with a ... death."

She pulled back and took his wrist, looking at his watch. "Only a wee bit past dawn. How long have you been up?"

"No' long. Where are the bairns? I was careful about making noise, but when I checked, their beds were empty."

"At Fern's. She was here when the siren sounded and stayed with me the day." Maggie hugged him, wanting to explain what a help Fern had been, how it had calmed them both, talking about their shared concerns, their fears. But now wasn't the time. If ever.

"What about Den?" His right eyebrow arched. "Did he spend the night at Fern's too?"

She stood and pulled on her dressing gown. "He's upstairs."

Rob raised his hands and quit the room, calling over his shoulder, "I could use some more coffee. Went through one pot."

Och, that man and his coffee. She laughed at herself as she set his coffee to perk and water to boil for her tea. Was she any better? There were times she thought she'd die if she didn't have a cuppa.

Cuppa indeed. She'd spent too long in England.

Coffee and tea in hand, she walked into Rob's office.

He sat at his desk, staring at a blank piece of paper. Wadded-up papers littered the floor at his feet. "I don't know what to say," he muttered as she handed him his mug. He took a sip and carried the coffee over to the window. He lifted a corner of the lace curtain and stared out at the slopes of Ben Innis, light green with new shoots of heather.

Most likely, the scene he saw was not the one before his eyes.

She took the mug, put it on his drafting table, and stepped into his arms.

He held her tightly, his cheek resting on her hair. "Why didn't he wait to be transferred, Maggie? I was on the way. There was still time."

His ragged whisper tore at her heart.

He wanted to save them all. Despite rescuing almost a hundred souls the past year, one death, especially such a senseless one, was devastating.

"We'll never ken why. Alcohol probably affected his judgment, or he may have panicked."

He held her away and looked into her eyes. "Until this mornin, I was blaming myself for making a mistake. But it occurred to me what he did—mebbe no' why—but what. He killed himself, just as sure as if he'd held a gun to his head. What a waste."

"You couldn't have known that then. You risked your life, luve. No one has the right to expect more."

He pushed a curl from her forehead. "I suppose you're right."

Such a weary smile. But her Rob was sharing his burden.

Chapter Sixteen

The inquest into the death of one Giovanni Alberto Rossi of Albany, New York, was brief and anti-climactic. Rob's written statement was read into the record, but he was not called to testify. Only male passengers gave verbal accounts, all filled with praise for Mr. Rossi's concern for their safety. A Royal National Lifeboat Institution official congratulated the crew of the *Maggie* for saving the lives of eight passengers, citing Commander Robert Savage's bravery in his attempt to save the victim. After five minutes of deliberation, the verdict was read. "Accidental death by misfortune," the sheriff's clerk declared in a sonorous tone.

Rob waited until they were outside on the pavement before pulling Den to a halt. "What a waste of time," he said, stabbing his fingers through his hair. "No' a word from anybody but me about the skipper being blootered."

"And the passengers," Den said. "Things aren't so different here in Scotland after all. I'm thinking Rossi must have been a rich big shot in the States." His sudden laugh held no humour. "With a name like Rossi, that cover-up smells like the long arm of the Mob to me."

Rob sat at his desk, knees crossed, one foot jiggling, while Den leaned back in a chair, chewing on a pencil, the sun creases beside his eyes crinkled in what looked like disgust.

"Hope that's yours." Rob gestured with his chin at the pencil.

"I don't like it." Den spat out the pencil, studied the line of teeth marks circling it, and wiped it on his denims before sliding it into his shirt pocket. "This a partnership or a monarchy?" He crossed his arms and frowned. "I don't like being told something after you've already signed off on it."

Rob kept his gaze on Den, not expecting an open-minded audience. Pulling rank in the service was easier than explaining a course of action in business, and that tight-lipped expression on his partner's face was becoming all too familiar. "Barra and Harris's first coxswains need to be aboard their new boats for the sea and capsizing trials. They're experienced navigators and rescue men, but on lifeboats, no' rescue boats." He held up a hand to cut off Den's interruption. "You've broken in a lot of new copilots the same way—by turning over the yoke and giving them an opportunity to get the feel of the Fort—no' just expecting them to know it all because they logged a few hours on multi-engines back in the States." He blew out an exasperated breath. "We can't just hand over those boats after the trials and leave it at that."

Den leaped up and began pacing. "What about the bugs we have to work out on those trials?" He scrubbed at his hair. "You want them privy to all our dirty laundry?"

"Dirty laundry!" Rob leaned forward, finger stabbing. "What makes you an expert? You've never taken a boat through sea trials." He'd had enough of having his decisions questioned. He pushed away from his desk and reached for his jacket. "If you want oot of this partnership, that's your privilege, but don't pick a wrong-headed fight with me and use that as an excuse." He strode toward the doorway and paused in front of Den. "I've sweated almost five years getting this business up and running. If that isn't enough for you, that's your problem, no' mine." Rob dodged through the cluttered shed, yanked open the door, and stepped outside. He unclenched his hands and took a deep breath.

He couldn't go home like this, belly cramping and thoughts in a muddle. Instead of taking the path, he walked along the sand at the side of the main pier and threw himself down on the stone bench, staring out at the harbour. He'd handled it all wrong, said some things he shouldn't have, but every word was true.

What was wrong with Den, up one minute and down the next? They'd weathered a lot of things over the years but always together, no' locking horns. Mebbe he was right on suggesting Den wanted out of the partnership. But why?

Was it Fern? Did Den regret giving up his love-'em-and-leave-'em way of life?

Rob cradled his chin in his palms. All these months he'd prayed and waited to hear Den say he was a believer, but no' a peep. Rob couldn't bear the thought of losing his companionship again. But losing him for eternity was far worse. *I've allowed my priorities to get muddled, Faither. 'Tisn't running the boatworks or even the rescues that count, but Den's soul. Speak to him. Show him the way. Plea—*

"Room on that bench for one more?" Den stood next to him, hands deep in his pockets, head bowed.

Rob scooted over.

"Have I gone too far, Rob, or is there a wee bit of time for an explanation?"

It was up to him now. His reply could either give him some answers or send Den away. *Your words, Faither.* He cleared his throat. "I'm no' going anywhere."

"'Tis a nice een. Hardly a breath of wind."

Patience, Savage. "It is that."

Den toed the sand, picked up a cockle shell, and held it up to the dying light. "This is the way I feel most of the time—empty." He tossed the shell aside. "The rest of the time I'm so full of ... of wanting, I feel like I'm going to explode."

Rob kept silent, guessing more would follow. Weighty problems needed time to be put into words.

"You're a believer, Rob. Why? You've always analyzed everything, turned it upside down and inside out before you accepted it as truth. I'm going crazy over this. I have to know what made you believe."

Rob sat back, the hard stone bench digging into his spine. So this was what had Den in such a fankle. Why hadn't Rob shared his childhood from the very beginning of their friendship instead of allowing Den to assume he had a mither and faither too? It might have opened a conversation about the faith he'd been raised in, how it had kept him from giving up. Should he tell him now, or would Den resent no' being privy to his past? Remembering Maggie's relief the night he had told her, he began to talk.

He made it brief, the words halting, then gaining momentum, becoming easier each passing minute. The orphanage's noise, the smells, the confusion that sent him seeking a spot inside himself where he could hide. Learning to read and the world it revealed. How only one couple had chosen him, then returned him to the orphanage months later without an explanation. Watching the barnstorming Jennies, his yearning to take flight, to lose himself in that vast sky. His prayers for a family he could call his own and his steadfast belief that sometime, somewhere, God would answer.

Finally, he said, "To answer your question, I don't remember a time when I haven't believed. It was always there, accepted by me and everyone around me, young and auld."

"I should have known." Den buried his head in his hands. "You only got letters from that senator you said sponsored you to the Point. Never had any visitors or phone calls. I'm sorry, Rob. Some friend I am."

"'Twas my choice to hide my past, Den. When I left Newton, I buried all that. Didn't want to think about it, let alone share it with anybody. And in a way I turned my back on God too, when I didn't tell you what He'd meant in my life." Rob squirmed, back beginning to sting. "I was what they call a lukewarm believer when I came to Innisbraw. But after listening to Hugh teach, I learned what a wonderful, faithful, luving Heavenly Faither I'd had all along. He's taken the place of the mither and faither I can't remember. And He gave me the family I always prayed for."

Den's laugh had a bitter edge. "In a way, you're luckier than I am. I told Elspeth last time I was here that my folks couldn't be heathens because they took us to church on Christmas and Easter. But they were. The only God they ever worshipped was the pacifist one who demonstrated against war and always turned his cheek." Again, that laugh. "I kept a few secrets from you too. Now you know why they didn't show for my graduation at the Point. Couldn't stand being around anyone in uniform. Even their son."

Rob flinched. Why had he swallowed Den's excuse that his parents were too busy?

Den studied his clenched hands. "Our partnership might be ending soon anyway. I can't stay here once Fern tells me she's waited long enough."

"Long enough? Long enough for what?"

"She told me the day I got here she wouldn't marry an unbeliever. That's why I've been trying so hard."

"You talked marriage the day you got here?"

Den's crooked grin dissolved beneath the tears trickling down his cheeks. "Yeah," he choked. "Pretty pathetic, isn't it?"

Now it all made sense. The mood swings, Den's rapt attention at kirk, the covert glances he and Fern sometimes exchanged, longing and sadness in their eyes.

Your words, Faither, no' mine. As his pal liked to say, time to cut to the chase. He tapped Den's knee. "Do you believe the Bible is the inspired Word of God?"

The tap, an Air Forces gesture for "heads-up" brought an immediate reply. "Aye. Fought it for weeks, but all of a sudden, it made sense." Den swiped a palm over his eyes. "Don't know why I believe that. But I do."

Almost there. "Then if 'tis the Word of God and it tells you the path to salvation, to becoming a believer, what's the problem? You expect bells to ring and drown out all the wee, niggling doubts that creep into your mind? Or mebbe you're waiting for the clouds to part and the heavens to open? We're living in the de'il's world, Den. Not often we see visions or hear words, only those we read in the Bible, showing us the choice between guid and evil." He handed Den his kerchief. "I'm thinking you may be close to being a believer and don't even realize it."

Two wide blue eyes met his.

He stood and rubbed his back. "If I'm any later, Maggie'll kick *me* off the island. I'll race you home." He took off at a trot, hoping Den would follow.

No folk on the path, just a few lights from the howff and post office piercing the gloaming. Had he said enough? Too much? But he'd prayed for God's words. Either he believed the Lord would answer, or he was a hypocrite.

A rabbit darted from Angus's drive and dashed across the path in front of him, scut raised in panic.

Pounding footsteps behind him. "No fair. You had a head start. Slow down, bucko. I'm coming."

Chapter Seventeen

The Harris rescue boat strained against the ropes holding her fast to the launching skids. Rob planted his feet firmly on the deck, raised his arm, and prolonged the suspense by scanning the hushed crowds gathered on the path, main pier, and lining the top of Innis Fell.

Maggie knew the island's folk better than he. She'd told him the successful launch of the Barra boat the day before would no' quench their thirst for excitement.

He dropped his arm.

Axe blades flashed in the sunlight. Ropes parted.

Loosed from her bonds, the boat's stern slid into the harbour. The deck rocked beneath Rob's feet. Within seconds, momentum carried her into deeper water. She was afloat.

Whistles and shouts from over two hundred folk competed with the boat's siren as Den engaged the two powerful diesel engines and steered the boat toward her berth.

The familiar, deep-throated purr and throbbing deck beneath Rob's feet trapped a breath in his throat.

The engines thrummed as if saying, "Treat us right and we'll take you anywhere—no matter how rough the seas or how high the waves."

Grinning, he stepped to the starboard railing and snapped a salute to the tiny figure standing on her cottage entry. Elspeth. Her prayers had made this possible. The Innisbraw Boatworks, only a dream for almost five years, had become a reality.

Once Den had the boat snug alongside the dock's rubber fenders, Rob tossed the stern and stem lines to Graham and Danny.

"Another grand launch," Graham shouted. "We're in business now."

"We are that." Rob shot him a grin and turned to peruse the young men surging onto the boatwork's pier. Only his building crew. Where was Maggie?

A skirt-clad figure darted its way to the front.

Before he could slide the gangplank in place, two of his lads picked Maggie up and lifted her over the railing.

She fell into his arms, laughing, hugging his neck. "'Twas

glorious," she breathed into his ear. "You've brought life back to Innisbraw."

He dove into the depths of those sparkling, blue eyes, inhaled the fragrance of heather clinging to that spill of wavy, black hair, tasted the sweet lips pressed eagerly to his—and was lost in a sensation of luve so overwhelming it drove the breath from his lungs. His Maggie.

Den stood in the cabin doorway, searching the dwindling crowd for a glimpse of Fern. Was she stuck at the infirmary? Or fast at home watching all the bairns, so Maggie could be here to share Rob's triumph? He ground his teeth.

No' fair, those thoughts. He might deserve some of the credit for the next boats launched, but what Rob had said in his office that night was true. It was Rob's ideas, his plans, his hard work that had made this happen.

And his prayers.

Den closed his eyes, thinking back to what Rob had revealed while they sat on the bench. An orphan. That had knocked him for a loop. He'd spent hours lying in bed that night, looking back at all the signs he'd seen but ignored: no letters from home for Cadet Savage, no visitors, no snapshots of family or friends tacked above Rob's desk.

Sure, Rob was so quiet their plebe year it took a lot of effort to find a topic of conversation that elicited more than a grunt. But as the inexplicable bond between loner and extrovert deepened into friendship, Den took the easy way out.

Keep it light. Joke a lot. Talk about girls and dances and the one subject sure to bring a response—flying.

The two taboos? Religion and family. The first was a given as far as Den was concerned, and the second, a new hurt that still stung too much for him to share. His folks had never been perfect, but until he enrolled at the Point, they'd nurtured him and showed pride in his accomplishments. His three older sisters teased, scolded, and drove him crazy with their coddling. Because they loved him.

And all that time, what did Rob have? Only the faith that God would give him a family … someday.

Faith.

Den's future hinged on that five letter, one syllable word. Could Rob be right? Could he already be a—

An explosive burst of laughter shattered his musings.

Standing on a crate, Paddy gripped Rob's arm, holding an open bottle of ale over the commander's head. "'Tis done all the time in County Cork," he roared. "Come on, ye don't want it said ye refused to be christened." He looked around at the building and rescue crew lads clustered around Rob, as though soliciting their support.

To a man, they backed away, shaking their heads.

The Irisher changed tack, brought the bottle to his lips, and emptied it in several long swallows.

Both crews waved their guidbyes, leaving Rob and Maggie alone at the railing.

What kept Den rooted to the spot, unwilling to move? Having to talk about the sea trials scheduled for the next day, that's what. He'd put his foot into it, and he'd never found it easy to climb out of a verbal pit he'd dug for himself.

Stop putting it off. He's the brother you always wanted. Act like it.

He made his way to Rob's side, tapped his shoulder, and flashed two thumbs-up. "Mission accomplished, bucko."

Rob's warm smile acknowledged more than gratitude for the support; it reached back and gathered seventeen years of memories into one brief moment of brotherhood.

Maggie pulled on Den's sleeve. "There you are. Fern wanted you to know she'll be here as soon as she can. The MacKenzies' lad, Kieran, has a sore throat, and Faither wanted to take a culture."

Before Den could thank Maggie for the message, Rob said, "Speaking of lads, where's ours? And Annie and Katie?"

"I left them sitting on Angus's cairt bench so they could see over the folk's heads. No' to worry, Flora's there too." She wrinkled her nose. "Though we'd best give heels to. We shouldn't keep them waiting when everybody's off to cottage and croft."

"Why don't you start walking, then?" Rob nuzzled her hair and helped her down the gangplank. "I'll catch you up in a tick, lass."

Den squirmed when Rob turned and pinned him with a steady stare. Here it came. Time to get out the shovel and start digging.

"Ready for the sea trials? They start on the morra's mornin."

He knew what his pal was waiting to hear—what he should have heard that night in his office. Swallowing around the lump in his throat, Den said, "Aye. Ready and eager to show off their boats to those coxswains."

Rob's answering grin made eating crow a sma' price to pay.

David Hamilton, first coxswain of the Barra lifeboat—stocky, barrel-chested, with soft grey eyes, and just as affable as he'd been on the telephone—was just the man Rob should pair with Den.

His counterpart on the Harris lifeboat, Bruce Cairns, was aulder and rail thin, with a long, weathered face that must have felt a smile when he was a lad.

Rob and Den alternated keeping their boats close to the island in case there was a shout. While one stayed close to the shore, the other went out into deeper water. Rob spent hours with both coxswains, testing radio and radar systems, pressing engines to the maximum, and giving advice, both technical and anecdotal.

On the evening of the third day, Rob called Den into his office. "Have a seat," he said. "I need to fill you in on how we'll handle the capsizing trials on the morra."

"So you've changed your mind about me taking one boat."

Och, that raised chin and icy stare again. He'd thought Den was over second-guessing his decisions. "I have no', so haud yer wheesht and listen up." Rob sat on a corner of his desk.

Den sat back in his chair, eyes lowered. "Go ahead."

"I want both you and Bruce with me on the Harris trial. Bruce will have the second coxswain's seat, and we'll have four of our rescue lads aboard, suited up and ready. Neil and the rest of our rescue crew will be aboard the *Maggie* on standby to assist if there's a need. You with me so far?"

"Why have me there if Bruce is your second?"

"Because you'll be hanging onto the back of my seat, watching every move I make. Remember, he's used to handling a capsizing lifeboat—which is verra different—and you and twa of our rescue crew have never been through one. Understand?"

Den's gaze locked onto his. "Confirmed."

How easy it was for Rob to slip back into the role of commander over subordinate. "I won't be aboard when you take the Barra boat through her trial. So watch what I do until I tell you to join the crew. Then hang on for dear life, because you're in for an experience you'll never forget."

"It's really that hairy?"

"Capsizing is as bad as having your Fort stall and go into a nosedive." Rob slid off his desk and paced. "I'll have to tell you this since you won't be watching, but I won't goose the engines till we're upright. Once we are, take your place behind me again and pay verra close attention. When 'tis your turn, you'll find making your way through that channel between Heuch Fell and the rocks is some of the hardest sailing you'll ever do." He stopped in front of Den. "Any questions?"

Den scuffed the floorboard with his toe. "You sure I can do this? I took a look at that surf off Heuch Fell the last time we were oot, and it's the roughest I've ever seen—even worse than the skerries."

"Nowt to worry about. You'll have another four of our rescue lads aboard. They all went through the *Maggie*'s capsizing. Make sure they're suited up properly and remind them all to hang on. And use them to spot for you after your boat recovers and you're traversing between the fell and the rocks." He tapped Den's shoulder. "Remember, I'll be standing by on the *Maggie*. Don't make your move till I'm in position for an assist."

The Harris boat performed exactly as she should. Rob timed the capsizing from his seat. Eleven seconds from full upright, to capsize, back to full upright. Might be able to shave off a second in future boats, but with as much water as these boats displaced, ten seconds was the minimum expended time the experts could predict.

He turned to Bruce in the second coxswain's seat. "Satisfied?"

The twitch of a lip was the perfect reply to a perfect trial.

Den was more vocal. "I always doubted any boat could right herself. Wow! That was something!"

Fifteen minutes later, Rob steered the boat around the last rock, breached the final large wave, and sailed into calmer waters, bracing himself for the congratulations of his crew.

Late the following morning, Den climbed over the Barra boat's railing and raced up the dock to where Rob waited. Adrenaline running, heart still racing, he pounded on Rob's shoulder. "She did it, bucko—och, sorry I was too kittled up to time her, and it might have seemed like a lifetime, but I know it was only a few seconds. And that was only the beginning. Getting through that narrow channel to open sea took so much concentration, I thought my brain would explode." He held out his hands. "Look, I'm still shaking."

Rob flashed his watch. "Eleven and a half seconds was all it took. And you're on your feet. I was afraid I'd have to crawl off the *Maggie* after she capsized. What did David think?"

"He was wearing the biggest grin I've ever seen. All the way back to the harbour, he blethered on about finally having a boat built to rescue people no matter the weather." Den stepped back, looking over his shoulder at the Barra boat. "It was an experience I'll never forget, but I hope I never have to go through it during a shout."

"Amen to that." Rob turned away and walked toward the pier. "I have a thermos of coffee, if you'd care to share it."

Den hurried to catch up. "You're on. A shot of caffeine is just what I need right now."

"Maggie can't understand why that's so." Rob chuckled. "But she always heads for the teapot when she's kittled up or fashed. Mebbe no' as much as coffee, but it always calms her down."

Den slapped Rob's back. "Ready to take your transition course in Oban tomorrow? 'Tis way past time to get you rated on our floatplane."

Rob pulled Den to a stop. "Between the launches, sea trials, and capsizing trials, I've been so busy I forgot about it. You sure it will only take a few hours? Don't want to leave Neil alone too long in case there's a shout."

"I'm sure. With all your experience in single engine P-47s, plus over eighty missions in multi-engines, you'll ace it."

He watched the expressions flitting across Rob's face. Apprehension mebbe, resolve definitely, and joy that clogged Den's throat.

The wakes cut through the harbour water by the departing Barra and Harris rescue boats reminded Rob of contrails streaming behind B-17s. He looked up at the dove-grey sky, reliving oh-dark takeoffs and the first blush of dawn lighting the heavens far above the French countryside. He shivered with a thrill of anticipation. In a few minutes he would be up there in that infinite sky where he belonged, unfettered and free as the birds.

Though he'd memorized the check lists and operations' manual Den had given him, he felt edgy. Landing on tarmac or even grass was one thing. But water? *Give me confidence, Faither. I'm certain I can do this, but I want it so badly, I'm afraid I'll freeze.*

Den trotted onto the dock, whistling "Off We Go into the Wild Blue Yonder," sunglasses perched above his forehead, grin wide enough to swallow a cat. "Couldn't wait, huh?"

Rob shoved trembling hands into his pockets. "You're a little late to see David and Bruce off. They should be approaching Barra Head about now."

"On purpose, bucko. On purpose."

"Thought you said last night they'd make good commanders. Having second thoughts?"

"No' at all." Den dangled a key in front of Rob's face. "Their business was with you, no' me." He pocketed the key and stepped onto the ladder to the lower dock. "But from now on, this day is for playing." His head disappeared, then popped up again. "You coming? Need to show you how to pre-flight check this baby."

Baby, no' bairnie. Den's Scots was getting more fluent, but he still used his favourite American expressions. Rob climbed down the ladder.

There she was, that sleek floatplane, riding the soft swells, the first rays of a newborn sun glinting off her red wings.

His breath caught. *Soon.*

"'Tis the same as ground-checking any land plane except for the floats," Den said, nudging a pontoon with his toe. "You check oot the exterior and I'll take anything to do with the wheels and floats."

Once inside the plane, they went through the pre-start and start-up checklists, then Den started the engine and allowed the plane to drift away from the dock. "Remember the manual? Full back on the controls at 1700 rpm. A little rudder and aileron to turn us into the wind, pull back on the throttle to 1000 rpm, and we're ready to taxi."

Rob rested his hands on the yoke and touched his feet to the rudders, anticipating, feeling every adjustment Den made, mentally performing them himself.

He had to stop himself from taking over when Den opened the throttle to take-off power and pulled the stick all the way back. Once the nose was up as far as it would go, his fingers itched to move the stick forward to a neutral position.

The plane rose on the floats. *Verra soon.*

They raced across the harbour until the floats hit a large wave that bounced the plane into the air. As Rob expected, Den took advantage of the lift, applied rudder, and they were airborne.

Rob closed his eyes. The sensation of flight was so familiar, so natural. Like an eagle released from its handler's arm, soaring higher and higher toward the sun. Maggie was right. He was born to fly. *Thank Ye, Lord, thank Ye.*

No chatter on the flight—just two pairs of eyes scanning the horizon with an occasional check of the instrument panel. When they reached the harbour at Oban, Den turned control over to Rob and had him practice two water landings and takeoffs. Rob sweated the first, but the second was far less nerve-racking.

Den contacted the airstrip at Oban and announced their approach. "You handle the landing, bucko. Wheels down and locked. She's all yours."

The landing was smooth and easy.

While he waited, Den read every dog-eared aviation magazine, drank three cups of tea—ugh—and filled out the application to apply for a British instructor's license. When the floatplane still hadn't reappeared, he wandered outside and looked over the few planes tied down nearby. He wasn't worried about Rob passing, but he wished they'd hurry it up. He was gleg as a gled.

A speck appeared in the western sky. Moments later, the red-and-black amphibious plane circled the airstrip, lined up with the runway, and its wheels kissed the grass. A perfect landing.

At 1000 hours, the C.A.A. inspector handed Rob his single engine amphibian rating.

"Well, was he hard-nosed or reasonable?" Den asked as they walked toward their plane.

Rob laughed. "By the book. What else did you expect?"

Den left Rob to do the ground check alone and climbed into the right seat. He'd kill for a cup of coffee and a fry-up. Another half an hour and they'd be home. Fern had said she'd try to join Maggie on the dock for their arrival. But would she really? Every day he expected her to give up on him, to tell him she was tired of waiting.

Waiting for what? For him to fall on his knees and tell her was a believer now, that she could marry him? He grimaced and fastened his harness. How could he do that when he wasn't sure himself?

Rob slipped into the left seat, locked the door, and shrugged into his harness. "Ready?"

Flying right seat was going to be a pain. "That was a mighty quick ground check. Certain you didn't miss anything?"

That maddening eyebrow shot up. "Biddy certain. The one we did this mornin and another verra thorough one before I took the inspector up were thorough enough too."

"Then I'm ready." Once they reached cruising altitude, Den glanced at Rob.

He looked like a little boy who had just received everything he ever wanted from Santa Claus: joy, wonder, delight. Rob's chest rose and fell rapidly, like he'd run several miles, and he swallowed every other breath. What was he feeling right now? How many times had he looked up at the sky, remembering how it felt to chase the clouds, to climb and climb until the air thinned and he saw spots before his eyes? How many dreams of soaring free had he awakened from, crushed to find himself still earthbound?

Den looked away. Even happy emotions could be too painful to watch when one knew the cost of such a long wait. “Try some banks.” He laid his head back. “She responds pretty well, even with the floats causing some drag.”

The plane tipped and hurtled downward, left wing slicing through the air.

Den grabbed his harness. “Hey, this isn’t a P-47. Watch your airspeed.”

Rob’s sudden laugh was confident, exultant. “And she’s no B-17. The ball’s in the center, Den. I still remember how to use the rudders.”

Den’s face burned. In less than an hour of flight time, Rob probably knew more about this plane than Den would ever learn. He knew he was a good pilot—maybe even as good as Rob. But Den had to work at it. And Rob? Flying came as naturally as breathing.

A climb to regain lost altitude, then a steep bank to the right.

Den unclenched his hands and rested them in his lap.

Another climb.

Which way would his empty stomach lurch this time? He sneaked a keek. Rob was running his long fingers over the faces of the instruments, as though reading their numbers and diagrams through his fingertips.

At least they were level again and back on course.

“She’s light and very responsive, Den. ’Tis almost too easy.”

“I told you she was a nice bird. How does it feel?”

“I ... I haven’t the words to describe it. ’Tis like when I learned to walk again, but even better in so many ways.” He swiped a sleeve across his eyes and gave a crooked grin.

Tears pricked Den’s eyelids. The look on Rob’s face was so radiant, he felt like rouping. Even if they never used the floatplane for business, the happiness it would bring Rob made it more than worth every cent.

Maggie and the bairns waited on the boatworks dock when they taxied in. And there was Fern, pressed against the dock’s railing, smiling down at him, the breeze toying with her shiny black hair.

Den’s heart did a little slide and shuffle.

Rob closed the throttle, killed the engine, and sat quietly, hands resting on the yoke.

What was he waiting for? Den stowed his harness and sat back, tapping his fingers on his knees.

A hand pressed his shoulder. “That was better than the first time I soloed,” Rob said with another crooked grin. “Thank ye, Den. I’m whole again.” Without waiting for a reply, Rob popped the door and climbed down onto the dock.

Den scrambled after him, vowing he'd never take flying for granted again. He helped Rob tether the plane and followed him up the ladder.

Maggie leaped into Rob's arms and hugged his neck. Their kiss would have made Scarlett O'Hara and Rhett Butler green with envy.

Though Den wanted to kiss Fern like that, wanted to breathe in her sweet scent, his greeting was a lot more subdued. He had to be satisfied with Fern and Katie's hugs. He and Fern weren't merrit, and he wouldn't risk embarrassing her. He kissed Fern's cheek and ruffled Katie's hair.

"Did Rob get his license?" Fern asked.

"What do you think? He aced it—I mean, he didn't have a single problem."

The Savage family walked down the pier, Robbie's excited questions and Maggie's musical laughter waltzing back on the breeze.

Katie grabbed Den's hand. "When can I fly? Is it skeery?"

"No' a bit. Do birds look skeered?"

She giggled and dashed off to catch up with Robbie, her hair catching the sun like dancing leaves on a copper beech tree.

Den looked around.

Nobody watching.

He pulled Fern into his arms and kissed her—not as long as he wanted, but it would have to do until this een. "I couldn't wait," he said, when she smiled up at him.

"What makes you think I wanted you to?" She laughed and raised her face for another.

A much longer kiss this time, filled with luve and longing—at least on his part.

She slipped her hand into his as they made their way past the *Maggie* and onto the pier. Could it get any better than this?

Och, with so much happening, he'd forgotten his news.

"I applied for my British instructor's license this morning. I'll have to pass a couple of tests in a few weeks, but as soon as that's over, 'twill be your turn to fly." He waited for her reaction. Had she really meant it when she said she wanted to learn?

Her radiant smile was answer enough. "I can't wait. But what about Maggie? Are you going to teach her?"

"With Rob around? He'd be none too happy. Do I look like I have a death wish?"

Chapter Eighteen

A light breeze rippled the lace curtains at the open window, perfuming the room with scents of salt and sea and casting intricate shadows across the walls. Maggie's favourite time of night. Supper over, bairns bathed and fast asleep, and she and Rob smooriching 'neath a light bedquilt. She closed her eyes, fingering the dimples beside his lips. He'd been so kittled up after his flight she hadn't been able to get a word in.

All the way up the fell his words had poured out: how the cloudless blue sky reached from horizon to horizon, endlessly reflecting sea and sun; the thrill of a steep bank with the wing slipping closer and closer to the sea; the longing to climb higher and higher until the golden radiance shining from the face of God blinded him with its glory.

He'd never spoken so long, or with such passion. That last piece of what he was—who he was—beyond his reach for so long, had been fitted into place by their luving Heavenly Faither. Thanks to His using Den, her Rob was complete again.

His dimples deepened and a smile warmed his voice. "What are you thinking about, luve? It must be guid."

She rested her face against his neck. "How glorious this day has been. You, up in the sky where you belong ... and a bit of news I received this mornin."

Soft lips trailed across her forehead. "What news?"

Make him guess. "How do you feel about the name 'Elizabeth'?"

He reared up on one elbow. "You're biggen?"

Och, she shouldn't have made it so easy. "Aye, I'm biggen."

He gathered her into his arms and showered her face with kisses. "I luve the name Elizabeth," he murmured in her ear, "as long as we can call her Beth."

How perfect. "Elizabeth" for her mither and "Beth" for the lass at the orphanage who had been so kind to Rob. "It could be a lad."

"Then we'll call him Will."

"'Tis no' too soon for you?"

"Too soon?" A chuckle rumbled in his chest. "I've been thinking for weeks it was time for another bairnie. Robbie's growing like a mayweed and even Wee Annie's running all over. I want another wee one to hold and luve without it always squirming to be put down. When will it be birthed?"

"Around the first of the new year."

"I almost hope we don't have time to reach the infirmary." He caressed her flat belly. "I never thought I'd say this, but I want to help this wee one into the world too."

Tears flooded her eyes. "Whether at the infirmary, or in this bed, 'twill be your hands this bairnie feels first. 'Tis only fitting."

Hugh stepped into the infirmary foyer, so kittled up it was hard to breathe. He couldn't wait to share the guid news. Who better to hear it first than John? The man dealt with so much pain and suffering in his career.

John skirted the admitting desk, hand extended. "Hugh! What brings you up here? I released Hamish Sinclair early the day. No' ailing, are you?"

Hugh clasped John's hand.

The guid doctor's body was tense, his dark brown eyes probing.

This would never do. "No' at all. I'm so healthy, my guardian angels must fall onto a cloud every now and then, halos askew and wings ragged from all their hard work."

"What a picture you paint with words." John laughed, pressed Hugh's shoulder, and guided him down the hall. "Let's go to the kitchen. Fern brewed a pottle of tea."

"Where is the lass?"

"She's cleaning Hamish's room."

Hugh plonked into a chair and accepted the cup of tea. "Thank ye." He took a healthy swallow. "No' coffee, but it still tastes grand." He nodded at a chair. "Fauld yer fit. I have some news to share." He couldn't wait much longer, would explode if he couldn't deliver his news soon.

John brought his tea to the table and sat leaning back, hands laced across his belly. "Oot with it. If your face gets any redder, I'll have to take your blood pressure."

"Twa weddings a week apart."

"Twa weddings? Who? And when?"

"Graham MacDonald and Rinait MacPhee on Saturday, the twenty-first, and Colin MacRay and Bridget MacGinnis on Saturday, the twenty-eighth. We haven't had a wedding on Innisbraw since those just after the war ended." Hugh reached across the table and squeezed John's hands. "After I leave here, I'll drop by Elspeth's cottage and have her call some of those guid with a needle to make new altar cloths. Next, I'll visit Morag and ask her to round up some of the womenfolk to clean the sanctuary and wax the pews." He lifted his teacup, but his hands were shaking too hard to chance a sip. "Just think, John. Twa new families for Innisbraw."

"I share your excitement," John said, rubbing his beard. "But that doesn't leave much time for making handsel gifts. This is the busiest time of the year. The crofters are tending their new crops, fishing is picking up, and there's the rest of the peat to cast."

"But the women make most of the handsel gifts. The lads already have kilts and the lasses their mither's plaids, so there's no weaving required."

"'Tis just that I spent last Sabbath afternoon with Rob and Maggie. She's run ragged, what with being biggen, overseeing the weaving, and taking care of Katie and her own bairns. And don't forget, the Proctors will be coming for their holiday the first week of July. She's already airing oot their rooms and fretting about meals and such." John's sober face broke into a smile. "She's also busy trying to bring Rob back to earth after his getting his license to fly."

Fern attacked a tea stain at the bottom of the jawbox to keep tears from falling. It wasn't like she'd been eavesdropping on Hugh and John's conversation. She'd been in the supply room getting fresh linens, and the kitchen was just across the hall.

Hugh's triumphant words rang in her ears. "Twa weddings. Twa new families for Innisbraw."

Four happy young folk, believers all, who would become husband and wife. Why couldn't she have fallen in luve with a Christian? What should she do about Den? She'd let it go on far too long. To lose him now would be like losing a part of herself. And Katie? The lass adored him.

She pulled a kerchief from her sleeve and wiped her eyes. What was taking him so long to see the truth? Sabbath after Sabbath, he listened to Hugh's teaching from the Word, taking notes on scraps of paper that he shoved into his pocket before the benediction. He was surely too young to have his heart so hardened, to have the Holy Spirit leave him to his fate.

He would have to say something soon, or she would be forced to make that final decision—one that would drive him away from her forever—and, most likely, from Innisbraw. Memories of her life with

Edward paraded through her mind—happy memories, filled with luve and laughter and a shared faith in Christ.

Until that dreadful day it had all been taken away by four words in a telegram. *Missing and presumed dead.*

She'd worked so hard to make a guid life for Katie. Wasn't she meant to be a wife? Was she lacking something the Lord deemed important? Would she turn into one of those wizened, auld widows who enlivened their empty lives with gossip behind raised aprons?

She dropped into a chair and buried her face in her hands. "Help me know what to do, Lord. I thought by bringing Rob and Maggie into my life, by reminding me what being merrit truly means, Ye were preparing me for a new life. Give me the strength to fulfill Your perfect will, Faither, no matter what it is."

Den pretended to be as pleased as the rest of the congregation when Hugh announced the marriages scheduled to take place in twa weeks. He returned Fern's smile, feeling like a hypocrite. Why should he be happy twa couples were going to be merrit when his own life hung by a thin thread? Even worse, hearing about the weddings would remind Fern it was time to cut him loose.

He couldn't concentrate on Hugh's lesson. He replaced the hymnary in its rack and sat back, gaze drawn to the stained-glass depiction of the "Risen Christ" above the altar. *I don't know what to do, God. You look so kind, Your arms outstretched like You're calling all of us to You. Help me. Please help me.*

After the service ended, Den held back, waiting until Rob and Maggie turned up the path, before nodding to Fern and Katie. "Ready for that long walk home?" He forced a smile.

"Aye." Katie laughed and slipped a hand into his.

Fern didn't reply. She ignored his outstretched hand, but she did stay by his side on the path.

He was right. The axe was about to fall.

A black future stretched before him, bleak and lonely. Saying guidbye to Innisbraw and everyone he loved, trying to find a flying job back in the States, moving into an empty apartment where he would become another anonymous presence to those passing on the stairs. He pictured himself standing at a window, face pressed to the glass, watching children play on the street outside—searching for a flash of copper-colored hair. Or in a line at the grocery store, gazing longingly at the black-haired woman in front of him, until she turned and his heart plummeted.

Shards of pain pierced his throat, splintering his breath. No. Somehow, he had to fix this. It was time to face his past, present, and future—but not with his usual jokes or playing the clown. Or carefully worded evasions. If he had to bare his soul, he would do it. He clasped Fern's elbow and pulled her to a stop. "We need ... to talk."

Her eyes searched his. "Here? Now? We'll be home soon."

"This can't wait."

Katie pulled on his hand. "Come on, Uncle Den. Mither's fixed chicken bree for dinner, and I'm hungry."

He slipped his fingers from hers and cleared his scratchy throat. "Can you skip ahead for a while, lass? Your mither and I want to talk."

Eyes rolling, she tossed her curls. "You just want to kiss again." She smirked and skipped off.

"I think a certain lassie's been keeking through the window when we say guidnight on the entry." Though Fern's words were teasing, there was no humor in her steady gaze.

His hands trembled when he rested them on her shoulders. "I was out of line when I hinted about us getting merrit. You were right when you said we needed time to get to know one another."

"I also said I'd never marry an unbeliever." A ragged whisper. She ducked her head, but not before he saw the tears in her eyes.

Here it was, soul-bearing time. "You were right about that too."

Her head shot up. "What do you mean?"

"Hugh gave me an auld English King James Bible. I looked it up. Second Corinthians 6:14: 'Be ye not unequally yoked together with unbelievers ...'" He'd read that verse so often it was permanently implanted in his mind—a constant reminder of all he had to lose.

"And?" Again that searching gaze. "Are you a believer, Den?"

Help me, God. "That's just it. I'm not sure." *Please, help me.*

"Would you be willing to talk to Hugh about it?"

Hugh. The very encounter he'd avoided, knowing that was the final step to rejection or acceptance. He swallowed and nodded.

"Now?" Her eyes were pleading.

"Aye. Right now."

"Then run ahead and see if Maggie and Rob will watch Katie. You don't have to tell them why, just that we need to talk. Privately."

A short time later, they knocked on the manse door just as Hugh finished changing out of his Sabbath clothes.

He smiled, tucking in his shirttail. "In you come." He led them into the chaumer. "What can I do for you?" he asked when they were seated.

Fern sat beside Den, fingers twisting in her lap.

No help there. But this was Den's show. He sucked in a deep breath. "I've been asked if I'm a believer. I don't know how to answer because I'm not certain exactly what that means."

Hugh leaned forward, that familiar smile rounding his cheeks into ruddy apples. "It means, do you believe that Jesus Christ is the Son of God? Do you believe that He was born in human form of the Virgin Mary? And do you believe that He died on the cross for all the sins of mankind, yours included? That He rose again?"

Stunned by the brief statement, Den stared at him. "That's all? I mean ... there's nothing more, like tithing and always turning the other cheek, and ... and never sinning?"

Hugh's smile broadened. "Never sinning is impossible in our imperfect human bodies, Den. Only our Saviour Jesus Christ attained that, and He was and is the Son of God." His smile faded. "As to tithing and turning the other cheek, or luving your neighbour as yourself, or helping those in need, those are the fruits—the results—of our belief, no' the criteria. We no longer live under the law, but in the Church Age. We cannot earn our way into Heaven by works. Only by faith."

Only by faith. Den closed his eyes. How could he have been so blind? Time to lay it on the line. "Then Rob was right. I am a believer. I just didn't know it."

"Were you a believer when you came to Innisbraw?"

At one time, Hugh's quiet question would have embarrassed Den. But it felt good to have everything out in the open. "No, I wasn't. My folks only took us to church—kirk—on Christmas or Easter. I went to chapel at the Point with Rob a few times, but it wasn't like it is here. You make things so plain, so cut and dried."

"'Tis no' my words, but those of the Holy Spirit."

Den wiped the sweat from his forehead, avoiding Fern's gaze. "I've done some pretty rotten things in my life. But when Rob was in the water, and I knew it was up to me to save him, I couldn't do it without help. So, for the first time in my life, I prayed—for strength and that Rob was still alive." He bowed his head. "I know God heard me because I'm no' a super strong swimmer, but He gave me the strength. And Rob *was* still alive. That's when I started paying attention to your lessons."

"Have you ever told the Faither you believe?" Another quiet question.

"Told Him? I thought you said He knows everything. Why should I have to tell Him?"

Hugh took Den's hands in his. "As an act of faith, Den, that's all. A simple act of faith."

"How do I do it?"

"Just bow your head and tell Him in thought only—no' aloud if you like—that you believe He is the Son of God, and that He died for your sins and lives again. 'Tis as simple as that."

"That's all?"

"That's all."

Fern put a hand on Den's shoulder as he bowed his head.

It is simple, so simple I can hardly believe it. A few minutes later, Den cupped Fern's chin in his palm and raised her gaze to his. The tears in her eyes mirrored his own. "Well, Fern MacNeill? There went your last excuse."

Her smile filled him with a joy so intense he felt faint. "Aye, Den Anderson. My answer is aye."

The words he didn't think he'd ever hear. *Thank the Lord.*

She groped for her handkerchief. "How does the mids of July sound? I've a million things to do first, and we have to have your kilt made."

Yikes. He had to wear a skirt? He looked into her blue eyes, so filled with luve and trust. Now he knew why Rob treasured his Maggie. This was his lass, the one God had saved for him, to share his life, his joys. Even his sorrows.

"Kilt? What's this about a kilt already?" Hugh asked.

Den laughed and turned to him. "You probably think we're daft, but we're talking about our wedding. Will you be free to marry us?"

Hugh leaped to his feet and embraced them. "Of course. Nowt could make me happier."

Chapter Nineteen

Stained-glass windows refracted the light of a butter-yellow sun, scattering rhomboids of blue, red, and green across the starched, white altar cloth. Maggie took a deep breath of the warm beeswax scent filling the packed sanctuary. Surely, that same sweet fragrance of worship surrounded the throne of God in Heaven.

Her gaze traveled over those sitting in the front pew across the aisle: Flora, Sim, Edert, and Elspeth, all clad in their Sabbath best, Edert and Sim's hair slicked back with Brylcreem, Flora's in a single braid, and Elspeth's wrapped around her head like a halo. Their smiles radiated joy—and hope.

Morag sat on Maggie's right, clasping Alec's hand, she with a kerchief pressed to her mouth, he with a bemused smile as he gazed at his son through tear-glazed eyes.

Maggie pulled Annie's blanket higher. Sweet lassie, keeping to her nap time. So far, Robbie was quiet, content to play with his grandfaither's watch fob. Her gaze turned to the dais where Rob stood next to Graham. How braw he looked in his kilt. Their eyes caught and held. His tender smile filled her with a warm glow.

Graham and Rinait's wedding signified more than the uniting of twa young folk in luve, grand as that was. It was the blending of the twa families who had been Rob's strongest supporters since he came to Innisbraw: the MacDonalds and the MacPhees. Prayers, advice, the loan of cairts and cuddies, watching the bairns when Maggie was needed away from home, gifts of cheese and butter and beef, and perhaps most important, the unwavering belief that he would succeed in bringing life back to Innisbraw.

And dear Graham. What a grand lad he was, and such a hard worker. The pleats of his red MacDonald kilt shook as if he danced a jig.

She stifled a giggle. Even an ex-Captain in the British Army could suffer wedding-day jitters.

Excited whispers faded away as the organ swelled with the beginning notes of the wedding march. Maggie pulled Annie over her shoulder as she and everyone rose and turned toward the door to the narthex.

Rinait, clad in a long green- and red-plaid skirt and sash—her mither's Campbell clan plaid—walked up the aisle in measured steps, hand resting on her faither's arm.

Angus, a true Innisbraw man, studied the floor carefully before each step, only the trembling of his green- and blue-MacPhee tartan kilt and high colour in his cheeks betraying his emotions.

Rinait's pert nose was in the air, but tears softened the fire usually present in her large blue eyes. Just turned seventeen, she should still be a child in so many ways, but it was a young woman who strode forward, head high, gaze never wavering from the young man who awaited her at the bottom of the stairs. No tossing her long, red braid over her shoulder this day. She wore her hair loose, pulled back from her bonnie face. It cascaded down over her shoulders and back in burnished curls that caught the candlelight and sparkled like fire.

Tears pooled in Maggie's eyes during the service. She held no doubt this was a union ordained in Heaven, just like hers and Rob's. Though opposites in nature—Rinait, stubborn and hot-headed; Graham, calm and dedicated to his work—they both used their hands to create wonders. Rinait, her weavings; Graham, his boats.

The young couple was obviously so in luve the service was a "two kerchief" affair. Tears trickled down Maggie's cheeks when Graham kissed his young bride tenderly after they were pronounced man and wife. She prayed their love would continue to grow as hers and Rob's had.

Rob's smile matched hers.

"I'm telling you, Den, you have to start paying attention to what you're doing." Rob stopped pacing his office and threw down a pencil. What was wrong with Den, mooning around like a luve-sick lad with fuzz on his chin? He'd made another daft mistake—one that could have held up production for over a week. "I ken you're kittled up about marrying Fern, but that's no excuse for ordering the wrong hardware. If there hadn't been some in that shipment from Harris Isl—"

"But I'm going crazy waiting, and it's still over three weeks away. I'll never make it without going daft. You know me, Rob. I never could just twiddle my thumbs."

Den's bloodshot eyes bored into Rob's. True, Den wasn't a patient man. Nor was Rob. But he could hide his impatience, could at least pace in private. Den's manifested in eyelid tics, bursts of manic activity, or long moments of staring into space, lost in a dream known only to him.

Rob grunted. What had happened to the level-headed, clear-thinking man he'd taken on as a partner only months ago? And the Proctors would be arriving in less than a week, taking him from the shed and interrupting his turns. Would things never get back to normal?

He stopped in front of Den's chair. "Consider this a direct order, Major Anderson," he said in American English. "Your mission is to marry the girl you love. Said objective has not been cleared for action. You will wait for orders to taxi and take off." Rob leaned closer. "Until that time, I expect you to execute your assigned duties. Is that clear, Major?"

Den's left eyelid jerked. Not that tic again.

"Confirm, Major." Rob's tone sounded harsh even to his own ears, but these mistakes had to stop. Now.

Den knuckled his eye. "Confirmed, Colonel."

Rob thumped Den's shoulder "Then get it in gear. We're late for dinner and we still have to shower and change before Colin and Bridget's wedding."

On their run up the path, Rob regretted his harsh words. He'd been fortunate. He'd asked Maggie to be his wife one een and the next afternoon they were merrit. He couldn't imagine having to wait six weeks for something he feared could never happen if he lived to be a hundred.

Their midday meal was interrupted by the shout siren's loud wail.

Both men bolted from their chairs. Rob kissed Maggie, Robbie, and Annie, and hustled Den out the door, prodding him down the path when Fern dashed down her entry steps, calling out, "Godspeed."

Fern joined Maggie in front of the radio. The tension knotting Fern's shoulders eased when Control informed Rob it was a tow for a trawler that had lost its engine. *Thank Ye, Faither. Only a tow.*

She and Maggie prayed for a successful tow, then finished feeding the bairns their dinner. They pondered showing up late to the wedding before deciding it would be rude to interrupt such a solemn occasion.

"Have you heard? Anna MacKinnon and several fishermen's wives are opening a general store next to the post office." Maggie clasped her hands. "Anna said their supplies would be meagre at first, but it won't be long before a trip to Oban is only a once-a-year event, more for clothing, furniture, or pleasure than necessity."

A frisson of joy moved through Fern's heart. "I'm so kittled up. Just think, a general store on Innisbraw."

Laughing with delight, Maggie said, "And with Rob bringing back another six lads to help build the trawler, it won't be long before we have even more weddings to attend. After that, Alice Ross will have more midwifery duties than she can handle."

During the shout, Rob stayed at the helm, while Den commanded the rescue crew on deck. Once the lines were secure, Rob goosed the *Maggie*'s engines to take up the slack, counting on Den to keep close watch on the tension, especially during the manoeuvre.

The helm suddenly torqued to the starboard, almost unseating him.

A line had snapped!

He pulled both engines to a full stop, turned the helm over to Neil, and raced out onto the deck.

Artair sat against the cabin wall, mouth open in surprise. A length of cable, wide as a man's thumb, snaked across the deck boards by his feet.

Rob knelt at his side, looking for a sign of bleeding. A line that large could shatter a man's leg—or worse. "Where are you hurt?"

"It didna touch me," Artair gasped. "I saw the tension skew and jumped back from the winch just in time."

Duncan went to his knees at his brother's side. "You certain it didna hit you?"

"It came so close, I'll never disremember the sound. Like the crack of a giant's whip. A giant from hell itself."

Den, face white and eyes wild, pushed his way through the group of stunned crewmen. "Are you all right, lad? It was my fault! I shouted a warning, but 'twas too late."

Rob gritted his teeth and scrambled to his feet. If he touched Den now, he'd do some damage. And if he said what was burning his tongue, he'd destroy the crew's trust in Den as a commander. He yanked open the cabin door. "Artair's fine, but you'll have to use Duncan to shoot the line again. I'll back up enough to engage a shorter line this time. Have the crew winch that other line in as we get closer to the trawler."

A subdued "Aye, Commander" was Den's reply.

Praying for control, Rob took his seat, while Neil reversed the

Maggie's engines and began backing up. *Help me get control of myself, Faither. I'm so biling mad I could strangle him. Daydreaming again, just when he needed to concentrate the hardest.*

The second tow attempt went without a hitch. Which was good, as Rob couldn't handle commanding all the shouts himself, especially when winter storms turned the sea into a seething cauldron of towering waves.

Once the *Maggie* was in her berth and the trawler secured at the dock, Rob nodded to Den and walked toward his office. He didn't look back to see if the redhead followed.

Den was never one to shirk a chewing-out when he deserved it.

Rob poked his head into the Control room and told Stephen to take a tea break.

The lad grinned and hurried out.

Rob sat at his desk as Den walked in. "Close the door, please." No longer as angry, he leaned back and blew out a long breath. How could he tell his best friend, the man who had saved his life, that he was off the rescue roster?

He couldn't—at least until he heard Den's account.

He studied Den's stiff posture, the set of his shoulders, the tilt of his chin, the direct eye contact. "What happened out there?" Rob kept his voice low, tone soft.

"I blew it."

Rob nodded. "I know that. I asked you what happened."

"I took my eye off the ropes. Didn't see them skew. By the time I noticed, it was too late. I shouted to warn Artair, wanted to push him out of the way, but I wasn't close enough. No excuse for it." Den's shoulders sagged. He dropped his gaze. "Like I said, I blew it."

"You've handled tows before. Why did you take your eyes off the ropes at the most critical time of all?"

Den looked up. Tears glazed his eyes. Not tears of self-pity. "I don't know why. I really don't. One minute I was concentrating on the ropes, watching the tension, then my attention sort of drifted. But I don't know why."

Rob couldn't stand this any longer. He stood and pushed his chair back. "You're off the rescue roster until after you and Fern are merrit. After that, 'tis up to you. Prove to me your thinking's back to what's important, and you'll resume command."

"They'll never trust me to command after today. The crew, I mean. I could have killed Artair. In fact, by the time this gets around, the whole island will mistrust me."

"The crew won't tell anybody. Even their own families. They

never share the dangers. None of us do."

Tears welled in Den's eyes again. "But you know."

Rob walked around the desk and draped his arm over Den's shoulder. "I've been chewed out by three-star generals. We all make mistakes. 'Tis what we learn from them that counts."

Busy pouring tea, Fern startled when Den burst through the door late that afternoon.

Ignoring Fern and Katie's greetings, he tossed his dark glasses on the bunker and headed to the jawbox. He drank three glasses of water, gulping them down so fast he slubbered all over the front of his shirt. Wiping palms on his pants, he looked at them. "What's everybody staring at? Never saw a thirsty man before?"

Fern set down the teapot.

What was wrong? Den's face was flushed, his eyes bright, like he had a fever.

She took his arm. "Did you go into the water? Is that why you're so thirsty?"

He swiped a sleeve over his lips and pulled her into his arms. "No water rescue. Just a long, long tow."

She evaded his kiss. "Something happened. What?" She framed his face with her palms. "And none of that false, little lad's smile you give to charm me out of expecting an answer." She poked his chest. "I want the truth."

Den's gaze darted to Maggie and the bairns watching from the living room. "Nowt happened, luve." He avoided her eyes and kissed her on the cheek. "But you'll be kittled up to hear I'll be spending my time in the office for a few weeks. No more shouts till I catch up on the ordering."

"Rob won't let you command any more shouts?" Fern fought the tears choking her voice. "Och, Den, what did you do?"

He jerked away, spiking his hair with his fingers. "I thought you'd be relieved, no' having to worry when the siren sounds."

Fern watched Maggie hustle the protesting bairns into Robbie's bedroom and close the door. *Bless her.*

Den pulled her around to face him. "I'll even be able to help you plan the wedding—you know, give you a man's perspective."

There it was, that smile she'd been talking about. Like a wee lad trying to get his way. And he hadn't answered her question. Why had Rob taken him off the rescue crew? Och, how could she expect an answer from a man who ran from an uncomfortable truth faster than a hen fleeing the butchering axe?

She poured a mug of coffee, grabbed her cup of tea, and nodded at the door. "The front entry's private enough for what we've to discuss."

He opened the door and followed her out.

Den stared at the mug she thrust into his hands. Why hadn't he told her the truth when she asked? Prolonging the agony tortured him far more than her. But he couldn't. Not until he figured out how to make it sound better. Or found some humor in it, a way to turn it into a silly mistake anybody could have made.

Silly? He'd almost killed a man.

Fern took his hand and led him to Rob's rocker. "Sit."

He sat.

She stood before him, shoulders stiff, eyes boring into his soul. "Why did Rob take you off the rescue crew? Tell me."

A groan built in his chest.

Her shoe tap-tapped on the stone flags. "I'm waiting." Her cold gaze cut through him.

His vocal cords froze. "I ... I ..." Coffee sloshed onto the flags.

Tap. Tap. Tap.

"I'm no' good enough for the likes of you." Just a ragged whisper. The tapping stopped, but he couldn't meet that icy gaze again. He set the mug on the table.

"Why would you think that?" A whisper no louder than his.

Did she have to ask why? A crazy laugh burst from his throat. "Because I'm a joke. Having to wait till the mids of July to marry you has me acting like a daftie. I trip over my own feet. I can't pour a cup of coffee without spilling it. I lose papers, find them, then lose them again. I order the wrong hardware. I can't concentrate on anything. Can't sleep, can't sit still, feel like I'm living in a fishbowl with everyone standing around waiting for me to do more than stare at them goggle-eyed, opening and closing my mouth and blowing bubbles. God must have crossed some wires when He made my brain."

Fern sat in Maggie's rocker next to him, soft fingers trailing the edge of his clenched jaw. "So you're tired of waiting. So am I, but planning a wedding takes time. Will you really help me? With the planning, I mean?"

He leaned back and closed his eyes. "I'll just mess it up like everything else I touch."

She kissed his chin, his cheeks. "You mean like whatever happened on the shout?"

He needed more time, a snappy retort, something to lighten things up. A joke leaped into his mind, something about a guy shaving his head before his execution in the electric chair so he could give *himself* a razor burn.

No. Too dark.

How about the minister killed in an automobile crash who tried to slip by Saint Peter at the gates of Heaven with an out-of-date driver's license?

Too dumb.

How could he ever tell her the truth? It would stand between them, maybe even make her change her mind about marrying him. She was solid. A woman who had tackled running a boatyard on her own. No eejit mistakes. No mistakes at all.

But she had to know. *Help me, Lord. I don't want to lose her.* He took a deep breath and told her everything.

No jokes.

Just the truth.

Maggie settled into Rob's lap and rested her cheek against his chest. "'Twas nice of Den to offer to stay at the manse while the Proctors are here. With his room free and their wee Chris on a cot in Jill and Stu's room, there'll be a separate bedroom for Brenna."

"Mmm."

So he was still chewing over what had happened the day. Time to get it out in the open. "So how did Den react when you told him you were taking him off the rescue crew till after the wedding?"

"Relieved, if anything." He wrapped a curl of her hair around his finger. "'Tis a guid thing I waited till after the shout was over and I'd cooled down before I told him. I was so biling when it happened, I wanted to knock him flat—and he knew it."

She toyed with the laces of his shirt. "What I don't understand is why he's so fashed about having to wait another three weeks. Graham and Rinait put off getting merrit for over a year."

"If I knew the reason, I'd have fixed it before the day." Rob blew out a long breath. "I don't ken why, but I keep thinking it has to do with something that happened when he was growing up. If you think it's hard for me to talk about when I was a lad, Den's so close-mouthed about his family that I didn't even learn his parents weren't going to show up for our graduation at the Point till after the ceremony. And even then, he just made a joke about them being so busy that if they made room in their schedules, it would take them years to catch up."

Maggie sat up straight, looking into Rob's face. "But he knows about your past."

A flicker of pain darkened his eyes. "That I grew up in an orphanage? Yes, I told him a month or more ago, mainly so he'd know how the Lord watched over me and finally gave me the family I always wanted. He said I was lucky. And he told me why his folks didn't attend his graduation from the Point. They were too busy marching in some war protest. I should have known how much that hurt. Their own lad and they refused to see him graduate one of the finest universities in the States because he wore an army uniform."

"Then we must pray he'll leave that hurt behind when he marries Fern and has his own family." Maggie kissed the tip of his nose. "Just like you did no' so many years ago."

Chapter Twenty

The *Sea Rouk* eased up to the dock, her starboard kissing the old tyre fenders with the soft brush of a familiar, oft-practiced greeting. Maggie hurried to Rob's side, then Rob and Den tied the mooring lines thrown from the trawler's deck around the bollards and rushed to help Sim MacPhee lower the boarding plank into place.

Maggie waved to the Proctor family. "Welcome back to Innisbraw!" she called, a bubble of happiness bursting in her chest. She squeezed Rob's hand. "They're finally here and how grand they all look."

"They do that, lu—"

The Proctors' lass, Brenna, raced down the boarding plank and threw herself at him, hugging his hips. "Rob," she cried, burying her face against his belly. "I'm here. I'm here, Rob!"

Rob was knocked back and his panic-filled eyes sought Maggie's.

Stu Proctor moved past Maggie and pulled his daughter away from Rob. "You almost knocked Rob into the water. We told you to act like a lady. Now go help your mother with Christopher."

"We'll both help Jill," Maggie took Brenna's hand and pulled her toward the plank. "That brother of yours is a braw lad, like our Robbie at his age."

Jill held out a hand of greeting when Maggie stepped aboard. "You're as bonnie as ever." Her grey eyes softened with warmth.

Grasping the proffered hand, Maggie kissed Jill's cheek. "And so are you." She gazed at her friend, soaking in the bond she'd felt from their first meeting.

The year had been kind to Jill. Her dark blond, shoulder-length hair and fresh complexion glowed with health. A light sprinkling of freckles on her slightly up-turned nose made her look even younger than her age.

The laddie in Jill's arms leaned over and planted a wet kiss on Maggie's cheek.

She held out her arms, and he slid into them with a husky chortle. "Och, I can't believe how you've grown—and changed," Maggie said, bouncing him on her hip. "And look at all that dark brown hair, just like your faither's."

"But his eyes are grey like mine and Brenna's." Jill laughed. "I no longer believe my biology teacher who said dark hair and eyes are dominant."

Maggie smiled. "I agree with you." She kissed the bairn's dimpled cheek. "Let's get you all up the fell. I remember how exhausting trawler travel can be." She hurried down the plank, catching Brenna's hand to include her.

Rob fell into bed with a groan. "It was grand visiting with Stu and Jill again, and your supper was perfect, but I'm all blethered oot." He reached for Maggie and fingered a curl of her hair. "And Brenna has me in a rare fash. Every time I glance her way, she's staring at me."

"Och, she's just a bit smitten with you, like Rinait years ago."

"But 'tis embarrassing. If she thinks of lads at all, it should be those her own age."

"'Tis just a thing most lasses go through. And I think she has verra good taste."

"Maggie!"

She laughed and cuddled closer. "I'll ask her to call you 'Uncle Rob' like Katie does. That should help."

"And if it doesn't?"

"Don't worry over a twelve-year-auld lass's fanciful dreams." She kissed his chest and rested her leg across his so she could nestle closer. "I have some news to share."

He looked into her eyes. Violet blue, they were, and filled with dancing lights, like the moon catching a froth of wave. He let out a ragged sigh. "This news, it can't wait until I rest?"

A flash of white teeth revealed by an impish smile. "It could, but you're so seldom home we have little time to talk."

"Let's hear it, then."

"Jill's biggen too. And, like me, she's due to birth her bairnie the first of the New Year. Just think, twa bairnies birthed—perhaps on the same day—to friends who live so far apart. 'Tis almost as guid as them naming their lad after you."

"'Tis a guid thing they called him Chris, no' Rob. I'd hate to think of spending three weeks wondering which Rob somebody's talking to—or about."

Thoughts of the chaos surrounding a breakfast fry-up with twa extra adults, a halflin, and another bairn all vying for a chance to be heard sent Rob to the shed earlier than usual.

Maggie caught him at the front closet. "But you can't leave before anybody is up." She crossed her arms. "'Tisn't mannerly."

"Tell Stu to meet me at the shed later." Rob shrugged into his A-2 jacket. "I pointed it oot to him last een." He pulled Maggie into his arms. "Working early will free me up for that basket supper you have planned on the fell strand." A lingering kiss, a fond pat on her bottom, and he was out the door.

The chill in the gauzy, early-morning air nipped the tips of his ears and clung to the back of his neck as he jogged down the path. Aye, he was a coward, leaving Maggie alone to face the bedlam. But she seemed to thrive in the company of friends, no matter the confusion. And he wanted to check those orders he'd assigned Den last week.

Gratified to find the orders—signed off with pending delivery dates noted—stacked on his desk, he decided to give his office a quick redding before the boatbuilding crew reported for work. He stood back and looked in dismay at the midden of papers covering his blotter.

Telephone messages, ideas for design improvements, old rescue crew schedules, a few scraps of wrinkled paper with notes he could no longer read, the stubs of twa pencils, a petrified scone unearthed beneath a paper, one of Robbie's drawings of an airieplane, and a small booklet of tide tables.

He set to work, filling the trash bin to overflowing, filing things to be saved, even neatening the drawers in his desk.

The door to the outer shed opened.

He glanced at his watch. 0530. Too early for the crew. Probably Graham coming early to make a work schedule for the day. He grabbed a notepad, fresh pencil, and small metric scale, plonked into his chair, and rested his heels on his clean desktop. Now he had the time to put to paper some of the deck design modifications he'd thought up for the trawler.

"Run away from home?"

Den leaned against the doorsill, cheeks ruddy, blue eyes glinting in the overhead light.

No time to think up a lame excuse. "Aye. Did you?"

"Nah. Just couldn't stomach that mud Hugh calls coffee. Want to grab a mug at Paddy's?" Den's keen gaze swept over the top of Rob's desk. "Or are you too busy doing the housemaid's work?"

"He's no' open yet."

"Lights on over there. Come on. It's on me. After all that

blethering at the supper table last night, I'm ready for a guid mug of joe and some quiet time with the king of quiet."

Rob leaped up and pulled on his jacket. "You said the magic words. Lead on."

Rob and Den enjoyed an entire pot of coffee, then spent several hours aboard the *Maggie*, checking for nicks to repair and supplies to replenish. When Den retired to his office to take care of the ordering, Rob settled back into his own chair, again turning his thoughts to the trawler. He had just started sketching when there was a tap at his office door. What now? He threw down his pencil. "Come."

Stu poked his head in, a sheepish grin on his face. "Sorry if I interrupted something important."

Rob stood and ran his fingers through his hair. "No' at all. Just putting some design ideas on paper." He pulled an extra chair up to his desk. "Glad you could make it. Sit yourself down." He studied the man for a moment.

As always, he was neatly dressed and fresh-shaven, his dark eyes filled with interest. Stu ignored the chair and walked to the back of the office, studying the pictures on the wall. "So, these were your planes in the war? And your crews?"

"Aye—yes. Two planes, many different crews."

One more brief scan of the pictures before Stu settled into his chair. "I've always regretted not being in uniform. Right after I graduated from San Diego State, the military hired me to do accounting for naval shipyards. I tried to enlist a couple of times, but they wouldn't let me go."

Rob settled onto a corner of his desk. "Don't be sorry you didn't see action. You did your part and, now it's over, you have no bad memories to give you nightmares."

Thinning lips showed Stu's disagreement, that this was still a sore spot. He picked an invisible piece of lint off his knife-pleated slacks and leaned forward. "You know I'm a CPA?" He flushed. "A certified public accountant."

"I didn't know about the certified public part, but you told me before you're an accountant."

Stu rose and clasped his arms in front of his chest. "I realize this could be construed as a snoopy imposition, but I'd like to help you set up your books." His Adam's apple bobbed. "That is, if you don't already have an accountant."

He couldn't mean it. "But you're on holiday."

"I never take what you call a 'holiday' from numbers, Rob. If I believed in reincarnation, I'd swear I was an abacus in a previous life."

This man had traveled halfway across the world to visit him and Maggie. As for seeing his "books" … Rob twirled around and opened a desk drawer. "I don't mind you looking at what I have, but I don't keep books. Just scraps of paper." He held a fat manila envelope out to Stu.

Stu snatched the envelope out of his hands, untied the strings, and spread the contents across the desk. He sorted through receipts, lists of orders stamped with the time of delivery, time sheets, several used checkbooks filled with tiny printing, and innumerable scraps of paper with figures jotted on them. His eyes held a wild look when he glanced up. "This is all you have? No contracts, no billing information?"

"The contracts are in a separate envelope."

"Rob, you've no head for business. These scraps of paper will never stand up to an audit. You need to hire yourself a bookkeeper to handle all the taxes and payroll. It'll free up a lot of your time too."

"There's just one wee problem." A worm of embarrassment burrowed deep inside Rob's stomach. "There isn't a person on this island with the training to do the job. And I can't see it helping much to bring somebody over from the Mainland or Scotland once a month. I pay the lads weekly."

"How about asking whoever does your contracts to recommend someone? Even help once in a while would be better than this mess." Stu returned to his chair, eyes glazed.

Rob rubbed the side of his nose. "I draw up the contracts myself. Fly them to Oban to be recorded."

"You don't use an attorney or solicitor or whatever they call them here? Good grief, Rob, somebody could take you to the cleaners."

Rob pushed the pile of papers back into the envelope. "You're right, I'm not a businessman. I thought when I brought Den aboard as a partner things would get easier. But what with the rescue work and boats to be built, there just aren't enough hours in the day to do everything that needs to be done."

Stu leaned back in his chair. "How do you structure it now? You've got Graham and Den. How do you divide the workload?"

"Graham pretty well handles the shop work, but he won't be able to do that and train a green crew when we start three boats next month, so I'll have to spend more time here. Den's running his legs off procuring all the fittings, radios, engines, and radars we'll need. I've been filling in when needed, plus running the rescue operation."

"It won't work, Rob." Stu shook his head. "You need more help. You have a growing family, Graham just got married, and Den's taking the plunge in a couple of weeks. You all need time off occasionally. How is your rescue operation set up?"

"What do you mean?"

"How do you meet expenses? What's your source of revenue?"

"This isn't America, Stu." Rob blew out an exasperated sigh. "Over here, the Innisbraw Coastal Rescue Service is all volunteer work with the exception of one full-time mechanic, who also doubles as a second coxswain."

"So nobody gets paid but him?"

"That's right."

"How about repairs to the *Maggie*? Who foots that bill? And who pays your mechanic?"

Rob squirmed and rubbed the side of his nose again. Why did he feel like a school lad who'd turned in a poor assignment? "I do."

"Out of your own pocket?"

"Aye."

"Is that the way all the Coastal Rescue Services are run?"

Not a poor assignment. A failing test paper. "They have a board that raises donations to cover expenses. I haven't had time to set one up."

Stu jingled some coins in his pocket. "What a mess. I hope your pockets are really deep."

"After building the Maggie and meeting the first year's building payroll, they're about as empty as a liar's promises."

"Have you been paid for those two rescue boats you just built?"

"We'll be paid sometime next week. But a lot of that money will go to pay for the lumber and supplies we need to build the next three boats, plus payroll."

Stu scratched his head. "Did you ever sit down and figure out what kind of a profit you make on each boat?"

"A ballpark figure, aye."

"Can you and your partners live on that?"

"Aye. It's just all the juggling that drives me crazy." Rob paced. "Graham, Den, and I, none of us expects or even wants to get rich. All we need is to be able to provide for our families and to help the economy of the island." He whirled around. "'Tis growing, Stu. By leaps and bounds, 'tis growing."

"And maybe growing more than you think."

"What do you mean?"

"I'm interested in moving my family here … and buying into

your business."

Two hours later, Rob and Stu were on their way up the hill to the house, and Rob was still shaking his head. Afraid the Proctor family would regret the move, he'd used every argument he could think of to change Stu's mind: the windy and rainy winters, the lack of adequate transportation, the culture shock of moving one's family from an affluent city in America to an isolated island over seventy miles from the coast of Scotland.

All for nowt.

Stu and Jill had done their homework. They knew the mean temperature of each month, had investigated the school system. They even knew what their income would have to be to live here comfortably.

As they walked, Stu rubbed his hands together. "We've been unhappy where we are for a long time. The commute to work's a nightmare, the social life demands we attend one party after another—all boring—the kids' classes at school are becoming so crowded no child gets enough attention. We even thought about packing it all in and moving to someplace like Alaska, but that would mean as many changes in lifestyle as coming here. This is a beautiful place, and I've never met finer people. We've talked of little else since we were here last year."

"What about Brenna? Surely she'd miss all the excitement of living in a large city in the richest country on earth."

"We don't think so. She's never really fit in with the other girls at school. Doesn't have a social bone in her body. She'd rather be reading a good book than partying it up."

"And you've run this idea past her, have you?"

"Yes. She's all for it."

For biddy certain she was. But he couldn't open that can of worms now. And he was out of arguments. It wasn't that he didn't like the idea of having Stu as a partner. The very possibility excited him. He just didn't want the man moving his family across the Atlantic only to have them miserable and disillusioned within a year.

Stu gripped Rob's elbow. "I know you'll have to talk to Den and Graham, and I'll understand if they say no, but I think I have something to offer. I can handle all of your paperwork, including invoices, billing, contracts, taxes, and payroll. With the sale of our house and two cars—which we own free and clear—plus what I've got in savings, we could give your boatworks some much needed working capital. But the main thing is you'd get an accountant, which you badly need. And I'm not exaggerating that need just to convince you to take me on."

"I know you're not. I just hope and pray you know what you're getting into. I couldn't live anyplace else, but my family's already here. I don't have anyone else."

"The two sets of grandparents'll have a cow, but they'll adjust. My parents may even join us here. They hate living in Florida."

"You'll all have to learn Scots and even the Gaelic if you move here. It's too hard to communicate if you don't. Too few of our people speak English."

"Tha mi airson Gàidhlig ionnsachadh."

Rob stopped and stared at Stu. "Where did you learn that?"

"Did I say it wrong? Jill and I ordered Gaelic tapes from a university library in L.A. I was trying to say, 'I want to learn the Gaelic.'"

"You did say that, and well." Rob laughed and unlatched the gate. "Just remember, here the 'ae' in Gaelic is pronounced like the 'a' in father, no' with a long 'a.' Elspeth's going to be delighted."

"Elspeth? She's the old lady who sent the flowers to Jill when Chris was born, right?"

"Aye, and she's our Scots and the Gaelic teacher."

"Then you think there's a chance for us here?"

"A guid chance. We'll get together with Den and Graham in the mornin. I can't think of a single reason they won't welcome you with open arms."

The following evening, there was an impromptu party at the Savage house with the Proctors as guests of honour. Brenna had loosed her hair from its braid. It twined in blond ringlets down the middle of her back.

First, Rob ushered in Den, Fern, and Katie, then John and Calum.

Graham and Rinait arrived a little late. "'Tis my fault," Rinait said. "Graham's had me picking oot things for our new house. The time ran away from us."

The men gathered in Rob's office while the women busied themselves in the kitchen. Rob lifted his bottle of ale and nodded at the others to do the same. "Here's to our new partner and his family. Slàinte mhath."

They all echoed the toast and drank.

"When are you hoping to move here?" John asked Stu.

"That's up in the air right now. We have to sell our house, but the market's red hot. I think we can be here by late September or early October."

John smiled and shook his head. "Och, the thought of all you have to do tires me oot. 'Tis a guid thing you're young."

Stu laughed and took another swig of ale. "I've never felt better. I only wish we'd visited Innisbraw when we were first married, but I suppose things wouldn't have been the same then."

Calum laughed. "That's for certain. Rob and Maggie have changed the island completely."

"For the better, I hope." Rob grinned.

"That goes without saying." John clapped Rob on the back. "I can see a time when we have ferries coming to our shores with tourists eager to see our birds, sea life, and wildflowers. Innisbraw is coming of age. In fact, that calls for another toast." He raised his bottle. "To Innisbraw. Slàinte mhath!"

The men's shouts echoed through the house.

Chapter Twenty-One

"The Proctors have decided to cut their holiday short and leave for America the day after Den and Fern's wedding," Rob said in the Gaelic, addressing the Island Council. "They don't think it will take them long to sell their house in San Diego, so I'd like your permission to build their home next to Fern's." He tried to read their faces.

Impossible. They were Scots, after all.

"I'll have the plans completed by the time the men have Graham and Rinait's stone walls in place."

A unanimous vote granted permission.

Rob rubbed the side of his nose and contemplated the faces before him. "I feel badly I haven't followed the tradition of helping raise walls for others since our home was built, and I—"

Elspeth tapped the flagged floor with her walking stick. "There is no reason to address this issue. You have been labouring for years to build our rescue boat and to bring prosperity to our island. I speak for all of Innisbraw when I say we would not accept your help even if you insisted." Her faded blue eyes glinted with resolve. "Your time is far too valuable to be wasted working with stone. This meeting stands adjourned."

Several folk voiced their agreement

Rob's face burned.

"Priorities, lad, priorities." Elspeth patted his arm with gnarled fingers.

The screech of a saw and babble of voices drifted into Rob's office from the shed. He signed the last check and rubbed it, facedown, on his blotter.

Last payment to a supplier. Now he could begin the payroll and—

A light tap on his door propelled him to his feet.

"Come."

Stu stepped in, juggling a tea towel-covered plate and large thermos. "Grab the thermos before I drop it." He placed the plate on Rob's desk. "Maggie sent some fresh scones and more coffee. Said you missed your breakfast."

The spicy scent of Stu's aftershave competed with the warm aroma of buttered scones. "You didn't have to walk all that way." Rob rummaged in the lower drawer of his desk for an empty mug. "But now you're here, join me, please."

"Couldn't eat another bite, but I will have some coffee." Stu accepted the mug and sat in front of Rob's desk, stretching out his legs. "I don't see how you stay so thin with the breakfasts Maggie serves—sausage, eggs, beans, fried bread, and sweet scones."

He'd find out soon enough that such breakfasts were usually reserved for Sabbath morning. Rob picked up a scone and bit off half, catching a drip of butter with a finger. He took a swig of coffee and sat back. "Since you're here, I've a question about your bedroom. I don't know what furniture you have, so I'm wondering if you want more windows than the one at the front of the house."

Stu sipped his coffee. "I like the layout of your bedroom. Let's stick with just the one window." He pointed to the open checkbook on Rob's desk. "Payroll?"

"Just finished paying a few suppliers. Payroll's next."

"Give me time sheets and your pay scale and a small table to work on. I'll do it for you."

The relief loosening Rob's taut muscles was short-lived. Stu was on holiday. "You don't have to do that."

"Isn't a matter of having to, just wanting to." Stu finished his coffee and set the mug on the desk. "I was coming down here later this morning, anyway. I'll start organizing what you have and see if I can set up some sort of system before I leave for home. I'm sure you don't have the ledgers, folders, and other supplies I'll need once I'm working here, so I'll bring them with me when we come back."

Hand hovering over another scone, Rob stopped and stared at Stu. "But you've already cut your holiday short."

"How long has it been since you've taken what you call a 'holiday'?"

"Me?"

Dark eyes drilled him.

He rubbed the side of his nose. "If you consider military sick leave, over four years. If you don't count that, I did catch a week's leave in Wales sometime in nineteen and forty-two."

"Don't you get tired? You know, want to get away from it all?"

Rob thought for a moment. "No, never. Och, I get physically tired, but not tired of what I'm doing. It's too varied to be boring, except the paperwork. I don't see how you can stand it day after day."

"Numbers." Stu poured another mug of coffee. "They've always fascinated me. That, and order. I can't stand things out of order."

"No wonder you almost passed out when you saw what was in that envelope. I'm surprised you didn't run out of here as fast as you could."

"What, and miss the chance to bring order out of chaos?" Stu leaned back and sipped his coffee. "That's my fun in life."

Chapter Twenty-Two

Katie giggled. "If you don't stop dropping things, you'll never get ready."

Fern fought a growing panic. "I found my hairbrush and sash pin, but I don't see the other pearl earring Den gave me anywhere." She knelt and brushed a hand over the floorboards. "Och, where can it be?"

Katie dropped to her knees beside her mother. "If this is what it's like, I'm never getting merrit."

"Och, don't say that. Help me look."

"Lift the quilt. I'll look 'neath the bed.

"But I wasn't near the bed when I dropped it." Fern heard the rising hysteria in her own voice and took a deep breath before pulling the quilt to one side.

Katie crawled 'neath the mattress and disappeared into the darkness. Only seconds later, a muffled shout of triumph came from below.

Fern collapsed onto the bed and hugged a pillow. What would she do without her lass?

A rapping sounded on the front door.

Och, no' already. Where had the time gone?

Maggie and Jill rushed in, laden with ribbons and flowers.

"We've come to help you dress," Maggie said. "I'm no' ready." Fern's voice trembled.

Excitement? Nerves? "Of course you aren't. But you soon will be." She eyed Fern's bare feet. "We'd best hurry. Stu and John took Chris, Robbie, and Annie down to the shore to get them out of the way while Rob helps Den dress."

The usually unflappable Fern rushed about the house in her dressing gown, eyes wide, breath coming in gasps. "I thought I had everything organized." She panted. "But I can't think straight. What should I do first?"

"Have you bathed?" Jill asked.

"Aye. Early."

Maggie handed Jill a spool of wide, blue ribbon and pushed Fern into her bedroom. "Then get oot of that dressing gown and put on your tights, slip, and sweater. We'll do your hair next so we don't ruin it pulling your sweater over your head."

"Aye. Tights, sweater."

"And slip."

"Slip. Of course."

The ensuing hours were no less frantic. By the time the men returned with the bairns and Fern was on her way to kirk in Alec's cairt, Maggie and Jill barely had time to oversee Katie's hair and dress, and hurry to the Savages' home to prepare themselves.

"If your Viking forebears could see you now, they'd no' believe it." Rob helped Den into his jacket and straightened the sporran chains.

"They'd hack me to pieces and have me for minced pudding."

"On you come." Rob laughed and clapped him on the back. "'Tis your wedding day. Alec's waiting ootside in his cairt."

"You'll stay right beside me the whole time, won't you?" Den's voice trembled like leaves on a sapling caught in a blowsterin wind. "Have you got the ring? Och, Rob, please don't tell me you've lost the ring."

Rob pulled the gold band from his sporran. "'Tis right here. Calm down before you jump oot of your skin." He started out the front door.

Den grabbed his arm. "Level with me. Am I doing the right thing?"

"Do you luve her?"

"Of course I luve her. Why do you think I've—?"

"Then you're doing the right thing. On you come, or you're going to be late for your own wedding. I've heard brides don't like that."

A noisy swallow before Den pulled to a stop again. "My knees show. They didn't make this kilt long enough."

"Och, for ..." Rob yanked Den's arm and marched him to the cairt. "That much of your knees is supposed to show. Just be thankful you don't have my scars."

"I'd take your scars if it meant this was over," Den muttered, climbing onto the bench.

"Thank ye for biding, Alec." Rob swung up beside Den. "We had a bit of a problem getting dressed."

"'Tis always that way the first time," Alec said with a grin. "It's easier each time you wear it."

Den slapped his thighs. "I'll never wear a skirt again. Once and only once."

Maggie pulled Katie close and hugged her as Den and Rob took their places on the dais. "Doesn't Den look grand in his McGrath kilt?"

"Aye, but why is his face all wet? It isn't raining."

"He's in a bit of a swither. He's never worn a kilt before."

Katie snickered. "No' as much a swither as Mither. She acted like a daftie all mornin."

Jill leaned forward on the pew and gave Maggie a conspiratorial wink.

Neil MacLean, holding his violin, took his place beside Sheila MacNab at the organ. The haunting notes of the violin playing the descant joined the swell of the organ as Pachelbel's "Canon in D" filled the sanctuary.

Den's gaze darted to the door to the narthex.

Alec stepped in, Fern on his arm.

The sight of her, head held high, dark and light-blue plaid skirt swirling around her slim ankles, filled him with such luve. No woman on earth could be so beautiful. Her black hair was pulled back from her face and caught in a blue ribbon covered with wee white flowers. The pearl earrings he had given her for Christmas gleamed in the candlelight. Her lips and cheeks were so rosy she looked as if she were wearing face paint, though Fern would never do that.

I luve you, Fern. More than I've ever luved anybody before, I luve you.

When she and Alec reached the steps to the dais, Rob prodded Den to move.

He floated down the steps.

Alec placed Fern's hand over Den's arm.

Shaking, it was. Like his.

She smiled up at him, large blue eyes shiny with tears.

The wedding ceremony passed in a blur. Den spoke at the right time and accepted the ring from Rob when he should, but Fern's bonnie face stole his concentration. How had he ever won her heart? He breathed a quick prayer of gratitude to the Lord, who'd surely had a hand in this. Why else would this gorgeous creature ever have consented to be his wife? He was a clown, an irreverent buffoon with unruly red hair, an overactive sense of humor, and no real goal in life.

Correction. He'd *had* no real goal. Now he did. To make this bonnie lass as happy as he possibly could.

When Hugh pronounced them man and wife, Den felt as if he had awakened from a long dream. The candlelight seemed brighter, the air fresher, the colors more vivid. He gathered Fern into his arms and kissed her tenderly. Even her lips tasted sweeter. She was his wife. Fern Lamond MacNeill Anderson was his.

After two more hours of festivities, Rob corralled Den and Fern and told them they could leave any time they wanted.

"You certain? Don't want to step on any toes."

"I'm certain. On you go now. Your overnight bags are already on the plane, so we'll see you on the morra's een. Enjoy your honeymoon in Oban, short as it is."

Den pulled Rob aside as Maggie and Fern embraced. "I want to apologize for being such an eejit these past few weeks. I finally figured oot what was happening." He leaned closer. "The de'il was trying to take control, and I didn't know how to fight him."

Like with Rob's bad dreams about the rescue boat sinking when she was launched. "Don't worry about it. You've taken a stand for the Lord now, so Satan knows he's lost."

"And he'll keep on losing." Den clasped Rob's hand. "Thank ye for everything. Tell the Proctors I'll see them in a couple of months. Ciao, bucko." Den pulled Fern away from Maggie and hustled her toward the hall door.

Rob grinned at Elspeth, who sat nearby. "I think he's in a bit of a hurry."

"As he should be." Her eyes sparkled with laughter. "'Tis only fitting."

Chapter Twenty-Three

The Proctors were back in America, Den had moved in with Fern, and for the first time since their Christmas celebration, Maggie was free to spend a Sabbath afternoon at their special cove with just Rob and her bairns.

The marram grass's needles whispered secrets to the onshore breeze, and white clouds scudded overhead. Herring and great, black-backed gulls rode the light breeze, while a single oystercatcher swooped overhead, piping its *pik-pik-pik* song.

Shep stood guard between Robbie, who was poking a stick at the rocks glistening in the bottom of a tidal pool, and Annie, who knelt beside a clump of sea pinks and wrinkled her nose as she inhaled their pungent fragrance.

Such peace.

And joy.

Rob caressed her belly with his huge palm. "'Tis getting larger," he said, voice soft and deep as eiderdown. "Won't be long till our new bairnie makes itself felt."

"Aye, only a month or so."

He grasped her hand and kissed each knuckle. "Do you have any idea how much I luve you?"

Much more than an idea. "You give me a hint now and again."

He sat up beside her. "Only a hint?"

"Mebbe a wee bit more."

"A wee bit?"

She laughed and swatted at him. "All right, a lot more."

He kissed the tip of her nose. "That's better. You had me thinking I'd lost my touch."

"If you live to be a hundred, you'll never lose your touch, luve." Her fingertips traced the message across his braw face.

"Mmm, you're making me even sorrier I've been so busy."

"Och, we're both busy. You with the boatbuilding and rescue service and now the Proctors' house, and me with the garden, bairns, and weaving ... it seems to get more complicated every day."

"But when Stu returns, he'll take a big burden off my shoulders. I spend hours on the payroll alone."

Dare she tell him now? What better time? "I want you to spend more time flying."

A deep sigh. He took her into his arms. "There's too much to do."

"'Tis a joy you need." She tapped his chin. "It renews your soul."

His right eyebrow rose. "And how do you know that?"

"I've seen the calm deep inside you after you've been flying."

Another sigh. "I suppose you're right."

"'Tis something you need, Rob. You have so little time to yourself."

"You have none." He kissed the tip of her nose again.

No' that auld argument again. "That's no' true. When the youngest bairns nap, I have time to spend at my loom or in the garden. That's my time alone, to seek the inner peace I need. We all need that special time, Rob, even you. As busy as you are, especially you."

A muscle knotted in his jaw. "Why *especially* me?"

"Because you have a quiet soul, luve. I've always known that. There's something deep inside you that draws strength from flying alone, up in the sky."

"But that means more time away from you and the bairns."

"'Tis time well spent." She rested her forehead against his. "Please, Rob, do this for me if no' for yourself."

He looked out at the sea, shoulders slumped. So tired, he was. But he wrestled with those inner demons that drove him on and on, regardless of how it damaged him.

"I'll try," he said at last. "If you're certain that's what you want."

She smiled and rested her cheek against his chest. "Biddy certain."

Rob took the floatplane up alone early the following morning. How would she handle when he was solo? As soon as he reached altitude, he pulled her nose up until the aircraft stalled, then lowered the nose and added power.

The small plane recovered quickly.

He rolled his head from shoulder to shoulder. No sign of the stiff neck he'd awakened with. He turned the plane north.

Barra Head passed below, its lighthouse standing proud atop the rocky peak. Then the awe-inspiring fells on the Isle of Mingulay appeared, the scree tumbling over one hundred metres into the sea.

Banking closer, he could make out the slitterie twig and feather nests the guillemots and kittiwakes had made early that spring. He lowered the nose and cut speed.

Seals engaged in a never-ending battle for space on the large, flat rocks at the edges of the islands. A large pod of dolphins, sleek, undulating bodies catching the sun, stitched their way south.

He laughed aloud, feeling free as the golden eagle floating in a vast sky of brilliant blue far off to his left. Passing over a few sheep crofts on Sanderay, he circled Castlebay, the Isle of Barra's main village, before doing a slow bank to the west.

The machair on the western shore above the high-water line was carpeted in brilliant patches of blue squill, wild geraniums, and orchids. Ringed plovers pecked for limpets along the shore.

There was so much more to see, but he checked his watch and his fuel gauge, reluctantly pulled the nose up, and did a broad bank to the southeast. Time to refuel in Oban.

The fuel attendant at the Oban airstrip was a displaced Scots-speaking north Heilander. When Rob returned his grunted greeting in Scots, the man's eyes lit up and his tongue loosened. He blethered on about how much he missed hearing Scots and the Gaelic.

Rob switched to the Gaelic.

The husky young man's grin widened. "What's your name, sir?"

"Rob Savage."

The man's mouth fell open. "You're that American from Innisbraw," he said in the ancient language. "The man with the rescue boat?"

"That's me."

"Why, you're a legend around here, saving souls and helping birth babies. I'm not surprised to find you so very tall and fine-looking. Wait until I tell my wife I met Rob Savage. She'll never believe me."

His wife? People were talking about him in Oban? Rob pulled at his collar. "Got any coffee around here?"

"Sorry, no, but I've a touch of stewed tea left in my thermos. I'd be most proud to share it with you."

"No, thank you." Rob walked off a ways, cheeks burning.

Next time it would be all business. Birthing bairnies, indeed.

The refueling finished, Rob did a ground check and took off as quickly as possible. He did some touch-and-go landings on the Isle of Mull's Tobermory Harbour before heading home. As he turned the plane west, he passed over the steamer ferry on its way to the Isle of Barra.

Something John had said the other night niggled at the back of his mind.

Ah, a ferry to Innisbraw. Rob grinned. Why no'? All they needed was a wide enough dock to accommodate the length of the ferry so the boat could drop gangplank to offload passengers.

Circling the Innisbraw Harbour, he studied the configuration of the main pier and docks. If the western dock was elongated to accommodate the island's fishing fleet, that would leave the center dock free of berthed vessels.

His heart rate increased. It was doable, he knew it was.

After landing, he taxied up to the boatwork's dock, turned off the engine, and sat for a moment, hands shaking. He'd make some telephone calls to the Island Council.

Ferries brought tourists. Tourists brought revenue. Even with the boatworks and the weaving, Innisbraw needed more revenue.

He whistled as he tethered the plane to the dock and climbed the ladder.

Maggie stood on the flagged entry of the weaver's shop until the floatplane landed safely. She rushed down the steps and helped Annie into the cairtie in front of Robbie. "On you come, Shep," she called, hurrying across the path.

Had Rob a guid time flying?

She met Rob as he trotted off the pier. The dancing green flecks in his eyes and his broad smile played a jig on her heartstrings.

"Maggie, you were right." He picked her up and twirled her around. "It was wonderful."

His kiss was so exuberant, she fought for breath. "Och, if it made you feel this guid, I'm thinking you should start each day in the sky."

"I already do, lass. With you."

"I want to hear all about it. Have you time now, or are you late for another meeting?"

"I wouldn't care if I was." He patted her bottom, picked up the cairtie tongue, and pulled it toward the bench by the main pier. "I have to share the wonders I saw." Rob kissed Robbie and Annie, and pulled Maggie close, nuzzling her neck. "Wait a minute. What are you doing down here?"

"Checking on the weaving." She poked him in the ribs and settled back. "Now tell me everything. Every single sight."

He spent fifteen minutes telling her all about his flight. "Those dolphins were acting just the way I felt, luve. Free and at one with sea and sky."

Thank Ye, Faither. "It sounds so peaceful. I'm grateful you enjoyed it so much."

He ordered Shep to round up Robbie, who was straying too far.

The dog leaped to the task, eyes eager.

"That's no' the best of it." He squeezed her hand. "I'm thinking your faither gave me an idea that will finally put Innisbraw on the map—literally."

A small alarm sounded deep in her mind. An idea? Surely no' another pull on his precious time. "What are you talking about?"

He pulled Annie into his lap and kissed her bonnie cheek. "I disremembered you weren't in the office the other night when he talked about the future when ferries would come here just like they do to the larger islands."

The alarm clanged. "Ferries?" Her voice cracked. "Why? Malcolm brings our post and any food or packages we need delivered."

His smile stretched to a grin. "Tourists. Do you realize how much silver tourists spend?"

Tourists? "But what would they spend it on here? We have no inn or hotel."

"What about this? Folk can open their homes. Just the other day, Hugh said what a waste that huge manse is with only one man living in it."

Though his excitement was catching, the alarm had not stilled. "What would tourists do here? Many of our strands are too rocky for enjoyment."

"But think about that wide cove on the western shore with its white sands and shallow surf. And the harbour strand itself. And we have Ben Innis to climb, and even the broch—those auld ruins on Heuch Fell—to explore." He put Annie in the wagon. "On you come, Robbie. Faither'll pull you up the path." He helped Maggie to her feet. "We'll talk more on the way home."

Maggie considered the possibilities. "I suppose if things really worked oot, the weavers who aren't part of the Cottage Weavers could sell some of their original pattern. And the women would have a market for the woolen sweaters they knit."

His fingers tightened around her waist. "And you know auld Sandy MacIver's wondrous wood carvings of seals and pewlies and dolphins? They'd sell in a heartbeat."

A sudden thought slowed her steps. "You're forgetting one thing. There's no transportation here. How would folk get around?"

"Shank's mare, of course. We could have cairts meet the ferry to help with the baggage, but I'll warrant there are a lot of folk who'd luve to get away from car exhausts and horns honking day and night."

Maggie could no longer drown out that alarm clamouring in her head. "I send you off in your airieplane for some relaxation, and you come back with yet another turn to do. I suppose you'll want to head this up."

Her bitter-sounding tone must have been obvious, for he pulled her to a stop. "Of course I'd like to have my say, but I'm thinking the Island Council should be in charge. Let them form a committee to look into it."

Couldn't he see the problems in that? "No' all of them will want our island to change so much. It would mean giving our summers over to strangers, and there's still the problem of Innisbraw no' having a public eating house."

Rob was silent as they continued up the path.

Mebbe he'd give it up. If he didn't, Island Council or no', he'd still find a way to be involved.

"There's Paddy's howff," he said, as they passed the auld McGrath cottage. "He could expand his menu. And we could hold ceilidhs so the tourists could see how we entertain ourselves. The few auld-timers who oppose owt new are always saying nobody understands our culture. This could change that." He unlatched their gate. "You know me, luve, I don't like strangers poking into my business any more than the auld-timers do. Just think about it, Maggie. If it could mean Innisbraw prospering, I could put up with it four or five months oot of the year."

If tourists came, he might regret those confident words.

Rob sat in the back of the room, all his attention on Alec, who looked around the crowded room at the raised hands of his fellow Island Council members.

Only Fergus and Alistaire fiddled with their bunnets, staring at the floor with obstinate scowls. Och, why did those twa auld-timers always have to disagree with any new idea for improving the island?

Whispers rose to loud conversations.

Elspeth tapped her walking stick.

Silence.

"The motion to look into bringing a ferry to Innisbraw is carried by a majority vote," she said. "Because we need a loan to elongate our western dock, I suggest we appoint Alec to spearhead the effort.

He has several banking contacts in Oban where he has sold his beef for many years."

A voice came from the crowd. "It won't be easy, getting a loan."

"Once my banker hears Rob Savage's name," Alec said, "he'll agree to a loan. Everyone in the business knows how fast our Innisbraw Boatworks is growing."

Rob met Alec on the dock outside the boatworks and thumped the crofter's back. "Didna take you long to get that loan."

"Och, remember, the loan's ours only if we get the ferry to add Innisbraw as a destination."

"You'll get it."

"No' if I'm late for the meeting with those folk who decide the ferry's routes."

Helping Alec into the floatplane, Rob said, "We'll be early, if anything." He turned the ignition. "Ever been up in an airieplane before?"

Alec tugged at his seat belt. "First time, and I'm so kittled up I hardly slept a blink."

Rob allowed the floatplane to drift away from the dock, then turned her nose into the wind. "Then hang onto your bunnet. You're about to soar like a bird."

While Alec made his case before the ferry officials, Rob nosed around the Oban ferry terminal. Maybe talking to the tourists would give him an idea of the desire of the masses. He could make a proposal like he had to Wing Command before a bombing mission.

A lone male with a large backpack over his shoulder strolled by.

"Excuse me. I wonder if I could interest you in visiting the Isle of Innisbraw. 'Tis small but—"

"I sprechen wenig—uh, poor Englisch."

A German? Rob relaxed. This he could handle. He spoke to the man in his own language, extolling the birdlife, wildflowers, untamed natural beauty, and the pleasure of visiting a primitive island with no cars.

"All those birds and no autos would be a delight," the tourist said, eyes wide.

Rob thanked him for his time and moved to a large group, binoculars and cameras around their necks. Americans, by the looks of their casual dress and expensive gear.

They all expressed an interest, if they could be assured of seeing plenty of birds.

"We've ospreys and golden eagles on Heuch Fell," Rob said, "and you'll find every kind of seabird that's in the Hebrides on Innisbraw, like mergansers, oystercatchers, puffins, and black-backed and pewlie gulls, no' to mention the land birds like ravens, lavrocks—och skylarks—and wheatears."

"And there really aren't any auto-mo-biles?" drawled an American woman with a broad, southern accent.

"None. Never have been, never will be. We have no roads, only wide paths."

The only teenager in the group pressed his way to the front. "Could we really go to one of your Scottish parties? With kilts and bagpipes and everything?"

"Aye." Rob broadened his Scots burr. "Ye could even lairn to dae a jig or reel."

Later, when Rob met Alec at the airstrip, the crofter's broad grin and hearty handshake erased any doubts about a successful meeting.

Rob clapped his shoulder. "You did it."

Alec scuffed the sparse girse with his toe. "They agreed to three trips a week, starting next June. They even said they'd notify newspapers and such and put up poster boards in their terminals."

"Grand. That'll save us trying to get the word oot." Rob removed the wheel chocks. "Let's get aboard. I don't like being away too long in case there's a shout."

Alec boarded the plane with a nod.

"They say anything about how many passengers we have to pull in to keep the ferry coming?" Rob asked as they taxied down the runway.

"Didn't mention it. They'll use the same ferry they use to Barra, so some of the tourists who stay on Innisbraw can continue on later, if they want." Alec rubbed his fingers together. "More silver in the ferry owners' pockets."

"That means you can firm up the loan as soon as the ferry authorities put it in writing. We'll have to get to work on that dock while the weather's still guid."

"Aye." Alec looked at the sea below and tapped Rob's arm. "Do you suppose you could do another of those thingummys like you did before? When the wing drops down?"

"You mean like this?" Rob put the plane into a steep bank.

Alec held onto his bunnet, teeth flashing. "Aye! Like this."

Den, Fern, and Katie joined the Savages for supper that een.

Den, who'd had a successful day procuring fittings, felt on top of the world. "This island's going to rival any in the Hebrides. We might just become *the* place to holiday." He held up his hands to frame his words. "I can see it now, this huge poster with a picture of Ben Innis on it. '*Come and get away from it all. No cars or traffic, no department stores or theatres. Just heather, sheep, a few coos, and plenty of sky and ocean.*'"

Rob groaned and threw a napkin at him. "We've more to offer than that. Like peace and quiet, the best ale in the Hebrides, lots of birds for the 'birders,' and"—he nodded at Maggie and Fern—"some of the bonniest lasses in the Western Islands."

"The first tourist who makes a pass at my lass'll wish he'd never heard of Innisbraw."

"Och, Den, I'm no' a lass anymore." Fern gifted her husband with a pert smile. "I'm a wife."

"Aye, and if I have to, I'll make you carry a sign that says 'Taken, do no' apply here.'" Den ducked as another napkin came his way, this one from Fern.

Maggie laughed as she brought some shortbread to the table.

Fern poured Rob and Den more coffee. "Where are the bairns off to?"

"They went into Robbie's room. Katie wanted to practice bandaging."

Rob sipped his coffee. "That lass has it bad. It looks like there's going to be another nurse in the family."

"No' a nurse." Den couldn't help a smug smile. "Our Katie wants to be a doctor."

Rob stared at him. "A doctor?"

"Aye, a doctor. She wants to operate and do all that bloody stuff doctors do."

"Den," Fern said in that scolding tone, "'tis guid to have her set her sights high."

"I think 'tis grand," Rob said. "I just never thought of her wanting something so—so difficult."

Den slapped down his coffee mug. "It is grand. And she's smart enough to do it."

❧

The loan came through on the fifteenth of August. A large group of adults and every bairn auld enough to walk gathered to watch the pylons being driven into the seabed. By the twenty-eighth of the month, the addition to the western dock was finished. The first day of June the following year, Innisbraw would welcome its first ferry to its shores. The folk of Innisbraw, most happy, some reluctant, and a few dragging their heels and screaming, were finally entering the twentieth century.

Chapter Twenty-Four

"I can't believe we've finally finished lofting the trawler." Rob waved a hand over the full-scale plan drawn on the planks. He struggled to his feet and held out a hand to help Graham up from the shed floor. "A week of this torture was enough."

"Sitting instead of kneeling like we used to should have been easier." Graham kneaded his back and rolled his shoulders. "Mebbe easier on my knees, but the rest of me feels like I've been overrun by a cairt full o' paving stones—especially my behoochie."

Rob's grimace turned into a tortured grin. "Behoochie? You sound like my wee Robbie when he's been paddled for acting the skellum." He reached for Graham's shoulder. "Don't move till I try a step."

"Move? Who can move?" Graham grabbed for Rob's shirt. "I'd like to have those Krauts who put that bullet in my leg here right now. I'd grind 'em to mince."

"With about as much success as me dropping a load of bombs on that flak that tore up my airieplane." Rob flexed his knees and ankles. "Can you move now?"

"Slow as a snail in a Sassenach rose garden."

"As they say in the States, get a move on. I'm about dead for a cup of coffee."

They staggered across the path and collapsed into the first vacant chairs in the howff.

Fifteen minutes later, Paddy brought a second pot of coffee to Rob and Graham's table. He grinned, eyes full of Irish devilment. "You twa look stone-tired. I still say you've a flask o' John Barleycorn hidden in that shed." He laughed and smacked his knee. "At least you're no' screechin' oot a ditty about some yeller-haired lass like you did the last time."

Rob's eyebrow rose. "I'll remind you 'twas Graham screechin' like a raven with his beak caught in a nail hole. I don't screech, I sing."

Graham spewed a spray of coffee across the table. "Sing? I sit in front of you at kirk. You croak like a bullfrog with a bee stuck in his throat."

Paddy swiped a cloth over the tabletop and shambled away, shaking his head and muttering. “Eejits, that’s what they are. Eejits.”

Two coffee mugs were raised in unison and clicked together.

“Another day of sun we’ve missed.” Rob sighed.

“And the crops are ready for harvest a guid month earlier than usual,” Graham said, nodding. “Faither and the other crofters are already putting a scythe to the oats, barley, and hay.” He leaned back in his chair. “And no’ wanting to lose their crops to an early gale like last year, they’re cairting it to their byres as its cut.”

“Cannie thinking.” Rob drained his mug. “How’s your new house coming along?”

“We’d be finished if Rinait didn’t keep changing her mind.”

“Changing it how?”

“She’s no’ used to having so much room, so she scrimps on things like shelves, then when they’re up, she realizes her mistake and they have to be done over.”

“Sounds like what I tried to keep Maggie from doing when I was building our home.” Rob’s gaze drifted to the window. ’Twas almost gloaming. Violet-blue eyes, voice soft as a bairnie’s breath, and rosy lips beckoned him home.

Graham freshened their mugs. “A guid idea, putting the new trawler crew to work finishing the inside of my house till that shed addition was built and the plans lofted.”

Och, why was Graham bringing this up now? Rob sat on his impatience. Concentrating on getting every measurement perfect meant any talk had to wait until moments like this. “How are they working oot?” After all, Graham had pulled all the newcomers from surrounding islands.

“Verra well. No’ a slacker in the bunch, and one lad, name of Paul Murray, looks like he’ll make foreman material with a little more experience under his belt.”

“That’s guid. With three boats going at once, we’ll be stretched rather thin.”

“I’ll use the same crews I used on the boats for Barra and Harris.” Graham kneaded the back of his neck and winced. “The trawler’s so large and complicated, ’twill most likely be us spending our time overseeing the new crew.”

“Once Stu’s aboard full-time, I’ll be spending more hours in the shed. You need to concentrate on the rescue boats. I’m thinking of turning our rescue operation over to Den. I’ll still command shouts, but he can handle everything else.”

Den pulled a chair up to the table. “Did I hear my name?” He slapped Rob's shoulder and signaled the bartender, Jack Ferguson, for an empty mug.

Rob groaned loudly, aching to feel Maggie's soft skin beneath his fingertips. "Whatever we were sayin', I don't think I can repeat it." He filled Den's mug.

"All this clean living has rendered you incapable of bad language, bucko." Den waggled his eyebrows. "You don't even swear when you stub your toe."

Graham pushed back his chair. "This is getting too raw for my tender, young ears. I'm going to check on my house. See you."

"Thanks for the help, Graham," Rob said.

"See you," Den echoed.

Face impassive, tone nonchalant, Rob said, "How would you feel about taking over the day-to-day rescue operation?"

"We about finished with the supplies we need for the new boats?"

"The last was the radios you took care of yesterday."

Den took a deep swig of coffee and smacked his lips. "Then why no'?"

Almost payback time. "It'll mean you'll have to work with Stu on setting up a donation committee."

"One of my specialties. Nowt I like better than schmoozing with prospective donors."

"The committee gets to do the wining and dining. You have to do the paperwork."

"Paperwork? Where's the fun in that?"

"Tell you what I'll do, auld friend." Rob patted Den's arm. "As senior partner, I'll authorize allocating funds for a once-a-year ceilidh. You get to organize and run it. Better?"

Eyes narrowed, Den stared at Rob. "What's the catch?"

Suspicious, was he? "No catch. You want to do some wining and dining. Here's your chance."

Den raised a hand, spreading his fingers. "Only if there's no storytelling in the Gaelic." He ticked off one finger.

"All right, no storytelling."

Another finger. "And we'll at least serve ale for those like me who detest lemon skoosh or Irn Bru."

"Ale it is." Rob could no longer suppress the grin begging for release.

The redhead's hand dropped. "I don't like that smile on your face. There has got to be a catch."

"I'm telling you, no catch." Rob sat back. "Of course, you will be expected to keep up the tradition of charity ceilidhs by wearing your dress kilt."

"My kilt?" Den choked on his coffee, thumped his chest, and rasped, "You know how I hate that monkey suit. That's a huge catch."

Rob pushed away his empty mug and tamped down a snort. "'Tis tradition, no' a catch. Don't disremember, as a partner in the Innisbraw Boatworks, you have to set an example. 'Tis a formal occasion, and in Scotland, formal occasions call for the dress kilt."

"Traditions were made to be broken." Mournful as the plea from a dying man.

"No' when you're going with your hand out. Folk expect a grand ceilidh for their silver. You can't disappoint them."

Chapter Twenty-Five

The next morning dawned dreich. High, black clouds spilled their contents across the sky like overturned inkwells, and icy air, heavy with the scent of incipient rain, sent the crofters racing to bring in the last of their crops.

Rob ignored his tepid coffee and sat back in his office chair, caught up in the magic of the isle. And in the magic of his wife, who embodied her birthplace. Her touch, her scent, her voice, all wove a spell around and through him, like a soft, fragrant mist borne on a breath from heaven.

The discordant ring of the telephone startled him.

"Savage," he grunted.

A garbled, almost incoherent noise assaulted his ear. Alec's voice, but no' a word understandable.

"Calm yourself down. I can't hear you."

"Och ... och, Rob. I need you to come now. Right now!"

"Are you at your cottage?"

"Aye, but I only came back to use the telephone. I need you to meet me at Una Hunter's auld croft." Alec took a deep breath.

Morag's voice came over the line, telling her husband to put his head between his knees and breathe slowly.

"Rob, the men tearing down that auld sheep fauld at the Hunter croft have found something most terrible."

Rob steadied his rapid breathing. It was unlike Alec and Morag to be in a fash over nowt. "What have they found?"

"They've found ... they've found human bones."

His hand tightened around the receiver. "Human?"

"Aye. And I know it's not uncommon to unearth some when one puts plow to sod on a croft. That isn't what has us in a swither. They're the size of a ... a small bairn."

"A bairn? Maybe that spot was an auld burying place."

"No burying box, no stone to mark the spot, just bones laid oot in a sma', peaty hole, and it no' verra deep."

"And this is Una Hunter's auld croft?" Hens-flesh crawled over Rob's arms. Una Hunter, the daft, auld woman who had tried to poison him and kill Maggie. He still turned his head away every time he passed her cottage, not wanting to remember her evil deeds.

"Aye. Since she's locked up in that place for dafties, the Council decided to divide the croft and put in three more cottages. Nobody wants such a sma' place to raise sheep." Alec's voice rose. "Och, Rob, please say you'll come. We don't ken what to do!"

"I'll find Den and we'll give heels to." Rob replaced the receiver. His stomach knotted. Whose dead bairn lay in the Hunter's sheep fauld?

Rob and Den soon reached the Hunter cottage, which had been completely refurbished with a new thatched roof and fresh emulsion on the door and windowsills. Alec's cairt stood nearby, his cuddy blowing steamy gusts into the chill air.

"The sheep fauld's back here." Rob jumped a low, stone dyke and trotted through a girsy area cluttered with weeds and rusty, discarded food tins.

A group of men stood huddled beside a partially demolished stone wall, their faces unnaturally pale.

Alec came toward Rob and Den, his relief palpable. "Thank ye for coming in a tick. We're in a rare fankle."

Sweating from the run, Rob removed his A-2 jacket and tossed it onto a pile of stones. "Lead the way."

Alec stopped just inside the fauld and pointed. "The grave—for lack of a better word—is right here, beside what's left of this wall. Colin had just put his digging fork in to lift out the foundation stones, when he hit something what felt strange. He dug around with his hands and uncovered the bones."

Rob nodded at Colin Stewart, owner of the largest sheep croft on the island. A guid, levelheaded man, Colin.

"My Betty and her Martin are planning on putting up a cottage here since she's biggen and 'tis never guid having a merit daughter and mither living together too long." Colin's weathered face cracked a wee smile. "Martin took Betty up to the infirmary to see Doctor John, so I came over to put a hand to." The smile faded. "But I never gave thought to finding what I did. Death brings unforgettable images."

Did the crofter still dream about knifing that German invader on the southwestern shore when he and Rob had guard against a U-boat invasion? A man of peace and of the land, the horror of what he had been forced to do, the coppery scent of fresh blood, must have haunted him for years.

Rob patted Colin's arm. "Let's have a keek then." He beckoned to Den and stepped over the rubble.

They stood back a moment, eyeing the two moldy, lichen-covered walls still standing.

Though the thatched roof had been removed, an unpleasant, fetid odor of damp and decay burned Rob's nostrils. He knelt beside the shallow grave.

No flesh on the bones, or rotting cover. The bones were laid out most proper-like, but the head was smashed and the legs bowed in till the feet crossed.

Rob shivered. "'Tis less than a metre long and about thirty centimetres wide. You're right," he said over his shoulder to Alec. Rob had expected it would be a wee bairnie, mebbe birthed in secret, then lived, died, and buried in secret.

But these bones were larger.

Rob pushed aside thoughts of his Robbie and Annie. Surely Den and he had seen worse during the war ... He forced himself to study the skull. "I'd be thinking it was only a poor lad or lass who died a natural death—but for the damage to the head." If the head injury had been caused by an accident, surely the wee one would have been buried in the cemetery. He looked around for Colin and beckoned him closer. "You're certain your digging fork didn't do this?"

"Biddy certain," the crofter said, breathing through his kerchief. "My fork went in somewhere in the mids. Soft it was, no' like owt I'd felt before. I used my hands after that."

Rob swallowed the bile in his throat. "I'd like John to see this, and I'm thinking we'd best call the polis in Oban. I'll talk to Elspeth." He turned to Alec. "And mebbe you should bring Alistaire or Fergus here for a keek." He got to his feet and brushed the soil from his denims. "They're the auldest men on the island who can still get around well. Mebbe they've heard of a bairn gone missing over the years."

"I've already put in a call to John. He'll be here as soon as he can get away from the infirmary."

Rob looked down at the bones. "Was Una ever biggen?"

"Och, no, and we'd have known if she had a bairn, what with seeing her about all the time."

"What about her mither?"

"Her mither?" Alec's broad forehead creased in thought as he rubbed his chin. "She was a strange one, Ishbel was, though I was only a sma' lad when she died. Kept to herself, never even went to kirk. Una had a wicked tongue, as you well ken, but I remember

Elspeth saying she was meek as a wedder lamb compared to her mither."

Nothing meeker than a lamb yeaned before its time. "And Una's faither? He must have kept sheep, though it can't have been an easy life, this croft being so sma'."

Alec fidgeted as though uncomfortable. "Kenneth had a rare hard time after he merrit Una's mither. She was one of them uppity Monroes and moved here from Skye. But he was a gentle soul, never one to raise his voice, let alone his hand." He raised his face to the louring sky. "But I do remember my faither once telling me, when I complained about having to cast peat, that he'd heard Kenneth say 'twas too bad the Lord never blessed them with a strong lad."

Den stepped back into the fauld, his usually florid face pale, kerchief crumpled in his palm. "You're going to call the polis, aren't you, Rob?"

"I'm thinking Alec should since he's on the Island Council."

They all looked over as Angus pulled his cairt up in front of the cottage, John beside him.

The doctor dismounted and trotted toward them, wind riffling his hair, arms wrapped around his body. "What's this about some auld bones you've found?" he asked Alec. "We didn't always have a cemetery, you ken. You'll most likely find graves behind every cottage on every path—and even scattered across the machair."

Rob gripped John's shoulder. "This is a bit different. Better take a keek, then Den and I'll ride back with you as far as the shed." He shivered in the wind. It had a bitter bite to it. Why had he taken his jacket off?

Angus followed John but stopped and turned away the moment he caught sight of the bones.

John knelt beside the hole. "Och, I see what you mean." He studied the skeleton for a long time, hands clenched into fists, then sat back on his heels. "We'll need an expert to make sense of this muddle. The remains look verra auld, but with all the peat in the soil, they're well preserved." His eyes probed Rob's. "Anything strike you as strange?"

"About the bones?"

"No' just the bones. The grave, the way the body's laid out—all of it."

"No burying clothes, or a cover of some kind, unless 'tis so auld it's long rotted. And why is the hole so shallow?"

John blew out a long sigh. "That's exactly what has me so flummoxed. It looks like the hole was dug in a hurry, but the poor wee one was put in the ground with some degree of care."

Rob pointed to the legs. "There's something no' right about the bones themselves."

"That's an understatement." John studied the bones again. "I'd say 'tis a lad, since the pelvis notch is so narrow. And if I had to guess, I'd put his age between twa and three. See that protuberance on the forehead and how wide apart the eye sockets are? Also, the shoulders and ribs are extremely narrow and the spine's twisted, to say nowt about the bowed legs." Eyes bleak, he looked up at Rob. "If it was just the legs, I'd say he could have died of malnourishment or suffered from rickets, but this is far worse." He stood and brushed the dirt from his knees. "This poor wee one was grossly malformed. With no room in that small chest for growing lungs and heart, he couldn't have lived much longer. So why would someone have bashed his head in?"

Rob leaned forward for a final look. "What's that? Beneath the bones of the right hand. Looks like a piece of wood or stone."

John knelt again. "I see it too, but don't have a glimmer of what it is. We'll have to wait till the bones are moved."

Angus nudged Rob and handed him a large piece of waxed cotton. "The rain's about to pish doon. Mebbe you'd best cover that before it starts."

After waiting until the bairns were abed, Rob told Maggie about the gruesome discovery.

She shivered. "'Tis enough to give you hens-flesh. But nobody could have had a bairn so deformed without everybody on the island knowing it." Her chin rose, a sure sign she'd made up her mind. "Those bones are surely a hundred years auld."

"You're most likely right." Rob blew a long sigh. "But the polis are going to investigate. They'll be here on the morra with their pathologist so he can make sure the bones are packed up and transported withoot damaging them."

Rob sneaked out of bed after the turn o' the night for another keek at Robbie and Annie.

The rain tapped a muted tattoo on the slate roof, and the wind howled around the eaves, sounding like the moans of the dying. The hairs on the back of his neck stood on end.

He made certain both bairns were covered, then stood over each, thanking God for their strong bodies and the joy they brought to his life. Making his way back to bed, he blinked away tears, eyes burning at the thought of some poor, wee laddie, already burdened with a twisted, deformed body, being struck on the head with a blow strong enough to shatter his skull.

Och, Faither, I pray one of Your angels is holding that wee one verra close.

Slipping carefully in beside Maggie, Rob rested his head on his pillow. A scripture about heaven leaped to mind. ... *And he shall wipe away every tear from their eyes; and death shall be no more; neither shall there be mourning, nor crying, nor pain, anymore: the first things are passed away.*

He fell into a deep, dreamless sleep.

Detective Inspector Grant of the Oban polis arrived on the island late the next morning, accompanied by two constables and one seasick pathologist, Doctor Thomas Rankin.

Rob, who had met Grant when he came to the island as a detective sergeant in 1942 to investigate Una Hunter's threats against Maggie, congratulated Grant on his promotion to inspector.

The detective's grey eyes widened with surprise. "So you're walking again, Colonel. And you came back after the war?" Same gruff, no-nonsense voice.

"A bit before that, but aye, Innisbraw is my home now."

"And that bonnie lass?"

"Maggie. She's my wife."

"Now, why doesn't that surprise me?" A rare smile lit his craggy face, then faded. "Because the remains were found on Una Hunter's property, I called the head doctor at Stoneyetts Mental Institution in Lankarshire to see if she was capable of being interviewed. He informed me she committed suicide over a year ago." The corners of his thin lips turned down. "Apparently one of the orderlies was lax, and she was left unchecked in her room long enough to strangle herself with a sheet from her bed."

So it was truly over.

Unfortunately, it wasn't surprising she had taken this way out of a life tormented by insanity.

"I hope she's at peace now." A hoarse whisper, but all he could manage.

"That's hardly what I expected you to say after what she did to you and your wife."

It was Rob's turn to try a smile. "The grace of the Lord covers a multitude of sins, even those from a sick mind."

Alec's cairt pulled up with John on the bench beside him.

John turned to the pathologist, who mopped his pale face with a monogrammed kerchief. "Would you like a bit of rest before we start?"

Doctor Rankin pushed the kerchief into his pocket and straightened the lapels of his expensive tailored coat. "I'm feeling much better now I'm off that dreadful boat. Lead on. We've a long day ahead, and I'm most eager to see what you've found."

"At least the rain's stopped," Alec muttered as he helped the pathologist onto the cairt's bench.

"Did you cover the remains before the rain started?"

Rankin's sarcastic tone in a pseudo-cultured Edinburgh burr irritated Rob.

Alec stiffened. "Of course. We're no' eejits."

Rob turned his head to hide a smile at Alec's gruff Scots reply.

Grant issued curt orders to his constables during the busy afternoon of studying, photographing, and gathering soil samples. At last, the bones were brushed off, a thin piece of wood placed beneath them, and they were moved to a small, coffin-like box.

As they were finishing up with the site, the pathologist pulled on a clean pair of gloves and picked up the object Rob had seen earlier. "What have we here?" He turned it toward the light.

Grant leaned over his shoulder. "Looks like a marking of a sheep."

Rob stepped closer. About the size of his palm, the carving that had been under the bones was skillfully executed, with swirls of curly hair, four legs—one missing a hoof—and a stub of a tail. "These bones can't be that auld, then. No' if a carving of a sheep survived, even if no flesh did."

"True, true," Rankin said. "It does look like a sheep, doesn't it?"

That's what Grant and I said, eejit. "Aye, and if it looks like this after being buried so long, it must have been a remarkable likeness when 'twas new."

Grant handed the pathologist a small evidence bag.

He placed the carving inside and tucked the bag into the box beside the bones and stood. "I've a schoolmate who's taken a keen interest in dating old bones. He's a forensic anthropologist with a laboratory in Glasgow." He brushed his soiled suit pants with vigor. "I'm certain he'll be willing to come to Oban when he hears of your find. Perhaps he can at least give us a general time frame for how long these bones have been buried." His scowl deepened. "There's little doubt as to the cause of death."

Grant ordered his two constables to stay at the croft with the group of crofters to fork up the entire earthen floor of the fauld. "Do it with care," he said, "and to a depth of no less than two metres." He ignored the constables' groans and brushed his palms together. "I want everything you find placed in evidence bags, no matter how small."

Later that night, Rob joined John, Alec, the polismen, and Rankin in Hugh's chaumer.

"Though it's going to take some time to determine the lad's age at time of death, I'm certain you're spot-on about the sex of the bairn and deformities of the bones," Rankin said to John.

John took a cup of tea from Hugh and directed his question to Grant. "What happens next? I don't expect you remember them after all this time, but we have Alistaire MacIver and Fergus MacCrae thinking back to see if they can recall anyone in their lifetimes who might be tied to that poor laddie's murder."

Grant graced him with a grimace. "Och, how could I forget those two—erm—gentlemen. Just remember to have someone available to translate. I still don't speak the Gaelic."

"Alec here will go with you."

"Is there perhaps an older woman we can interview? Sometimes we find the best witnesses are women who have a propensity for a bit of ... well ... gossip."

Hugh refilled Rob's coffee mug. "I'm sorry to say there are quite a few who fit that description on this wee island of ours. I'll make a list and give it to Alec on the mornin before he picks you up."

Nothing of importance was found in the fauld, and Grant's interrogations did not reveal any names of missing bairns. The only encouraging bit of news was that all of the auld-timers were certain that, before Una was born, there was a period of over three years when Ishbel Hunter was never seen outside her cottage. Even her husband, though he was always a taciturn loner, had kept completely to himself.

Fergus recalled that, though the poor man always worked his croft from dawn to long after gloaming, one of those years had been unusually hard, with a bitterly cold winter and frost on the ground at lambing. A strong, young man in his prime, Fergus had gone to the Hunter cottage to offer his help, only to be turned down by an angry Kenneth, his large hands fisted, black eyes flashing.

"But you never saw a lad?" Grant asked again, "or even clothes on a line what might fit a laddie?"

Fergus lost his temper and Alec had to calm him down before he replied with a spate of Gaelic, his normally rheumy eyes sharp with anger, cheeks splotched with red.

"He says he never did," Alec translated.

Though that was certainly not all Fergus said.

"Well, I suppose it's possible they hid her pregnancy—and the lad, once he was born. But it isn't much to go on." Grant snapped erect. "However, that's neither here nor there. They're all dead, so there's nowt to it, even if we could prove them responsible."

Rob and Maggie talked for hours that evening before deciding that Grant was right. Even if the bones were those of a Hunter lad, it was much too late to take legal action.

Maggie nestled deeper into Rob's lap. "I do hope they return him to Innisbraw. He deserves a well-tended grave, no' a hole in a sheep fauld."

"At least somebody cared enough to carve him that sheep." Rob gazed into the flickering peat fire. "But we can't put up a stone to mark the grave. We don't even know his name."

"Of course we can. It might no' have a name on it, but at least it can say something like 'Here lies an Innisbraw lad, known by few but mourned by all.'"

He buried his face in her hair. Trust his Maggie to bring this entire heartbreaking event to a proper end.

Chapter Twenty-Six

"I canna believe how long it's been since our last shout." Rob studied Den, who stood in his office doorway. Up to his auld standards, he was. Not a single blunder or mishap since his marriage to Fern. Rob pointed a pencil at the redhead. "I'll be tied up here tighter'n a wild-eyed cuddy till the new trawler crew is broken in, so you'll handle the next shout withoot me. Meantime, go over the *Maggie* with care. Don't want a malfunction with a new commander on board."

No' a smirk, no' a pause, just a crisp, "Aye, Commander."

Keep him focused, Faither. And I'm so whummled with work, I need focus too. Give me Your words to motivate the new crew.

Fifteen minutes later, assured that Graham and his seasoned crews were hard at work on the rescue boats in the old section of the shed, Rob gathered his lads around the plan he and Graham had lofted on the floor planks.

This wouldn't be easy. Though all were woodworkers and intelligent and eager to please, these lads knew nothing about boat construction.

"Take a guid look. Then I'll hear your questions."

They milled about, foreheads creased, taking care not to smear the pencil marks or dimensions noted on each board.

Once they'd all had a look, Rob leaned against a workbench. "Questions?"

A hand shot up. Paul Murray, the lad Graham had mentioned.

"What's your question, Paul?"

"If we've already got a paper plan, why do we need another on the floor?"

Exactly the question Rob hoped to hear. "Just think of it as a prototype boat. Instead of building from a plan on paper only, you now have the complete boat with every board, no matter how large or small, drawn on the floor."

He picked up a piece of lumber he'd cut earlier and walked to the lofted plan. "Once you cut your lumber to size, you lay it out on the floor and make sure it's a perfect fit before you put it into place on the boat." He slid the board into place. "Saves having to redo a section of planking because you cut a board wrong at the beginning."

The lads all grinned and nodded at one another.

"Just remember to mark the plan with an *X* when you've cut the board properly." He pointed at a smaller drawing. "Now to the cra—"

The loud wail of the shout siren brought gasps of surprise and open mouths.

Of course the lads were alarmed. The siren hadn't sounded since they'd come to Innisbraw.

Rob smiled reassuringly and waited until the siren's dying note before explaining when it was used and how it alerted the rescue crew, no matter where they laboured on the island. "Den Anderson will be commanding this shout," he said. "So back to where we were. The cradle. As any of you who grew up around boats knows, the—"

A hand waved. One of the youngest of the lot, if his smooth, beardless chin was any indication. "But ... but I heard you commanded the rescue boat."

Rob sat on his impatience. "We usually command together, but as you can see, I'm a wee bit busy. Now where were we? Och, aye, the cradle. The word describes it perfectly. It will serve as a—"

"But can the other commander help birth bairnies like you?"

Rob whirled around.

Den lounged in the doorway, grinning like a daftie. "'Twas a false alarm, Commander. Our first." He saluted. "Carry on, sir."

Despite an inauspicious beginning, Rob's instructions were followed with diligence, and just two days later, the large cradle stood in place, ready to receive the keel post.

His crew learned that exact measurements were a must and that it paid to measure and mark a piece of lumber at least twice before cutting it.

Graham was right about Paul Murray. The lad had a natural ability to help others who were struggling, and his no-nonsense approach fit with Rob's preference to always use the fewest words possible when issuing directions or orders. By the end of the week, Rob appointed him foreman.

The Proctors arrived on the tenth of September, the *Sea Rouk*'s deck stacked with boxes.

"You hear horror stories about pictures and important papers disappearing into the bowels of a ship, never to be seen again," Stu said when he saw Rob's raised eyebrow. "All these items are irreplaceable. Everything else was shipped on a merchant vessel."

Rob should have expected that. Anyone who craved order would never trust his dearest belongings on a merchant ship. "'Tis a guid thing I borrowed Angus's cairt. We'll take those labeled 'Personal' up to our home, and I'll have a few lads move the others to the infirmary storeroom later." He pressed Jill's shoulder, ruffled wee Chris's dark hair, and nodded a quick greeting to Brenna.

Maggie waited on the entry, hugging herself against the cold breeze. The moment the cuddy's hooves sounded on the path, she raced down the flagged path and threw open the gate.

Jill fell into her arms, laughing and fanning her face. "What a horrid trip. I didn't think it would ever end."

"In you come." Maggie waved Brenna toward the back of the house. "You'll find Katie, Robbie, and Annie in Robbie's room." She kissed the laddie's cheek and hugged Jill's arm. "We'll get you settled into your room while our strong men unload your boxes. Fern will be over soon as she's finished at the infirmary. She and Den will be joining us for supper."

After depositing Chris into the care of his older sister, Maggie and Jill climbed the stairs to Jill and Stu's room.

Jill took one look at the large bed and threw herself down on her back, heaving a loud sigh. "This bed has been calling my name. But we'll be out of your hair the minute we can. I can't thank you enough for offering us your spare rooms again."

Maggie sat beside her. "'Tis what they're for. And that's what friends do."

Jill patted her belly. "You're showing more than I."

"You're a wee bit taller. Gives you more room to spread things oot." Maggie leaped up and brought an extra quilt from the closet, folding it at the end of the bed. "Have you been sick at all?"

"Not a day. But I'm going to be in trouble here. All I think about is hamburgers—not the thick, juicy ones, but the thin ones you get at a cheap five-for-a-dollar burger shack. How about you?"

"No mornin sickness. But like you, I've a craving, and 'tis for lemon curd, of all things. It's never been my favourite, but now I want to eat it by the spoonful." Maggie laughed and put a finger to her lips. "Don't tell Rob or he'll call Harrods and order a crateful."

The shout siren interrupted supper.

Maggie gave Rob a pleading look.

He nodded. "You're still up," he shouted to Den. "False alarms don't count."

Fern and Katie hugged Den before he dashed out the door.

When the siren fell silent, Maggie turned to Fern. "Why don't you, Stu, and Rob monitor the radio? We'll enjoy the sticky toffee pudding you brought later."

Jill waited until Rob closed the door to his office. "How about you kiddos playing a game in Robbie's room?"

Brenna pursed her lips and glared at her mither, but she scooped young Chris from Jill's lap with a "humph" and followed Robbie and Annie into the bedroom.

Katie hung back for a moment, face bleak, before sighing and joining them.

Heart aching, Maggie gathered some of the dirty plates. "I'm thinking your lass resents being treated like a young one."

Jill picked up the rest of the plates and joined her at the kitchen bunker. "She'll get over it. It's just her age. One minute she's still a needy little girl, and the next she's a rebellious young woman." She scraped the dishes and set them into the soapy water. "It's hard, isn't it? I mean when that siren goes off? Even for Katie, as young as she is."

"Den's the only faither she's ever known," Maggie said, pouring tea. "Let's sit for a spell. Rob will be oot to tell us as soon as he learns what kind of shout they're facing."

"I couldn't bear waiting for hours, knowing Stu was in danger and there was nothing I could do to help him."

Maggie stirred her tea. "'Tis more a matter of learning to lean on our Lord." Her cheeks burned. "I'm no' a verra guid example. I ... I faced the same problem when Rob was flying in the war."

Jill's warm fingers closed over her hand. "We all have our own problems with trusting God to answer our questions and fears." Her dry laugh sounded more like a cough. "Like Brenna's crush on Rob, for instance, and how to handle it."

"As long as you know Rob's done nowt to encourage it. In fact, he—"

The door to Rob's office opened.

Fern stepped out, gaze darting about the living room. "Where's Katie? I need to put her fears to rest."

"She's in Robbie's bedroom. 'Tis a tow, then?" Maggie's gaze went to Rob, Stu fast on his heels.

"A medical emergency, luve." Rob nuzzled her ear and reached for the coffeepot. "Sit you down," he said to Stu, handing him a mug. "An aulder woman passenger on the ferry from Barra to Oban took a fall. They think she broke her hip."

"But they should be almost to Mull Sound by now. Why was Innisbraw called?"

"The ferry was late sailing from Barra because a large troke broke down on the loading ramp, holding up boarding. But the ferry's well oot in the Minch by now, so we're closer."

Fern joined them, a smile softening her worry lines. "'Twill be a long shout, but at least our crew won't be going into the water." She breathed a sigh as she poured a cup of tea. "We need to pray. It can't be easy transferring an auld woman with such an injury from the ferry to the *Maggie*."

"I agree," Rob said. "They'll have to use the inflatable, and though the sea's no' running verra high yet, 'twill test our lads, keeping the stretcher steady."

Maggie knelt beside her chair. "Then, pray we shall."

A week later, a routine of sorts established, Maggie could finally relax and enjoy their guests. Stu accompanied Rob to the shed every morning, Jill helped with the cleaning and cooking, Brenna either mooned about or doted on Annie, dressing her sock doll and teaching her songs. Robbie surprised everyone by including Chris, who'd gone from toddling to running, in his games.

One morning, Shep followed the two lads, barking, tail wagging and eyes adoring.

"Shep, stop that bowfing." Maggie removed her palms from her ears and ordered the dog to his spot on the hearth rug. She caught the tail of Robbie's sweater. "And you stop running in the house."

"But we're playing chase."

"Quit your whinging and go to your room. You sound like a herd of coos on the loose."

Chris swatted her skirt and ran off, giggling.

She scooped him up and carried him to Robbie's bedroom. "You lads play with the cars, or roll a ball—anything but running about like dafties."

Annie looked up from her favourite place near the hearth and rocked her sock doll, singing a song in her wee, soft voice.

Maggie closed the door on Robbie's protests.

"Sounds like they've run you ragged." Jill shook the rain from her coat and hung it in the closet. "Sure you still want eight kids?"

Only if they're mine. "Where's Brenna?"

"At school, taking placement tests. I passed Morag on the path, and she said Alec would bring her home when school's out." Jill hurried into the kitchen, filled the teakettle, and set it to boil. "Isn't there some kind of magic Scots incantation to make this water boil faster? That wind's so cold I'm numb."

"Certain you still want to live here?"

Jill's nose wrinkled as she smiled. "I deserved that." She jumped when a loud thump came from Robbie's bedroom. "Sounds like it's my turn to lay down the law."

Maggie grimaced, poured boiling water over the tea leaves, and settled the cosy over the pot before setting it on the breakfast table. "I said they could roll a ball. Let's ignore it while we can."

"I'll get the milk and honey. Then I want to tell you about a decision Stu and I made last night."

"Och, Rob's learning to cope with Brenna's—"

"We're still wrestling that one. It's about her schooling next year."

"Next year?"

"Her teacher looked over all the school records I brought, then listened to her read aloud. According to Mrs. Stewart, she'll likely be put in the top form, meaning this is the last year she can attend primary school."

"So she'll be going off to boarding academy next August."

"Over our dead bodies."

Jill's adamant words alarmed Maggie. "You're going back to America, then?"

"Of course not. But she's been uprooted enough. I'll homeschool her."

Maggie poured their tea and added milk and heather honey. "What does 'homeschool' mean?"

"It's the way parents used to teach children, before communities were large enough to support schools—before the States mandated public schooling. The parents are the teachers, and the children learn at home." Jill prepared her tea, took a healthy swallow, and leaned forward. "We'll have to see what the laws are here in Scotland, but in the States, you don't need a teaching degree to homeschool your own children."

Annie tugged at Maggie's skirt. "Oop, oop," she pleaded.

Maggie picked her up and kissed her cheek. "There's my lassie. Want a spoonful of Mither's tea?"

Annie grabbed the spoon and guided it into her mouth. She smiled and pounded the spoon for more.

"It looks like we'll have to talk later, when there are fewer distractions," Jill said. "I'll start chopping vegetables for the bree."

Stu came running in just before supper, apologizing for getting tied up in his work. "I spent over an hour convincing Den to have the Rescue Boat Fundraising Foundation's treasurer bonded. Couldn't get it through his thick head that I wasn't questioning the honesty of the man he'd chosen, just covering our partnership if an audit shows a discrepancy." He shook his head. "And I thought Rob was stubborn."

After supper was over and bairns were bathed and settled into bed after prayers, Rob still hadn't shown up. Jill and Stu disappeared upstairs with Brenna to talk about her afternoon at school, while Maggie paced, stopping only to lift a corner of the lace curtain to peer through the rain at the empty path.

He always called when he was going to be verra late. And her phone was working. Her faither had rung just after supper.

She telephoned Fern. "Is Den home yet?"

"No' yet, and I'm about to skite his lug. Katie went to bed in tears because he promised to help her with her maths."

"Rob's no' home, either. Let me know if you hear anything."

Maggie hung up and jiggled the receiver. "Two-oh-four," she said to the operator.

Rob's office line was busy.

She hung up.

The shout siren had been silent, and he hadn't mentioned any meetings this een. Why hadn't he called?

She added peats to the fireplace, pulled out a pile of mending, and sat in her rocker, sewing basket at her side. Might as well do something useful while she waited. She cut a patch for a tear in a pair of Robbie's breeks and threaded a needle. Her mind wandered back to what Jill had said about homeschooling. She shared Jill's concern. When it came time to send her own lads and lasses off to academy, she didn't see how she could bear to do it. It was such a shame that Innisbraw didn't have its own academy.

The door opened.

She whirled around.

Rob stood in the doorway, looking like a dirty, near-drowned beastie. Grease smeared one cheek, wood chips glistened on his drenched hair, and his shoulders stooped with fatigue.

She dropped Robbie's breeks onto the pile and rushed across the room. "You're so late, luve. What kept you?"

He pulled off his dripping waxed jacket and shook it on the entry flags before closing the door. "I tried to call you, but the line was busy."

Maggie hung his jacket in the closet. "I called your office phone, but it was busy too. When did you call?"

"Right after we finished rearranging the machinery in the trawler section of the shed." Rob wiped the back of a hand over his mouth and kissed her cheek. "I knew from the first day the flow wasn't right. The lads kept running into each other, and it slows things when they dance back and forth, apologizing." He ladled a bowl of bree from the pot on the stove and ate a spoonful. "Then Graham came in with a question, and we walked it through, spotting the problems. Any bannock, luve?"

Maggie handed him a piece of oat bread.

He broke it into the broth and mashed it with his spoon, and took another giant bite. "I'd be even later, but Den showed up and we talked him into helping us. We had to unbolt every saw, the planer, sander and drill press, move them, drill new holes and rebolt them to the floor."

"Sit at the table, Rob. I'll pour your coffee."

"You're giving me that look. Am I in trouble, then?"

"What look?"

"The one with the raised eyebrows."

She took his bowl, set it on the bunker, and threw hers arms around him. Och, he'd spent eighteen hours at hard labour and she'd no' even welcomed him home. "I'm sorry, luve," she mumbled into his shirt. "I'm no' in a fash. 'Tis just ... I've never seen you eat supper without a cat's lick first."

His fingers left her shoulders as though burned.

She sneaked a keek. Studying his greasy hands, he was. And looking ashamed.

He ducked his head. "I'm the one who's sorry. My good sense must have been drowned oot by my growling stomach."

"You didna have dinner?"

"No time."

No dinner. And he wondered why he had to pull his belt tighter to keep his denims from slipping. She hugged him again. "Then wash your hands and we'll sit at table while you finish your supper. There's pumice 'neath the jawbox."

Hands clean and equilibrium restored by Maggie's fond smiles, Rob kissed her soundly and sat beside her. "Tell me about your day." He gulped half a mug of coffee before attacking his bree again.

"Faither called to tell me that auld woman with the broken hip is complaining about being tied to a chair instead of lying in a bed."

His spoon stopped halfway to his mouth. "Tied to a chair? That sounds like torture."

Warm fingertips brushed his cheek. "'Tis so she won't get pneumonia from lying prone. She's no' tied with ropes, luve, just soft pieces of cotton. She's sitting on a pillow with another at her back—and Fern's been staying with her, asking questions about her family to help keep the poor auld soul's mind off the discomfort."

He grunted. "Shows you how little I know about medicine." He drained his mug. "So why isn't her family here where they belong?"

"Den didn't tell you? Her son and his wife are flying in from America. They'll stay at Fern and Den's. 'Tis closer to the infirmary than the manse." She filled his bowl with more bree, poured fresh coffee, and set a plate of bannocks at his elbow. "Now for some news that'll leave you dumbfoondert."

Her fingers gripped his arm.

"Jill's no' going to send Brenna off to academy. She'll teach her at home."

Again, his spoon halted between bowl and lips. He didn't like the gleam in those violet-blue eyes. "Don't you be getting any ideas about teaching our bairns at home. With as many as we're having, you'd be run ragged."

The wrinkling of that pert nose presaged her ready answer. "That's why we'll ask the Island Council to build an academy on Innisbraw."

Chapter Twenty-Seven

Elspeth fanned her face with her kerchief—she was no' warm—just excited by Rob's proposal. She scanned the faces of the council members, hoping to read their reactions.

Morag and Alec looked flummoxed. Tormad MacKinnon and Colin Stewart shook their heads and studied the floor. Alistaire and Fergus sat upright in their chairs, lips clamped tight, cheeks blotched with rancor. Those twa would fight their own shadows. Only Sheila MacNab smiled at Rob, blue eyes sparkling with approval.

No' a time to sit by in silence. "Our Rob has presented a most unusual request," Elspeth said in the Gaelic. Her fingers tightened around her walking stick.

Dear Rob, standing so straight and tall against the wall beside Hugh, had no idea the skep of bees he'd kicked over this een.

She slipped her kerchief back into her sleeve. "I have expected this proposal for years, yet not once have any of our folk petitioned for an academy here on Innisbraw, despite the economic and emotional hardships suffered by parents of those young ones desiring a higher education."

Fergus snorted. "A waste of our time, that's what it is. I had no schooling. Never needed it. In my day, a man worked with his hands and the thews of his body, not his head."

One muted snicker as every eye raked over the old man's ragged breeks, offal-coated newspaper sticking from holes in his wellies, and long, white hair flying about his head like feathers from a molting gull.

He hawked up phlegm and spat into his kerchief. "If Rob can build a house fit for a king, he has enough money for that academy on Harris."

Alec leaped to his feet. "If you stopped fighting progress on Innisbraw, you'd have time for improving your own cottage, Fergus. Rob has been respon—"

Elspeth pounded her walking stick on the floor flags. "We're all aware of how hard Rob has worked for our folk. Please take your seat." She gifted Alec with a wee smile.

Fergus moved to stand.

Her steely glare stopped him halfway out of his chair. "Fergus MacCrae, you have forgotten our rules of conduct. At no time are council members to demean or belittle a suggestion brought before us. We may disagree with an idea, but we never speak ill of a petitioner."

The old man leaned toward Alistaire, obviously expecting a word of support, but Alistaire edged away and plucked at a loose thread on the knee of his worn, tweed trousers.

Elspeth took a deep, cleansing breath. Too bad those crabbit, auld men never found a wife. They both needed a sharp-tongued, no-nonsense woman to show them what crabbit really meant.

There was a time when she would have delighted in the prospect of a verbal battle. These days, dissension consumed her carefully-hoarded energy at an alarming rate. Living to an auld age might seem like a blessing to the young, but to the auld, it was a frustrating burden. She opened the meeting to discussion and sat back, calming her ragged breathing with prayer. *My precious Heavenly Faither, give me the strength to guide this meeting toward the fulfillment of Your perfect will.*

Questions were raised and discussed until a consensus evolved. All the board members—with the exception of Fergus—agreed about the growing need for an academy on Innisbraw. Financing such an endeavor, however, brought a more dour exchange.

Taking another deep breath, Elspeth prepared to interject some ideas, but Rob stepped forward, wearing his military bearing like the officer he had been for so long.

"Only a few of our people have the funds to send their bairns to Harris." His deep, low voice commanded attention. "And those who do often go without food in their stomachs to pay the tuition." His eyes narrowed. "I've put figures to paper. One month's tuition at Harris for a single student could pay a teacher's yearly salary right here on our island." He handed a sheet of paper to each board member.

Leave it to Rob to use simple, understandable logic and back it up in writing.

But she needed to voice the largest impediment to higher education on Innisbraw. "I agree about the cost of a teacher," she said, nodding at Rob. "But we'd have to pay for new facilities. When our school was built, we couldn't afford room for an infant school, something we regret. The building is large enough for the primary students but would have no room for academy students."

Rob's eyes darkened, shoulders straightened. "I think we're all missing something. There's no more important time in a young person's life than those four years we send them off to be educated—and perhaps even more importantly, raised—by strangers. That's the time they need to be with their own families, learning from their example. In their own homes, where they can feel at ease among their kin. Attending their own kirk, where Hugh teaches directly from the Word. On our own Innisbraw, where they are not forced to learn English, but can speak Scots proudly."

There were several raised eyebrows, but it was Alec who broke the uneasy silence. "You surprise me, Rob. I should think that you, of all people, should realize how important it is that our young people learn English. It's the language of commerce and so much more."

"It is important." Rob crossed his arms and widened his stance. "But not the way it's taught on Harris, as though it's superior to Scots. As soon as my bairns are fluent in the Gaelic and Scots, I'll teach them English." He paused, gaze probing each face. "But as a language, not a way of life."

Those almost translucent hazel eyes locked with Elspeth's.

"If we keep our young ones on Innisbraw, they won't be made to feel like second-class citizens because they speak Scots."

Sheila MacNab waved her hand. "I agree. We heard our daughter-in-law, Siobhan, was in tears her entire first term because everyone made fun of her Scots. By the time she went off to university, she never spoke Scots at all and didn't like it when her family did. Said it was 'low class' or some such nonsense." A sudden smile chased away her frown. "Of course, that was before she returned to Innisbraw and gave her heart to our handsome Lachlan."

Everyone was spent and rising time came early for most of these folk. Elspeth tapped her walking stick for order. "I commend Rob for bringing this need to our attention. I want you all to go home and think very hard about how to raise the money for a new academy building." She shot Fergus a stern look.

He closed his half-open mouth and swallowed, Adam's apple convulsing.

"As I have heard Rob urge us," Elspeth said, "to think beyond the usual. Any idea, no matter how ridiculous it may seem, should be considered."

Maggie stepped out onto the entry and looked down the path. She couldn't believe it—only a bit gone 1800 hours, and Rob had called to say he was on his way home. She hugged herself, not against the icy bite of the wind this time, but from joy.

These past few weeks had been glorious. Only intermittent rainy days, another woman in the house to blether with, and —if she dared admit it—Robbie much easier to handle with a younger, guid-natured laddie to share his play.

A gibbous moon cast a timorous light on the soft swells of the harbour moving its inky surface like a mither's arms rocking her bairnie.

Thank Ye, Faither, for bringing Den and Stu here to Innisbraw to help Rob. Which means I finally have a husband to share my eens. Aye, he's spent from all his physical labour, but the green flecks are back, dancing in his eyes.

The latch on the gate clicked.

She rushed to meet Rob on the steps.

"There's my lass." His husky growl sent her pulse pounding. He caught her up and hugged her, pressing cold lips against her throat. His palm caressed her belly. "How are we the een?"

"We're grand." She grasped the back of his head and pulled his mouth down to hers. Cold lips and hot breath assailed her senses. His kiss softened, moved over her cheeks, forehead. He smelled of wood shavings and salt-scented sea air, and the feel of his lithe, muscular body brought tears to her eyes. "Welcome home, luve," she breathed.

Rob carried her into the house. A perfect beginning to a perfect een. His muscles ached, and he was so hungry his stomach cramped, but nothing mattered more than this perfect minute of time. He sat in his rocker and pulled Maggie's head against his chest so he could bury his face in her fragrant hair. "I'm thinking you had a verra guid day." He rubbed his cheek against her silken hair. "Care to share it with a spent, auld man?"

She stiffened. "Spent? Mebbe. Auld? Never."

He tweaked a curl. "If you won't go first, I will." He waited a long moment, prolonging Maggie's suspense, knowing how she hated any pause in conversation. When she opened her mouth to speak, he covered her lips with his palm. "I had a verra guid day, thank ye for asking. Alec has volunteered to oversee a crew of men to do the carpentry and plumbing work on Stu and Jill's home." He chuckled. "A bit slow, our Alec, but if he's satisfied with the work, it's well done."

She sat up, violet-blue eyes sparkling in the firelight. "May I speak now?"

That wrinkled, pert nose and saucy smile brought a laugh. "You may—if you have anything to say."

"Och!" She swatted his arm. "We held our Women's Aid Society meeting at Rinait and Graham's new home." Her smile widened and pearly teeth flashed. "You should see the way she's decorated the walls with woven hangings. The colours are glorious. 'Tis obvious the lass is an artist with the loom."

"Graham appears to take to merrit life." He stared into the flickering peats. "If only Rinait could be more understanding about the long hours keeping him away from an early tea or supper."

"She'll learn. 'Tisn't an easy lesson to master, but she will … in time."

Her quiet words shredded his heart. How many times had she waited supper, only to have him come home long after the bairns were abed? How many nights had he found her asleep in her rocker, a pile of mending in her lap, tears dried on her cheeks? He laced his fingers through hers. "I'm sorry I've failed you so often, luve. It hasn't been a'purpose, but I've hurt you by my own long hours."

"Haud yer wheesht." She kissed his knuckles. "Early or late makes no never mind, for you always come home. That's what's important—to all of us."

"I don't know what I'd do if I didn't have your support. And it's so hard on you, especially with the weather turning so cold and the storms moving in so you can't take the bairns outside, besides on the porch 'neath the overhang." He rested his chin on her head.

"Even Annie, as much as she hates the cold, would rather be oot there than inside all day. With both Brenna and Katie off to school, she misses their attention."

"How does Katie like school?"

"Fern says they're going to have a real scholar on their hands by the time she's advanced beyond primary. It seems our Katie will already settle for nothing but a perfect mark on every paper."

No surprise, that. Katie MacNeill Anderson would be a fine doctor someday. He looked around, chagrined not to have asked before. "Where are all the bairns?"

"Robbie's in his room, playing with his troke, and Annie's in hers, rocking her baby to sleep in that wee cradle you made her."

"Jill and her twa?"

"She had Angus drop them all off at Elspeth's. Jill wants to advance in Scots and the Gaelic as quickly as possible, and Brenna's formed quite an attachment to Elspeth. Says she reminds her of her Grandmither Proctor."

His body tingled. "You mean we're alone with our bairns?"

"Aye." She nuzzled his chin. "Where's Stu? He didn't come home with you."

"With Den. They're working out the final plan for an Innisbraw Rescue Boat Foundation."

"Och, sounds verra important."

"No' as important as this." He kissed her deeply, savoring her sweet taste.

"Faither, want oop."

Rob's lips reluctantly left Maggie's.

Annie waited at his side, large hazel-brown eyes pleading.

Maggie stood and straightened the pleats in her skirt. "I'd best finish supper."

He waggled his eyebrows. "I'd like to carry on with what we started a wee bit later."

Soft fingertips brushed his hand. "So would I."

He picked up Annie and cradled her in his lap. At twenty months, she was still such a wee lass with a winsome, shy smile and quiet personality.

She rested her head against his shoulder and patted his back with her tiny hand. "My faither."

He lifted her curls and kissed the back of her neck. "My Wee Annie," he whispered.

A loud crash and howl from Robbie's room shattered the comfortable silence.

Rob grabbed Annie and leaped from his rocker.

Maggie met him at Robbie's door. "Give me the lass."

Robbie was on the floor, his large wooden troke on top of him, face screwed up in a scowl.

Rob pulled the troke off, knelt on the floor, and took his son into his arms. "Where do you hurt?" he asked, anxiously scanning the lad for blood.

"My behoochie!" Robbie roared. He kicked the troke, blinking back tears.

Rob grabbed his foot. "No more of that." He set the lad on his feet and ran his hand over the lean bottom. "Is this the only place you hurt?"

Robbie nodded, lower lip pushed out.

"And what were you doing with your troke that made you fall on your behoochie?"

"Flying." The lip trembled.

"That's a troke, no' an airieplane." Rob turned his head to hide a grin. "Trokes can't fly."

"But I don't have a big airieplane. I climbed on the bed and held my arms oot like wings, but it didn't fly."

Rob picked him up. "That wasn't a verra guid idea, was it?"

The lad buried his face against his faither's chest and shook his head.

"I know you've never seen a real troke driving on a road, but you've ridden in cairts. Cairts can't fly and neither can trokes, lad. They stay on roads and paths."

"I hate paths. I want to fly like you."

At a loss for words, Rob looked at Maggie.

She shook her head and smiled, rocking a whimpering Annie in her arms. She wouldn't come to his rescue this time.

He sat on Robbie's bed, his precious laddie in his lap. "Someday you'll fly like Faither. But Faither didn't fly until he was a grown man, no' a bairn. Flying isn't easy. It takes training and you have to be verra big to do it."

Robbie keeked out and gave a skeptical look.

He needed to use an approach a bairn could understand. "Can Annie climb as high as you, or run as fast?"

A glimpse of blue eyes framed by swooping, black lashes. Then a frown. "She's too wee."

"Aye, she's too wee. Now, can you climb as high as Faither, or run as fast?"

A deeper frown.

Rob shook him lightly. "Well?"

"No." A whisper.

"Why no'?"

"I'm no' as big as you."

"Aye, you're no' as big as me." He turned Robbie so he could look him in the eyes. "You see, lad, there are certain things you can't do until you're big enough. Flying is one of those things. Do you understand?"

A reluctant nod.

"I'll tell you what." Rob tapped Robbie's chin and smiled. "When you're six years auld, I'll take you flying in my floatplane. How many fingers is that?"

"Don't know."

"'Tis this many." Rob held up six fingers. "How many fingers are you now?"

Three fingers shot into the air.

"Verra guid. So, in three more years you can fly with Faither."

"That's too long!" Both lips trembled and tears flooded his

flushed cheeks.

Rob held him close, kissed his forehead. "I know it seems like that. But just think, when you're as auld as Katie is now, you get to fly with Faither. All right?"

"My behoochie hurts." The lad sobbed.

"I'm sorry about that, but you mustn't ever try to fly your troke again, no' ever." Rob carried Robbie into the living room, squeezing Maggie's arm when they passed. This was only the beginning. Rob wanted to carry his lad to the ends of the earth, anywhere to protect him from the agony and ecstasy that lay ahead. He knew exactly how his son felt—the frustration, excitement, longing too deep to voice. Robbie had been bitten by the flying bug and, like his faither, he wouldn't be satisfied until he was soaring free in the vast, unlimited sky.

Chapter Twenty-Eight

Maggie snuggled Annie in her lap, listening to the raucous laughter coming from the bathing room. Robbie's first shower, and from his reaction, he'd never be satisfied with a bath again. She nuzzled Annie's neck, inhaling her clean scent, remembering Robbie's dirt-smeared face, hands, and clothes when he held a large tattie Rob forked up.

What a lovely Sabbath een. An early tea. Rob pulling late carrots, harvesting cabbages and the last of the tatties from their garden. Robbie crowing with delight as he placed each new trophy in the straw-lined storage pit. There'd be no lack of fresh vegetables this winter.

She tried a deep breath. Impossible with her lass's weight pressing on her growing belly. Only three more months and Rob would have his new bairnie to cuddle.

The bathing room door crashed open, and Robbie dashed to her rocker, towel wrapped at his waist, face wrapped in a smile. "I took a shower with Faither!" he shouted, shaking her arm and hopping from foot to foot. "'Twas fun."

"So you're a big lad now." Maggie patted his bottom. "Into the bedroom. Your nightclothes are 'neath your pillow."

He grabbed Shep's ruff and pulled him to his feet.

The dog yawned, stretched, left his favourite spot on the hearth rug, and trotted after Robbie.

"Faither says to no' have a keek till he cleans up the water," Robbie said over his shoulder. A husky laugh. "We made a rare midden."

His door slammed, startling Annie from a light sleep. The lassie smiled, blew a saliva bubble, and closed her eyes again, long lashes sweeping her rosy cheeks.

"I'll take the lass to her bed." Rob leaned over, smelling of heather soap and that man-scent she so luved, and brushed his lips across Maggie's cheek.

She felt a need to set those dimples beside his lips dancing. "But you've a midden to wipe up."

No' only the dimples danced. The green flecks in his eyes

sparkled to the same lively tune.

She caught her breath, watched his braw face come closer. A flush warmed her body.

"Later, lass. Much later."

She drowned in the depth of his voice, rode the swells of anticipation. His face filled the space before her eyes, blurred.

Lips moved on hers, soft with longing, deep with luve, ripe with promise.

Hugh rapped on Elspeth's door. He rocked on his feet, impatient to share a blether with his dearest friend. How could so much happen in less than a week?

The merchant ship carrying the Proctors' belongings had arrived the very day their house was finished. He himself had helped—och, no' loading or carrying anything, but he had unpacked books and placed them on shelves in Stu's office. So many books, on so many subjects. An interest in higher mathematics was understandable, but dog-eared copies of Goethe, Plato, Virgil, Dante's *Divine Comedy*, Bunyan's *Pilgrim's Progress*, Milton's *Paradise Lost*? Even volumes of poetry by Anne Bradstreet, Keats, Wordsworth, Ralph Waldo Emerson, the complete works of William Shakespeare, and a new-looking collection by Robert Burns.

"Stu has a fine library," he told Elspeth after bringing her up to date on all that had happened. "'Tis obvious he's well-educated."

"That doesn't surprise me." Elspeth's lined face softened into a smile. "I'm thinking that entire family realizes the importance of reading. Brenna's far above average for an upper primary student."

Hugh sipped his coffee. "Any ideas about how we can finance an academy?"

"No' a one that will work. But the council hasn't given up yet."

"I hope no'. I want you to know I'm prepared to offer my time as headmaster."

A sharp clack of china as Elspeth set her teacup into its saucer. "Och, Hugh, you have no time for that."

But he longed to stretch young minds, to make them eager to go beyond their classwork and seek the thoughts, the words, the genius God had given the human mind. "I'll make time. And I've decided to turn over my visiting to the Women's Aid Society—no' carrying the lesson to those who can't attend kirk, as I'll still tend to that. Just the times I drop in for a blether. But I've been doing less and less of it these past few years. The Lord seems to be leading me down other paths—like the academy."

"But your studying. 'Tis too important to skimp on that."

"Och, I've no intention of ever cutting back on studying the Word. But I do that best late at night when I've no interruptions. 'Tis guid I've no family. Wouldn't be fair to them with me up half the night with my nose in a Hebrew, Greek, or Aramaic translation—another example of our Lord's luving omniscience."

Her faded blue gaze seemed to turn inward, as though looking for a comparison in her own life. Surely she wouldn't have far to look. If she had been blessed with a husband, bairns, grandbairns, even great-grandbairns by now, how much time would she have lost on her knees in prayer, how many lives would not have been changed by practical advice gleaned from her long, sometimes arduous journey on earth? Like he, she had filled the void left by no family to nurture by giving her heart to the few she trusted to treat it gently.

Her head snapped erect, gaze pinning him. "Then, 'tis time we prayed together. Somewhere, in God's perfect plan, there must be a place for an academy on Innisbraw." Her eyes regained their sparkle. "You'll make a fine headmaster."

Rob threw down his pencil and pushed back from his desk. No use trying to work on that list of orders for Stu until he faced the idea he'd been wrestling with for several weeks. He, Den, and the Proctor family—with the exception of young Chris—were all Americans by birth, but they only celebrated Christmas and Ne'ers, holidays recognized in most of the world.

He rubbed a hand across his face. Why couldn't he get the idea of celebrating Thanksgiving out of his mind? His background in celebrations of any kind was meagre.

Orphanages had no money to spend on special holidays.

Birthdays? Never mentioned—but mebbe that was understandable—too many foundlings with unknown birth dates. Halloween? A pagan ritual to be avoided. Christmas? A delicious cup of cocoa with a marshmallow melting on top—and a reading of the virgin birth from the Bible. New Year's? Ignored.

But Thanksgiving? The only day out of the year when the tantalizing aroma of turkey, dressing, and gravy drifted from the kitchen, up the stairwell, and into his room, bringing spurts of saliva to his mouth. Aye, it was always provided by charity, but that didn't affect his appetite. One memorable year, Missus Pointer, the director's wife, made apple pies.

With the first bite, tart, spicy juice spilled over his tongue, the buttery crust crumbling between his teeth. He'd been at least ten, old enough to set an example of table manners for the younger kids. But when every tiny, treasured bite was only a memory, he swiped a finger across his plate and sucked the last bit of sweetness into his mouth.

Missus Pointer joined the angels in heaven only months later. At her funeral, the cook, a kind, yet formidable woman with a huge bosom and stiff chin hairs, revealed the secret of "The Missus's" famous apple pie. No apples. Just buttery crackers.

As an adult, every time Rob tasted real apple pie, the first bite disappointed. Missus Pointer must have taken the recipe with her.

Rob grabbed his A-2 jacket and bolted from his office. Thinking about all that food had set his stomach growling. A bowl or twa of Paddy's tattie bree would go down a treat, but—his steps slowed.

The Proctors were having a wee party at their new house the een. Nothing special, Stu had stressed, just sweetenins, tea and coffee, and a chance to blether with Brenna watching the bairns.

And no' staring at me. He smiled. What better opportunity to scratch this itch that was driving him crazy?

"I like the thought of celebrating an American holiday." Stu waved his drink at Rob. "The Fourth of July would be a wee bit oot of line in Great Britain, but I think a day of thanksgiving would be grand. Are you thinking of the fourth Thursday in November?"

Rob leaned back and scanned the neat, orderly bookshelves lining Stu's home office. Orderly mind, orderly surroundings. "Aye. Why no'?"

"With turkey and all the trimmings?" Den licked his lips.

"I wouldn't go that far. For one thing, I don't know where we could find a turkey."

Den gulped down the last of his drink. "You may have to come up with one. What's Thanksgiving withoot turkey?"

"How about roast chicken?" Stu asked. "I haven't had time to build our coop, but you both have chickens."

"You kill one of Maggie's laying hens and she'll roast you for supper." Rob snorted. "You know she only raises extra hens so she can make bree. Besides, some Americans don't eat turkey. Some have gammon—ham to you, Stu—or even roast beef or lamb."

"We could get a large beef roast from Alec." Den's blue eyes glittered.

Rob groaned. "My stomach's starting to growl, and I had supper only twa hours ago. What say we ask our wives what they think? After all, they'll be doing the cooking."

Stu gathered the empty cups and lined them up neatly on his desk. "Why did you choose Thanksgiving, Rob?"

"The main reason was to go back to the original idea of the holiday—being thankful." No' a lie, exactly, but the buried memory that had finalized his idea was his alone. "I'm thinking we could ask others to come as well. If we use our living room and borrow your dining room tables, we should have room for several more families."

"Use our living room for what?" Maggie asked from the doorway.

"'Tis time for dessert?" Den's tongue slicked his lips again. "My Fern brought sticky toffee pudding."

All three wives were delighted with the idea, though it being on a Thursday dimmed their enthusiasm.

"What about your men at the shed, Rob? Are you going to give them the day off?" Maggie asked.

"And the infirmary? John can't just no' show up for his patients," Fern reminded him.

"Don't forget the bairns," Jill said. "Katie and Brenna have school that day."

All were legitimate arguments. "Then, how about moving it to the fourth Sabbath in November? That would take care of everything."

Stu pulled out his wallet and extracted a pocket calendar. "This year, that would be the twenty-eighth. Any reason that wouldn't work?"

Maggie turned to Jill. "Since you're the only American woman here, you should be in charge of the menu. You can run ideas past Fern and me to see if there's a problem with finding something." She blew Rob a kiss. "I think this is a grand idea. Our bairns need to celebrate their entire heritage, no' just a part of it."

"I'd be happy to handle the menu." Jill hugged Maggie. "Then you and Fern can come up with a guest list and mebbe some decorations."

Fern grabbed Maggie and Jill and herded them toward the kitchen. "Katie and Brenna can help with a lot of things too."

Den poked Rob in the ribs. "You just scored a touchdown, bucko."

Maggie and Fern narrowed the guest list to close friends and family. John and Calum were invited, as were Elspeth, Hugh, Graham and Rinait, Alec and Morag, Angus and Flora, Sim and Edert, Malcolm, Tormad and Anna and their Kaitlin, and Mark and Susan Ferguson and their wee lassie, Sorcha. All received invitations designed and handmade by Brenna and Katie.

"Be grateful the island folk are closemouthed," Maggie told Rob the Friday evening before their holiday. "I'd hate to have hurt feelings because we didn't include someone."

"I've never seen so much visiting going on between you, Fern, and Jill." Rob waited until she had finished a row of knitting before he picked her up and settled her on his lap. "Surely one dinner can't be keeping you so busy."

She placed the yarn and needles on the table and molded her body against his. "There's so much to do, and with Fern working most of every day, we have to use part of the eens to make certain we don't forget anything."

"How can you forget what food you'll be cooking?"

If that didn't sound just like an ignorant man. "No' just the food, though that's taken a lot of planning. 'Tis a guid thing we've had three weeks to get ready. Anna ordered evaporated milk, a bag of milled flour, and sugar for her store. And Jill's mither sent a box with a jar of sweet pickles, tins of olives, yams, pumpkin, spices, and pie tins." She laughed and poked his thigh. "You should have seen Fern's face when she saw those tins of olives. She's never tasted them."

Long fingers gently tweaked her ribs. "Sounds like an Innisbraw lass who whispered the same thing to me in the chow hall at Edenoaks."

She wrinkled her nose. "And I remember an American lad who'd never tasted haggis, partan bree, cullin skink, or even clootie dumplings."

"I ken when I've been bested. Truce, luve. What else has you so busy?"

"Decorations."

"For Thanksgiving?"

"Of course. Brenna and Katie have been busy colouring and cutting oot paper leaves, turkeys, and something Jill called pilgrim hats. She showed them how to stick them together using flour thinned with water for paste."

His deep chuckle tickled her back. "So that's why Katie's been pestering Den to tell her about those 'redskin guests' at the first pilgrim's dinner. He pumped me for everything I remembered studying in school."

Maggie turned and threw her arms around his neck. "Och, luve, this is a tradition that will enrich our bairns' lives. They need a part of their American heritage celebrated. 'Twas a grand idea."

The kitchens in the three homes were redolent with mouth-watering aromas all day Saturday. Rob, Den, and Stu had dinner at the howff so they wouldn't interrupt the flow of baked pies, rolls, and sweets being produced in amazing quantities.

Six pumpkin pies sat on the bunker when Rob walked into the kitchen that night. "I think I died and went to heaven." He leaned over and smelled one. At least it was certain not to be another disappointing apple pie. "Mmm, guid. I'm glad Jill thought of pumpkin pies. I'd disremembered that's what most people serve on Thanksgiving."

Maggie laughed and made a face. "You forgot the sweetenins? A likely story." She put toasted cheese and skirlie on the table. "Nowt fancy the night, luve. I'm all cooked oot."

"How about if I just eat whatever I like?" He nibbled on her earlobe. "I'll start with this sweet morsel."

She returned his hug before pulling away. "The chef's no' on the menu if you want your dinner the morra."

He smoothed damp tendrils of hair from her forehead. "You look stone-tired, luve. This has been too much for you."

"Away with ye. I've learned so much and we've had a grand time. However, I wouldn't turn down a wee backrub later this een."

"You've got it."

John arrived early the next afternoon. What better time to spend with his grandbairns? He scooped Annie into his arms and held tight to Robbie's hand as they stood against the wall, watching Rob, Den, Stu, and Calum come through the front door, laden with twa pans of roasted beef joints, bowls of mashed tatties, gravy, and candied yams.

Robbie launched into a loud protest about his bedroom being full of living room furniture. His nattering turned to wide-eyed amazement when Brenna and Katie scattered colored leaves and pilgrim hats across the tablecloths.

Mark and Susan were the first guests to arrive, soon followed by Hugh.

Annie spotted wee Sorcha. “Doon, Grandfava. Doon!” The second John set her down, she ran to Sorcha, touching her black curls and fingering her sweater, embroidered with frolicking lambs. “Lammies,” she said, smiling at Susan.

“Aye, lass, lammies.” Susan patted her other knee, and Annie climbed into her lap.

“Bairnie and lammie.”

Susan’s soft laugh encouraged her own lassie to reach out to this interloper who shared her mother’s embrace. “Ba,” Sorcha said, smile so wide her four teeth sparkled in the light.

What a bonnie picture that makes. The black-haired, blue-eyed lassie and our own Annie with her long, light-brown curls and soft hazel eyes. But where had Robbie gone off to?

John checked the bathing room, Rob and Maggie’s bedroom, Maggie’s weaving room, and Annie’s room before eyeing Robbie’s closed door. Of course, wee skellum. He eased the door open and peeked in. He clamped his hand over his mouth and retreated, pulling Hugh to his side. “Take a keek,” he whispered, stifling a laugh.

Hugh leaned inside, before ducking out again. He shook his head, grin as broad as John’s.

Rob had exchanged greetings with guests and hung coats and jackets in the closet, while the women had all bustled off to help put the rest of the food on the table: home-canned peas, cabbage slaw, small bowls of olives and sweet pickles, plates of butter, jars of bramble jam, pots of heather honey, and pitchers of milk.

Elspeth had sat in front of the fireplace, telling the bairns a story that compared the lives of the American Colonists with the earliest settlers on Innisbraw. “So you see,” she concluded as coffee, tea, and milk were poured, “the story of the first Thanksgiving in America and our own colonists is no’ so different. All were brave, resourceful people. We have much to be thankful for. All our forebears persevered through so many hardships.”

On Maggie’s signal, Rob called everyone to the table. At last, after much jockeying by all to read the names printed on the paper turkeys, Annie was lifted into her highchair, Sorcha settled into Susan’s lap, and everyone else stood behind their designated chairs—save twa. Where were Robbie and Chris—and Shep?

The lads must have sneaked ootside with the dog in all the excitement.

Rob held up his hand to quiet the blethering. “We’re missing

Robbie and Chris. Did anyone see them sneak off with Shep?"

John tapped Rob's shoulder. "They're in the lad's bedroom. You and Maggie should follow me—and Jill and Stu."

The parents joined John. They opened Robbie's bedroom door and stepped quietly inside.

Robbie and Chris rocked side by side in Rob and Maggie's chairs, facing away from the door, while Shep lolled on his back in the middle of the bed.

"It's been a midden of a day," Robbie said, shaking his head. "I wonder if those twa boats will ever be built."

Young Chris nodded. "Midden," he echoed.

"How was your day, luve?"

Maggie gripped Rob's hand.

The hairs on his arms stood on end. Just the right inflection, caring and soft. But how many conversations between him and Maggie had Robbie overheard? What would his lad say next? Afraid to find out, he cleared his throat. "If you twa are ready, dinner's on the table."

Robbie jerked and leaped up. "'Tis about time." He patted his belly. "I'm gleg as a gled."

"Gleg as gled," Chris parroted, waving his short legs to reach the floor.

Certain he had just averted major embarrassment, Rob pulled Shep from the bed and ushered everyone back to their seats. He smiled at the clever seating arrangements. Katie and Kaitlin were sat side by side, Annie's highchair was next to John, and Robbie and young Chris sat on stacked books between Calum and Edert, twa of their favourite folk. His smile faded. It might be proper putting Maggie, as hostess, at one end of the long, joined tables and him, as host, at the other, but he wanted to squeeze her hand or finger a curl when the need overcame him, no' send a smile over twenty feet away. He returned to his chair and nodded at Elspeth standing to his right, and to Hugh, at Maggie's right.

Hugh smiled, brown eyes twinkling, round cheeks red as a summer sunset. "What a grand idea this was," he said heartily. "Shall we bow our heads in prayer?"

Everyone followed his lead.

"Our gracious Heavenly Faither, we gather together the day with grateful hearts filled with thanksgiving. Ye have blessed every family present at this table. Ye have poured out Your blessings upon our entire island. Prosperity has replaced poverty and a place of work has busied idle hands. Let us never forget where these blessings come from. The Psalmist David said it best when he wrote, 'Let us come before his presence with thanksgiving, let us make a joyful noise unto him with psalms.' We ask Your special blessing upon the hands which have prepared this food, and upon the food itself. Help us to be as faithful to Ye as Ye are to us. In Jesus's name we pray, amen."

Chapter Twenty-Nine

Den added his hearty "amen" to those around the table. If he had to put a name to his feelings, *contented* might do it. Yikes, Den Anderson, content to live on a primitive piece of rock miles off the coast of Scotland? Next, he'd take to smoking one of those cuttie pipes and puffing away, staring into space and counting blessings.

Fern's slim fingers pressed a napkin over his thigh and stroked his hand, filling him with a glow warmer than peat embers in the hearth. Aye, blessings. He had a wife he loved so much, the thought of her took his breath, the sight of her sent him soaring higher than any bird. And he had a daughter with a bright, inquisitive mind, copper curls, and dimples in her bonnie cheeks—who gifted him with her love every day—and called him "Faither."

If only the Lord would give them their own child, lad or lass, black hair or red, a buffoon like him or calm and level-headed like Fern. Didn't matter.

Fern watched Sorcha's wee, dimpled hands clutching her mother's shoulder.

Don't give up, luve. Look how long it took Rob to have his prayers for a family answered. And us with a bonnie lass already.

Fern looked back at him and nudged his arm. "Head oot of the clouds. This is heavy, luve."

He shot her a grin and took the bowl of tatties from her.

Katie tapped his knee. "We're ready." She giggled, cheeks red, dimples deep.

Den half-stood and cleared his throat.

Bowls and platters were set down and the happy buzz of conversation died.

"Folk, some of our lads and lasses would like to show you a Thanksgiving tradition from America." He sat down and nodded at Katie.

Small hands shot up around the table.

Fingers waved.

Each tipped with a shiny, black olive.

Even Annie and Sorcha sported an olive on each forefinger.

Susan whipped out her napkin and captured Sorcha's olive

before it disappeared into her open mouth. "No, no, lassie. You'll choke."

Robbie crowed, young Chris laughed so hard he fell off his chair, and Katie and Kaitlin giggled, their blue eyes glistening like newborn stars.

The adults clapped and laughed.

"I wondered what them shiny black thingummys were guid for," Tormad said, reaching for the lamb.

Anna elbowed him, but nobody took affront at the good-natured, honest comment.

Den leaned over and kissed Fern's cheek. Blessings. Rob wasn't the only one who'd gained a large family on Innisbraw.

Plate piled high, Rob looked at the small slice of lamb nestled between peas and slaw. His antenna quivered.

Sure enough, Maggie was watching, a tiny smile tilting her lips. Since she'd done the roasting, he'd best get it over with.

He cut off a piece, put it in his mouth, and waited to quell the gag reflex sure to come. But wait—this was tender, no' tough—and sweet, no' rank like mutton. He swallowed, sent Maggie a thumbs-up, and reached for another bite.

The conversation around the tables soon centered on the changes to Innisbraw.

"As a member of the Island Council, I have to tell you, we've never had to call so many meetings," Alec said.

Elspeth, Morag, and Tormad nodded.

"We have requests for building sites almost every week, and our store needs to expand. If all this building keeps up, the island's men are going to be hard-pressed to find the time for their own crofting and other turns, what with all the stone work they're doing."

Rob nodded at Den.

He wiped his lips on his napkin and stood. "The partners in the Boatworks are thinking of expanding into another business. There are some fine craftsmen on Innisbraw, and plumbers and roofers." Den's words flowed like water over polished pebbles. "We're thinking of starting a construction business to put even more lads and men to work." Den sat down amidst a flurry of conversation around the tables.

Elspeth tapped her spoon against her teacup. "'Tis a grand idea. This way, the cottages will no' go up shilly-shally, but the building can be planned and supervised."

The seed had been planted. Rob could water it. "We've one lad in particular on the boatbuilding crew who would make an excellent building supervisor. Of course, we'll have to replace him on our crew, but after the trawler's finished, I think we can free him up to help head this new enterprise. His name's Paul Murray."

"We all know the lad," Hugh said. "He's a fine, upstanding young man."

"What about the stone work?" Angus asked. "Would that be included?"

A question Rob had expected. "No' under our business. But we think there should be some sort of organization and payment. Like Alec said, the island's men are being stretched thin with all the new building."

Alec scratched his chin. "The organization, I admit, is needed. But it's always been a tradition here on Innisbraw for the men to erect the walls of a cottage with no thought of payment. I don't want to see that change."

There were many nods around the table.

No surprise there, either. "Then that tradition won't change." Rob rubbed the side of his nose. "We'll just have to arrange the building schedules around lambing and calving season and, of course, peat casting, planting, and harvest time."

Hugh turned to John, who was sitting next to him. "And speaking of work, how is the infirmary?"

John's broad smile tilted his eyeglasses. "Verra guid. The way things are going, Fern's running her legs off. We'll soon need another full-time nurse. Maggie, here, will have her hands full with three small bairns, so it isn't fair to ask her to help at the infirmary anymore."

"Or acceptable," Rob said quickly.

John nodded.

"You did a fine turn setting the broken arm of one of our lads," Tormad said. "I've even been able to keep him on the crew."

"So, how's fishing?" Stu asked. "It seemed you were gone to sea all season."

Tormad nodded at Calum. "This lad here has made some changes in the way we set our nets—something he picked up from the crew of a Danish trawler. What with the guid weather and calm seas, we've never had a better season. We even had a record herring catch."

"You'll have to let me in on your secret." Mark grimaced. "We had our best summer yet, but no' much herring."

Maggie made more tea and coffee while the women cleared the table and sliced the pumpkin pie, clootie dumplings, and sticky toffee pudding. She smiled to herself when Den was the only adult who reached for the pudding. He'd often told her nothing could compare to the rich, dense taste of dates and melted caramel. Her Rob's hand hesitated over the clootie dumpling before reaching for the pie. Och, these men and their eating habits.

The pumpkin pie was an instant hit.

"I'm thinking this should be included in our ceilidh celebrations," Elspeth said, after eating every bite. "'Tis too guid no' to share with all our folk."

Even Wee Annie, who was not normally a sweet-eater, opened her mouth eagerly for more.

"We're going to have to find a source for canned pumpkin," Maggie said. "No' only is it grand tasting, but 'tis a healthy sweetenin for the bairns."

"I'll see if we can find a supplier," Anna said. "And those olives were a marvel. The general store could use some supplies you wouldn't normally find on Lewis or Harris."

"I was delighted to hear you already have to expand." Morag reached across the table to pat Anna's hand. "Your store was an idea too long in coming. I ran out of wheat grain for my flour the other day and didn't have to make a trip to the mainland. Are you planning on stocking more cotton and thread for sewing, also?"

"Aye. And needles and scissors, and even some of those knitting needles that let you knit in the round."

"Och, what will they think of next!" Elspeth laid a hand on her cheek.

Rob handed out the men's and aulder lads' jackets and herded them to the front entry, while the women busied themselves washing and drying the dishes. Brenna had been staring at him all afternoon, making him feel like a man walking a tightrope over the English Channel seeded with German mines.

His concern with Brenna's behavior pressed into the background as soon as Malcolm spoke.

"I'm thinking of retiring. The *Sea Rouk*'s worn oot, and I'm too auld to think about buying a new boat."

"But what about the post?" Alec asked. "You've done a grand turn, making sure we get it every twa days."

"That's up to the government. 'Tis about time they added our post to that going on the daily steamer to Barra. If no', I'm certain they'll find someone else who will take the turn seriously."

Angus's face creased. "What about Sim, here? He'll be oot of a turn."

Sim darted Rob an anxious glance. "I was thinking of joining the boatbuilding crew. There's more of a future in it than fishing."

"We can use you, lad," Rob said. "Any time." He turned to Malcolm. "Is there owt we can do to help the *Sea Rouk* last a while longer? Some refitting or keel work?"

"Thank ye, but no. I'll take her as far as she can go, but it won't be much longer. I'm thinking early spring should do it."

"Is she still safe in high seas?" Den asked. "This mild weather won't last much longer."

"Aye, for a time. My engine's still guid. To tell the truth, I'm more spent than she is."

"I've been telling you to cut back for years," John said.

An undercurrent of tension ran between the two men.

A rare scowl darkened Malcolm's rugged face. "There's nowt wrong with me, John. I'm just ready to settle down on land. My cottage needs some work, and that'll keep me busy a guid long time."

The holiday season was soon upon them. Once again, Hugh opened the kirk hall for a 'Ne'ers Eve, island-wide Hogmanay ceilidh. Anna made good on her promise and stocked several cases of canned pumpkin and evaporated milk—a miracle with rationing still so punitive—plus cinnamon, nutmeg, and ground cloves.

Jill's mother sent another box of metal pie tins, an unheard of luxury in the UK.

The island folk gathered around the refreshment table, eager to taste this treat from America. The shiny new pie tins, the recipes Brenna had printed laboriously by hand, and the pies themselves were soon gone.

Rob kept a close eye on Maggie. Due to give birth in a little over a week, she shouldn't be overextending herself, holiday season or no'.

"I'm no' an invalid," she grumbled as he bundled her into Alec's cairt for the ride home. "We only danced one strathspey."

"And I'm thinking that was one too—"

The siren high on Innis Fell wailed its warning.

"I'll see Maggie home safely, and Morag will stay with her and the bairns," Alec said, pressing Rob's shoulder. "Godspeed."

As the rescue crew poured out of the hall, Rob kissed Maggie. "I'd rather you didn't turn on the radio the night," he said. "You need to go to bed."

She clung to him. "I'll be fine." Tears shone in her eyes. "I need another kiss."

He kissed her deeply, then rubbed the tip of her nose with his. "No need to worry. The weather's still guid and 'tis most likely another tow, but pray anyway. We can always use your prayers, and it helps you through the waiting." He pressed her fingers. "Promise you'll call your faither if you feel any pains."

"I promise. Godspeed, luve."

Rob raced after Den and the lads, down the path toward the pier.

The moment he reached the *Maggie*, Rob radioed the shed. "What do we have?" he asked James, who was manning the radio.

"'Tis an assist call from Barra Rescue. The last ferry to run this year has collided with a ... *trawler*." His voice broke. "'Twas Malcolm's *Sea Rouk*, Rob. This is a bad one."

Chapter Thirty

Rob donned his wetsuit. His hands shook as he dialed the radio to the Barra Rescue frequency and hit Broadcast. "*Flora MacDonald*, *Flora MacDonald*, this is *Maggie*. Do you copy? Over."

"*Maggie*, this is *Flora MacDonald*. We read you loud and clear. Over."

"*Flora*, what are the coordinates of the rescue? Over."

"The coordinates are fifty-six-point-six degrees north by seven degrees west. They should have called you first because you're closer. We're still twenty-five to thirty minutes out."

Rob stuck a pin on the map, marking the coordinates. "Can you give me any details?"

"We called you the minute the ferry radioed her distress call. She hit the trawler *Sea Rouk* amidships about twenty minutes ago. Several people on the ferry's deck were knocked into the sea by the collision. The ferry, the *Lismore Lady*, is taking on water fast, but we don't know the condition of the *Sea Rouk* or her crew. The ferry's carrying about thirty-five passengers and its crew. Far as we can figure, there are five or six souls in the water now."

"Roger that. Any other rescue vessels responding?"

"We still have our old sister lifeboat, so she'll be there along with another out of Tiree, though it'll take her a while to arrive at the coordinates."

"What is the radio frequency for the ferry?"

After the *Flora* provided it, he asked, "Do you need any more information? Over."

"Negative. Just keep monitoring our frequency. I'll want to coordinate with you during the rescue. *Maggie*, oot."

"Understood. *Flora,* out."

Den gripped Rob's shoulder, face grim.

Rob nodded and dialed the ferry's radio frequency. "*Lismore Lady*, *Lismore Lady*, this is the Innisbraw Rescue Boat, *Maggie*. We're only ten minutes from your position. Do you have your lifeboats in the water? Over."

"*Maggie*, this is *Lismore Lady*. We're readying our passengers, and are preparing to launch the minute we can. We have four lifeboats. Over."

"Copy that, *Lismore Lady*. Have you picked up the people knocked overboard? Over."

"With the exception of one crew member we canna find. Over."

Rob took a deep breath, felt it explode in his lungs. "Have you picked up any souls from the *Sea Rouk*? Over."

"Negative. We must have about cut her in half, considering the damage we received. She sank immediately. There's still some debris in the water, but we haven't seen any sign of survivors. Over."

No sign of survivors. Rob struggled to speak. "I ... read you. Make sure your passengers and crew have life vests and keep evacuating them. We'll sound our siren when we see you. Over."

"Pray God you arrive soon. Some of our folk need medical aid. Over."

"We'll be there in less than seven minutes. *Maggie*, oot."

"Thank ye. *Lismore Lady*, oot."

Rob sat back and put his head in his hands. No survivors from the *Sea Rouk*. He shook himself and turned the helm over to Neil so he could concentrate. There was debris in the water, so there was still a slim chance Malcolm and Sim were alive. *Och, Faither, help them find a plank, a life ring, even the wheelhouse door to cling to.*

A few minutes later, Neil sounded the siren and the ferry's deep-throated blast responded.

The crew ran from the cabin.

Rob activated the search lights and cautioned Neil to stay clear of the ferry. "She's so big. If she goes down, she could suck things close-by down with her. Get on the radio and warn the ferry's captain to have his lifeboats put as much distance as they can between themselves and the ferry. Also, have him ready to transport his injured. We'll launch the inflatable."

"Aye, Commander."

Rob eyed the damage to the ferry.

Several feet of the prow were mangled, and she was listing as if she was still taking on water rapidly.

He ran outside where Den was in position at the port railing. "See owt?"

"Just some small debris. Nowt large enough to support a man." Den knuckled his eyes. "I'm afraid 'tis hopeless, Rob. Malcolm and Sim must've gone down with the boat."

Rob called to Artair and Neil to release the inflated life raft from the top of the cabin. "When you have her in the water, take her to the ferry and transport their injured. Don't take chances. If the ferry starts to go down, get oot of there fast."

They untied the clamps as he spoke.

Rob ran to the starboard side and scanned the water carefully.

Several crates bobbed on the surface, along with small pieces of planking. It had been well over forty minutes since the collision, far too long for a swimmer to stay alive in that icy water without a wetsuit.

But he couldn't give up the search. He raced into the cabin and returned with a hand-held search light. Making his way slowly along the railing, he scanned the sea for anything large enough to support a man.

What was that?

His heart lurched.

A wave pulsed under the debris. Only an empty crate. He inched his way around the *Maggie*'s deck.

Stopped suddenly.

Something there.

Large, but too far away to make out clearly. "Duncan," he called to the fantail. "Get up here and retrain that starboard spot farther oot."

A few moments later, the light's illumination extended farther.

Rob's heart pounded.

A large section of planking—with something on top.

"Den!" he shouted. "Over here!"

Den raced to his side.

Rob pointed. "Twa o'clock high. What do you see?"

Den focused his binoculars. "A piece of decking … with twa men lying on top!"

Rob turned to order the inflatable back, but it was already at the ferry's side. He grabbed Den's arm. "We're going in."

They raced to the fantail, tied their lifelines and slipped into their flippers.

"Matthew, get to the cabin and prepare to receive injured from the ferry," Rob ordered. "Have Paddy help you. Stephen, you and Duncan stay by these lines. Don't leave for any reason."

Rob and Den jumped into the water. They surfaced and both struck out toward the debris, dodging small planks, pieces of net, and a cushion from the wheelhouse.

Lord, let them both be alive and no' injured, please, Lord, alive and no' injured. Rob crested the top of a swell. Almost there, but the waves were carrying the section of decking away from him at an alarming rate. He reached out even farther and kicked his feet faster. His hand hit something hard. He grabbed it and raised his head.

They were almost out of range of the light. All he could see was the outline of two bodies lying on the planking he now grasped. He inched his way around the planks, praying they would hold together a while longer. When he reached the closest body, he reached out and touched a leg. Icy cold, it was, and didn't respond to his touch.

"Malcolm!" he panted. "Sim!"

No reply.

Den reached the opposite side.

"On you come, but verra carefully!" Rob shouted. "It's about to break up." He wanted to climb onto the planking, but knew it would never support his weight. He pulled on the pants leg.

Still no response.

Sirens wailed nearby. The *Flora MacDonald* and her sister lifeboat had arrived. They could help with the ferry's passengers, while he concentrated on saving Malcolm and Sim.

When Den joined him, he leaned in close. "We can't push this back to the *Maggie*. It's breaking up. We'll each take one man, and they'll have to pull us in. Get next to me and be ready to catch one when I tip the planks. I'll take the one in front of me, you take the other."

"I'm ready."

Rob eased his upper body onto the planking and the bodies slid closer. He grabbed a handful of clothing and pulled. The far planks broke off. He yanked as hard as he could with both hands. The weight of the man knocked them both underwater. He held his breath, pushed away a splintered piece of wood, took a firm hold under the man's arms, and kicked as hard as he could toward the surface. Rob placed his arm around the man's chest and pulled him close, keeping his face out of the water.

It had to be Malcolm—too bulky to be Sim. Den must have the lad.

The planks drifted off in the waves.

Rob used his left hand to take the slack out of his lifeline and, when it was taut, gave three hard pulls.

It immediately tightened around his waist.

He fought to keep Malcolm's face out of the water as they were being pulled to the *Maggie*. As they neared the fantail, Rob's right arm cramped. He tightened his grip and looked up to see Duncan's arms reaching out. He wrapped both arms around Malcolm and lifted him up as high as possible.

Duncan struggled before finally pulling the skipper up onto the fantail deck.

Den appeared at Rob's side, holding tightly to Sim.

The lad's eyes were closed, and he was a dreadful grey colour.

Rob helped Den lift him into Stephen's waiting arms before they climbed the short ladder to the fantail deck.

"I need help down here," Duncan called to the main deck.

Paddy climbed down the ladder. The two men hoisted Malcolm up the ladder, where Matthew and Artair waited with a stretcher. Paddy climbed down again and put Sim over his shoulder, scaled the ladder, and disappeared into the cabin.

Rob kicked off his flippers and forced himself to climb to the main deck. His heart pounded in his throat. *Please, Faither, let them be alive.* When he reached the top, he pulled off his hood and made his way quickly into the cabin.

Matthew bent over Malcolm with a stethoscope. He straightened when Rob reached his side. "I'm sorry, Commander. He didn't make it."

Rob went to his knees.

Malcolm's face was dusky blue, his eyes slightly open, but he was long past seeing anything on this earth.

Hot tears scalded Rob's cheeks as he held the body of the first of the Innisbraw folk to befriend him. Instant pictures of a robust, grinning Malcolm paraded before his eyes. There was no way he could recall all this friend had done for him over the years. The list was too long. His shoulders shook as he tried to close Malcolm's eyes—he couldn't.

"He's been gone too long," Matthew said, voice hoarse.

Stephen called to Matthew. "I need you over here."

Matthew jumped to his feet and went to Sim's stretcher.

The lad was choking and vomiting up seawater.

"Turn him on his side," Matthew ordered. He stripped Sim's wet sweater and shirt from his body. "Help me cut off his breeks," he called to Rob.

Rob forced himself to leave Malcolm's side and take the scissors Matthew was holding. He soon had the sodden pants off, and they covered the lad quickly with the blankets Den shoved into their hands.

Rob uncovered one arm and massaged it briskly, and Den did the same with the other arm.

After a few minutes, Sim shivered. His teeth chittered.

They covered his arms and massaged his legs.

Sim moaned and thrashed, but they didn't try to stop him. Any kind of movement helped circulate the lad's blood.

Matthew moved away and Rob took stock of the situation.

Every stretcher in the cabin had an injured person on it. All the stretcher holders were full and several stretchers were on the floor.

He might be needed elsewhere, but he'd stay where he was until Matthew asked for him. They had to pull Sim through this. They had to.

The lad retched again.

Rob picked him up, laid him on his stomach on the deck, and knelt, straddling Sim's legs. Den knelt in front of him to monitor Sim's pulse as Rob pressed his hands on Sim's sides, just below his rib cage. He pressed and released, time and time again until the lad quit vomiting seawater.

Den tapped his arm. "Pulse is stronger."

Rob and Den lifted Sim onto the stretcher again and worked for over half an hour, briskly massaging his limbs.

At last, his breathing eased.

Rob grabbed a stethoscope and listened to the lad's stomach and lungs.

No liquid sounds. The heartbeat, though slow, no longer fluttered.

"I think he'll make it," he told Den.

"Commander!" Neil called from his position at the helm. "Barra Rescue wants to talk to you."

Rob motioned to Den to stay put, made his way forward, and took the mike from Neil's hand. "This is Rob. Over."

"How many injured do you have aboard? Over."

Rob counted. "We have six injured and twa near-drownings, plus one fatality. Over."

"Copy that. We need to put a few of the ferry passengers from the lifeboats aboard your boat. Both our boats and Tiree's are filled to capacity. Can you handle three more?"

"We can, but make it quick. Some of these people need to reach a doctor fast."

"I'm sending our inflatable with three elderly passengers, all complaining of chest pains. They're on their way now. Over."

"Copy that. We've been busy over here. What's the condition of the ferry?"

"Still afloat, though listing badly. Thank God for calm seas. And thanks for the assist, Rob. I'm sorry about the *Sea Rouk*. I just heard she's one of yours."

A cramp knifed Rob's belly. "We saved the deckhand but the skipper's gone. We'll be underway the minute those last three are aboard. *Maggie*, oot."

"Godspeed, Rob. *Flora MacDonald*, out."

Rob couldn't say Malcolm was dead. He couldn't even acknowledge that to himself. Somehow "gone" was less final. He'd deal with it later, when lives didn't depend on his clear thinking. He ordered Paddy and Stephen to help the new passengers aboard and got a triage report from Matthew: several broken bones, one of them among those who had nearly drowned. Sim and the lad with the splinted leg would be put in the first cairt.

Paddy reported that the new passengers were aboard. The *Maggie* was out of stretchers, so Stephen issued blankets to the new arrivals and seated them on the floor of the cabin. Matthew examined all three and reported they were fit to begin the trip back to Innisbraw. He then inserted saline drips in each of their forearms.

Rob keyed his mike to Broadcast. "Innisbraw Control, this is the *Maggie*. Do you read me, James? Over."

"This is Innisbraw Control, Rob. Are you starting back?"

"Aye. We have six injured, some with broken bones and twa near-drownings. Also, three aulder passengers with histories of heart problems. We'll need at least six cairts."

"Roger that. We'll have Angus as lead cairt. He's got Feona in the traces, and he can take your near-drowning victims. We'll have five more cairts ready for the others."

"Tell Angus that Sim is one of the near-drownings, but he's responding well. And you'd better make that seven cairts. We have one fatality. We'll transport him last."

"Did you say fatality?"

Did Rob want to give Malcolm's name over the radio? But Maggie and the other islanders with radios couldn't pick up his transmission this far away, and James would likely telephone only Hugh.

He cleared his throat. "Aye. Malcolm ... Malcolm was gone before we arrived on the scene."

"Och, I'm sorry. He was a guid man."

Rob dropped his head for a moment.

"How long before you arrive?"

"About twenty-five minutes. *Maggie*, oot."

"We'll be ready. Control, oot."

Rob slumped in his seat, body numb, mind churning with memories so painful he gritted his teeth to keep from weeping. So many lost over the years—some his own crew members, others pilots he'd known for years. He'd thought that had stopped with the end of the war.

But it hadn't.

Who would be next? Elspeth? He ground his teeth so hard his jaw cramped.

Den?

Or ... Maggie?

He leaped up and raced out of the cabin, leaned over the railing, and retched. A gibbous moon flaunted its light over the waves, mocking his bleak, black thoughts. *Help me, Lord! Take these terrible thoughts away, please.*

Chapter Thirty-One

The *Maggie* pulled into her berth with a soft burble of dying engines. Rob quit the cabin and walked to the railing, gaze drawn to the folk lining the pier. The outside lights of the boatshed bathed both the pier and dock in a hazy, other-worldly glow, casting light and elongated shadows over the crowd. Stoic men scrubbed stubbled cheeks with calloused hands, and women held kerchiefs to their faces.

So everyone knew.

The heavy stone weighing on his heart shifted, recognized the luve that motivated these hard-working folk to leave their warm beds hours before dawn.

Den gripped Rob's arm. "The crew's readied the stretchers." His voice sounded hollow, bled of substance, the way Rob's bones felt.

Together, they lifted the railing and set the gangplank in place.

Flora rushed up as Sim's stretcher appeared. "He's doing fine, Flora," Matthew assured her, "but we want John to have a keek as quickly as possible."

She nodded and trotted beside the stretcher, one hand held out toward her eldest son, the other clutching a kerchief to her lips. Rinait, Graham, and Edert appeared at the end of the pier and joined the procession.

The second patient was carried out immediately, and both stretchers were loaded into Angus's cairt. It tore up the path and disappeared, swallowed by darkness.

The other survivors were transported in the next five cairts. No voices broke the stillness, only the soft snort of an impatient cuddy and the splash of the incoming tide against mussel-encrusted pilings.

When only Alec's cairt remained, Rob returned to the cabin, his legs obeying some involuntary command to move. He felt like one of those windup toys he'd seen in store windows when he was a lad—at the mercy of the one holding the key—except this one had thrown the key away. A familiar feeling. The same he'd had when he watched a plane go down, engulfed in flames, or the flight surgeon emerge from the operating room, shaking his head.

But Rob was no longer the group commander who'd climbed inside himself to hide from sorrow. He had to pull himself out of this miasma of grief and self-pity. Aye, self-pity—just like guilt—a destructive emotion inspired by the de'il to cripple humanity. A member of a large island family, he needed to be strong for those who suffered from the loss far more than he.

He squatted beside one stretcher handle and Paddy, Den, and Artair did so at the others. "On the count of three." His first words in almost an hour. Deep, steady, firm. "One, twa, three—lift."

They carried the stretcher bearing Malcolm's blanket-shrouded body off the dock and down the pier. Bunnets were swept off, heads bowed, and only an occasional sob pierced the pall of grief.

Hugh, who waited on the path, hurried forward and trotted to match their pace. "Courage."

His word of comfort echoed in Rob's mind before it was lost in the sound of footfalls on sand.

The four men lifted the stretcher into the cairt. Without a word, Rob, Den, and Hugh climbed in beside it. Malcolm would not take his last ride alone.

Paddy and Artair sat up front beside Alec.

The infirmary foyer hummed with activity. John was absent, but Maggie trotted from stretcher to stretcher, helping Matthew triage victims. Her red-rimmed eyes met Rob's for a second before turning to the grey blanket covering Malcolm. Her dark blue eyes filled with the grief of generations of Innisbraw women who welcomed home the bodies of those they luved.

James stepped forward and took Rob's place. "I'll take it from here, Commander. We know where to go."

Rob waited until the stretcher passed into the hall before taking Maggie into his arms.

She shivered.

He cradled her close. "You need to go home to bed, luve. We don't want our bairnie birthed this night." He kissed her cold lips and rested his forehead against hers. "Please, Maggie, let me take you home."

She clung to him, taking deep breaths. "In a minute. I'm almost through here, then I'll go. I promise." Wriggling from his arms, she turned to another patient.

He let her go. She needed the activity to get her mind off her loss. She had known and luved Malcolm all of her life. His grief must be miniscule when compared with hers.

A hand gripped his shoulder. "I need a strong man to help me set a broken leg." John's gaze was filled with purpose, yet dark with the same grief Rob had seen in Maggie's.

"Then Sim and the other lad are all right?"

"They're stable now. I have them in the same room, with Fern on duty. She'll let me know if their vitals change."

Rob helped at the infirmary until daybreak. The inside of his wetsuit was drenched with sweat, but there had been no time to go home to change. Matthew told him Maggie had left as soon as triage was finished, but Rob had been helping John, so he could only pray Morag was with her. He didn't want her alone now.

The first sun in weeks cast its cloud-smeared rays above the horizon as he made his way down the infirmary steps. How dare the cheerful sphere make an appearance on such a dreadful day?

John called his name, stopped him in mid-stride with a grasp of his arm. "'Tis guid I caught you up. I'll walk with you. There's something I want to tell you and Maggie."

The two men walked to the house in silence.

Maggie sat in her rocker in front of the fireplace, Morag beside her.

Rob bit back a protest. She should be in bed.

Both women rose as Rob and John stepped inside.

Maggie's eyes were so swollen, she must have been weeping for a long time. She came into Rob's arms with a cry.

He held her as tightly as he dared, rocking her back and forth. "I'm so sorry," he said, "so terribly sorry. He was gone ... long before we arrived."

Morag brushed tears from her cheeks and asked for John's help in gathering up Robbie, Annie, and Katie. "I'm going to take them home with me for a few hours. Maggie has agreed. She and Rob, Den and Fern, they need to sleep without interruption."

Maggie nestled into Rob's lap. So warm, his body.

He rocked slowly, wiped her face with her sodden kerchief, and caressed her hair and shoulders.

At last, her sobs diminished and she lay quietly against his chest, body exhausted, heart filled with a dull, throbbing ache. "He was too young." Her voice was so hoarse she barely recognized it. "He didn't even get to enjoy his auld age."

"I know, luve."

His deep voice, luve softening it to a whisper, echoed in her mind, easing for a moment the painful questions bombarding her thoughts. She rested, drawing strength from his soul, so entwined with hers.

John came back into the house after seeing Robbie and Annie and Katie off in Morag's cairt. Head bowed, steps slow, he took a place in front of the fire.

Maggie suddenly remembered that her faither and Malcolm were the same age, that they had grown up together. She wanted to cry at the depth of her faither's loss, but no more tears would come.

Rob had never seen John look so tired.

The doctor stood with his back to the fire, dark hollows beneath his eyes, and lines of fatigue and grief aging him far beyond his years. "I've something to say to the both of you." Voice thick with unshed tears. He cleared his throat. "Malcolm didn't drown. He died of coronary occlusion—a heart attack. That's most likely why the *Sea Rouk* was in the ferry lane. I'm certain he was dead for some time before the collision. There was no water in his lungs."

"A heart attack?" Rob shook his head. "He never mentioned having a bad heart."

John blew out a long sigh. "The same kind of massive heart attack killed his father at the age of forty-three. I've been trying to get Malcolm to slow down for years, but he always said life was for the living and death for the dying, and he wasn't about to get the twa mixed up." He ran a hand over his face. "He died doing what he luved. He didn't want to retire. He wanted to die exactly the way he did—at the wheel of the *Sea Rouk*."

"Thank Ye, Lord." Rob felt a knot in his chest relax. "I knew there'd be an inquiry, especially with a ferry involved. I didn't want Malcolm's reputation as a skipper dragged through the mud."

"It won't be."

John cupped his hand beneath Maggie's chin and looked into her eyes. "Will you be all right if I go now, lass?"

She nodded.

"Guid. Then I'll take my leave. I've patients to see to."

"How's Sim?" Rob said.

"He'll be fine. I'll keep him at least overnight to rule out pneumonia, then he can go home. You'll get your boatbuilder a bit earlier than you expected, Rob. Are you certain you can use him?"

"Absolutely."

"Guid. He'll need something to occupy his thoughts." The two men clasped hands silently before John quit the house.

Rob added peat to the fireplace and flicked the switch to heat the shower water. Maggie could slip and fall in the tub. When the water was hot, he undressed her, peeled off his wetsuit, and guided her into the shower, where he bathed her with care. Her body felt so cold, he directed the water on her while he soaped himself quickly, rinsed, and turned the water off. He blotted Maggie dry, wrapped her in a towel, and dried himself.

So quiet, she was.

His own heart must be shedding tears of blood, filling his chest, making each breath difficult. He led her into their bedroom, pulled back the quilts, and settled her into bed. After climbing in beside her, he pulled up the covers and cradled her cold flesh against his warm body. "We need to talk, luve. I know 'tis hard so soon, but we can't wait, for our bairnie could come any time." He buried his face in her hair. "Tell me what you're feeling, lass. Please."

A tremor ran through her body. "'Tis such a waste." A whisper raspy as a breeze scudding through tall girse. "He was such a guid man."

Rob ran his lips across her cheek. "He was that."

Icy fingers groped for his hand. "Why, Rob? Why did God allow this to happen?"

"We may never know." He laced his fingers through hers. "But we do know our Lord luves Malcolm even more than we do and welcomed him into heaven with open arms."

A tear slipped down her cheek, salting his lips. "I'll miss him so terribly. He was always there when I needed him."

"We'll all miss him."

She shivered and placed her leg over his. "That last time I brought you home on the *Sea Rouk*, he was such a strength. He didn't say much, but he was there, close by. I don't think I could have made it without him."

"He made me realize my flying experiences, guid and bad, were worth remembering. Did you know that?"

"No. When?"

"When those boxes arrived from Edenoaks, after I was invalided oot of the Air Forces. I wanted them pushed to the back of the infirmary storage and disremembered. Malcolm said we should drink a toast to those memories. It was then my heart started to heal, and I could begin to look back without regret."

A fleeting smile. "That sounds like Malcolm. Did you know he used to hold me on his lap when Mither died? He told me stories about when they were bairns and young lads and lasses and even had me laughing about some of the things he and Mither and Faither did when they got aulder."

"I'm thinking all those hours he spent alone at the wheel gave him time to grow verra wise."

"Aye. He knew human nature and how fragile the heart can be." She smiled.

"Can you sleep now?"

"I'll try."

"Then I'm going to turn over. I want to feel our bairnie moving against my back while you coorie doon. 'Tis our hope for the future, Maggie, and a sign from our luving Faither that life goes on."

The creak of a cairt awakened Rob. He pulled on his denims and a shirt and leaned over to kiss Maggie's shoulder. "The bairns are home, luve."

Morag came bustling into the kitchen, carrying a large pot. "I've some tattie bree for the both of you. The bairns have all eaten. Alice has Katie and she'll walk the lassie home when Fern's finished at the infirmary."

Annie enjoyed her parents' hugs and kisses, but Robbie soon tired of it, pushing their faces away. "Faither, I got to feed the coos."

A small ray of sunshine pierced the cloud filling Rob's mind. He tousled his son's hair. "Did you, now? And what did you feed them? Tattie bree?"

"Hay, of course. They don't eat tattie bree, Faither."

"They don't? Who would have thought that?"

Satisfied, Robbie ran into his room and emerged with his ball. "I'm going to play with Shep."

Annie hesitated, then followed him outside.

Morag smiled and shook her head. "I've never seen a lad with more energy, and I thought Graham was full of it."

"We stopped by the infirmary for a minute on the way here," Alec said. "John said that Sim wants to talk to you, Rob. He says there's no hurry, just sometime before he discharges the lad on the morra's morn."

"How is he?"

"Fine and already nattering to go home."

Morag stirred the pot of bree heating on the stove. "If you want to go now, we'll stay with Maggie and the bairns."

"You should go." Maggie laid her head on Rob's chest. "Perhaps Sim wants to tell you what happened."

"Are you certain?" Rob tilted her chin up. "I can go later when the bairns are abed."

She nestled closer. "Go now. Sim needs to talk, just like we did."

He tried to tell her with a kiss how proud of her he was. "I'll no' be gone long, then."

When he reached Sim's room at the infirmary, the lad was sitting up in bed talking to his faither. "Rob," he exclaimed. "'Tis guid to see you." Though his voice was hoarse, Sim looked good. His hand trembled as he pushed back a shock of red hair falling over one eye. "Faither, I need to talk to Rob alone."

"Of course." Angus patted his arm. "Your mither wants me to run home for some fresh clothes for you, and now is a guid time." He rounded the bed and clasped Rob's hand. "There are no words to thank ye." Tears welled in his eyes. "You saved our lad. We'll be forever in your debt."

"It was Den who pulled him from the water."

"But Den said you're the one who spotted him after everyone gave up hope. Thank ye again." Angus quit the room, wiping his eyes with his sleeve.

Rob pulled over a chair and straddled it. "Feel like talking?"

The lad nodded. "Aye. I have to tell somebody, and it seems to me it should be you. After all, ye're the commander of the *Maggie*."

"I am that."

Sim's blue eyes swam with tears. "John says Malcolm had a heart attack and was dead afore the ferry hit us."

Rob nodded.

Sim swallowed convulsively, his prominent Adam's apple bobbing. "I didn't ken he was dead, no' at first." He pulled up a corner of the sheet and wiped his eyes. "The skipper ... sent me oot on deck to fasten down some ropes that had unfurled and were slapping in the wind. I had trouble with one of the ropes. It was wet and kept slipping through my hands, and I kept losing sight of it in the dark. It took me a guid long time, and when I went back in the cabin, he ... he was sitting all slumped over at the wheel, no' moving." He stopped and took several deep breaths.

Rob handed him a glass of water and helped him drink.

"Anyways ..." He wiped his mouth with the back of his hand. "I tried to wake him up, but I couldn't. So I laid him down on the deck, there in the cabin, and reached for the radio." A shudder shook his body.

"That must have been when the ferry hit us. I remember hearing this blowsterin, swoofin noise, louder than a hurricane, then everything went black. I woke up when I hit the water, I suppose. I kept reaching oot for something to catch hold of, but nothing was big enough. Then something bumped my legs. I reached down and felt Malcolm's arm, so I pulled him up. He was so heavy." The lad wept openly.

Rob didn't interrupt.

"He kept pulling me under the water. I'd do all I could to reach the surface for a quick breath, but then he'd pull me doon again. I suppose it was about then I kenned he was ... dead." He wiped his eyes and nose on the sheet. "But I couldn't leave him to the fishes and crabs, Rob. I couldn't! I just kept trying to stay afloat. All I remember after that is crawling up onto some planks. I worked and worked to get Malcolm up with me. Then everything went black again."

Rob gathered the lad into his arms.

Sim sobbed for several minutes. "I tri ... tried, Rob, I really did," he said at last.

"You did guid, Sim." Rob held the lad tightly. "I'm proud of you."

"Why? Malcolm's dead."

"He was dead when you found him, lad. But you didn't leave him to the sea. You made sure he'd come home where we could give him a proper burial."

Sim's body sagged. "I'm so spent."

Rob laid him down. "You did what few men could have done." He raised Sim's chin with his palm and looked into his tear-blurred eyes. "Last een, when you left Innisbraw, you were still a lad. In the mids o' the night, you came of age. Now you're a man, Sim."

On the third day of January, everyone on the island attended the funeral service for Malcolm. Hugh gave an uplifting message and several men spoke at length about the unique qualities of the man they all loved. John even told some funny stories about the pranks they had pulled when they were young. Laughter mingled with tears as the eulogies were given.

Finally, Graham MacKay stepped to the side of the coffin and readied his bagpipes. The haunting strains of "Oft in the Stilly Night" skirled through the sanctuary.

The first stanza of the familiar, auld song drifted through Rob's mind.

Oft, in the stilly night,
Ere Slumber's chain has bound me,

Fond Memory brings the light
Of other days around me;
The smiles, the tears,
Of boyhood's years,
The words of love then spoken;
The eyes that shone,
Now dimm'd and gone,
The cheerful hearts now broken!

Many wept as the last notes faded and the slow *dong, dong, dong* of the death knell rang out over Innisbraw.

Six men, including John and Rob, lifted the simple, wooden coffin onto their shoulders and carried it out of the kirk, past the MacCrae, MacNab, and MacDonald crofts and up the narrow path to the burial ground.

It was Rob's first time to be part of "The Lift," a tradition unique to the United Kingdom.

A snell wind rattled bare rowan branches and scattered sodden leaves across clumps of dried heather and simple gravestones, their etched words often too eroded to read.

The graveside service was short. Hugh quoted in the Gaelic from Isaiah 41:10. "'Fear thou not, for I am with thee; be not dismayed, for I am thy God: I will strengthen thee; yea, I will help thee; yea, I will uphold thee with the right hand of my righteousness.'"

The six men lowered the casket into the ground. Those closest to Malcolm each placed a spadeful of dirt onto the top of the casket, including Rob.

After the spades were put aside, Maggie tossed in a spray of dried heather as the traditional final tribute. Several crofters picked up the spades to finish filling the grave. The service was over.

Later, when everyone gathered in the kirk hall, the talk was subdued but comforting. Stories swirled of Malcolm's youth, of his marriage, and the death of his wife in childbirth. Rob hadn't known that both John and Malcolm had suffered such devastating blows as young men, or that Malcolm, unlike John, had also lost his newborn son. So much grief to endure at such a young age. Rob held Maggie close, legs weak, heart lurching. *Keep her safe, Lord. Och, Faither, thank Ye for my Maggie.*

Chapter Thirty-Two

Maggie's labour began just after midnight on Sunday. As with Annie, everything had been prepared since before Christmas. Though Rob thought about calling Fern or Alice, he decided he could always do so if something went wrong. He was soon much too busy to think of anything but the imminent birth of their bairnie.

Though the labour was a little longer this time, Maggie finally progressed to the point where Rob could see the top of the bairnie's head. "Almost there. One more guid push."

She strained and cried out as the tiny head emerged.

Rob quickly helped the shoulders out, and the baby slipped into his waiting hands. "'Tis a lass. A bonnie, bonnie lass!" He brought the baby up to Maggie's chest.

The bairnie let out an angry cry, then screamed lustily.

Rob grinned through tears. He tied and severed the cord, then covered their lassie with a towel.

Maggie smiled as she looked down at the squirming bairnie. "She looks like Annie, only she's no' so wee."

"Aye." Rob choked. "Our Beth's both bonnie and braw. Listen to her roup."

Rob bathed their daughter, and Maggie dressed her and swaddled her in a blanket.

Rob helped Maggie wash up, rolled up the soiled bedding, then took her hand and kissed her palm. "I'm fixing you a cup of tea, and I'll no' listen to any blethering. You need the liquid."

She laughed but didn't protest. "Listen to you. You're getting to be an expert."

He trailed his lips over her damp cheek. "Just as long as nowt goes wrong. You're the expert here." He looked at her, a swell of tenderness threatening his breath. "Thank ye for another bonnie daughter, Maggie. You're the luve of my life, you ken that."

She returned his smile. "I do. And you're the luve of mine."

The kirk bell rang five times early on the morning of January 4, 1948, to herald the arrival of Elizabeth Savage. That afternoon, it rang five times again for the birth of Amy Elspeth Proctor. Alice was called the moment Jill's labour started, but it was Fern who delivered the bairnie moments before the midwife arrived.

The next evening, Maggie nattered at Rob to take their new lassie to visit the Proctors.

"But 'tis too much for you," he grumbled. "Hasn't even been twenty-four hours since you birthed our Beth." Yet he gave in.

The two women laid their newborns side by side on the bed.

"I swear they must weigh exactly the same." Jill touched Beth's toes.

"That's no' the only likeness," Maggie said. "They both have light-brown hair and so much of it."

Rob brushed his fingers through Beth's curls. Soft as eiderdown, they were. "You realize they'll probably be best friends all their lives."

Stu laughed. "When they're not having one of those little arguments lasses have."

"How's Beth suckling?" Jill asked.

Maggie made a wry face. "Like she's waited days since the last feeding."

"Amy started slowly, but she's improving. Brenna was like a bottomless pit that couldn't be filled. Even when I was trying to wean her, she'd follow me around the house, hoping I'd sit down so she could climb into my lap and suckle."

"Mother!" Brenna's horrified cry took them all by surprise. She fled the room, face crimson.

Jill pushed the pillow from behind her back. "Och, that was thoughtless. I keep forgetting she's no longer a child." She reached for her robe. "I'd best go apologize."

Stu pressed her back into bed. "I'll go." He looked at Rob. "We all know why she was so embarrassed. 'Tis time for me to put a stop to this nonsense."

Rob's face burned. "I'm thinking we should go home."

"This is none of your doing. She needs to be told once and for all it isn't proper to moon over a merrit man."

Maggie laid a hand on Stu's arm. "We all know Rob's done nothing to encourage it, so I think you should let it work itself oot. If you forbid it, it'll only make her moon all the more, just in secret, and that'll blow it all oot of proportion."

Jill plumped her pillow and sat up straighter. "I agree with Maggie. Every lass has her bouts of luvesickness. In time, 'twill be some lad closer to her age."

Stu crossed his arms and rocked back on his heels. “I don’t like Rob embarrassed every time we’re all together.”

“It’s no’ that bad,” Rob said.

“Brenna’s always had her wee infatuations. You’d think she didn’t get enough luve at home.”

“Nonsense.” Jill stroked Stu’s hand. “You and Brenna have a guid, luving relationship. Some lasses’ heads are more easily turned by a braw man. You remember her fifth grade teacher, Steven Morris? She luved the ground he walked on until Rob saved our lives, then it was ‘Steven Who’?”

Rob had a sudden vision of Annie sending luve-blinks at an older man. “Maybe I should talk to Brenna.”

“It would do no guid. Time’s the only answer.” Maggie chewed her lower lip. “But Jill can still apologize for embarrassing the lass and let it go at that.” She smiled at Rob, eyes sparkling. “I’m thinking you’d better grow a thicker skin, luve. When the ferry comes, there’ll be many a tourist lass who takes a fancy to a verra tall, braw-looking Scotsman, merrit or no’.”

He’d suffered admiring glances from women passing on the street in London during the war—even when flashing his wedding ring—but he’d thought it had been his uniform.

“She’s most likely right,” Stu said. “You’d better face it, Rob. Most men are like me—average—but a few are cursed with guid looks.”

Rob’s face burned. “This room’s a bit close. Think I’ll step oot onto your entry.” He squeezed Maggie’s hand. “Be back in a tick.” He rushed out the front door and stood on the entry, gulping in air. Guid-looking? Stu must need eyeglasses. Rubbing the scar on his forehead, Rob leaned against the railing and looked down at the harbour.

A waxing moon tipped the crests of waves with sparkling diamonds—like his Maggie’s eyes when she voiced her luve.

Maggie. She must be exhausted. Och, he’d been selfish, running off like that. He’d best go back in and take his family home.

Once Robbie and Annie were abed, Maggie placed Beth in her cradle and went into Rob’s arms. “I’m sorry all that happened. Stu was so upset he talked to Brenna, and it seems this entire episode was all a dreadful mistake. Brenna wasn’t embarrassed just because you were in the room, but because we both were.”

“I don’t understand.”

"She said that was private, for family only."

"Are you certain?"

"Brenna left us alone, and Jill told me Edert MacPhee turned Brenna's head at our Thanksgiving dinner. She thinks he's verra braw."

He'd never again suffer suggestive smiles and long, soulful stares? He threw back his head and laughed. Blessings on Edert MacPhee.

"I can't imagine opening our home to tourists," Maggie said one een when Fern came to pick up Katie after work. "But I suppose using the dark, stormy months to prepare is wise."

Fern set down her teacup and looked around Maggie's comfortable living room. "It must be hardest on those having to weave new linens and patch worn bedquilts." She sighed. "We're so fortunate. Morag told me at kirk last Sabbath that those who can afford it have ordered new china or fresh lace curtains from Ireland, where they're more plentiful, but that's only a handful of those opening their cottages."

"And don't forget the menfolk." Maggie jumped up to move a pot of simmering bree to a cooler spot on the stovetop. "Graham told Rob that Tormad and Calum made a run into Oban for some new emulsion for limed walls and cairts. They wanted saddle soap for their cracked harnesses, but with rationing on, they had to settle for rendered poultry fat." She giggled. "Can't you just see a cairt loaded with tourists rumbling down the path with a flock of squawking hens following?"

"Or Den, waving a bottle of ale." Fern laughed at Maggie's puzzled expression. "Dougal MacArthur's stepped up his production, bottling twice his usual amount of ale. That was one bit of information Den couldn't wait to share."

Rob relaxed when Robbie seemed to take Beth's arrival in stride, with no signs of jealousy. The lad was much too busy to let the little stranger interrupt his life, and he paid her scant attention.

Annie's reaction was entirely different. She wanted to mither the tiny bairnie, and her greatest joy was sitting in Maggie's rocker with Beth in her lap. She called her sister "Beff," gave up her cradle willingly, and welcomed having her own new "big lass's bed" in the girls' bedroom.

"Someday, she'll be a perfect mither," Rob said to Maggie. "Our

Wee Annie's just like you."

The procurator fiscal's formal inquiry into the collision between the *Lismore Lady* and the *Sea Rouk* was held during the third week of January. Because the sky was only overcast, Rob flew Sim to Oban for the hearing. The lad was so nervous on the flight to Scotland, Rob was careful to make it as smooth a trip as possible. When they reached the hearing room, he realized it wasn't the floatplane flight that had frightened the lad but having to testify before so many strangers.

He took Sim aside in the hall. "Just speak as slowly and clearly as you can. These men are no' blaming you for owt. They just want to hear what happened before the collision."

Sim gulped a breath. "Aye, Rob. I'll try hard." On the way into the room, he pulled Rob to a stop. "My English isna verra guid. What if they dinna ken Scots?"

"Then they'll call for an interpreter and ask you to speak in the Gaelic. Don't fash yourself."

Commander David Hamilton of the Barry rescue boat and Captain Evan MacNamara of the *Lismore Lady* both testified before Rob was called. Because he had spoken before them in English on several occasions, he couldn't pave the way for Sim's Scots but told exactly what had transpired once the *Maggie* had arrived on the scene.

When Sim was called, the pale lad shook as he made his way forward.

It didn't take long for the board to realize they were dealing with a lad who spoke very little English. They called one of their Gaelic-speaking assistants forward to ask Sim questions and translate his account of what had transpired before the collision.

John McGrath's affidavit stating that Malcolm MacNeill had suffered a "massive myocardial infarction" was read into evidence.

Every member of the board was familiar with the doctor's reputation. They quickly squelched any attempts by the ferry line's representatives in both questioning the diagnosis and demanding the corpse be dug up for a proper postmortem.

The entire hearing was over in less than an hour, and no fault was leveled, much to the chagrin of the ferry company advocates.

"An accident, pure and simple," was the way the procurator fiscal put it.

Now the whole dreadful event could be put to rest. Though they had never found the body of the crew member who had been knocked from the deck of the ferry, surely he was gone. Malcolm was gone too. Though Rob's heart still ached with the loss, it was time to move on.

Sim was a different lad on the flight home. He asked Rob if he could do one of those things that made the wing dip like Alec had told him about, and he whooped with laughter when Rob obliged by putting the aircraft into a steep bank.

The rescue crew averaged four to five rescues a month. Many were minor mishaps or medical emergencies, but a few involved in-water rescues. One occurred when a large yacht out of Mull, with nine adult males aboard, plowed into the rocks at the southwestern end of Innisbraw during a thundering rain squall. Ironically, it was the same spot where Gregor Boyd's trawler had wrecked six years before, with all hands perishing.

The *Maggie* was at the scene of the yacht's accident twenty minutes after the siren first sounded. Rob couldn't risk moving her in close enough for the sling, and the rain was coming down so hard and the waves pounding so loudly, he couldn't use the bullhorn. He kept the yacht's captain, an American, on the radio as long as he could, but when the boat began to break up, he told the man to have his passengers abandon ship.

Every crew member but Matthew and Neil was ordered into the water. It was a rough rescue fraught with danger for victim and rescuer alike, and Rob was grateful he had Den along. Under the circumstances, an extra crew member could spell the difference between success and disaster.

Rob, Den, and Paddy pulled in two victims apiece. Artair and Duncan each saved one. Paddy suffered an injured shoulder when he was thrown against a rock, but his was the only injury among the rescuers.

All the survivors were at the infirmary in under an hour from the first distress call. The captain of the yacht pulled Rob aside and congratulated him on "the finest rescue I've ever seen or hoped to see. I thought we were all goners for sure."

"Your passengers kept their heads and followed orders. Withoot that, it could have ended very differently."

"I should hope so. They're all presidents and vice presidents of construction companies, and they all came up the hard way."

Rob exhaled loudly. "No wonder they were strong enough to

swim with us. What were you doing oot in our waters in the mids—middle of winter?"

"We just flew to Scotland from California yesterday. We're doing some development at Salen on Mull and thought we'd take a look at the Outer Hebrides. That squall caught us completely off guard. I've been in squalls before, but that one beats anything I've ever experienced. Couldn't see a thing from the moment it hit."

"Our squalls can be like that." Rob touched his arm. "Now if you'll excuse me, Captain, I need to check on an injured crewman. I'll catch you up later if I can."

"Of course, go ahead. And thank you again."

Rob went into the examining room where John was treating Paddy. "How's the shoulder?"

"Nowt broken," John said. "Just a deep bruise."

The Irishman grinned, displaying his sling. "I can still hold me bodhrán. Lucky it was me left shoulder."

John growled. "It could have been your head. Bodhrán, indeed."

"'Tis how I make me life enjoyable, boyo." Paddy laughed. "The howff just pays the bills. Playing me bodhrán makes me happy, that it does."

Elspeth fell ill during the last week in March, when a cold settled in her lungs.

John immediately told her she needed a short stay at the infirmary.

"But I feel more comfortable in my own wee cottage."

"I can't leave my other patients to come see you as often as I should. They need me too."

"Och, how many patients are at the infirmary?" Her chin rose along with her eyebrows.

"Four, as you well ken from your prayer requests: one appendectomy, one tonsillectomy, one broken collarbone, and an inflamed gallbladder."

She studied her hands. "All right then, as long as you understand I think 'tis a lot of bletheration over nowt."

Once John let on to Hugh, he immediately called for a prayer service. "Our Elspeth's been on her knees for us most of her life. 'Tis time we reciprocated."

Their prayers appeared to go unanswered as Elspeth's condition worsened over the next two days.

John voiced his concern. "At her advanced age, her body has few resources to fight off pneumonia."

Hugh caught an occasional nap on the couch in the foyer, while many of the island's folk kept a constant vigil outside the infirmary, bundled in bedquilts or knitted haps against the chill. Maggie stayed during the day. Rob paced the hall outside Elspeth's room every night.

Rob could not remember ever being so frightened.

"Go home," John told him on the third night. "She knows you're oot here, and she can't rest."

"Then tell her I'm gone, but I'm no' going anywhere," Rob whispered. "I can't leave—no' until I know she's better."

"Och, then go in and sit with her. That way you can both get some rest. Just don't let her talk."

Rob opened the door and tiptoed in.

An oxygen tent covered the bed to Elspeth's waist. An IV was in one arm, dripping saline and penicillin, while the other arm lay on top of the bedquilt.

Though her eyes were closed, he sensed she was awake. He pulled up a chair, tears stinging his eyes at the thought of all she had done for others during her long life.

She opened her eyes.

"Go to sleep," he whispered. "I'll just sit here with you for a spell."

Smiling softly, she nodded off.

He fought for control. This woman meant so much to him. From their first meeting in 1942, she had whetted his appetite for spiritual food, then fed him a bit at a time, leaving him hungering for more.

After his last B-17 crash, she had believed he would live when no one else, no' even Maggie, had a glimmer of hope. Perhaps it was her prayers above all else that had kept him alive those first crucial days.

She had encouraged him every time he doubted the first rescue boat would float. And the only reason he spoke Scots and the Gaelic was because of her competent, luving teaching.

He studied her tiny, gnarled hand. The veins stood out prominently, and her fingers were misshapen from arthritis, yet she still tended her garden and shared its produce, knitted bonnie sweaters for his bairns, baked him almond scones, and made him coffee.

Tears pooled in his eyes and spilled down his cheeks, unheeded. "Och, Faither, Elspeth is Yours, I ken that. But I don't think her journey on earth is finished. Heal her body, Lord, for her spirit is needed here on Innisbraw." He leaned over her, willing the strength of his body to somehow transmit itself to hers. "Come back, Elspeth," he whispered. "Come back where you are needed."

Chapter Thirty-Three

At dawn, John came into the room. He unzipped the oxygen tent and put a stethoscope to Elspeth's chest, moving it around, listening. At last he straightened and smiled. "She's better. The fluid drowning her lungs is finally abating."

Tears ran down Rob's cheeks and dripped onto his shirt. "Thank Ye, Lord." He reached for her hand and gently squeezed it. "We need you a while longer, Elspeth."

She opened her eyes. "I ... had the strangest dream." Voice weak, trembling. "I was ready to step into a boat to take me across the great water when a voice stopped me. 'Your spirit is needed on Innisbraw far more than it is in heaven,' the voice said." She paused and took several shallow breaths. "'Come back, Elspeth. Come back ... where you are needed.' The boat left me and returned, empty, to the other shore." She looked at Rob. "'Twas your voice I heard, lad. 'Twas your voice."

She heard me. Rob wiped his face on his sleeve.

She closed her eyes and slept.

John squeezed Rob's shoulder and re-zipped the tent. "She's improving, lad. Go home and sleep."

On the fifth day, Elspeth opened her eyes again and squeezed Rob's hand. "'Tis time you went home where you belong, my precious lad. Your work here is finished."

He lifted her hand and pressed his lips on her knuckles. "Aye, you're back to stay."

"For a while, Rob, only for a while."

The ferry, a large steamer, made its first stop on Innisbraw on the second of June. It was a perfect spring day with a light onshore breeze and sunshine sparkling on the turquoise water close to shore. Many of the seabirds were frightened away by the large vessel, but the bolder pewlie gulls circled and keened overhead, searching for a morsel of food someone had dropped. Thirty-four passengers waited eagerly at the railing for the gangplank to be put into place.

Rob stood on the dock, heart swelling with pride at the smiles on the tourists' faces. He'd known it—one look at the beauty of Innisbraw and the most jaded traveler's heart would be touched. He heard his name called from the bridge and looked up.

Captain Evan MacNamara stood at the upper railing, the sun sparkling on his immaculate white uniform. "Commander!" he called, snapping a smart salute.

Rob saluted in return. "Captain!"

"How do you like our new ship?" MacNamara called in the Gaelic.

Rob grinned. So the captain spoke both Scots and the Gaelic. "She's grand. It's good to see you're back in command."

"It's good to be here. Are you folk ready?"

"We're ready."

MacNamara turned and ordered the gangplank lowered into place.

The passengers filed off, cameras around their necks, baggage in hand, chattering and laughing.

Rob was surprised to see a familiar face in the crowd—the German man he had talked to at the Oban ferry terminal. He pressed forward through the throng and greeted the man in his native language.

The tourist shook his hand vigorously and introduced himself as Gunther Schwartz. "The beauty of this island is tremendous." The German pulled a companion up to Rob. "This is Herr Stephen Kornfeld. He is a physician who spends his holidays looking for unusual birds, so we have decided to combine our efforts."

Rob shook the doctor's hand, drawn to the man's heartfelt smile and warm handshake. "I trust you won't be disappointed."

"This is a dream come true," Kornfeld said, eyes dancing with sparkling lights. "I can't wait to begin."

When Rob discovered that they would be staying at the manse, he pointed out Hugh, who stood on the path at the side of Alec's cairt. The two picked up their unwieldy baggage and trotted down the pier, obviously eager to begin their search.

Rob mingled with the people, helping to point out their hosts who waited on the path beside their cairts. Finally, baggage and tourists loaded, the cairts moved off to their destinations. Ferry crewmen trundled stock for the general store out of the hold and up to the pier.

Rob was turning to go back to the shed when he noticed two passengers standing alone on the dock.

A tiny, slender, young blonde clasped the hand of a small lad.

She looked familiar—how could that be?

He stopped in front of her, dismayed to see tears streaking her cheeks. "Can I help you?" he asked in English.

She smiled up at him, grey eyes wide. "You're Colonel Savage."

Not a question. A statement. Had she said colonel?

The lad tugged on her hand. "Is it really him, Mom?"

She extended her right hand. "I don't expect you to know me, but I know you very well. I'm Ellie Florey, Rich's sister."

Rich? His tail gunner who'd died when their B-17 was attacked? Rob stared, not believing what he was hearing. His palm swallowed hers. "You're Ellie? You're really Rich's sister, Ellie?"

She laughed, nervous. "Rich sent pictures of the crew when he wrote. I knew you immediately. You stood almost a head taller than anyone in the pictures, and you do here as well."

He pulled her into a hug. How often did a breath from the past surround one's heart with such bittersweet memories? "Ellie. No wonder you looked familiar." His vision blurred with tears. "You look just like Rich."

She took a kerchief from her pocket and dabbed at her eyes. "It's so good to know this wasn't just a wild goose chase. You really are here on Innisbraw."

Rob turned to the boy. "And this is your lad?"

"Yes, this is Richie Florey. Actually, Richard Robert Florey."

Rob's eyes blurred again. The lad had blond hair and his mither's grey eyes, though he looked like a young Rich. He felt a stab of renewed grief at Rich's death when German Focke Wulf-190 fighter planes attacked their plane in the spring of '42. He and Rich had spent many an evening playing darts and drinking ale at an Edenoaks pub with "Gunny" Hastings, another member of Rob's crew aboard the *Liberty Belle*. He had never allowed himself to bond so closely with members of his crew after Rich's death. It hurt too much. "Did you make a reservation with a local family? Because if you did, we're going to have to cancel it. You're staying at my home."

Her cheeks flushed. "I'm afraid I didn't. This was sort of a last-minute trip, and the plane was late getting into Heathrow, and we almost missed the train to Oban."

"Guid. We have twa—two—extra rooms that will be perfect. Is this your baggage?"

"We really don't want to put you out. Perhaps we'd better stay at a hotel."

He smiled and picked up their bags. "There isn't one, and you're not putting anyone oot. We have some catching up to do, don't we, Richie?" He winked at the lad.

The lad smiled. It was Rich's crooked smile.

Rob cut his stride short so they could keep up, though it was hard to do as he was so eager to tell Maggie the news. So this was Ellie Florey. What a small world. And what had brought her so far from home?

"This is such a beautiful island," Ellie said. "The colors are so vivid they almost hurt your eyes."

"Aye, 'tis that," he said, before kicking himself for speaking in Scots. "Maggie—that's my wife—was born and raised here," he added in his best English.

She laughed. "I notice you have quite a burr, but I can understand you just fine."

"Sorry about that. I don't speak English much anymore. I'm out of practice."

"Oh, don't apologize. It's charming. I picked up a brochure at the railroad station. Is it Scots you speak, or the Gaelic?"

"Both, actually. Few of the folk on Innisbraw speak much English."

Her eyes widened.

"But that shouldn't be a tickler—problem. My wife, Maggie, speaks it, and there are twa—two—other American families here on the island. They live very close to us. One, Den Anderson, was also with the 396th."

"The name sounds familiar. What brought him here?"

He chuckled. "'Tis a long story, but we'll have a time for talking. How long are you planning to stay?"

"I don't know. I bought open-ended return tickets. I just had to meet you in person. Rich wrote so much about you." She stopped suddenly and looked him straight in the face. "Do you know some people think you're dead?"

"Dead? Who?"

"Pete and Caroline Hastings, for one example. Pete heard you were killed when your plane crashed almost a year after Rich was killed."

"You know Pete?"

"Oh, yes. We correspond regularly, and they even came for a visit two years ago."

He tucked the smaller bag beneath his arm and resumed walking. "I hope you set him straight. I've always wondered what happened to Gunny—that's what we called him, since he was my right waist gunner on the *Liberty Belle*. He, Rich, and I had some good times in Edenoaks."

"Pete had written from the Eastern Theater that he'd heard you'd been killed, so I contacted the International Red Cross. It took over a year before I heard from them that last you were alive, you were living here. I wanted to make sure you really were alive before I called him and Caroline. It wasn't easy to get us to this island, but I knew Rich would want me to find you."

"I'm glad you made the effort." Rob unlatched the gate. "Here we are."

Ellie hesitated. "I hope your wife won't be upset by unexpected company."

"Och, she'll be happy to meet you. She was stationed at Edenoaks too, though I don't think she knew Rich."

"She was in the Air Forces?"

"Maggie was in the Royal Air Force Nursing Service." He led them up onto the entry. "She worked at the base hospital—something involving a trade-off with the Brits to pick up different methods of treatment."

"This is a beautiful house." Ellie looked around. "And so large."

"There's a reason behind its size, but we'll have to leave that for later." He put the bags down and opened the door. "In you go, then."

Shep was the first to greet them.

Richie's eyes lit up. "They have a dog."

"His name's Shep. And, if you're no' careful, he'll lick the freckles right off your nose."

Richie laughed and held out his hand.

Shep nosed it, eager to make another friend, especially a young lad.

"Maggie!" Rob called. "Maggie, lass, where are you?"

"In the bedroom, luve, changing Beth's hippen."

"Out you come when you can. A surprise came on the ferry. There's someone here I want you to meet." He took Ellie's elbow. "I'll take your things up to your rooms in a minute. That was quite a walk. Sit you down and rest."

Ellie looked around. "This is so welcoming."

"I hope so. That's what we wanted when we built it." Rob ordered Shep to lie on the rug. "He loves bairns so much he can be a real scunner—och, pest."

"But he belongs here. He completes the picture."

Maggie came in carrying Beth.

Rob gave her a kiss and pulled Ellie forward. "Do you remember me talking about my tail gunner, Rich Florey? This is Rich's sister, Ellie, and her lad, Richie."

Maggie smiled warmly, handed Beth to Rob, and embraced Ellie. "Of course I do. This is the lass you wrote the letter of condolence to from the Royal Infirmary."

"It is. Can you believe it? She's come all the way from America to make sure I'm still alive." He smiled at the blank look on Maggie's face. "It seems some of my old crew think I died in that last crash."

Maggie hugged him. "You almost did, luve. I'm sorry I missed meeting the ferry, but Shep had a splinter in his paw that needed tending. Sit you down, Ellie. You must be exhausted. 'Tis a long, long journey."

Ellie fingered Beth's curls. "What a beautiful child. She favors you both."

"No' like your lad," Rob said. "He's the image of you. Which means the image of Rich too."

"I guess the Florey genes are strong."

"Did your husband come with you?" Maggie asked.

Ellie's cheeks flushed. "No. No husband. It's just Richie and myself."

"You need a cup of strong, hot tea," Maggie said quickly. "Rob, put Beth in her cradle and take their bags upstairs. I just took the bed linens off the line. They have a wee smell of heather."

"Is that the fragrance I smelled in the air? I noticed it on the walk up the hill."

"Aye, the bell heather is already blooming between the rocks by some of the burns. Soon, most of the island will be covered with common heather, and the fragrance will be much stronger." Maggie led Ellie into the kitchen. "We have milk or a bottle of lemon skoosh for Richie. 'Tis a kind of lemon soda."

"The milk sounds fine. He's been so excited about finally seeing Colonel Savage he hasn't eaten much."

"Rob, please," Rob said from the living room. "Have you scones or shortbread, luve? I'm sure both Ellie and Richie could use a piece."

Maggie laughed. "And I'm sure you could too. Am I right?"

He came into the kitchen and kissed her cheek. "You know you are. I'll take the bags upstairs. Where are the bairns?"

"At Fern's. She has the day off, and Katie's playing doctor again."

"Och, that lass."

Ellie watched Rob leave the room. He was so tall, the top of her head would barely reach his shoulder. He was even better looking than in the pictures Rich sent, but it was Rob's deep, soft, caring voice that made the strongest impression. And Maggie was beautiful with her milk-white skin, black hair, and violet-blue eyes—and so tiny. What a striking couple. It made her feel warm all over that the colonel—Rob—was happily married.

"I gather 'bairns' are children," she said as Maggie took a teacup from the cupboard. "So you have more than this little one?"

Maggie set out a plate of shortbread. "We have three. Robbie will be four in September, Annie's almost twa and a half, and our wee Beth is five months auld."

"Do the others look like Beth?"

"Och, Annie does, though she favors her faither even more. Robbie has my black hair and blue eyes, but that's all. Other than that, he's so much like Rob, 'tis almost frightening."

Ellie laughed. "That's what people say about Richie. He's the image of my brother. In fact, if you place pictures taken when they were both three side by side, you'd swear they were the same boy."

Maggie poured them both tea and added honey and milk. "That must please you. I know Rob was verra fond of your brother. He liked all of his crews, but Rich and Gunny Hastings are the only ones he still talks about."

"According to Rich, Rob was an exceptional commander. I was surprised to hear from him so long after Rich's death."

"There was guid reason for the delay." Maggie sipped her tea. "Rob was critically injured in that crash the day your brother was ... killed. He wasn't strong enough to ask about his crew, or even think about writing you, until he had time to heal—his legs were paralyzed. It took him months to learn to walk again."

"I'm so sorry. I didn't know."

Rob walked into the kitchen and poured himself a mug of coffee before sitting down. "I'm thinking I should go get the bairns. Richie, here, is the perfect age to play with Robbie."

Maggie shot him a warning glance. "Ellie, would you like the lad to rest first?"

Ellie shook her head. "He's quiet now, but this isn't his usual self. He's go, go, go from the time he gets up until he goes to bed."

"Sounds familiar." Rob laughed. "Our Robbie's exactly the same." The phone rang and Rob excused himself to answer it. When he returned, he gulped down his coffee and reached for a piece of shortbread. "That was Graham. The trawler crew needs some help interpreting the plans." He touched Ellie's shoulder. "I'm sorry to run off, but this is important. You twa get acquainted. I'll fetch the bairns when I get back. I shouldn't be gone past an hour."

"Then plan to stay home long enough for dinner," Maggie said. "I've fixed Scotch eggs, and we'll have toasted cheese."

"Sounds guid." He kissed Maggie and tousled Richie's hair. "See you later."

"What's a 'trawler crew'?" Ellie asked as the door closed behind Rob.

"Rob owns the Innisbraw Boatworks. You may have noticed that large shed by the pier. He has three boats under construction right now, and one is a fishing trawler."

"He builds boats? How extraordinary. Rich never mentioned that in his letters."

"This is a rather new endeavor. When your Air Forces invalided him oot after his last crash, Rob designed and built the Innisbraw Coastal Rescue boat. She's the red and black boat down at the harbour."

"I'm sorry, I didn't notice." Ellie squirmed. "There were rumors of Rob's death. I was so afraid I'd come all this way on a fool's mission."

"But you didn't." Maggie patted her hand. "Anyway, the boat was such a success, he's building more rescue boats and also the fishing trawler I mentioned."

"From the way Rich wrote, I didn't think the colonel—Rob—would ever do anything but fly. Does he have some physical impairment that keeps him from it?"

Maggie poured more tea. "He and Den have a floatplane. Rob flies every chance he gets."

A loud wail from the bedroom.

Maggie put down her teacup. "Come into the living room with me, and bring your tea. I have to feed a certain lass before she works herself into a frenzy. She takes her nursing verra seriously." She paused. "Richie, now that you've finished your milk and shortbread, go into Robbie's room over there and grab a ball. I'm sure Shep would love a game of fetch."

The lad grinned. "Can I, Mom?"

"As long as you don't go out of the yard."

"He can't," Maggie said. "We have a stone wall all the way around, and Shep won't let Richie climb it. 'Tis one of his duties, keeping the bairns off the dyke."

Sighing as she sipped her delicious tea, Ellie sat in Rob's rocker, while Maggie nursed Beth. What a warm welcome. Orphaned at young ages, she and Rich had been shunted from relative to relative, never truly belonging to a family. For the first time in her life, Ellie Florey felt like she had come home.

Chapter Thirty-Four

Rob hung up the telephone and walked into the bedroom, shaking his head. "That was Morag. They've had so many tourists saying they plan to attend, they're holding the ceilidh at the kirk hall instead of Paddy's howff."

Maggie, busy laying his kilt on the bed, gazed up at him, eyes wide. "Surely they'll no' serve ale in the hall."

"You know Hugh would never allow that." He grinned. "And I think it's a grand idea. No' so crowded. And no alcohol means no tourists getting blootered and upsetting our folk." His grin faded. "I agree with Stu and Den that we should all go but leave early." He fingered his kilt. "I'll only dance with you."

Maggie straightened the ruffles on his shirt and handed it to him. "You have to dance with the tourists, luve. After all, it was you mentioning it to the Island Council that brought the ferry here. Ellie's looked forward to the ceilidh since the day she arrived, and I'm loaning her one of my plaid skirts." She clasped her hands. "I just wish I knew about Richie's faither—why he isn't here."

"Have you asked her?"

"Aye. This mornin, when Robbie and Richie were playing ootside. She mumbled something about him no' longer being a part of their lives and turned away."

Rob dropped the shirt on the bed. "Mebbe he was killed in the war—like Rich—and she can't bear to think on it."

She sighed and worried her lip. "I've a feeling 'tis more than that. She doesn't wear a wedding ring, but I don't want to force her to talk."

It would be playing dirty to take advantage of her pensive mood, but if it got him out of dancing with strangers … "We don't have to go the night."

Her shoulders squared and that pert nose shot into the air. "Calum and Faither are going too, so they'll help entertain Ellie, and you can dance with some of the tourists when I'm busy with her."

"I'm no' a guid dancer, lass." A stab of panic lanced his belly. "Och, Maggie, what have I gotten myself into?"

"You are a guid dancer. Just think of it as business, Rob. You'll be helping entertain the people who are providing added income for our folk, that's all. On you go now—into your kilt. I have to dress and get the bairns ready. 'Tis growing late."

Maggie dressed Richie in a kilt Robbie had outgrown. Though Richie was nine months aulder than Robbie, he was much shorter, so it fit well. Annie danced around the living room, whirling her green and blue plaid skirt, hazel eyes flecked with green. Beth fussed and kicked at the plaid blanket restricting her legs.

Maggie tried to soothe her with a bit of rocking, but the lassie's whinging grew louder.

Rob grabbed the bairnie, lifted her high into the air, and blew on her belly. "We're going for a walk, lassie," he crooned. "A long, long walk."

She smiled and cooed, arms waving.

When the families living on the fell gathered on the path to walk to the kirk hall, Den greeted Ellie with a warm smile. "I knew your brother well. Rich was the best dart player I ever saw. He talked about you all the time."

Tears misted Ellie's eyes. "I'm so happy you remember him. He and I were very close."

Robbie, young Chris, and Richie ran ahead, their shrill laughter carried back on the evening breeze. Shep pranced behind the lads as he herded them toward the hall. Brenna stayed with the adults.

Maggie, at the thought of music and visiting, laughed and lifted her face to the salted sea air. "What a glorious een. If Rob gets over his fash about having to dance with someone other than me, I'm predicting a grand ceilidh."

Fern uttered an uncharacteristic grunt and pointed ahead.

Den and Stu, looking very Scots in a kilt he borrowed from Angus MacPhee, walked at Rob's side, heads lowered.

"Rob's no' the only one in a fash." Fern lowered her voice. "Den was in such a fankle about having to wear his kilt *and* dance with the tourists, his face turned red and his eyes spit fire."

"He doesn't like wearing a kilt?" Ellie asked. "But why?"

"'Tisn't only wearing the kilt, but what he does or doesn't wear 'neath it."

Brenna made a strangled protest and raced ahead to join the bairns.

When they arrived at the hall, Rob estimated more than half the island was already inside. Locals, clad in their plaids, stood on one side of hall, while the tourists—och, so many of them women—wearing both casual and dressy clothing, gathered on the other. Expected or no', duty or no', how could he dance with a stranger?

Elspeth sat in her usual chair placed against the back wall.

Rob took Ellie over and introduced her, then asked, "Are you sure you're strong enough to be here, then? You haven't been up and aboot verra long."

"Och, quit your blethering. I want to talk to this young lass from America."

Rob grinned and kissed Elspeth's cheek. "Aye, Grandmither."

She tapped her walking stick. "Remember your duties, lad. You're cutting a fine figure the een. On you go—entertain our visitors."

He touched his forelock, smile fading. "Aye. My duties."

Elspeth watched him shamble away. "There goes a verra unhappy lad. 'Tis too bad Rob canna live on a deserted island with only those he luves about him. Strangers always make him uncomfortable."

"But he's so warm and friendly. And he and Maggie have gone out of their way to make me feel welcome."

"You're no' a stranger, Ellie. You're a friend. That's different."

"I feel like I've known him for years. My brother was fond of Rob and always mentioned him in his letters home."

"Your brother was one of his lads in the American Air Forces?"

"Rich was Rob's tail gunner. He was killed on his twenty-fifth mission."

The tears shimmering in Ellie's eyes required a quick change in topic. "Tell me, lass, how do you like Innisbraw? Does it live up to your expectations?"

"Oh, it's so much more than I ever hoped for. When I first learned Rob was alive and living here, there was no ferry service, or I'd have come sooner. This island and its people are like something out of a fairy tale. I've never met nicer people."

Elspeth smiled and patted Ellie's hand. "You're a warm, luving person yourself, and ye have much to offer. I assume that lad with Robbie is yours. They look like they get on well."

"They're so much alike, they've played nonstop since we got here."

"I hope you're no' planning to go home soon. I'm thinking ye've been in need of a bit of a rest for a guid long time."

"Oh, I hope it doesn't show. I haven't had a vacation since Richie was born. His father isn't in the picture. I teach school and clerk in a store during the summer vacation."

Elspeth patted her hand again. "I think it takes another woman to recognize when a lass is overworked. Now, here comes Calum, Maggie's brother. Have you met him?"

"I haven't. He and Doctor John were going to walk with us, but there was a last-minute problem at the infirmary. You can certainly tell they're related. They look so much alike."

"Aye, they do that." Elspeth grasped Calum's arm as he neared. "Calum, lad, I'd like you to meet Ellie Florey. She's a friend of Rob's all the way from America." Her heart fluttered. She didn't believe in playing matchmaker, but it couldn't hurt to give a gentle nudge. A bubble of expectation rose in her chest as the two young people shook hands.

"I'm verra—very happy to meet you at last." Calum tried a smile as he frantically sought to remember the English he'd learned at academy.

"I understand you're a fisherman," Ellie said. "It sounds like a lot of work." Her voice was soft as a mourning dove greeting the dawn.

Calum's smile broadened. "It is that. Are you enjoying your visit?"

"More than I thought possible, though I'm a bit worried about this 'kaylee.' I don't know a single Scots dance."

Elspeth thumped her walking stick. "That's easily corrected. The music's about to start, lad. On you go, then. Show this lass some steps so she can see how easy they are."

Calum felt his face flush. So wee, this lass, with her soft, grey eyes. "Mebbe Rob would rather do that."

"He's going to be verra busy the een. Now on with the both of you. I want to sit here and rest a spell."

Tourists eyed them as they made their way to the dance floor. Calum's mouth felt full of cotton wadding and his pulse pounded. He hadn't felt so gangly since he was at academy.

Paddy announced the first dance would be a strathspey. Its uncomplicated, gliding step would be easier for the tourists to master.

Calum hesitated, then took Ellie's sma' hand in his.

Her hand trembled.

So he wasn't the only one flummoxed. He tried another smile.

"'Tis a very simple dance. We start it side by side. Just watch my feet and hands for a minute, then you'll see how easy it is."

Ellie quickly mastered the gliding step, with its slight skip, seldom faltering as the other local dancers guided her through the patterns of exchanging hands. She felt like she was floating. Here she was, on a magical island, dancing with a shy, handsome Scotsman. Who would have dreamed it possible? Only a week ago, she had started her summer break from teaching kindergarten in a small town in New Hampshire. Tonight she was in Scotland, living a dream.

Rob insisted he dance the first dance with his Maggie. He soon became aware of the eyes turned his way.

Those tourists who weren't trying the dance ringed the dance floor, and every eye seemed to pierce his chest.

Maggie appeared to take the stares in stride.

Rob forced himself to concentrate on Maggie and how her eyes sparkled when she smiled up at him. Halfway through the dance, he began to relax. This was his lass, the luve of his life, and this dance was theirs. He leaned down and kissed her cheek.

A few whistles from the sideline brought him back to reality.

Maggie squeezed his hand. "'Tis all right. Just be yourself."

He groaned. "I can't. Everybody's looking at us."

"That's what they're here for, luve, to look. After all, that's what this ceilidh is for—to show them what we're like."

When the music ended, Rob took Maggie's hand and led her toward the refreshment table. "There'd better be coffee."

"You know there is. Morag's in charge of the refreshments the een, and she always makes coffee now."

Rob grabbed a lemon skoosh for Maggie and poured himself a mug of coffee.

"I thought they drank tea," a woman tourist said at his elbow. "That's coffee just like we drink at home."

Her male companion rolled his eyes. "Some Americans drink tea, so I suppose Scottish people have different tastes too." He reached for a scone. "Try one of those big cookies. They have almonds in them."

Rob looked for an escape. What had he gotten himself into? "I'd better check the bairns."

Maggie grabbed his sleeve. "Jill's watching them right now, and I'll spell her in a bit. The music's starting again, and 'tis an easy reel, so you'd better choose a partner and earn your keep."

He wiped his forehead. "I can't do it, Maggie."

"Yes, you can. Business, Rob. Pretend 'tis one of your general's wives you're dancing with."

"Won't make it any easier. I hated dancing with them also."

"Och, I've had enough." Maggie pushed him away. "On you go. Now!" She walked off, shoulders straight, nose in the air.

He gulped down his coffee and scanned the room.

Several women tried to catch his eye.

He squinted and ignored them. What was wrong with American women these days, acting like brazen young lasses with no manners and fewer brains? The Scots had a saying that described them perfectly—"Mutton dressed as lamb."

Then he saw her, an aulder woman wearing a tweed skirt and sensible shoes, with thick eyeglasses, taped at one corner. She looked safe. He forced himself to approach her. "Would you care to dance?" His voice choked with embarrassment.

The woman's hand flew to her throat. "Who? Me?"

"Aye, you." This time his smile was genuine. She appeared as flummoxed as he felt.

"But I don't know how."

"I can teach you. 'Tis simple, really."

Her cheeks coloured as she took his arm. "If you're sure."

She was as awkward as he had expected, but an eager student. He danced the reel with her before getting her a cup of tea and leaving her in the center of a group of blethering women sounding like a yard filled with laying hens. That wasn't so bad.

Den led a lithe, tanned young woman to the refreshment table. His buddy was sweating, and though he was smiling, his right eyelid twitched.

Rob wasn't the only one suffering for the cause, then. His gaze roamed the room.

Even John was talking to an American woman, though a glazed look in the doctor's eyes meant, most likely, he was wishing to be spending a relaxing een at home with his nose in the latest medical journal.

Stu appeared to be having a grand time. His Scots lessons had progressed to the point where he spoke it proficiently and, wearing Angus's kilt, it probably tickled him to have the American tourists assume he was an authentic Scotsman. He winked at Jill as he talked to a tourist woman clad in a long cotton skirt and clingy sweater.

Rob almost groaned aloud when Paddy announced that the

storytelling was next. With Elspeth still too weak to take part, Auntie Mairet would be filling in for her. In her tartan skirt and shawl, the frail auld woman certainly looked the part. But there was something almost fey about Auntie, and Rob didn't trust her to tell an appropriate story.

Paddy called Rob forward to do the translating from Auntie's Gaelic into English. Rob concentrated on Auntie's first words and breathed out when she announced the Selkie story. Mebbe he could make it through the ceilidh without blowing up.

The Selkie, a magical seal who turned into a beautiful woman when she came ashore.

Rob had a hard time not using Maggie's words, for this was a tale she had told him so many times when he was in pain from his wartime injuries. He lost himself in the telling, sometimes closing his eyes, picturing his Maggie instead of the Selkie.

The ending jarred him awake. Instead of remaining with her crofter-lover, the Selkie slipped back into her sealskin and returned to the Selkie male who called to her hauntingly over the waves.

No, that's not the way it ends. The Selkie and her lover were merrit and lived on their wee island in the sea forever and ever and ever.

Despite the unhappy ending, Auntie Mairet received a thunderous applause.

After the storytelling, Katie demonstrated the Highland Fling, with Graham MacKay on the pipes. The tourists appeared astounded by this young lass's poise and ability and rewarded her, too, with a long, sustained applause.

When the music resumed, Rob sought out Maggie. "One more for us, luve, please."

She smiled and took his hand. "Of course. I've missed you."

"Och, no' as much as I've missed you."

They danced the Eightsome Reel. No visitors took to the floor. This was a complicated, intricate dance for locals only.

Once again, the applause was deafening when the music ended.

Rob clutched Maggie's shoulder. "I'm ready to leave. How aboot you?"

"Dance one more, then we'll go."

"Och, I'm danced oot." He looked at the firm set of her lips. "I know—business. All right, lass, one more dance, then I'm through. By the way, where's Ellie? I was hoping to dance at least one with her."

Maggie stiffened. "She has Calum teaching her. It seems he's taken a special interest."

Rob shook his head, a smell of trouble addling his thoughts.

She pushed him away. "One more, Rob, don't disremember."

"How could I? I feel like a doomed coo on its way to the killing house." He spotted Brenna and Edert out on the floor, waiting for the next dance, looking very smitten with one another. "Thank you, Edert," he said under his breath. At least one trouble was taken care of.

Maggie caught his eye from where she sat along the wall and held up one finger.

He turned away, looked around, and spotted her immediately.

A mousy blonde stood alone, eyes downcast, shoulders slumped.

Help me, Lord, please. Ye know I don't want to do this, so make it verra plain if this is what I'm to do each time.

Though Rob was exhausted, the walk home energized him. He held Maggie's hand tightly, so thankful for their uncomplicated lives. He'd skip the ceilidhs from now on. He wasn't cut oot to be a dance instructor or to console unhappy women. He'd take half an hour out of his busy work schedule three times a week to meet the ferries … and that was all.

John had ridden home with Elspeth earlier, but Calum walked home with Rob and Maggie. He and Ellie laughed and talked nonstop until they reached the McGrath cottage, where he said his guidbyes. Rob carried Annie and Beth in and helped Maggie tuck them into their beds. Even Robbie and Richie were all tuckered out and went to bed without a fuss.

When Ellie excused herself and went up to bed, Rob added peats to the fireplace and collapsed into his rocker. "Och, I'm glad that's over."

Maggie sat on his lap. "You sound fashed."

"No' fashed, just spent. That's the hardest work I've done in years."

She cuddled closer. "I'm sorry it was so hard, luve, but the tourists seemed to enjoy it. I'd say it was a grand success."

He played with one soft curl. "Mebbe, but I've had my fill of it. I don't like being on display like an animal in a cage."

She smiled and kissed his neck. "I'm proud of you. You had every woman there wishing they were me."

"Don't start, Maggie."

"Don't start anything?"

"You ken what I mean."

"But you don't seem to ken what *I* mean."

He pulled her close and buried his face in her hair. "Och, lass, there are a lot of unhappy, lonely folk oot there."

"That last woman you danced with looked so sad."

"She was." He clasped her tighter, feeling her heart beat with his. "We're so blessed. We have each other. We have our luve, we have our bairns. I can't think of a single thing I could ever want that we don't already have."

Chapter Thirty-Five

Rob, aboard the Isle of Skye's rescue boat during its launch, missed greeting the next ferry. He backed the boat into the harbour and manoeuvred it slowly toward the empty berth next to the *Maggie*. As the starboard side nudged the dock, he pulled the rope dangling above his head and the shrill siren blasted out over the harbour. The crowd at the ferry's railing burst into cheers. This was one accolade Rob didn't mind receiving. Months of labour and thousands of pounds had gone into reaching this day.

The boatbuilding crew crowded aboard as the boat was tied up. Several of the lads hoisted Rob onto their shoulders and carried him across the dock to the pier. This was a grand day for the Innisbraw Boatworks.

Rob studied the calendar in his office. "Den, get on the phone and tell the people at Skye about the successful launch. As soon as she's passed her sea trials, they'll want to send someone over for the capsizing trial."

"When do you figure that for?" Den parked himself on a corner of Rob's desk.

Rob riffled through the pages of his desk calendar. "I'd say ... why don't we aim for the twenty-eighth? That'll give us time to get the sea trials oot of the way."

"The twenty-eighth it is." Den grabbed the phone and jiggled the receiver for the operator.

Rob was still so kittled up he couldn't sit still. He walked out into the shed and watched the crew busy at work on the trawler.

Launching that twenty-three-metre trawler would be a sight to behold. He'd have to try to arrange it to coincide with a ferry run if he could, but it all depended on the tide.

He brushed a lock of hair off his forehead. Though he had an order for one more rescue boat, he needed another to keep his crew busy through the winter. His negotiations with several coastal communities in Scotland would surely bear fruit soon. The *Maggie*'s reputation grew every month.

"Someone here to see you, Rob," Den called.

Rob hurried back to his office, hoping it wasn't a local waiting to congratulate him. Though he appreciated their continuing prayers and support, their effusive praise still made him uncomfortable. The visitor so startled him, he almost stopped in mid-stride.

A young man with black hair and piercing, dark eyes stood before him, dressed in a uniform.

What was the US Coast Guard doing here?

The officer snapped a salute. "Commander."

Rob's salute was automatic. "Commander." He stuck out his hand.

The American's handshake was firm.

"Welcome to Innisbraw. You wanted to see me?"

The man nodded. "Is there someplace we can talk in private?"

One of Rob's eyebrows rose. "Private? You're here on official business, then?"

The Coastie grinned. "As official as it gets, Commander Savage."

"Rob, please. We're no' formal here."

"Zeke Evans, but call me Zeke."

Rob returned the grin and introduced him to Den and Stu. "They're my partners. Whatever you've come to discuss is their business too."

"Well, in that case, perhaps I should have asked if there was a quieter place. All that power machinery makes conversation difficult."

Rob thought for a moment. "I suppose the howff—that's a pub—across the path will do. They have a corner table that's oot of the way. Let me get our other partner. 'Tis time to break for dinner, anyway."

"Dinner?" Commander Evans looked perplexed.

"Lunch—they call it dinner here."

The five men, now including Graham, crowded around the table and ordered coffee from Paddy.

"We've tattie bree, Rob, your favourite."

"Mebbe later. This is a business meeting."

Paddy eyed the American Coast Guard commander. "Oh, aye, I've got you. Coffee it is, Commander."

"Paddy McDonald's one of our rescue boat's crew," Rob said. "He owns this howff."

Commander Evans leaned forward. "That was quite a show you

put on today. Are all your launches timed so perfectly?"

"An accident. We usually try to launch in the afternoon, but the tide was right and we were ready."

Evans nodded. "The sea trials come next, right?"

"Right." Though Rob was curious, he didn't have time to waste on talk. "What is it you wished to see me about?"

"The United States Coast Guard is very interested in these rescue boats you're building."

"They are, are they?"

"Yes."

Rob tamped down his excitement. "And just how did ye hear about our boats? We aren't exactly a booming seaport here."

Zeke leaned back, smiling. "You're being modest. The rescue business is really a fairly small community. We heard about your first successful capsizing trial just hours after it happened."

"How?" Den asked. "I was in San Diego, California, at the time, and I didn't hear owt—anything."

"You weren't in the business then," Rob pointed out quietly. "What did you hear about the *Maggie*'s trial?" he asked Zeke.

"That you pulled it off, even when both of your engines failed."

"I was able to restart them."

"But not until after the boat capsized."

Rob was getting impatient. "What is it you want from us, Zeke?"

"We want to buy your design."

Rob exhaled noisily. He'd been expecting this—not from the Coast Guard, but from a boatbuilder in Scotland or even England. In fact, he and his partners had discussed it at length. "It's no' for sale."

"You haven't heard our offer yet."

Rob drained his coffee mug. "It's no' for sale at any price."

Zeke stared at him through narrowed eyes. "Any price?"

"That's what I said. Any price." Rob expected the commander to get up from the table and stalk off.

Instead, Zeke laughed. "That's what we thought you'd say."

Too busy to waste time on senseless blether, Rob's impatience turned to irritation. "Then why are you here?"

"To offer you a contract."

"For what?"

"For as many rescue boats a year as you can turn out."

The meeting lasted all afternoon. Graham and Den left early in the negotiations, Graham to return to the trawler crew, Den to firm up the travel plans for his San Diego electronics expert, who was finally coming to Innisbraw. A little after 1400, Paddy brought bowls of tattie bree and a large platter of bannock to their table in the corner.

Stu proved his worth that afternoon. He asked pertinent questions and made several changes in the wording of the contract.

"I'll have to get PRP to okay these changes," Zeke said, "but that shouldn't be a problem. They told me to be flexible."

"PRP?"

"Planning, Resources, and Procurement."

"I should think they'd have sent a negotiating team," Stu said, "not a single commander."

"They almost did." Zeke wiped his empty soup bowl with his last bite of bannock. "But they decided it'd be overkill. I don't think they wanted to take the chance of scaring Rob off."

"Do you want to be here for the sea trials on our latest boat?" Rob asked.

"You bet. But what I really want to see is that capsizing trial."

"We can pick you up in Oban for that. Save you the long ferry ride."

"Pick me up how?"

"With our floatplane. She's in that hangar at the end of our dock."

Zeke leaned forward. "That's right, I heard you were a pilot in the war. What did you fly?"

"P-47 fighters and B-17 bombers."

"Wow. Diverse. How'd you get into the boatbuilding business?"

"'Tis a long story and it's late. Do you have a reservation for your stay?"

Zeke pulled a piece of paper from his pocket. "I'm at the manse. Is that 'manse' as in 'church'?"

Rob smiled. "Aye, only here church is called kirk. You'll like Hugh MacEwan, our minister." He pushed back his chair. "Well, if you're ready, I'll take you there. Hope that bag isn't too heavy. 'Tis a bit of a walk."

"How do you survive without automobiles?"

"'Tis easy. No smelly fumes, no petrol stations, and no dodging a daft driver with what I believe you still call a 'lead foot.'"

Zeke stood and kneaded the small of his back. "Then lead the way. It's been a long, long two days."

Rob had a good reason for being late to supper. He was too excited to realize how tired he was. "Do you ken what this means, lass?" he asked Maggie. "We're in business and then some. We've agreed to up our production to four rescue boats a year. I don't know how, without hiring new lads and everybody tripping over one another, but I'm sure we can do it. Our future's secure now, luve. The Innisbraw Boatworks is in business to stay."

Maggie hugged him. "I can't believe the news traveled all the way to America. 'Tis a miracle."

"I don't ken about that, but it is remarkable. You'll like Zeke. He's friendly and outgoing and no' impressed with his rank, though he's obviously a real go-getter to have made Commander so young."

"'Tis too bad we don't have room for him to bide here."

"I'm enjoying Ellie's visit too much to wish that. Where is the lass?"

"She went down to the harbour to see Calum off. He's leaving for four days."

"Is there something there, or is it only wishful thinking on my part?"

A frown creased Maggie's brow. "Och, who knows. Ellie hauds her wheesht about the whole thing. And she's never said another word about Richie's faither."

"I'm wondering if they were ever merrit."

"Mebbe. Mebbe no'. I just don't want Calum hurt." Maggie lowered her head. "Now go get your shower. Your supper's on the warming shelf."

Zeke stayed for most of the sea trials and raved about how the Isle of Skye's boat performed. "I can't wait to get back for the capsizing trails," he said.

He and Rob met the ferry on June 16.

"I'll pick you up in Oban the day before the trials." Rob walked him up the gangplank. "Let me know when you arrive. I can be there in half an hour."

"Oh, the miracle of modern travel. I know it's ridiculous to go home for only a few days, but my wife hasn't been well. I need to be with her."

"I'm sorry," Rob said. "If there's a problem, let us know. The capsizing trial date can always be changed."

The date didn't have to be changed. Rob flew to Oban to pick up Zeke on the afternoon of the twenty-seventh. "How's your wife?"

Zeke grinned. "Everything's A-Okay. She's having a difficult pregnancy, but the doctor says things are back on course."

"That's guid. We've been fortunate. Maggie's had no problems with any of our bairnies—babies."

"Lucky man. We lost our first two. Anyway, Carol's doing well now. All we can do is keep our fingers crossed."

"And pray," Rob said as they taxied down the runway.

"Yes, and pray."

When they reached Innisbraw, Rob invited Zeke home to supper. Zeke was congenial and appeared taken with the Savage children. "You hit the jackpot," he told Rob as they relaxed on the entry, while Maggie and Ellie did the dishes. "I don't care whether we have a boy or a girl, just as long as it's healthy. Did you have any preferences?"

"I've felt the same way each time as you do." Rob scratched Shep's neck. "The Lord's blessed us and we know it."

Zeke went to the railing and looked out toward the blazing sunset colouring the sky with vivid red, oranges, and yellows. "I've noticed you mentioning prayer and God several times. You're a Christian?"

"Aye. I would say most of the folk on Innisbraw are."

"I thought you must be. There was something about the way you negotiated that contract. You weren't greedy, and you made sure it was fair for both parties involved."

Rob joined Zeke at the railing. "'Tis only fitting. The Lord's blessed the Boatworks from the beginning. We aren't about to ruin a guid thing by getting greedy now."

The capsizing trial was scheduled for 0800, when the tide would be at its apex. Rob kissed Maggie guidbye at 0700 and headed for the harbour. After he passed the infirmary, he waved to Elspeth on her front entry.

"Godspeed," she called.

He turned in at her gate and quickly climbed the stairs. "So you ken about the trial this mornin?" He kissed her tissue-thin cheek.

She ran a palm along the side of his face. "Of course. I need to ken how to pray."

"The Lord bless you, Elspeth."

"Och, He already has. On you go, lad, and don't disremember, this is the Lord's endeavor too."

"I'm no' about to disremember that. Thank ye for your prayers. A lot rides on this trial."

"On you go, then. It will be perfect."

The Isle of Skye's boat capsized in a deep trough of water between Heuch Fell and a large rock, and righted herself almost immediately. The *Maggie*, which was standing by, sounded her siren. The moment the new boat entered calm seas, Rob gave her voice an opportunity to be heard.

Zeke acted as excited as a lad at a carnival. "I've never seen anything like it. You've really done it!"

Zeke was called back to the United States early the next morning. His wife had gone into premature labour.

Rob flew him to Glasgow, where he could catch a train to London. "Don't fash yourself," Rob told him. "Our minister's let the folk know, and they'll be praying. You're no' alone."

Zeke's dark brown eyes softened. "I know that, Rob. I just hope God hears them."

"You know what the word 'hope' means in the original language of the Bible?" Rob asked. Before Zeke could answer, he said, "Absolute confidence that the Lord will do the right thing. Keep that thought, Zeke, and call me when your bairnie's born. We have a custom here on Innisbraw. If it's a lad, the steeple bell rings four times, and if a lass, five. We'll ring the bell for your bairnie, so let us know."

The next afternoon the steeple bell rang four times. The folk of Innisbraw rejoiced that Carol Evans had delivered a tiny but healthy lad far away in America.

Chapter Thirty-Six

Ellie needed time to be alone and pray. She left Richie in Maggie's capable hands and walked down to the kirk. Why did the people of this small island care so much about what happened to strangers on the other side of the Atlantic? When she entered the sanctuary, her heart plummeted.

Hugh busied himself at the altar, replacing candles. "Guid day, Ellie," he said, smiling. "'Tis a bonnie mornin, isn't it?"

She smiled in return. How could she not? He was as warm and cuddly as a teddy bear.

"I'll leave you alone in a moment." He lifted a large box of candles. "I'm almost finished."

"There's no hurry. I just wanted to spend some time in prayer. I've noticed how close I feel to God when I'm here."

"I'm happy to hear you say that. I find it a perfect place for prayer myself."

Ellie pulled out a kneeler and settled herself, gaze drawn to the stained-glass portrait of the Risen Christ behind the altar. This was so hard. She should never have come to Innisbraw. Why hadn't she anticipated the questions people might ask—or her reluctance to explain?

Tears welled in her eyes, fracturing the brilliant blues, reds, and yellows of the glass. She bowed her head and tried to pray, but she was so confused she didn't know where to start. "Help me, Lord," she begged, "please help me." She sat and waited in silence, hoping for guidance.

A hand settled on her shoulder as Hugh slipped into the pew and knelt beside her. "Our luving Heavenly Faither, only Ye and Ellie ken the reason for her tears. She has asked for Your help, and that prayer never goes unanswered. Quiet her soul so she can hear Your voice as Ye speak words of comfort through Your Holy Spirit. In Jesus's name we pray. Amen." He started to rise.

Ellie put a hand on his arm. "Please stay. I'm so torn, I don't know what to do."

"Then I'll bide a while." He patted her hand. "Would it help to talk about it?"

"I have a secret I've kept for years." Tears trickled down her cheeks. "I haven't told anyone, and now I feel I have to, and it's tearing me apart. I don't know what to do."

"Does this secret involve somebody else—somebody dear to you?"

"The two people I treasure the most."

"I heard someone open the front door." Hugh grasped her elbow and helped her stand. "My office is more private." He led her through a small door at the side of the sanctuary. "It's just ahead."

The warmth of his office drew her in. With the window drape open, the morning light glinted off shiny surfaces—a glass-covered picture of school children centered on a wall, the green shade of an Anglepoise lamp, the gilded edge of an ancient-looking tome on his book-cluttered desk. The pleasant, brittle scent of old paper bindings anchored her to a place of timeless sanctuary.

He settled her in a chair and pulled another up across from her.

She wiped her eyes with her handkerchief. No more tears. These walls had surely heard much worse than what she had to tell.

"Now," Hugh said, leaning forward. "Ye don't have to tell me your secret, for that's your own private business, but there must be a way for me to help ye. After all, our Lord led ye here today for a reason, and He doesn't make mistakes."

"I do need your help."

That teddy bear smile again. "What ye need is our Lord's help, no' mine."

"I've prayed and prayed for an answer, but I still don't know what to do." She took several deep breaths. "I don't want to ruin my brother's reputation when he isn't here to defend himself."

"Was your brother's sin so great that others would judge him unfairly?"

"I don't know. I only know I can't ruin his name when he gave his life in the war. And he died not even knowing he had a son." She covered her mouth.

"So your lad, Richie … he's no' your son, but your brother's?"

A pain pierced her chest. "Please don't tell anyone. I've had Richie since he was three days old."

Hugh pulled his chair closer and took her hand.

The warmth of his touch soothed her fears. He was a man of God. He wouldn't betray her—or Rich.

"And does Richie no' wonder about his faither—who he is, where he is?" The lilting cadence of Hugh's voice softened his words.

"I've told him from the beginning he was adopted and that my brother died in the war. Last year I gave him the medals the War Department awarded Rich. They're his most prized possessions—those and the letter of condolence Rob wrote from Edinburg. Rich was killed on the same mission that wounded Rob the first time."

A knowing look came over Hugh's features. "Rob's spoken to me often about his grief over your brother's death—that he wasn't able to say guidbye."

"They were close."

"And now you're here on Innisbraw, staying with Rob and Maggie, seeing Calum, Maggie's brother, and ye have no explanation for your absent husband. Why haven't ye told them ye adopted Richie, that he isn't your natural son?"

"Because Richie's the exact image of Rich. Even Rob commented on it. Rich and I looked alike, so everyone's assumed it's only a family resemblance. If I tell them he's adopted, they'll guess the truth immediately. I don't want that."

Hugh settled back in his chair, making a steeple of his hands. "Perhaps if ye tell me how ye were able to claim Richie as your own, I'll have more understanding."

If only Hugh would take her hand again. She needed his touch to bring her courage. "Rich and Linda went to the same high school. He had a crush on her, but she was beautiful and popular and acted like he didn't even exist. Her father's a judge, and she only dated the sons of her parents' country-club friends. Do you understand the kind of people I'm talking about?"

Hugh grunted. "Of course. False pride elevates many above their real station in life."

"When Rich quit college, enlisted in the Air Forces, and returned from training, the girls in town flocked around him, flirting, wanting to touch his uniform. The night before he shipped out, some of Rich's buddies threw him a party—and guess who showed up, wearing lip paint, real nylons, high heels, and enough perfume to overwhelm a skunk?"

"Linda."

Ellie nodded. "I left the party a few minutes after I saw her pulling him toward her Mercury convertible." Her cheeks burned. How catty that sounded. What would Hugh think? She looked up from beneath lowered lashes.

"Ye paint a vivid picture."

"After I saw Rich off at the train station, I never thought about Linda again—until her father barged into my apartment months later, accompanied by two lawyers." Her lips thinned at the memory.

"Butter could have melted in his mouth, though his eyes showed contempt when he looked around my shabby living room. He spread some papers on my table and asked me to read them."

"Adoption papers?"

She swallowed around the bitter taste in her mouth. "Yes. Adoption papers stating that I was now the legal mother of an unnamed boy, father Richard Andrew Florey, mother's name sealed by court order, who had been born at Elliot Hospital in Manchester, New Hampshire, that morning." She lifted her head, anger fueling her words. "That very morning, Hugh. No questions about what I wanted, no doubting my ability to be a mother to his grandchild, no thought about my shock at hearing that Rich had a son—nothing." She leaped to her feet. "And on top of that, the judge had the nerve to push an envelope filled with money across the table. 'To help find a better apartment and for unexpected expenses,' was the way that horrible, pompous ..."

"And ye signed the papers."

She threw herself into the chair, trembling at a memory she'd tried so long to bury. "I know the Lord was with me that afternoon. I told him I wouldn't sign a thing until I saw the baby and prayed for guidance." Her sudden laugh sounded brittle to her own ears. "And I pushed the envelope back. 'You might buy the court's cooperation,' I said, 'but you won't buy mine.' Then I stalked into the bathroom, slammed the door, and lost my lunch."

"Ye're a verra brave woman, Ellie." Hugh removed his glasses and polished them on his handkerchief. "I take it ye recognized something of your brother in the wee lad?"

"The second I looked at him, I knew. There was so little of Linda, only Rich." Tears overflowed onto her cheeks. "The hospital let me take him home two days later. And he'll be mine forever."

"He never bothered ye again? The judge, I mean."

"He was appointed to the New Hampshire Supreme Court by Governor Blood and the family moved to Concord. Apparently the judge covered his underhanded dealings well."

Hugh handed her a clean handkerchief and waited while she dried her face. "But how have ye survived? Raising a bairn takes silver. I understand ye're a schoolteacher but, here in Scotland at least, they don't earn what they deserve."

"I was the beneficiary of Rich's military insurance. It wasn't much, but I was able to move to a nearby town, find a small apartment above a garage, and pay the landlady to watch Richie while I taught school. Even so, it's been hard." Her laugh held a sarcastic edge. "Peanut butter, bruised fruit, and oatmeal can keep an adult healthy for a long time."

A long sigh escaped Hugh's lips. "What ye've told me took courage, Ellie. I didna ken your brother, but many of our lads served in that terrible war, and some made the ultimate sacrifice. One night of indiscretion could never make me think less of them. None of us are withoot sin."

"Rob's the one I'm worried about. I don't want anything to taint his memories of Rich."

Hugh rose and gripped her shoulder. "Ye don't ken Rob if ye think that possible. He's not a naïve lad, Ellie. Tell him the truth and allow him to treasure the gift ye've brought from America—Rich's son. Take as long as ye want to pray aboot this. And I'm here for ye whenever you need." He left, closing the door behind him.

Ellie remained alone in Hugh's office for over an hour. When she left, the burden she had been carrying no longer weighed on her heart. She would tell everyone who had known Rich as soon as possible. Hugh was surely right. Rob would be pleased. He already looked at Richie with such fondness.

And Calum would hear the truth as soon as he returned from fishing. She'd been so secretive, he may think she was the one with a past.

She had asked for God's guidance. No matter what happened, it would turn out the way He wanted.

Chapter Thirty-Seven

The thrice-weekly ferry arrivals brought many changes to the island. Paddy added to his howff's menu and renovated the kitchen. "This winter, we're goin' to add a room at the back for bar customers," Paddy told Rob the afternoon Zeke Evans left. "Then, the front can be used for a dinin' room only. I'm thinkin' people eatin' want to look out at the harbour, so we'll add more windows."

"'Tis a grand plan, Paddy. Get together with Paul Murray. He can give you a price and timetable."

"How's the construction business comin', then? Are you busy?"

"Och, so busy I'm about worn oot. What we need is another partner who knows construction. One of my auld waist gunners is in the business in the States. I'm going to call and see if he knows somebody who might be interested."

"You're lookin' a might peaked, Rob. How about a pasty?"

"Maggie'll kill me if I don't eat my supper at home." Rob got to his feet. "I'd best give heels to. We're still working on how to turn out four rescue boats a year."

"'Tis a thorny problem," Paddy grinned and winked. "All this business."

Rob slapped him on the shoulder. "But a guid problem if it can be solved, isn't it? See ye, Paddy."

"Why did Ellie ask Jill to watch the bairns?" Rob toweled his hair dry. "She said she only wanted to see us all for a few minutes."

Maggie chewed her lip. "Keep your voice down, luve. She'll hear you. She was most insistent that only Den, Fern, and John be here with us. And no bairns. I've never seen her like this, all full of backbone one minute, then looking like she was about to weep a burn the next." She turned to leave, then whirled back. "And hurry. Everybody will be here in a tick."

Rob dressed, grumbling about having to wait for supper. He was so hungry he felt light-headed. He should have eaten that pasty at the howff. He pulled on clean breeks and a shirt, then padded out into the living room.

Ellie, standing at the head of the dining room table, nodded at Rob to take a seat. Everyone she had asked to attend was there. Would they understand her secret—and agree to keep it? Or was her dream vacation about to come to an abrupt end? *Hold me up, Lord. Give me strong legs and an even stronger purpose.*

All eyes were on her. Fern and Maggie smiled, but Den and Rob looked disgruntled. The light caught John's glasses, hiding his eyes.

John. Calum's father.

She groped for the edge of the table and held on. One deep breath, a swallow. "Before I start, I want to thank you for being here tonight." Why did her voice quiver so? Another swallow. "It's so hard to catch each of you alone, and what I need to say is meant for you and only you. This isn't something you can spread around the island. It's private. Deeply private."

No smiles now. Only concerned and penetrating gazes.

"I know you've all wondered why Richie's father didn't accompany us to Innisbraw. I'm sorry I haven't been brave enough to tell you all of this before, but it's something I've kept secret since the day Richie was born." She hesitated.

A sudden peace washed over her, bringing strength.

Thank You for Your blessing, Lord. She met each curious gaze without hesitation. "I've told Richie that his father was killed in the war, which is the truth. He also knows that I adopted him. All I've kept from him are the circumstances leading up to his birth."

Rob leaned forward, a sad smile playing across his lips as if he'd already guessed the truth.

She related Rich's futile infatuation with the lovely Linda, and how she had taken him away from the party the night before he left for war. She told about Linda's father visiting Ellie's apartment and the papers he demanded she sign. Her voice didn't waver and her gaze didn't falter until she described seeing Richie for the first time. "He was the image of my brother." Tears escaped her eyes and streamed down her cheeks. "I would have signed every paper in the world to claim him as my own."

Rob started to rise, but thankfully, Maggie held him back.

Ellie regained control long enough to add. "Please, I beg you, never breathe this to another soul. I'll not have Richie upset, nor one indiscretion stain Rich's memory." She sank into the nearest chair and buried her hands in her face, weeping. *Forgive me, Rich, but they had to know.*

Rob still reached her first. He pulled her into his arms and rocked her back and forth. "Hush-a-baw, Ellie. There's no' a soul here who would break the trust ye've placed in us. And there is no stain on Rich's name. We've all sinned. It was all covered on the cross." He laid his cheek against her hair. "And ye've brought the verra best part of Rich to us, to treasure forever."

Everyone voiced murmurs of agreement as Ellie was passed from one person's arms to another.

John was last to embrace her. "Tell Calum, lass," he whispered. "It will bring him peace."

She hid her smile against his chest. "The minute he docks."

Rob often worked far into the night at his drafting table, turning out remodel plans for several of the more affluent families who were adding bedrooms and another bathing room to their cottages so they could take in more tourists.

"What I need is another man to do this," he said to Maggie. "There aren't enough hours in the day to see it all done."

"You're losing weight again, luve." She frowned. "I don't like it."

He took her into his arms and rested his chin on her head. "I'm eating you out of house and home."

"I ken." She sighed and pressed closer. "Call Gunny. You should have done it when Ellie suggested it."

"I'll do it." He looked at his watch. "No' now, though. I'll have to wait until around fourteen hundred to catch him at home before he goes to bed. I'll get to it as soon as I can."

"Och, I forgot to tell you. A man called from Mull earlier today. He said he was the captain of the yacht that ran aground on the south side of the island. He wanted you to call him as soon as you could."

"Now?"

"Aye. He said it was verra important. I wrote his name and number by the phone in your office."

He kissed her. "Did anyone ever tell you what a grand secretary you are?"

She laughed. "You—every time I take a message for you."

Rob gave the operator the number, tapping his fingers on his desk.

A man answered.

Rob identified himself.

"Commander Savage, I'm glad you returned my call. I have some good news for you."

"Guid news?"

"You'd better speak clear English tonight, Commander. This connection's bad."

"I don't understand what you mean by good news."

"You will shortly. How's that crew of yours? All well, I hope."

"Verra—very well. What can I do for you?"

"Nothing, absolutely nothing, but we want to do something for you."

He didn't sound blootered. "I still don't understand."

"Listen, Commander, all of the fellows you pulled out of the drink want to give you a little something for your trouble."

Rob stood and paced as far as the telephone cord would allow. "That isn't necessary. We render a volunteer service. There's no charge."

"We understand that. We've been told that the coastal rescue services in Scotland are all run on a volunteer basis. Even you, as the commander, don't receive pay for what you do. Right?"

"Aye—yes."

"But you do take donations to keep your operation afloat—no pun intended."

"We do. Donations are used to defray the cost of replacing equipment and repairs to our boat, and to pay our mechanic."

"Well, we have a little check for you. We all got together and threw in five thousand dollars. That's forty-five thousand dollars, American. I realize that amount drops considerably when converted to English pounds, but it should still help."

Rob couldn't speak. Forty-five thousand dollars?

"You still there, or did you fall off your chair?"

Rob hadn't fallen off his chair—he'd collapsed into it. "I ... I'm here."

"Good. I'll send the check directly to you to be spent for whatever you need."

"I can't imagine it." Rob wrote *$45,000* on his blotter. "Are you certain you want to do this? 'Tis so much money."

"How do you put a value on a human life, Commander?"

"You don't." A stunned whisper.

"What was that? I couldn't hear you clearly."

"You can't put a value on a human life. It's too precious."

"Exactly. Well, I have another meeting to get to, so I'll have to hang up. Thank you again, Commander Savage. I hope we meet again under better circumstances."

"Of course. I ... I thank ye and the others."

"Goodbye then. Happy sailing."

The line buzzed.

Rob hung up the phone and sat back in his chair, running his fingers through his hair. What were they to do with forty-five thousand American dollars? He picked up the receiver to call Stu, thought better of it, and hung up. He needed to sleep on this.

Calum's boat docked early the following afternoon.

Ellie asked Maggie to watch Richie and ran down the path, pulse racing faster than her feet. "Help me speak the truth, Lord. I know I shouldn't be, but I'm so nervous."

Calum stood on the dock waiting for her. He picked her up and twirled her around. "It was the best fishing ever. You've brought me luck, lass."

Her cheeks heated at the fervor of his embrace. "That's wonderful, but I'm sure it was your skill, not luck."

"Mebbe a wee bit of both." He grinned. "I'll walk ye home, though I need to go bathe straight after that." He squeezed her waist. "I'm going to ask Faither to have Rob's company install one of those showers in the cottage. I'm tired of trying to fit these long legs of mine into something no' much bigger than a washtub." He took her hand as they walked onto the pier.

Surely he could hear her heart pounding. "There's something I want to tell you. Can we stop at that bench on the beach over there?"

He studied her face. "You look pale. Are you sick, then, lass?"

"Not sick. I just have something in my past you need to know about."

"On you come. You're too young to have much to tell."

"I'm two years older than you, Calum."

"What's two years?" He led her to the bench. "All right, I'm listening."

She sat down and adjusted her skirt over her knees. "This is going to be difficult, so bear with me, all right?"

He nodded and took her hand.

"You know my brother, Rich, was Rob's tail gunner during the war."

"I remember Rob talking about him. He considered him a friend as well as a member of his crew."

"They were good friends."

"This has something to do with your brother?"

"Yes. Everything to do with Rich."

"Och, go on."

"My brother was killed in action on his twenty-fifth mission. If he'd survived, they might have let him come home for a while before sending him somewhere else."

"I'm sorry, lass."

She studied his strong, calloused hand. "I was devastated. Rich was more than an older brother. He filled the gap left by my father's death. I walked around in a daze for weeks. I couldn't believe he was gone." She withdrew her hand from his and knotted her fingers. "But now I have to go back a bit." She quickly told him what had happened.

"Adoption papers? I don't understand. Did he claim your brother forced himself on her?"

"You're the first one who's asked that. I suppose she waited so long to tell her parents, they couldn't have convinced a court. Anyway, I went to see the baby and knew at once he was Rich's. So I signed the papers, and Richie's been mine since that day."

"But hasn't he asked aboot his faither?"

"When he was old enough, I told him his father was my brother—that he was killed in the war. I also told him that I adopted him. Richie's too young now, but someday, he'll ask about his real mother, and I'll try to be as kind as I can. But I don't want my son to know he's a ... he was conceived out of wedlock. I dread the day he asks questions." She hid her face in her hands.

"His faither was a hero. Nothing will ever take that away." Strong hands pulled her to her feet. "You'll never ken how relieved I am. I'm ashamed to say I—"

She lifted her face and searched his eyes. "Thought I was a woman with lax morals?"

"Och, no' that. Never that. I just wondered if your husband had left you and would want you back someday. Surely he'd realize what a treasure he abandoned."

She couldn't believe the smile on his face.

He lowered his lips to hers. Such a gentle kiss, so filled with love.

Tears flooded her eyes as her lips responded.

After a long moment, they drew apart and Calum stroked her cheek. "Don't go home to America. I canna bear the thought of losing ye."

"But we hardly know each other."

"Then give us the chance. If ye go away, it can never happen." He pulled her back into his arms. "I love you, Ellie. I want to grow auld with ye, with Richie beside us."

Chapter Thirty-Eight

Rob phoned a banker in Oban the next morning and was told the 45,000 American dollars were worth about 12,000 English pounds.

His next call was to his partners, asking them to meet him as soon as possible.

He prowled his office, dodging chairs, straightening pictures, running fingers through his hair as he related his telephone conversation the night before.

Den flashed a thumbs-up. "That's a lot of silver, bucko. It'll cover Neil's wages and the *Maggie*'s maintenance for more years than she'll be seaworthy."

"Bide a wee." Stu leaned forward and cleared his throat. "With all the donations we've taken in from the large fisheries, I'm thinking you've other plans for that silver, Rob."

Leave it to Stu to see more potential than the obvious. Rob planted himself on a corner of his desk. "I do. But we all have to be in agreement."

The meeting lasted an hour.

When it was over, Rob struck out for Elspeth's cottage. He found her in her garden deadheading spent blossoms.

"Lad, what brings you here at this time of mornin?" She slipped her secateurs into her apron pocket. "Is owt wrong?"

"'Tis business, Elspeth." He took her elbow and helped her up the stairs. "I've a proposition for you." When she settled into her rocker, he sat opposite her and reached for her hands.

"What is it? You're about to give me heart palpitations, you're that kittled up."

He couldn't help grinning. "You ken me too well. I *am* kittled up."

"Aboot what?"

His smile broadened. "As head of the Island Council, I want you to be the first to hear the guid news."

Her gaze sharpened. "Stop blethering and get to the point."

And folk thought *he* was impatient. "Remember how you told the Council to stretch their minds concerning where to come up with the money to build an academy here on Innisbraw?"

She nodded.

"Well, the most amazing thing has happened. Do you recall that American yacht that ran afoul of the rocks on our south shore?"

"Of course I mind. I may be auld, but I'm no' senile."

"The survivors are donating money to the rescue fund. A lot of money. Twelve thousand pounds."

Her mouth opened and closed. She removed her hands from his and pulled her kerchief from her sleeve. "But what has that to do with the academy?" Her voice quavered as she wiped her lips.

"Stu needs to do the right paper work, but the Innisbraw Construction Company is going to donate twelve thousand pounds worth of supplies and labour toward building an academy. We'll have to pay an architect to draw up the plans, but with the stone walls being provided free, and us donating our labour to do the roofing and finish the inside, we should be able to make it."

She groped for his hand. "But that's rescue money." Her fingers trembled. "Shouldn't it be spent on the rescue boat and its expenses?"

"It will be, in a way."

"I don't ken your meaning."

"We don't need that much money, Elspeth. We've already taken in several large donations from the owners of the big fishery boats, but we have to keep it in the rescue fund so the donors can claim a tax deduction to a charity." Rob leaned forward, "Stu's got it all figured out. We won't be out a farthing for rescue work for a long, long time. So we turn around and donate the money to the school. I know 'tis complicated, but 'tis legal."

She fanned her face with her kerchief. "I'll have to take your word, lad. I've never had a head for business."

"If we can find the workers, we can have the school built in time for next year's enrollment."

"Och, you'll find the workers, never fear." Tears softened her gaze. "Our folk want that academy. The men will gladly give their time and labour. Of a fact, Hugh's already volunteered to be headmaster."

Rob kissed her cheek. Fragrant, it was, with the scent of heather—the fragrance that had brought him his Maggie. It was time to show his gratitude. "This comes with one condition. That we get to name the school."

"What's in a name?" Her voice quavered. "Isn't that what Mister Shakespeare said?"

"It will be called the 'Elspeth NicAllister Academy.'"

Elspeth was struck dumb.

Rob called Pete Hastings in Columbus, Ohio, at exactly 1400 the following afternoon.

"Hastings."

The familiar voice caught Rob unprepared. "Uh, this is Rob Savage, Gunny."

A pause. "What kind of a sicko are you? I oughta call the police."

Gunny didn't believe him? Didn't recognize his voice? "Our Fort was the *Liberty Belle*," Rob said quickly. "During a single-plane strike on Metz, we took a lot of flak. I told you to bail out just after we crossed the Channel. Still doubt it's me?"

Pete choked and sputtered. "Why, you son of a gun. I heard you were killed a year after that crash."

"I almost was, but thanks to a lot of prayer and nursing from my wife, Maggie, I made it."

"You're married? This has to be a prank. Where are you calling from?"

"A wee island off the coast of Scotland. I've married a Scots lass and make my home here now."

"Scotland! No wonder you sound different. You're talking with a brogue."

"It's called a burr here. You're thinking of Ireland, Gunny."

"Gunny." He snorted and choked again. "I haven't been called that in years. Wait till I call Ellie. You remember Rich's sister. She lives—"

Rob chuckled. "You don't have to call Ellie. She's here on holiday right now."

"You can't mean it. Why didn't she let me know you were alive? I'll tan her little hide for this."

"She'd heard rumors about me, but wanted to see for herself before she let you know. She traced me down through the Red Cross."

"Why didn't I think of that? I should have known you were too ornery to die so young."

Rob wanted to climb through the telephone wires, wanted to throw his arms around the lad he still luved, wanted to tell him how much his friendship meant. "How are you doing, Gunny?"

"Oh, fine, fine. You remember me talking about my wife, Caroline? We knock around in this great, big house I built. I'm a contractor, but Ellie probably told you that. Anyway, no kids but lots of success. I got in at the beginning of the building boom after the war, so we've got nothing to complain about. You got any kids yet, Rob?"

"Three. One lad and twa lasses."

"You're a lucky man. Caroline's an adoption counselor, but we're like the cobbler whose family had no shoes."

"Give yourself a little time. Things have a way of working themselves oot." Rob tried to remember the wording of his well-rehearsed question. But he didn't have to mince words with a man who'd faced death with him. "I've a favor to ask. I need some advice."

"Advice? From me? That's a good one. Fire away. This I have to hear."

Half an hour later, when Rob hung up the phone, his jaw ached from a perpetual smile. He called Den into his office. "I just talked to Gunny Hastings."

"He give you a lead on a contractor?"

"No' yet."

"What does that mean?"

"It means he has to check a few people oot. But that's no' the guid part. He and his wife, Caroline, are coming here the last week in August, Den. Gunny's coming here."

"For a holiday or to stay?"

What was that wee sideways look for? "A holiday, of course. He said Caroline's been nattering at him to take some time off, so he's bringing her to Innisbraw."

Den chuckled. "Well, well. Dale will be here in twa weeks to install the trawler's radar and now Gunny's coming. If we're no' careful, the Island Council will chase us off for overrunning their paradise with Yanks."

Deep purple bled dark blue and red smears across the darkening sky as the sun plunged recklessly toward the horizon. In the side yard, a hen clucked the birth of her daily egg, and Shep raised his head from the entry flags, scented the air for any nearby creatures, then sighed and returned to sleep.

Maggie settled into Rob's lap on the front entry with a satisfied sigh of her own. Bairns abed, dishes done, and a long een to look forward to. She closed her eyes and buried her face against Rob's bare chest. Fresh from the shower, he was, chest hairs still damp and tickling her cheek. "I can't believe your auld friends are coming all the way from America to Innisbraw."

"No' only mine, but Den's friend will be here first. Den's hoping he'll decide to come back to stay." His deep chuckle reverberated in her ear.

"But he's coming for business, no' pleasure."

Soft lips trailed her forehead, bringing a warm flush of luve and gratitude. How heartbroken she'd been when leaving Innisbraw for nursing school in Edinburgh. If only she'd had a wee glimpse of what the Lord had prepared for her future—three perfect bairns and a husband who made a mockery of her childhood fancies, he so outshone them.

His cheek brushed hers. "I've never met Gunny's wife, Caroline, but from her pictures, she's a bonnie lass with a sonsie smile. I'm hoping you'll like her."

She laced her fingers through his. "You're happy, aren't ye?"

"I am that. I never thought I'd see Gunny again—till heaven, that is."

"He's a Christian, then?"

"He and Rich both were. I didn't consider it at the time, but that's what must have cemented our friendship, knowing we shared the faith that, though the war might separate us on earth, would bring us together through eternity." His voice had dropped to a whisper. Still grieving for Rich, he was.

"But you haven't really lost Rich entirely here." She sat up and smiled, tears misting her eyes. "You see him every day in Richie. You'll watch him grow into a halflin, and then a man, until one day he'll marry and have his own lad, and 'twill all begin again, a perfect gift from a luving Faither."

A finger traced her eyebrow. "You're right. I almost lost it the first time I saw Richie's crooked grin. A part of me wanted to run and hide from memories of ... but I couldn't." Rob's voice cracked. "'Twas like I had a second chance to spend time with Rich—to show him how much I luved him—without the sound of machine guns and the smell of cordite being constant reminders that just one .20 millimetre shell could shatter the physical bond between us forever." A shudder shook his body.

Pain spread through her chest, freezing her breath.

How could any man forget the horrors of war when he had lived through them day after bitter day? Perhaps a man couldn't on his own, but with the Lord's help, those dreadful memories could be blurred around the edges, softened by new memories of luve and family and life in a new, free world.

She hugged his chest. "Only the physical bond, Rob, but you ken that."

"Aye, thank the Lord." He rocked her, fingers tangled in her hair.

A question leaped into her mind. "Who do you want to see first in heaven?"

"Jesus." No pause to consider, no hesitation. "I'm going to throw myself at His feet and thank Him for giving me eternal life—and you."

"Och, you can't put me and eternal life in the same thought."

"Why no'? Our Lord's grace no' only provided me forgiveness and a never-ending future, but He gave me a taste of heaven right here on earth."

How could he say that after all the times her faith had faltered—even failed? And the times they'd disagreed—the hurtful words she'd spoken. Surely there were no arguments in heaven. "You frighten me." She buried her face against his chest. "I can never live up to such perfection."

A chuckle rumbled beneath her cheek. "I said a *taste* of heaven, luve." He raised her chin with his palm. "And never change. You're Maggie, my luve, my all. If I didn't have your luve to lift me up when I come near crashing, or to bring me doon when I fly too high, I'd have nowt to tie me to the now, to reality."

The luve in his eyes bathed her in warmth. Och, and he apologized about never having words to express his luve.

Robert Burns himself could never make her heart sing with such joy.

He kissed her forehead. "And then I want to meet Saint Paul. He's shown me to keep my eyes on the Lord first, and all my other relationships will fall into line. And I like his descriptions that compare our battles here on earth to those soldiers he saw about Rome."

Spoken like a man—especially a military one. She raised her head and tapped a finger on his chin. "That's strange. He's my second choice too, and 'tis no' because he told the Ephesians to put on the belt of truth and breastplate of righteousness."

"Then why?"

"Because he spoke to the common folk, in simple words they could understand. About luve, about mercy, about being an example and putting our faith into action."

"Mmm."

"And the third person you'll seek out?"

"My mither."

Of course. A frisson of happiness brought a smile. "What a grand time that'll be, seeing luved ones and friends, joining them in worship at the throne of God."

"There've been times in the past when knowing that was all that kept me sane."

The haunting trill of a laverock floated on the soft edge of the gloaming.

"You'll be reunited with Rich, and all those lads and men who were believers, and we'll both see Malcolm—and Elspeth, who will be there long before us." Her lips trailed across his throat. "And we'll be together forever, Rob."

"Aye, my Maggie. You and I. Forever and ever and ever."

The End

Acknowledgments

From the Publisher~

In past books in the Thistle Series, we used Dianne's own acknowledgments, which she had penned before her death. However, she was not able to work far enough ahead to have that material ready for this fourth book.

Accordingly, we have to assume that she would be thanking the same people:

Paddy MacKinnon, for her hospitality.

All Dianne's children, for their love and support.

The Ashberry Lane Editors—Christina Tarabochia, Sherrie Ashcraft, Kristen Johnson, Tami Engle, Andrea Cox, Rachel Lulich, and Amy Smith—who are blessed to continue their work in bringing Dianne's legacy to print.

And to her readers. We know she loves you all!

Bio

Dianne fell in love with writing at the age of five. Because her father was a barnstorming pilot, she was bitten early by the "flying bug" as well. She attended the University of California, Santa Barbara, and met and married the man God had prepared for her—an aeronautical engineer. After their five children were in school, she burned the midnight oil and wrote three novels, all published by Zebra Press. When her husband died, only three years after he retired, she felt drawn to visit the Outer Hebrides Isles of Scotland, where her husband's clan (MacDonalds) and her own clan (Galbraiths) originated. Many yearly trips, gallons of tea, too little sleep, and a burst of insight birthed her *Thistle Series*.

PUBLISHER'S NOTE: Dianne, born August 1933, lived joyfully despite dealing with terminal cancer and died in August 2013, a mere week before the release date for the first book of this series, *Broken Wings*. Everyone involved with the production of the six books in the series has been blessed beyond measure to be part of giving readers a chance to meet Rob and Maggie and visit the beautiful, fictional isle of Innisbraw.

Leave a message for her family and sign up to hear the latest at
www.ashberrylane.com/dianneprice or
www.facebook.com/authordianneprice.

Glossary

All words are Scots, unless otherwise noted.

APC: headache medicine.
auld: old.

baffies: bedroom slippers.
bairn: child.
bairnie: baby.
bannock: oat griddle bread, similar to English muffins.
ben: mountain.
biddy certain: very sure.
biggen: pregnant.
blether: talk, visit. (In the plural, nonsense.)
blootered: very drunk.
blowsterin: windy, gusty, boasting.
bodhrán: Gaelic (pronounced *bo-rahn*), one-sided drum.
bonnie: beautiful.
bowf: a dog's bark.
braw: handsome, a pleasing sight.
bree: soup or broth.
breeks: pants or trousers.
brose: creamy oat porridge, soaked overnight.
bunker: counter, like in a kitchen.
bunnet: a flat cap.
burn: small stream.
buttery: biscuit made with butter.

cairt: cart pulled by a horse.
cannie: shrewd, expert, skillful, or lucky.
cat's lick: wash hands and face, short wash-up.
ceilidh: Gaelic (pronounced *kay-lee*), party with music, dancing, sharing of news.
chaumer: parlour or gathering room.
clootie: steamed, sweet dumpling pudding dessert served with clotted cream.
clothes-press: dresser for clothing or bedding.
coo: cow.
crabbit: crabby, cranky.
croft: piece of land.
crofter: farmer, or one who owns a croft used for agriculture.
cuddy: small, shaggy horse, usually used to pull a cart

daft: insane.
disremember: forget.
dreich: dreary, dull, grey, usually describing weather.
dumfoondert: confused.

eejit: idiot, fool.
een: evening, can be written e'en.
emulsion: UK, paint.
entry: porch, passage into house.

faither: father.
fauld yer fit: rest, sit down.
fankle: disorder, entanglement.
fash: worry, vex.
fell: mountain or hill.
flag: piece of stone used as the floor of a cottage.
firstie: West Point 4th year or senior.

girse: grass.
gleg as a gled: starving, keen as an eagle.
gloaming: twilight.
grandbairn: grandchild.
grandfaither: grandfather.
grandmither: grandmother.
guid: (pronounced *gid*) good.

halflin: adolescent, teenager.
handsel: gift, usually handmade for a special occasion, like marriage.
hap: knitted blanket, afghan.
haud yer wheesht: hold your tongue.
hippen: diaper.
Hogmanay: New Year's Eve.
howff: pub.
hoy: greeting.

infirmary: UK, hospital.
Irisher: Irishman or woman.
Irn Bru: soda with a taste of tangerine, very sweet, national soft drink.

jawbox: kitchen sink.
joint: UK, roast.

keek: look at, peek.

ken: know, understand.
kirk: church.
kittled up: excited, enlivened.

lemon skoosh: sparkling lemonade.
louring: dark, black, heavy clouds or sky.

machair: Gaelic (pronounced *ma-K-er*), alluvial plain, unique to Outer Hebrides.
mebbe: maybe.
medicaments: UK, medicine.
merrit: married.
midden: dirty, messy, untidy place.
Minch: arm of the Atlantic Ocean between Outer Hebrides and Scotland.
mither: mother.

natter: chat, talk, often nag.
neeps: turnips.
no': not.
nowt: nothing.

owt: anything.

piece: snack, usually a small sandwich or buttery.
plowtering: splashing, playing in water.
polis: police.
pottle: pot full.
press: cabinet.

redd: clean, organize, tidy (up).
rouping: Scots, crying, usually a baby or small child.

Sassenach: English person.
Siobhan: Gaelic (pronounced *Shi-vahn)*, woman's name.
skail: heavy, driving wind.
skellum: little imp or misbehaving child.
skirlie: recipe made with raw oats and chopped onions browned in meat fat.
skite one's lug: box on the ears.
sleeperie: sleepy.
slitterie: messy.

slubber: slobber.
sma': small.
smoorich: cuddle.
snell: cold, if wind, usually from the north.
strathspey: regal, gliding dance.
swither: bemused, perplexed.

tatties: potatoes.
the day: today.
The Lift: Outer Hebrides, bearers carry casket from kirk to grave after service.
the morra: tomorrow.
tick: a second in time.
trews: leggings, tight pants, worn by a male.
troke: truck.
turns: jobs, chores.
twa: two.

verra: very.

wedder lambs: lambs born prematurely.
whinging: complaining.
whummled: overturned, knocked down.

yean: birthing of a lamb.

BOOK 5

in the

Thistle Series

We Meet Again

Coming Soon!

BROKEN *Wings*

THE *Thistle* SERIES
BOOK ONE

DIANNE PRICE

He lives to fly—until a piece of flak changes his life forever.

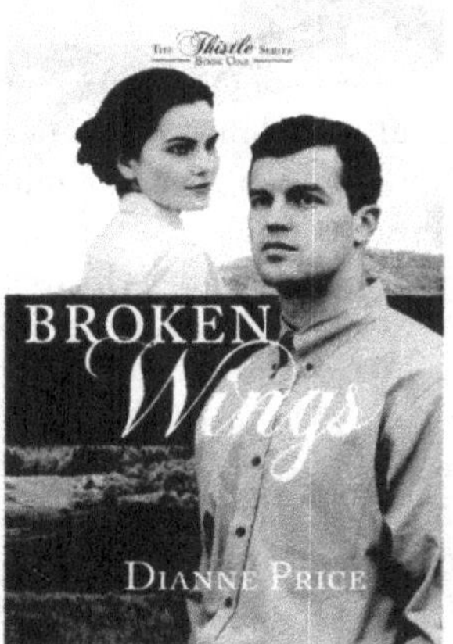

A tragic childhood has turned American Air Forces Colonel Rob Savage into an outwardly indifferent loner who is afraid to give his heart to anyone. RAF nurse Maggie McGrath has always dreamed of falling in love and settling down in a thatched cottage to raise a croftful of bairns, but the war has taken her far from Innisbraw, her tiny Scots island home.

Hitler's bloody quest to conquer Europe seems far away when Rob and Maggie are sent to an infirmary on Innisbraw to begin his rehabilitation from disabling injuries. Yet they find themselves caught in a battle between Rob's past, God's plan, and the evil some islanders harbor in their souls.

Which will triumph?

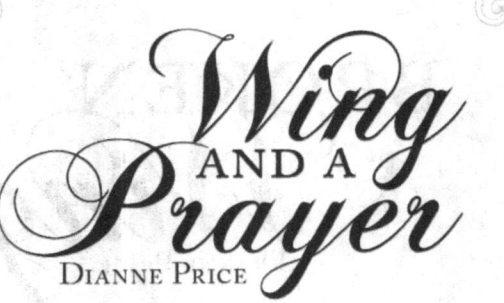

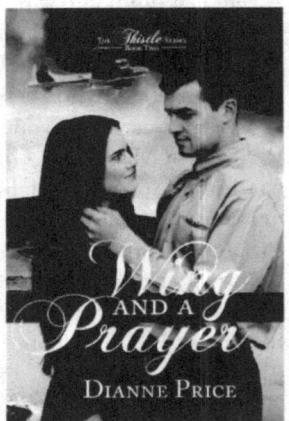

The Promise of Dawn

Dianne Price

Constant fear, piercing sirens, the darkness of war ... all that fades with

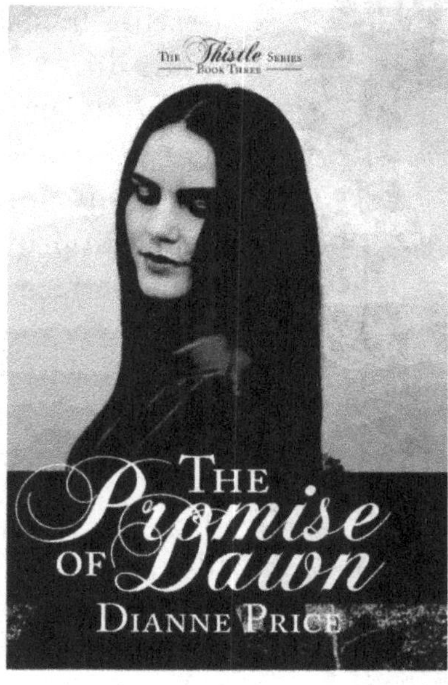

World War II is over, but there's much rebuilding to be done on the wee Scottish isle of Innisbraw. Now a wife and mother, Maggie Savage longs for other lasses to return to their island home, but how can they when there is no way to provide for themselves and their families? Her husband, Rob, driven by his unrelenting dream to build a rescue boat for the local fishermen, continues to be plagued by nightmares of impending disaster.

Will their simple faith in God and love for each other help them find a new dawn for their beloved community?

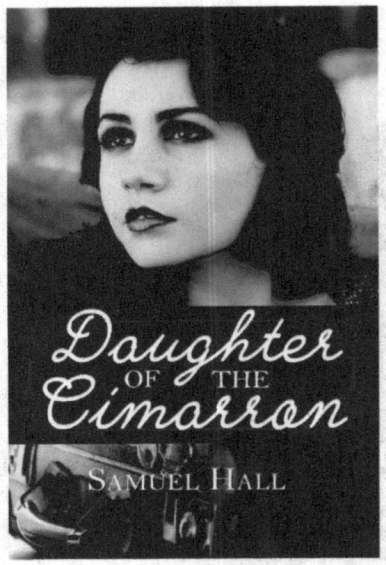

The Memoir of JOHNNY DEVINE

CAMILLE EIDE

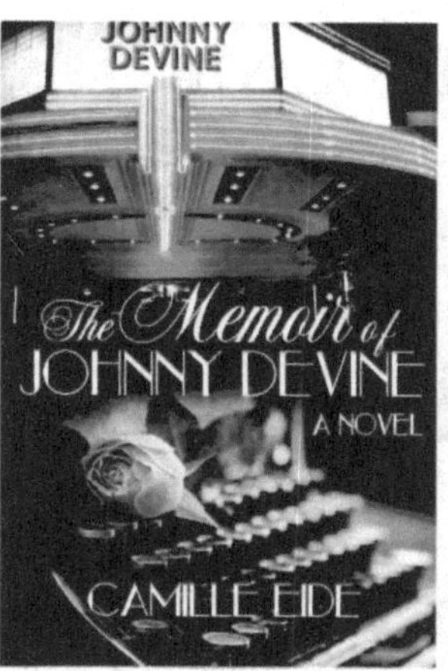

In 1953, desperation forces young war widow Eliza Saunderson to take a job writing the memoir of ex-Hollywood heartthrob Johnny Devine. Rumor has it Johnny can seduce anything in a skirt quicker than he can hail a cab. But now the notorious womanizer claims he's been born again. Eliza soon finds herself falling for the humble, grace-filled man John has become—a man who shows no sign of returning her feelings. No sign, that is, until she discovers something John never meant for her to see.

When Eliza's articles on minority oppression land her on McCarthy's Communist hit list, John and Eliza become entangled in an investigation that threatens both his book and her future. To clear her name, Eliza must solve a family mystery. Plus, she needs to convince John that real love—not the Hollywood illusion—can forgive a sordid past. Just when the hope of love becomes reality, a troubling discovery confirms Eliza's worst fears. Like the happy façade many Americans cling to, had it all been empty lies? Is there a love she can truly believe in?

The Journey of Eleven Moons

Bonnie Leon

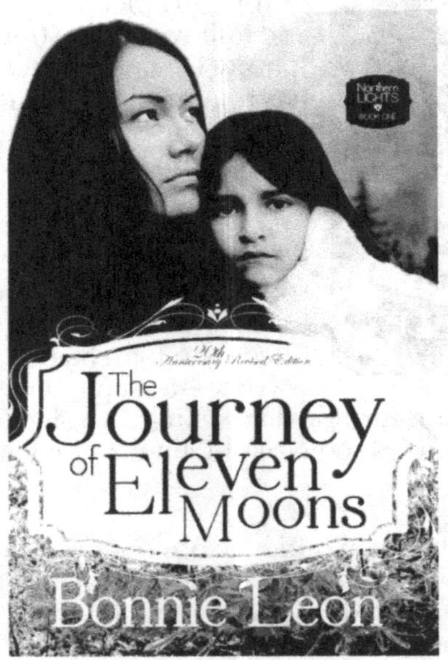

A successful walrus hunt means Anna and her beloved Kinauquak will soon be joined in marriage. But before they can seal their promise to one another, a tsunami wipes their village from the rugged shore … everyone except Anna and her little sister, Iya, who are left alone to face the Alaskan wilderness.

A stranger, a Civil War veteran with golden hair and blue eyes, wanders the untamed Aleutian Islands. He offers help, but can Anna trust him or his God? And if she doesn't, how will she and Iya survive?

Ashberry Lane

Ashberrylane.com

www.ingramcontent.com/pod-product-compliance
Lightning Source LLC
Chambersburg PA
CBHW011118050726
47495CB00021B/2893

* 9 7 8 1 9 4 1 7 2 0 2 7 1 *